Suddenly, out of nowhere, the fear came again. Not one of the stupid, personal fears, but something much, much greater. He clung to the windowsill with both hands as the sunlight turned as chill as a blizzard sweeping across the Plains, and his teeth chattered as he shook from head to toe, unable to move, scarcely able to draw a breath. His stomach clenched; his jaws locked on a cry of anguish. His heart thundered in his ears, and he wanted only to run, mad with terror, until he couldn't run any farther.

Mercedes Lackey was born in Chicago and began reading SF and fantasy at nine years old, when she decided she wanted to write for a living. After a succession of jobs, she became a full-time writer in 1990 and now has over a million books in print. She is a certified scuba diver, a member of the North American Falconery Association, and an amateur folk musician. She and her husband, SF artist and writer Larry Dixon, are avid conservationists involved in wildlife rehabilitation, specializing in birds of prey. They live in Oklahoma.

STORM WARNING

BOOK ONE OF
THE MAGE STORMS

Mercedes Lackey

MILLENNIUM

First published in Great Britain in 1994 by
Millennium
The Orion Publishing Group
5 Upper St Martin's Lane
London   WC2H 9EA

ISBN: 1 85798 297 5

Printed and bound in Great Britain by
Clays Ltd, St Ives plc

Dedicated to Elsie Wollheim
with love and respect

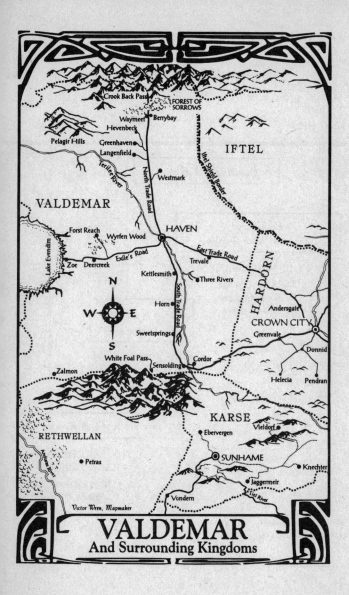

VALDEMAR
And Surrounding Kingdoms

Crook Back Pass

FOREST OF SORROWS

Waymeet   Berrybay

Hevenbeck

Pelagir Hills   Greenhaven   IFTEL

Langenfield

Terilee River   North Trade Road

Westmark

VALDEMAR

Forst Reach   Wyrfen Wood   HAVEN

Lake Evendim   Exile's Road   East Trade Road

Zoe   Deercreek   Trevale

Kettlesmith   Three Rivers   HARDORN

N
W—E
S

Horn   South Trade Road   Andersgate

CROWN CITY

Sweetsprings   Greenvale

Donnid

White Foal Pass   Sensolding   Cordor

Zalmon   Helecia   Pendran

KARSE

Vieldorf

RETHWELLAN   Ebervergen

Petras   SUNHAME

Knechter

Jaggermeir

Vondern   Tiel River

Victor Wren, Mapmaker

OFFICIAL TIMELINE FOR THE

by Mercedes Lackey

| 1000 BF | 0 | 750 AF | 798 AF |

Founding of Valdemar

Prehistory:
Era of the Black Gryphon

THE MAGE WARS
The Black Gryphon
The White Gryphon
The Silver Gryphon

Reign of Elspeth
the Peacemaker

THE LAST HERALD-
MAGE TRILOGY
Magic's Pawn

Reign of Randale

THE LAST HERALD-
MAGE TRILOGY

Magic's Promise
Magic's Price

BF *Before the Founding*
AF *After the Founding*

ERALDS OF VALDEMAR SERIES

Sequence of events by Valdemar reckoning

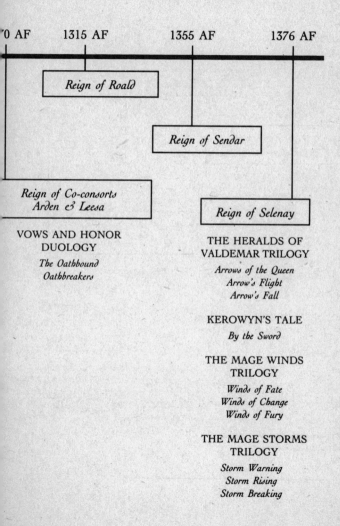

'0 AF   1315 AF   1355 AF   1376 AF

Reign of Roald

Reign of Sendar

*Reign of Co-consorts
Arden & Leesa*

Reign of Selenay

**VOWS AND HONOR
DUOLOGY**

*The Oathbound
Oathbreakers*

**THE HERALDS OF
VALDEMAR TRILOGY**

*Arrows of the Queen
Arrow's Flight
Arrow's Fall*

KEROWYN'S TALE

By the Sword

**THE MAGE WINDS
TRILOGY**

*Winds of Fate
Winds of Change
Winds of Fury*

**THE MAGE STORMS
TRILOGY**

*Storm Warning
Storm Rising
Storm Breaking*

Emperor Charliss

1

Emperor Charliss sat upon the Iron Throne, bowed down neither by the visible weight of his years nor the invisible weight of his power. He bore neither the heavy Wolf Crown on his head, nor the equally burdensome robes of state across his shoulders, though both lay nearby, on an ornately trimmed marble bench beside the Iron Throne. The thick silk-velvet robes flowed down the bench and coiled on the floor beside it, a lush weight of pure crimson so heavy it took two strapping young men to lift them into place on the Emperor's shoulders. The Wolf Crown lay atop the robes, preventing them from slipping off the bench altogether. Let mere kings flaunt their golden crowns; the Emperor boasted a circlet of electrum, inset with thirteen yellow diamonds. Only when one drew near enough to the Emperor to see his eyes clearly did one see that the circlet was not as it seemed, that what had passed at a distance for an abstract design or a floral pattern was, in fact, a design of twelve wolves, and that the winking yellow diamonds were their eyes. Eleven of those wolves were in profile to the watcher, five facing left, six facing right; the twelfth, obviously the pack leader, gazed directly down onto whosoever the Emperor faced, those unwinking yellow eyes staring at the petitioner even as the Emperor's own eyes did.

Let lesser beings assume thrones of gold or marble; the Emperor held court from his Iron Throne, made from the personal weapons of all those monarchs the Emperors of the past had conquered and deposed, each glazed and guarded against rust. The throne itself was over six feet tall and four feet in width; a monolithic piece of furniture, it was so heavy that it had not been moved so much as a finger-length in centuries. Anyone looking at it could only be struck by its sheer *mass*—and must begin calculating just how many sword blades, axes, and lance points must have gone into the making of it. . . .

None of this was by chance, of course. Everything about the Emperor's regalia, his throne, his Audience Chamber, and Crag Castle itself was carefully calculated to reduce a visitor to the proper level of fearful respect, impress upon him the sheer power held in the hands of this ruler, and the utter impossibility of aspiring to such power. The Emperors were not interested in inducing a *groveling* fear, nor did they intend to excite ambition. The former was a dangerous state; people made too fearful would plot ways to remove the cause of that fear. And ambition was a useful tool in an underling beneath one's direct supervision, but risky in one who might, on occasion, slip his leash.

There was very little in the Emperor's life that was not the result of long thought and careful calculation. He had not become the successor to Emperor Lioth at the age of thirty without learning the value of both abilities—and he had not spent the intervening century-and-a-half in letting either ability lapse.

Charliss was the nineteenth Emperor to sit the Iron Throne; none of his predecessors had been less than brilliant, and none had reigned for less than half a century. None had been eliminated by assassins, and only one had been unable to choose his own successor.

Some called Charliss "the Immortal"; that was a fallacy, since he was well aware how few years he had left to him. Although he was a powerful mage, there were limits to the amount of time magic could prolong one's life. Eventually the body itself became too tired to sustain life any longer; even banked fires dwindled to ash in the end. Charliss' rumored immortality was one of many myths he himself propagated. Useful rumors were difficult to come by.

The dull gray throne sat in the midst of an expanse of black-veined white marble; the Emperor's robes, the exact color of fresh-spilled blood, and the yellow gems in the crown, were the only color on the dais. Even the walls and the ceiling of the dais-alcove, a somber setting for a rich gem, were of that same marble. The effect was to concentrate the attention of the onlookers on the Emperor and only the Emperor. The battle-banners, the magnificent tapestries, the rich curtains—all these were behind and to the side of the young man who waited at the Emperor's feet. Charliss himself wore slate-gray velvets, half-robe with dagged sleeves, trews, and Court-boots, made on the same looms as the crimson robes; in his long-ago youth, his hair had been whitened by the wielding of magic, and his once-dark eyes were now the same pale gray as an overcast dawn sky.

If the young man waiting patiently at the foot of the throne was aware of how few years the Emperor had left to him, he had (wisely) never indicated he possessed this dangerous knowledge to anyone. Grand Duke Tremane was about the same age as Charliss had been when Lioth bestowed his power and responsibility on Charliss' younger, stronger shoulders and had retired to spend the last three years of his life holding off Death with every bit of the concentration he had used holding onto his power.

In no other way were the two of them similar, however. Charliss had been one of Lioth's many, many sons by way of his state marriages; Tremane was no closer in blood to Charliss than a mere cousin, several times removed. Charliss had been, and still was, an Adept, and in his full powers before he ascended the Throne. Tremane was a mere Master, and never would have the kind of mage-power at his personal command that Charliss had.

But if mage-power or blood-ties were all that was required to take the Throne and the Crown, there were a hundred candidates to be considered before Tremane. Intelligence and cunning were not enough by themselves, either; in a land founded by stranded mercenaries, both were as common as snowflakes in midwinter. No one survived long in Charliss' court without both those qualities, and the will to use both no matter how stressful personal circumstances were.

Tremane had luck; that was important, but more than the luck itself, Tremane had the ability to recognize when his good fortune had struck, and the capability to revise whatever his current plan was in order to take advantage of that luck.

And conversely, when ill-luck struck him (which was seldom), he had the courage to revise plans to meet that as well, now and again snatching a new kind of victory from the brink of disaster.

Tremane was not the only one of the current candidates for the succession to have those qualities, but he was the one personally favored by the Emperor. Tremane was not entirely ruthless; too many of the others *were.* Being ruthless was not a bad thing, but being entirely ruthless was dangerous. Those who dared to stop at nothing often ended up with enemies who had nothing to lose. Putting an enemy in such a position was an error, for a man who has nothing to lose is, by definition, risking nothing to obtain what he desires.

Tremane inspired tremendous loyalty in his underlings; it had been *dreadfully* difficult for the Emperor's Spymaster to insinuate agents into Tremane's household. That was another useful trait for an Emperor to have; Charliss shared it, and had found that it was just as effective to have underlings willing to fling themselves in front of the assassin's blade without a single thought as it was to ferret out the assassin himself.

Otherwise, the man on the throne had little else in common with his chosen successor. Charliss had been considered handsome in his day, and the longing glances of the women in his Court even yet were not entirely due to the power and prestige that were granted to an Imperial mistress. Tremane was, to put it bluntly, so far from comely that it was likely *only* his power, rank, and personal prestige that won women to his bed. His thinning hair was much shorter than was fashionable; his receding hairline gave him a look of perpetual befuddlement. His eyes were too small, set just a hair too far apart; his beard was sparse, and looked like an afterthought. His thin face ended in a lantern jaw; his wiry body gave no hint of his quality as a warrior. Charliss often thought that the man's tailor ought to be taken out and hanged; he dressed Tremane in sober browns and blacks that did nothing for his complexion, and his clothing hung on him as if he had recently lost weight and muscle.

Then again . . . Tremane was only one of several candidates for the Iron Throne, and he knew it. He *looked* harmless;

common, and of average intelligence, but no more than that. It was entirely possible that all of this was a deeply laid plan to appear ineffectual. If so, Charliss' own network of intelligence agents told him that the plan had succeeded, at least among the rest of the rivals for the position. Of all of the candidates for the Iron Throne, he was the one with the fewest enemies among his rivals.

They were as occupied with eliminating each other as in improving their own positions, and in proving their ability to the Emperor. *He* was free to concentrate on competence. This was *not* a bad position to be in.

Perhaps he was even more clever than Charliss had given him credit for. If so, he would need every bit of that cleverness in the task Charliss was about to assign him to.

The Emperor had not donned robes and regalia for this interview, as this was not precisely official; he was alone with Tremane—if one discounted the ever-present bodyguards—and the trappings of Empire did not impress the Grand Duke. Real power did, and real power was what Charliss held in abundance. He *was* power, and with the discerning, he did not need to weary himself with his regalia to prove that.

He cleared his throat, and Tremane bowed slightly in acknowledgment.

"I intend to retire at some point within the next ten years." Charliss made the statement calmly, but a muscle jumping in Tremane's shoulders betrayed the man's excitement and sudden tension. "It is Imperial custom to select a successor at some point during the last ten years of the reign so as to assure an orderly transition."

Tremane nodded, with just the proper shading of respect. Charliss noted with approval that Tremane did not respond with toadying phrases like "how could you even think of retiring, my Emperor," or "surely it is too early to be thinking of such things." Not that Charliss had expected such a response from him; Tremane was far too clever.

"Now," Charliss continued, leaning back a little into the comfortable solidity of the Iron Throne, "you are no one's fool, Tremane. You have obviously been aware for a long time that you are one of the primary candidates to be my successor."

Tremane bowed correctly, his eyes never leaving Charliss' face. "I was aware of that, certainly, my Emperor," he replied, his voice smoothly neutral. "Only a fool would have failed to notice your interest. But I am also aware that I am just one of a number of possible candidates."

Charliss smiled, ever so slightly, with approval. Good. Even if the man did not possess humility, he could feign it convincingly. Another valuable ability.

"You happen to be my current personal choice, Tremane," the Emperor replied, and he smiled again as the man's eyebrows twitched with quickly-concealed surprise. "It is true that you are not an Adept; it is true that you are not in the direct Imperial bloodline. It is also true that of the nineteen Emperors, only eleven have been full Adepts, and it is equally true that I have outlived my own offspring. Had any of them inherited my mage-powers, that would not have been the case, of course. . . ."

He allowed himself a moment to brood on the injustice of that. Of all the children of his many marriages of state, not a one had achieved more than Journeyman status. That was simply not enough power to prolong life—not without resorting to blood-magic, at any rate, and while there *had* been an Emperor or two who had followed the darker paths, those were dangerous paths to follow for long. As witness the idiot Ancar, for instance—those who practiced the blood-paths all too often found that the magic had become the master, and the mage, the slave. The Emperor who ruled with the aid of blood-rites balanced on a spider's thread above the abyss, with the monsters waiting below for a single missed step.

Well, it hardly mattered. What *did* matter was that a worthy candidate stood before him now, a man who had all the character and strength the Iron Throne demanded.

And what was more, there was an opportunity before them both for Tremane to *prove*, beyond the faintest shadow of a doubt, that he was the only man with that kind of character and strength.

"Your duchy is in the farthest west, is it not?" Charliss asked, with carefully simulated casualness. If Tremane was surprised at the apparent change of subject, he did not show it. He simply nodded again.

"The western border, in fact?" Charliss continued. "The border of the Empire and Hardorn?"

"Perhaps a trifle north of the true Hardorn border, but yes, my Emperor," Tremane agreed. "May I assume this has something to do with the recent conquests that our forces have made in that sad and disorganized land?"

"You may." Charliss was enjoying this little conversation. "In fact, the situation with Hardorn offers you a unique opportunity to prove yourself to me. With that situation you may prove conclusively that you *are* worthy of the Wolf Crown."

Tremane's eyes widened, and his hands trembled, just for a moment.

"If the Emperor would be kind enough to inform his servant how this could be done—?" Tremane replied delicately.

The Emperor smiled thinly. "First, let me impart to you a few bits of privileged information. Immediately prior to the collapse of the Hardornen palace—and I mean that quite precisely—our envoy returned to us from King Ancar's court by means of a Gate. He did not have a great deal of information to offer, however, since he arrived with a knife buried in his heart, a rather lovely throwing dagger, which I happen to have here now."

He removed the knife from a sheath beneath his sleeve, and passed it to Tremane, who examined it closely, and started visibly when he saw the device carved into the pommel-nut.

"This is the royal crest of the Kingdom of Valdemar," Tremane stated flatly, passing the blade back to the Emperor, who returned it to the sheath. Charliss nodded, pleased that Tremane had actually recognized it.

"Indeed. And one wonders how such a blade could possibly have been where it was." He allowed one eyebrow to rise. "There is a trifle more; we had an intimate agent working to rid us of Ancar, an agent that had once worked independently in Valdemar. This agent is now rather conspicuously missing."

The agent in question had been a sorceress by the name of Hulda—Charliss never could recall the rest of her name. He did not particularly mourn her loss; *she* had been very ambitious, and he had foreseen a time when he might expect her value as an agent to be exceeded by her liabilities. That she was missing could mean any one of several things, but it did not much matter whether she had fled or died; the result would be the same.

Tremane's brow wrinkled in thought. "The most obvious conclusion would be that your agent turned," he said after a moment, "and that she used this dagger to place suspicion on agents of one of Ancar's enemies, thus embroiling us in a conflict with Valdemar that would open opportunities for her own ambitions in Hardorn. We have no reason for an open quarrel with Valdemar just yet; this could precipitate one before we are ready."

Charliss nodded with satisfaction. What was "obvious" to Tremane was far from obvious to those who looked no deeper than the surface of things. "Of course, I have no intention of pursuing an open quarrel with Valdemar just yet," he said. "The envoy in question was hardly outstanding; there are a dozen more who are simply panting for his position. The woman was quite troublesomely ambitious, yes; however, if she uses her magics but once, we will know where she is, and eliminate her if we choose. No. What truly concerns me is Valdemar itself. The situation within Hardorn is unstable. We have acquired half of the country with very little effort, but the ungrateful barbarians seem to have made up their mind to refuse the benefits of inclusion within the Empire." Charliss felt a distant ache in his hip joints and shifted his position a little to ease it. A warning, those little aches. The sign that his spells of bodily renewal were fading. They were less and less effective with every year, and within two decades or so they would fail him altogether. . . .

One corner of Tremane's mouth twitched a little, in recognition of Charliss' irony. They both knew what the Emperor meant by that; the citizens of what had been Hardorn wanted their country back, and they had organized enough to resist further conquest.

"In addition," Charliss continued smoothly, "this land of Valdemar is overrun with refugees from all the conflict within Hardorn and from the wretched situation before Ancar perished. Valdemar could decide to aid the Hardornens in some material way, and that would cause us further trouble. We know that they have somehow allied themselves with those fanatics in Karse, and that presents us with one long front if we choose to fight them. Valdemar itself is a damned peculiar place. . . ."

"It has always been difficult to insinuate agents into Valdemar," Tremane offered, with the proper diffidence. Charliss wondered whether he spoke from *personal* experience or simply the knowledge he had gleaned from keeping an eye on Charliss' own agents.

From beyond the closed doors of the Throne Room came the soft murmur of the courtiers who were waiting for the doors to open for them and Court to begin. Let them wait— and let them see just whose business had kept them waiting. They would know then, without any formal announcements, just who had become the Emperor's current favorite. The little maneuverings and shifts in power would begin from that very moment, like the shifts in current when a new boulder rolls into a stream.

"Quite." Charliss frowned. "In fact, that *Hulda* creature was once one of my freelance agents in the Valdemar capital. I was rather dubious about using her again, despite her abilities, until I realized just how cursed difficult it *is* to work in Valdemar. As it was, her progress there was minimal. Most unsatisfactory. She was never able to insinuate herself any higher than a mere court servant's position, and she had more than one agenda and more than one employer at the time."

The corner of Tremane's mouth twitched again, but this time it was downward. Charliss knew why; Tremane never knowingly worked with someone who served more masters than he.

"Why did you trust her in Hardorn, then?" the Grand Duke asked in a neutral tone.

"I never *trusted* her," Charliss corrected him, allowing a hint of cold disapproval to tinge his own voice. "I trust no agents, particularly not those who are as ambitious as this one was. I merely made sure that this time she had no other employers, and that her personal agenda was not incompatible with mine. And when it appeared that she was slipping her leash, I sent an envoy to Ancar's court to remind her who her master was. And to eliminate her if she elected to ignore

the warning he represented. That was why I sent a mage, an
Adept her equal, with none of her vices."

"Your pardon," Tremane replied, bowing slightly. "I should
have known. But—about Valdemar?"

Charliss permitted his icy expression to thaw. "Valdemar
is peculiar, as I said. Until recently, they've had next to no
magic at all, and what they had was only mind-magic. There
was a barrier there, according to my agents, a barrier that
made it impossible for a practicing mage to remain within
the borders for very long."

"But how did Hulda—" Tremane began, then smiled. "Of
course. While she was there, she must have refrained from
using her powers. A difficult thing for a mage; use of magic
often becomes a habit too ingrained to break."

Charliss blinked slowly in satisfaction. Tremane was no
fool; he saw immediately the solution and the difficulty of
implementing it. "Precisely," he replied. "On both counts.
And that was *why* I continued to use her. In business matters,
the woman's self-discipline was remarkable. As for Valdemar—though they have begun again to use magic as we know
it, the place is no less peculiar than before, and many of the
mages they seem to have invited into their borders are from
no land that *my* operatives recognize! Well, that is all in the
past; what we need to deal with is the current situation. And
that, Grand Duke Tremane, is where you come in."

Tremane simply waited, as any good and perfectly trained
servant, for his master to continue. But his eyes narrowed
just a trifle, and Charliss knew that his mind was working furiously. A current of breeze stirred the tapestries behind him,
but the flames of the candles on the many-branched cande-
labras, protected in their glass shades, did not even waver.

"Your Duchy borders Hardorn; you will therefore be familiar
with the area," Charliss stated, his tone and expression allowing no room for dissension. "The situation in Hardorn
grows increasingly unstable by the moment. I require a personal commander of my own in place there; someone who
has incentive, *personal* incentive, to see that the situation is
dealt with expeditiously."

"Personal incentive, my Emperor?" Tremane replied.

Charliss crossed his legs and leaned forward, ignoring the

pain in his hip joints. "I am giving you a unique opportunity to prove, not only to me, but to your rivals and your potential underlings, that you are the only truly worthy candidate for the Wolf Crown. I intend to put you in command of the Imperial forces in Hardorn. You will be answerable only to me. You will prove yourself worthy by dealing with this situation and bringing it to a successful conclusion."

Tremane's hands trembled, and Charliss noted that he had turned just a little pale. How long would it take for word to spread of Tremane's new position? Probably less than an hour. "What of Valdemar, my Emperor?" he asked, his voice steady, even if his hands were not.

"What of Valdemar?" Charliss repeated. "Well, I don't expect you to conquer it as well. It will be enough to bring Hardorn under our banner. However, if during that process you discover a way to insinuate an agent into Valdemar, all the better. If you take your conquests past the Hardorn border and actually *into* Valdemar, better still. I simply warn you of Valdemar because it is a strange place and I cannot predict how it will measure this situation nor what it will do. Valdemar can wait; Hardorn is what concerns me now. We must conquer it, now that we have begun, or our other client states will see that we have failed and may become difficult to deal with in our perceived moment of weakness."

"And if I succeed in bringing Hardorn into the Empire?" Tremane persisted.

"Then you will be confirmed in the succession, and I will begin the process of the formal training," Charliss told him. "And at the end of ten years, I will retire, and you will have Throne, Crown, and Empire."

Tremane's eyes lit, and his lips twitched into a tight, excited smile. Then he sobered. "If I do not succeed, however, I assume I shall resume nothing more than the rule of my Duchy."

Charliss examined his immaculately groomed hands, gazing into the topaz eyes of the wolf's-head ring he wore, a ring whose wolf mask had been cast from the same molds as the central wolf of the Wolf Crown. The eyes gazed steadily at him, and as he often did, Charliss fancied he saw a hint of life in them. Hunger. An avidity, not that of the starving beast, but of the prosperous and powerful.

"There is no shortage of suitable candidates for the Throne," he replied casually, tilting the ring for a better view into the burning yellow eyes. "If you should happen to survive your failure, I would advise you to retire *directly* to your Duchy. The next candidate that I would consider if you failed would be Baron Melles."

Baron Melles was a so-called "court Baron," a man with a title but no lands to match. He didn't *need* land; he had power, power in abundance, for he was an Adept and his magics had brought him more wealth than many landed nobles had. His coffers bulged with his accumulated wealth, but he wanted more, and his bloodlines and ambition were likely to give him more.

He also happened to be of the political party directly opposite that of Tremane's. Tremane's parents had held their lands for generations; Melles was the son of merchants. Melles was, not so incidentally, one of Tremane's few enemies, one of the few candidates to the succession who did *not* underestimate the Baron. There was a personal animosity between them that Charliss did not quite understand, and he often wondered if the two had somehow contracted a very private feud that had little or nothing to do with their respective positions and ambitions.

Melles would be only too pleased to find Tremane a failure and himself the new successor. This meant, among other things, that if Tremane happened to survive his failure to conquer Hardorn, he probably would not survive the coronation of his rival, and he might not even survive the confirmation of Melles as successor. Melles was the most ruthless of all the candidates, and both Charliss and Tremane were quite well aware that he was a powerful enough Adept to be able to commit any number of murders-by-magic, and make them all appear to be accidents.

He was also clever enough *not* to do anything of the sort, since his political rivals would be looking for and defending against exactly that sort of attack. Melles was fully wealthy enough to buy any number of covert killers, and probably would. He was too clever not to consolidate his position by eliminating enough rivals that those remaining were intimidated.

That was, after all, one of the realities of life in the Empire; lead, follow, and barricade yourself against assassins.

And the first in line for elimination would be Tremane—if Melles were named successor.

Charliss knew this. So did Tremane. It made the situation all the more piquant.

Interestingly enough, if Tremane succeeded and attained the coveted prize, it was not likely that he would remove Melles. Nor would he dispose of any of the other candidates. Rather, he would either win them over to his side or find some other way to neutralize them—perhaps by finding something else, creating some other problem for them, that required all their attention.

Charliss had used both ploys in the past, and on the whole, he preferred subtlety to assassination. Still, there had been equally successful Emperors in the past who ruled by the knife and the garrote. Difficult times demanded difficult solutions, and one of those times could be upon them.

The entire situation gave Charliss a faint echo of the thrill he had felt back at the beginning of his own reign, when he first realized he truly *did* have the power of life and death over his underlings and could manipulate their lives as easily as the puppeteer manipulated his dolls. It was amusing to present Tremane with a gift of a sword—with a needle-studded, poisoned grip. It was doubly amusing to know that Melles, at least, would recognize this test for what it was, and would be watching Tremane just as avidly from a distance, perhaps sending in his own agents to try and undermine his rival, and attempting to consolidate his own position here at court.

The jockeying and scrabbling was about to begin. It should produce hours of fascination.

Charliss watched Tremane closely, following the ghosts, the shadows of expressions as he thought all this through and came to the same conclusions. There was no chance that he would refuse the appointment, of course. Firstly, Tremane was a perfectly adequate military commander. Secondly, refusing this appointment would be the same as being defeated;

Melles would have the reward of becoming successor, and Tremane's life would be in danger.

It took very little time for Tremane to add all the factors together to come to the conclusions that Charliss had already thought out. He bowed quickly.

"I cannot tell my Emperor how incredibly flattered I am by his trust in me," he said smoothly. "I can only hope that I will prove worthy of that trust."

Charliss said nothing; only nodded in acknowledgment.

"And I am answerable only to *you*, my Emperor? Not to any other, military or civilian?" Tremane continued quickly.

"Have I not said as much?" Charliss waved a hand. "I am certain you will need all the time you have between now and tomorrow morning, Grand Duke. Packing and preparations will probably occupy you for the rest of the day. I will have one of the Court Mages open the Portal for you to the Hardornen front just after you break your fast tomorrow morning."

"Sir." Tremane made the full formal bow this time; he knew a dismissal even when it was not phrased as one. Charliss was very pleased with his demeanor, especially given the short notice and the shorter time in which to make ready for his departure. There were no attempts to argue, no excuses, no plaints that there was not enough time.

Tremane rose from the bow, backing out of the room with his eyes lowered properly. Charliss could not find fault with his posture or the signals his body gave; his demeanor was perfect.

The great doors opened and closed behind him. Alone once again in the Throne Room, Emperor Charliss, ruler of the largest single domain in the world, leaned to one side and chuckled into the cavernous chamber.

This would be the most enjoyable little playlet of his entire reign, and it came at the very end, when he had thought he had long since exploited the entertainment value of watching his courtiers scramble about for the tidbits he tossed them. But here was a juicy treat indeed, and the scramble would be vastly amusing.

Charliss was pleased. Entertainment on this scale was *hard* to come by!

Firesong's Vale

2

Steam curled up from the water as An'desha gingerly lowered himself into the soaking-pool of Firesong's miniature Vale. *A Vale in the heart of Valdemar—no larger than a single Gathering-tent. I would not have believed that such a thing was possible, much less that it could be done with so little magic—yet here it is.*

It was amazing how much could be created without the use of any magic at all. Most of this enchanted little garden had been put together by ordinary folk, using nonmagical materials. There were only two exceptions; the huge windows, and the hot pools. The windows were not the tiny, many-paned things with their thick, bubbly glass, that An'desha had seen in all of the Palace buildings, which would not have done at all for the purpose. These eight windows, two to each side of the room, went from floor to ceiling in a single flawless triangular piece. Each had been made magically by Firesong, of the same substance used by the Hawkbrothers for the windows in their tree-perching *ekeles*. He had also created a magical source for the hot water for the pools. The rest, this garden that bloomed in the dead of winter, and the pseudo-*ekele* above it, was all built by ordinary folk, mainly due to Firesong taking shameless advantage of the Queen of Valdemar's gratitude and generosity.

Firesong felt that if he *must* remain here as the Tayledras envoy to primitive Valdemar, then by the Goddess, he would have the civilized amenities of a Vale!

Valdemar. An'desha had never heard of this land until a year ago. As a child and even a young man among the Clans, he had not heard of much beyond the Walls; indeed, the only places beyond the Walls he had learned of as a youngster were the Pelagiris Forest and the trade-city of Kata'shin'a'in. The Shin'a'in as a general rule cared very little for the world beyond the Plains; only Tale'sedrin of all the Clans had any measure of Outland and outClan blood.

In some Clans—such as An'desha's—such foreign breeding was occasionally considered a minor disgrace—not a disgrace for the child, but for the Shin'a'in parent. "Could he not draw to him a single woman of the Plains?" would come the whispers, or "Was she so unpleasant that no Shin'a'in man cared to partner her?" So it had been for An'desha, child of such an alliance—and perhaps that was why his own Clan had never so much as mentioned the lands outside the Dhorisha Plains. Perhaps they had feared that talking about the lands Outside would excite an un-Shin'a'in wanderlust in him, a yearning for far places and strange climes.

Well, I found both—without really wanting either.

The blood-path Adept who had flamboyantly named himself Mornelithe Falconsbane had never heard of Valdemar, either, until the two white-clad strangers from that land had come into the territory of Clan k'Sheyna of the Hawkbrothers.

An'desha had been a silent, frightened passenger in his own body, which Falconsbane had usurped by magic and trickery. With the Adept possessing him, he had learned just who those strangers were and something of their land. He'd had no choice in the matter, since he was a hidden fugitive within the body that Falconsbane had stolen years ago.

He should have died; that was what always happened before, when Falconsbane took a body. But he hadn't; perhaps the reason was that he had fled, rather than trying to resist the interloper.

A prisoner in my own body. . . . He closed his eyes and sank a measure deeper into the hot water. So odd . . . the memories of those years of hiding, when he had no control over the actions of his own body, seemed more solid and real than this moment, when the body he had been born into was once again his.

An'desha's had been only the last in a long series of bodies

Falconsbane had appropriated as his own. All that was required, or so it seemed, was for the victim to be gifted with mage ability and to have been a descendant of a mage called Ma'ar. If those remote memories were to be trusted, Ma'ar had lost his first life—or body, depending on your point of view—in the Mage Wars of so long ago it made An'desha dizzy to think about the passage of years between that moment and this.

He slipped down to his chin into the hot water, and closed his eyes tighter, letting the steam rise around his face. *His* face now, and not the half-feline face of Mornelithe Falconsbane. His own body, too, for the most part, though it was more muscular now than it had been when Falconsbane helped himself to it and tried to destroy the original owner. Falconsbane had made a hobby of body sculpting, trying out changes on his daughter before adopting them himself. He had indulged in some extensive modifications to An'desha's body, changes An'desha had been certain he would have to endure even after Falconsbane had been driven out and destroyed.

But his own actions, risking real soul-death to rid the world of Falconsbane, had earned him more than just his freedom. Not only had he regained his body, most of the modifications had vanished when the Avatars of the Goddess "cured" him of what had been done to him.

There were only two things they could not give him again; the original colors of his hair and eyes. His hair was a pure, snowy white now, and his eyes a pale silver, both bleached forever by the magic energies that Falconsbane had sent coursing through this body, time and time again. So now, when An'desha gazed into a mirror, it always took a moment to recognize the reflection as his own.

At least I see the face of a half-familiar stranger, and not that of a beast. However handsome that beast had made himself.

The hot water forced his muscles to relax some, but he feared he would have to resort to stronger measures to release all the tension.

This place is so strange. . . . Let Firesong wallow in being the exotic and sought-after alien; An'desha was *not* comfortable here. The only people he really knew were Nyara, the mage-sword Need, and Firesong, the Tayledras Adept. Of the three, the only one he spent any time at all with was Firesong. Nyara was very preoccupied with her mate, the Herald called Skif—and at any rate, it was hard to face her, knowing she was the offspring of his body when Falconsbane had worn it, knowing what his body had done to hers. Now that the crisis was over, Nyara seemed to feel the same way; although she was never unkind, she often seemed uncomfortable around him.

As for the ancient mage-sword that housed the spirit of an irreverent and crotchety sorceress, the entity called Need had her nonexistent hands full. She was engrossed in training Nyara, helping *her* adjust to this new land. Need was quite used to adjusting to new situations; she had been doing so for many centuries; in this, he had nothing in common with her.

After seeing changes over the course of a few hundred years, I would imagine that there is very little that surprises her anymore.

And as for Firesong—

He flushed, and it wasn't from the heat of the water cradling him. *I don't understand,* he thought, his logic getting all tangled up with his feelings whenever he so much as thought about Firesong. *I just don't understand. Why this, and why Firesong?* Not that the Shin'a'in had any prejudice about same-sex pairings, but An'desha had *never* felt even the tiniest of stirrings for a male before this. But Firesong—oh, Firesong was quickly becoming the emotional center of his universe. Why?

Firesong. Ah, what am I to do? Is he my next master?

His thoughts circled, tighter and tighter, like a hawk caught in an updraft, until he physically shook himself loose. He splashed warm water on his face and sat up straighter.

Don't get unbalanced. Concentrate on ordinary things; deal with all of this a little at a time. Think of ordinary things, peaceful things. They keep telling you not to worry, to rest and recover and relax.

He opened his eyes and deliberately focused on the garden around him, looking for places that might seem a little barren, a trifle unfinished. He had discovered a surprising ability in himself. It was surprising, because the nomadic Shin'a'in were not known for growing much of anything, and Falconsbane had been much more partial to destroying rather than creating when *he* had been active.

I never thought I'd be a gardener. I thought that was something only Tayledras did. He *loved* the feel of warm earth between his fingers; seeing a new leaf unfold gave him as much pleasure as if he had created a poem. Though the plants were cold and alien, in their own way they were like him. They struck a chord in him the way open sky and waving grass inspired his ancestors, and the scent of fresh greenery renewed him. An'desha had an affinity with ornamental plants, with plants of all kinds now, and a patience with them that Firesong lacked. The Adept enjoyed the effect of a finished planting, but he was not interested in creating it, nor in nurturing it. Though Firesong had dictated the existence of the indoor garden, planned the general look of it, and sculpted the stones, it was An'desha who had filled it with growing things, and given it life. In a sense, this fragile garden was An'desha: body, mind, and soul.

An'desha had not confined his efforts to the indoor garden surrounding the pools, hot and cold, and the waterfall that Firesong had created here. He had extended the plantings to cold-hardy species outside the windows, deciding that as long as the windows were that tall, there was no reason why he couldn't create the illusion that the indoor garden extended out into the outdoors. So, for at least the part of the year when the outside gardens were still green, this could have been a shady grotto in any Tayledras Vale.

The illusion was not quite perfect, and An'desha studied the intersection of indoors and outdoors, frowning slightly. He had matched the pebbled pathway between the beds of ornamental grasses indoors and out, but the eye still saw the windowpane before the vegetation outside it. He moved to the smooth rock edge of the pool and laid his chin down on his crossed arms to study it further.

There must be a way to make the window more of an accidental interruption to the flow of the gardens, the sweep of the planting.

Bushes, he decided. *If I have some bushy plants in here, and more that will outline a phantom pathway beyond the glass, that will help the illusion.* With just a little magical help, he'd accelerate the growth of a few more cuttings, and he'd have them at the right height in a week or two.

If I use evergreens, perhaps I can even take the edge off the transition between indoors and outdoors even in winter.

He had worried when Firesong came up with these clever ideas that the original "owners" of this bit of property might object to all the changes. Firesong's little home was in the remotest corner of a vast acreage called "Companion's Field," and the horselike beings that partnered the Heralds of Valdemar could very well have objected to their privacy being invaded. But they didn't seem to mind the presence of the Adept and his compatriots; in fact, they had contributed to the landscaping with suggestions of their own that made the *ekele* blend in with the surroundings, just as any good *ekele* should. From outside, the mottled gray and brown stone of the support pillars blended with the trunks of the trees masking it, and the second story was hidden among the branches. Firesong had chosen this particular place after he had heard of a legend that told of a Herald Vanyel, supposedly Firesong *and* Elspeth's ancestor, trysting with his beloved in this very grove of trees; after that, nothing would do but that his own *ekele* be here as well.

Firesong had insisted on building his "nest" in Companion's Field in the first place, rather than in the Palace gardens, precisely because he did not want any hint of the alien buildings of Valdemar to jar on his awareness.

Strange. I would have thought that Darkwind would be the one to feel that way, not Firesong. Darkwind was a scout; at one point, he could not even bear to live within the confines of a Vale! But Darkwind dwells quite comfortably in the Palace with the Queen's daughter, and it is Firesong who insists on removing himself to the isolation of this place.

Then again, Firesong was a law unto himself; he could afford to dictate even to a Queen in her own Palace how he would and would not live. Firesong was the most powerful practicing Adept in this strange land, and he did not seem to have a moment's hesitation when it came to exploiting that fact. Eventually Elspeth and Darkwind might come to be his equals in power, but he had been a full Adept from a very tender age, and had a great deal more experience than either the k'Sheyna Hawkbrother or the Valdemaran Herald.

And perhaps he has isolated himself for my sake, and not his own. That could very well be the case. An'desha stared into the tree-shadows on the other side of the window, and sighed.

He, more than anyone else, knew just how tenuous his stability was. For all intents and purposes, he was *still* the young Shin'a'in of fifteen summers who had run away from his Clan in order to be schooled in magic by the Shin'a'in "cousins," the Hawkbrothers. For most of his tenure within Falconsbane's mind, he had no more than brief glimpses of what Falconsbane had been doing. He had no real experience of those years; he might just as well never have lived them. In a very real sense, he hadn't. Most of the time he had been hidden in the darkness, snatching only covert glimpses of what Falconsbane was doing. *I was afraid he'd sense me watching through his eyes—and what he was doing was horrible.*

If he chose, he *could* delve into Falconsbane's memories now; mostly, he did not choose to do so. There was too much there that still made him sick; and it all frightened him with the thought that Falconsbane might *not* be gone after all. Hadn't *he* hidden within the depths of Falconsbane's mind for years without the Dark Adept guessing he was there? What was to keep the far more experienced and practiced Adept from having done the same? He had only Firesong's word that Mornelithe Falconsbane had been destroyed for all time. Firesong himself admitted he had never before seen anything like the mechanism Falconsbane had used for his own survival. How *could* Firesong be so certain that Falconsbane had not evaded him at the last moment? An'desha lived each moment with the fear that he would look into the mirror and see Mornelithe Falconsbane staring out of his eyes, smiling, poised to strike. And this time, when he struck at An'desha, there would be no escape.

Firesong was teaching An'desha the Tayledras ways of magic, and every lesson made that fear more potent. It had been magic that brought Falconsbane back to life; could more magic not do the same?

But by the same token, An'desha was as afraid of not learning how to control his powers as he was of learning their
mysterious ways. Firesong was a Healing Adept; surely he
should be the best person of all to help An'desha bind up his
spiritual wounds and come to terms with all that had happened to him. Surely, if there were physical harm to his mind,
Firesong could excise the problem. Surely An'desha would
flower under Firesong's nurturing light.

Surely. If only I were not so afraid. . . .

Afraid to learn, afraid not to learn. There was an added
complication as well, as if An'desha needed any more in his
life. The first time he had voiced his temptation to let the
magic lie fallow and untapped within him, Firesong had told
him, coolly and dispassionately, that there was no choice. He
must learn to master his magics. Falconsbane never possessed a descendant who was anything less than Adept potential. That potential did not go away; it probably could not
even be forced into going dormant.

In other words, An'desha was still possessed of all the
scorching power-potential of Mornelithe Falconsbane, an
Adept that even *Firesong* would not willingly face without
the help of other mages. The power remained quiescent
within the Shin'a'in, but if An'desha were ever faced with a
crisis, he might react instinctively, with only such training as
he vaguely recalled from rummaging through Falconsbane's
memories.

On the whole, that was not a good idea. Especially if the
objective was to keep anything in the area alive.

To wield the greater magics successfully, the mage must be
confident in himself and sure of his own abilities, else the
magic could turn on him and eat him alive. Falconsbane had
no lack of self-confidence; unfortunately, that was precisely
the quality that An'desha lacked.

*I cannot even bear to meet all the strangers here, and it is
their land we dwell in!* Stupid of course; they would not eat
him, nor would they hold Falconsbane's actions against *him*.
But the very idea of leaving this sheltered place and walking
the relatively short distance to the Palace, crowded with curious strangers, made him want to crawl under the waterfall
and not come out again.

So he remained here, protected, but cowering within that protection.

He found it difficult to believe that no one here would hold against him the evil Falconsbane had done. *He* had such difficulty facing those stored memories that he could not imagine how people could look at him and not be reminded of the things "he" had done.

And I don't even know the half of them ... the most I know are the things he did to Nyara. The truth was, he didn't want to know what Falconsbane had done—never mind that Firesong kept insisting that he must face every scrap of memory eventually. Firesong told him, over and over again, that he *needed* to deal with every act, however vile, and mine it for its worth.

He decided that he had stewed enough in the hot water; any more, and he was going to look like cooked meat. There were no helpful little *hertasi* here in Valdemar to attend to one's every need—a fact Firesong complained of bitterly—but An'desha had grown up in an ordinary Shin'a'in Clan on the Plains. That was a place where if a person did not do things for himself—unless he was incapacitated and needed help— they did not get done. He had brought his own towels and robes to leave beside the pool, with extras for Firesong when he should reappear, and made use of those now.

This hot pool was the mirror image of a cold one on the other side of the garden. It had a smooth backrest of sculptured rock, taller than the user's head; hot water welled up from a place in the center of the pool, and a waterfall showered cooler water down from above, from an opening at the top of the backrest. The whole was surrounded by screening "trees" and curtains of vines; Firesong did not particularly care if someone wandered by and got an eyeful, but An'desha was not so uninhibited.

Firesong's white firebird flew gracefully across the garden room as he climbed out of the pool and dried himself off. It landed beside the smaller, cooler pool that supplied the waterfall, in a bowl Firesong had built for it to bathe in. It plunged in with the same enthusiasm as the humblest sparrow, sending water splashing in all directions as it flapped and rolled in the shallow rock basin. When it finally emerged from its bath, it looked terrible, as if it had some horrible feather disease, and its wings were so soaked it could scarcely fly. It didn't even bother to try; it just hopped up onto a higher perch to preen itself dry with single-minded concentration. Hawkbrothers usually had specially-bred raptors as bondbirds, but in this, as in all else, Firesong was an exception.

An'desha got along quite well with the bird, whose name was Aya; especially after he had coaxed some berrybushes the bird particularly craved to grow, blossom, and bear fruit out of season in this garden. Aya was happy here; he did not seem to miss the Vales at all.

Even the firebird felt more at home here than he did.

He recognized the fact that he was feeling sorry for himself, and he didn't much care. The firebird paused in its preening, as if it had read his thoughts, and gave him a look of complete disgust before shaking out its wet tail and turning its back on him.

Well, let it. The firebird had never had its body taken over by a near-immortal entity of pure filth, had it?

He dried his hair and wrapped himself up in his thick robe, then went off to one part of the garden he considered his very own.

In the southwestern corner of the garden, near the window, he had planted a row of trees screening a mound of grass off from the rest of the garden. In that tiny patch of lawn he had pitched a very small tent, tall enough to stand in, but no wider than the spread of his arms. It wasn't quite a Shin'a'in tent, and it certainly wasn't weatherproof, but that hardly mattered since it was always summer in this garden. Here, at least, he could fling himself down on a pallet, look up at a roof of canvas, and see something that resembled home. And as long as he made no sound, there was no way to know whether or not the tent was occupied. Firesong had made no comment about the tent, perhaps understanding that he *needed* it, even as Firesong needed some semblance of a Vale.

A strand of his own damp white hair tangled itself up in his fingers as he pushed open the tent flap, and he shook it loose impatiently. White hair—he looked Tayledras. Just as Tayledras as Firesong or Darkwind. There was no way that anyone would know he was Shin'a'in unless he told them. Was there a reason for that? Firesong had told him it was because of the magic, but if the Star-Eyed had chosen, She *could* have given him back his native coloring. For a little time, at least.

He sat down on the pallet; it was covered with a blanket of Shin'a'in weaving—a gift from a Herald, who'd bought it while on her far-away rounds—and it still smelled faintly of horse, wood smoke, and dried grasses. The scent was enough, if he closed his eyes, to make him believe he was home again.

If the Star-Eyed could remake my body, couldn't She have taken away the magic, too?

Magic. For a long time, he'd wanted to be a mage. Now he wished She had taken his magic away, but there was always a reason why She did or did not do something.

He stared at the canvas walls, glowing in the late afternoon sun coming through the windows, and chewed his lower lip.

If She left me with magic, it is because She wants me to use it for some reason that only She knows. Firesong keeps saying it's my duty to do this, to Her as well as to myself. He felt a flash of hot resentment at that. Hadn't he risked everything to defeat Falconsbane—not just the pain and death of his body, but the destruction of his soul and his self? Wasn't that *enough?* How much more was he going to have to do?

Then he flushed with shame and a little apprehension, for he was not the only one to have risked all on a single toss of the dice. What of those who had dared penetrate to Ancar's own land to rid the world of Ancar, Hulda, and Falconsbane? If Elspeth had been captured, she would have been taken by Ancar for his own private tortures and pleasures. Ancar had hated the princess with a passion that amounted to obsession and, given the depravities that Falconsbane had overheard the servants whispering about, Elspeth would have endured worse than anything An'desha had faced.

Then there was Darkwind. Falconsbane hated Darkwind k'Sheyna more than any human on the face of the world, and only a little less than the gryphons. If Darkwind had been captured, his fate would have been similar to the one Elspeth would have suffered. And as for Nyara—

Nyara's disposition would have depended on whether or not King Ancar had recognized her as Falconsbane's daughter. If he had, he would have known she represented yet another way to control the Dark Adept, and she might have been kept carefully to that end. But if not—if Ancar had given her back to her father—

She would have been wise to kill herself before that happened. In her case, it would not have been hate that motivated atrocity, but the rage engendered by having a "possession" revolt and turn traitor. Motivation aside, the result would have been the same.

As for Skif and Firesong, the former would have been recognized as one of the hated Heralds and killed out of hand; the latter? Who knew? Certainly Falconsbane *and* Ancar would have been pleased to get their hands on an Adept, and given enough time, anyone could be broken and used, even an Adept of the quality of Firesong.

No, he was not the only person who had risked everything to bring Falconsbane down, so he might as well stop feeling sorry for himself. Still, it hurt.

That was precisely what Firesong would likely tell him, if Firesong had been there, instead of teaching young Herald-Mages the very basics of their Gift.

Firesong.... Once again, a wave of mingled embarrassment and desire traveled outward in an uncomfortable flush of heat. Somehow Firesong had gone from comforter to lover, and An'desha was not quite certain how the transition had come about. For that matter, he didn't think Firesong was quite sure how it had happened. It certainly made a complicated situation even more so.

Not that I needed complications.

He flung himself down on his back and stared at the peak of the tent roof. How did a person sort out a new life, a new home, a new identity, and a new lover, all at once?

It only made the situation more strained that the new lover was trying to be part of the solution.

Would it be easier if Firesong had been nothing more than a concerned stranger, perhaps even a tentative friend, as Darkwind or the two gryphons were?

He's being awfully patient, I suppose. Anyone else would have given up on me by now. Surely a stranger would have blown up at him more than once, have cursed him for his timidity, and consigned him to the ranks of those that could not be helped because they would not help themselves.

On the other hand, sooner or later Firesong's frustration was going to overcome his patience. He *wouldn't* be able to be impartial; he made no secret of the fact that he wanted, badly, for An'desha to reach his potential as a mage so that the two of them could enjoy a relationship of two equal partners, the kind that the gryphons had.

But is that what I want? Part of him longed for it with all his heart. Part of him shied away from the very idea. Firesong frightened him sometimes; the Healing Adept was so very certain of himself and what he wanted. *Sometimes I don't think he's had a single doubt in his life. How could I ever have anything in common with someone like him?* Powerful, charismatic, blindingly intelligent, and handsome enough to be a young god, Firesong was everything An'desha had imagined he *could* be, back in that long-ago day when he had run away from his Clan. No longer; he had endured too much, and he could never be that naive or hopeful again.

But Firesong *was* all those things. He would *never* lack for bed partners. An'desha could not imagine someone like Firesong being willing to wait around on the mere chance that a frail Shin'a'in half-breed *might*, one day, regain some of the spirit he had lost. Why should he? Why should he waste precious time that way?

And yet—

He's kind, he's patient. In fact, Firesong had been coaxing, courting, and cajoling him with a gentle awkwardness that seemed to bespeak a distinct lack of practice in those three skills. *Then again, why would he ever need to coax or court anyone? He could have anyone he wanted, I'd think. They must be throwing themselves at his feet, over there in the Palace.* So it was all the more confusing that Firesong was willing to take the time to lead An'desha along like a spooked and frightened colt, time he could, without a doubt, spend more pleasurably elsewhere, with other people.

His thoughts muddled together at that point. He didn't *want* to consider all the ramifications of this. He didn't *want* to think that Firesong meant everything he had said in the dark of the night. He certainly didn't want that kind of devotion.

Did he?

This was getting him nowhere. Rather than face further uncomfortable thoughts, he rose from his pallet and took himself back out into the garden.

The firebird had preened all the water from its feathers, and busily fluffed them, holding its wings away from its body in order to make certain that they dried fully. The bird paid no attention to him as he passed it and went to the far side of the garden, and the wrought-iron staircase that led to the second floor and the *ekele* he shared with Firesong.

He climbed the stairs and emerged in the middle of the central room of the *ekele*, a room intended for socializing. This room looked exactly like the "public" room of any Tayledras *ekele*; it was light and open despite little free floor space, furnished with a number of flat cushions for sitting and lounging, a pair of perches for bondbirds, and some low tables. The floor was a herringbone pattern of two different hardwoods, amber and pale honey.

An'desha passed through this room to reach his own room, one draped with cloth against all the walls, and gathered up in the middle of the ceiling, supposedly to resemble a Shin'a'in tent. Firesong's idea, and he couldn't spoil Firesong's pleasure by telling him it no more looked like the inside of a Shin'a'in tent than the Palace gardens looked like a Vale. It contained the chests that held his clothing, the few personal possessions that he had managed to accumulate, and a more comfortable bed than the pallet in the tent in the garden. He didn't use the bed much, except to lie on and think.

He pulled aside the cloth covering the windows on the outer wall, and looked out into the branches of the tree just outside. He found himself wondering if that story Firesong had heard was true—and if it was, how had it ended? In tragedy, or in happiness?

And how could it matter to me, either way? Oh, I think too much.

He turned back into the room, dropped the robe, and pulled out a shirt and breeches from the chest that held his clothing, pulling them on and trying to ignore the slightly odd cut.

These were not Shin'a'in, and there was no getting around the fact. They would never feel exactly "right."

But it was clothing, and it worked very well; it didn't matter if it felt like Shin'a'in clothing or not.

He turned back to the window—

And suddenly, out of nowhere, *the fear* came again. Not one of the stupid, personal fears, but something much, much greater. He clung to the windowsill with both hands as the sunlight turned as chill as a blizzard sweeping across the Plains, and his teeth chattered as he shook from head to toe, unable to move, scarcely able to draw a breath. His stomach clenched; his jaws locked on a cry of anguish. His heart thundered in his ears, and he wanted only to run, mad with terror, until he couldn't run any farther.

Something is wrong. . . .

Then, abruptly, the fear left him, gasping for breath, as it always did.

But the message remained.

Firesong sat under a crocus-patterned lantern in the gathering dusk, scratching the crest of his firebird. The bird weighed down his other arm, its eyes closed with pleasure, and Firesong's eyes were distant as he concentrated on An'desha's hesitant words.

". . . it was the same as the last time," An'desha concluded, the memory of that terror calling up a chill all over again. "That's three times now, and the circumstances I was in were different all three times."

Firesong nodded slowly, brushing a lock of white hair back behind his neck. The firebird slitted one sleepy eye in disapproval, until Firesong's hand came back to scratch his crest again. "I don't think this is coming from within you," he said, as a night-blooming flower beside An'desha released perfume into the air. "I believe your own impression is right; there is a menace approaching that we are not yet aware of, and this feeling of fear of yours is a presentiment."

An'desha sighed with relief; the first two times that this had happened, Firesong had been inclined to think it was nothing more than a delayed reaction to all that An'desha had been through. Still, he was troubled. "F–F–Falconsbane had no such prescience," he stammered.

Firesong only shrugged. "Falconsbane never wished to know the future," he pointed out. "He assumed it would follow the course that *he* set. And you are not he; the Star-Eyed could well have granted you such a gift along with all else."

A very real possibility and, if so, it was yet another "gift" he wished that She would take back. His face must have reflected that thought since Firesong smiled slightly.

"The most likely direction for threat is east, of course," he continued. "This Empire that the Valdemarans fear so much is rich with mages; I think it likely that they will not end their conquest at the Hardorn border."

As An'desha sat there dumbly, Firesong expanded his speculations. The Empire *was* a good prospect; the Adept was right about that. But An'desha could not rid himself of the surety that the danger was not coming from the Empire.

This was something more than mere warfare; something much, much worse.

When I was still hiding in Falconsbane's body, and the two Avatars of the Star-Eyed came to teach me the way toward freedom, did they not say something about this?

Now that he came to think about it, he believed that they *had*. He had been guided by a pair of spirits, who had once been fleshly. One had been a Hawkbrother, the other, a Shin'a'in shaman. They had helped and taught him how to gradually insinuate himself into his enemy's mind in such a way that Falconsbane thought the thoughts directing his actions were his own. They had also taught him how to gain access to the memories of Falconsbane's many pasts.

At least once, and perhaps more often, they had hinted that if he succeeded in regaining the use of his own body again, there was an even greater peril to be faced.

If only he could remember what they had said! But he had been too busy worrying about his own survival to pay much attention to vague hints of terrible danger to come. He'd had quite enough terrible danger on his plate at the time!

Firesong continued his speculations concerning the threat of this Empire, and he tried in vain to suggest that the peril *might* be coming from elsewhere. Finally, he just gave up;

when Firesong had the bit between his teeth about something, there was no hope for anyone else to get anything in. It was best to just nod thoughtfully and let him continue to expound.

But inside, his thoughts had a new target to circle around in worried, dizzy spirals. The danger was *not* from the East, but from where? What could be worse than an army, full of powerful mages and larger than anything Valdemar had ever seen, bearing down on the border?

If only he could remember. . . .

Karal

3

Karal patted his horse's damp neck nervously and tried not to be too obvious about watching the Valdemaran Guards out of the corner of his eye. The horse fidgeted and danced in place as it picked up his unease, and he dismounted to hold it by its halter, just under the chin. It snuffled his chest but calmed as soon as he got down on the ground beside its head; a light, warm breeze played across both of them, gradually drying the horse's sweating neck.

He continued to stroke it, his nose full of horse scent, the familiar aroma calming his own nerves. Nothing really bad had ever happened to him when he was around horses, and he kept reminding himself of that, holding it to him as if he held to a luck-talisman.

This was a good little gelding, and someone had trained it well before tithing it to Vkandis Sunlord. The sun shone on a perfect, glossy coat, skin without scars or disease, an eye bright with intelligence. Karal had no idea why the gelding's first owner had sent it in as part of his tithe, but it was obviously someone who took his duty to the Sunlord seriously, sending "the first and best fruits of his labor" as the Writ urged, rather than trying to cheat as so many did, sending only the unwanted and unusable.

A good thing for both of us that they did, Trenor.

The gelding was too small and light to go to the cavalry, and too nervous for a scout or skirmisher, so it had gone to the Temple. Karal had known quality horseflesh when he saw it, and requisitioned this youngster the moment his master and mentor suggested that he was entitled to a mount of some kind from the Temple herds.

This gelding was a lovely bay, otherwise perfect except for the slight flaw of high-bred nerves, and he'd named it after his little brother Trenor, who danced in place in much the same way when he was nervous. Trenor the gelding was, without a doubt, the best piece of horseflesh currently in the novices' stables, and every time he rode the gelding, Karal gloated a little under the envious eyes of his fellow novices. None of them were mounted nearly as well as he, although the horses they had requisitioned might look more impressive than little Trenor. *They* were gentlemen for the most part, and were certainly above choosing their own mounts—assuming any of them could tell a spavined breakdown from a sweet little palfrey like this one. And none of them would have stooped to asking for *his* advice. Doubtless, they had sent servants down to the stables, with orders to select beasts "suited to their station." Well, they paid the penalty of pride in their rumps, every time they rode, for the rest of the horses in the stables were a collection of sorry misfits. Most of them were showy pieces, huge creatures with long manes and tails, rejected from some noble warrior's string. Yes, they were lovely to look at, shiny and high-stepping, but they had iron mouths, bad tempers, or gaits that were pure torture to sit.

Not that all these traits were incurable. Karal could have settled an iron mouth or a bad temper quickly enough—but why should he, when his fellow novices neither asked for his help nor deserved it? Let the others suffer; Sunlord knew they'd made *him* suffer in other ways all through his training.

But that was behind him now. By the time he completed this assignment as his mentor's secretary, he would be a full Priest of Vkandis, and the equal of anyone in Karse save the Son of the Sun herself. *No one* could deny him that rank, no matter what his antecedents were.

He squinted up at the sun in the cloudless sky above. *We are all equal in Vkandis' Light,* he reminded himself. *Oh, surely, and cows will take to the air and soar like falcons any day now!*

Trenor tried to dance, this time with impatience, but Karal held him steady, and soothed him with a wordless croon.

How long had it been since he'd seen the human version of this fidgeting bundle of nerves? Three years? No, it was only two.

But if this Valdemaran escort doesn't show up, he may be grown before we ever see home again!

It was an exaggeration, of course, but it felt as if he had been standing here for days beneath the carefully dispassionate gaze of these two young men in their blue and silver uniforms. He and Ulrich waited on a stretch of newly-cut road that was only a few leagues long, one of the tangible evidences of peace with Valdemar. These bits of roadway linked Karse and its former enemy, bridging the distance from a Karsite road to a Valdemaran one, and giving real traffic a place to cross. On the Karsite side was a gatehouse and a pair of guards where the old road joined the new one. On the Valdemaran side were facilities and guards nearly identical to their counterparts at the Karsite border-crossing behind him, except for the color and cut of the uniforms. The Valdemaran version seemed rather severe to Karal, accustomed as he was to the flowing scarlet and gold of the Karsite regulars, with the embroidered sashes of rank, feathered turbans, and brocaded vests. Plain tunics, plain breeches, only the tiniest bit of silver trim and braid . . . these men might have been mistaken for someone's lowest-rank servant, a stable sweeper or horseboy.

Like I was . . . even Father dressed more handsomely than these men do.

Karal's father had never worn such unadorned clothing in Karal's memory; the Chief Stableman of the Rising Sun Inn could boast beautifully embroidered garments from the hands of his loving wife and daughters. His pay might be meager enough, but he could put on a show fit to match anyone of his own station and even a little above. The clothing Karal had worn before the Sun-priests came for him had been plain enough, but he *had* been a stable sweeper, and anyway, he had only been nine. Not nearly a man, and in no way needing to prove his worth the way a man did.

I wish that there was some shade here. The sun that was so kind in the mountains, countering the chill of the breezes, was a burden here. His dark robes soaked it up and released none of the heat. But the situation was too new, too delicate, for any real amenities for the few who wished to cross from Valdemar to Karse. All brush and trees had been cut back from the road for a distance of twenty paces, so that the guards at either gatehouse had a clear view of anyone coming or going. Karal could understand that. This was not a job he would care to have, himself; the guards at the Karsite side were clearly nervous, and the ones here probably were as well. This was only the second time that he had seen a real Valdemaran up close, one of the Hellspawn themselves—

No, not Hellspawn. Her Holiness, the Son of the Sun, High Priest Solaris has said that was all a fiction created by corrupt priests. They are not Hellspawn, they never were. Just people, different from us, but people.

Hard to undo the thinking of a lifetime, though, and if it was hard for him, it must be incredibly difficult for people like the officers in the Army. How must that be, to go to sleep, only to wake up the next day and find that your demonic enemies had become, by Holiest decree, your allies? To learn that they were not demonic at all, and never had been?

To discover that a terrible war that had killed countless thousands over the course of generations should never have taken place and *could have been ended* at any time?

Karal sighed, and his master Ulrich dismounted from his mount, a placid and reliable mule. Ulrich was no horseman, and moreover, he was a most powerful Priest-mage. He might need to work magic at any time, and needed a riding beast that would stand stock still when the reins were dropped, no matter what strangeness it heard or saw. The mule—which Ulrich called "Honeybee," for she was sweet, but had a sting in her tail in the form of a powerful kick when annoyed—was older than Karal, and looked to live and carry her master for the same number of years. Karal liked her, trusting her good sense to bring Ulrich through any common peril. Storms didn't spook her, uncanny visitations could not make her bolt, she knew when to fight and when to flee, and she was surefooted and wise in the way of trails and tracks.

But she was boring to ride, and while he could not have

wanted a better mount for his master, she was the last one he
would have chosen for himself.

"Patience, Karal," Ulrich said in an undertone. "Our escort
is probably on his way this very moment, and will be surprised to see us waiting. We are early; it is not even Sun-
height yet. You may worry when it lacks but a mark or two
before Sundescending."

Karal bowed his head in deference to his master's words.
Ulrich was surely right, yet—

"It seems ill-mannered, sir, to have us cool our heels at the
border-crossing, when you *are* the envoy from Her Holiness,"
he said doubtfully. "And to send only a single escort—it
seems a deliberate slight to me. Should we not have many
guards, perhaps a Court Official, or—"

Ulrich raised his hand to halt his young protégé in mid-
thought. "We are two, coming from the south, wearing the
plain robes of some sort of priest," he pointed out. "If the
Queen sent an escort of a score of her Guards, what would
the obvious inference be? That we *are* envoys of Her Holiness, of course. There are perils along the way, not the least
of which are those who will not believe that the war between
our lands is over."

Ulrich waited patiently while Karal thought out the rest of
the perils for himself. Mobs of angry border people, or even a
single, clever madman could plan to kill old enemies; assassins hoping to eliminate the envoys and thus the alliance
were a real possibility. Even mercenaries could try to slay the
envoys, hoping to start up the war again and thus ensure continued employment. For that matter, the threat need not
come from a citizen of Valdemar; it could come from someone from their own land, hoping to rekindle the flames of the
"holy war against the Hellspawn."

Karal shook his head mournfully, and Ulrich just chuckled.
"That, my son, is why I am envoy and you are a novice. *I* requested that we be met by but a single escort, though I also
requested one who could be trusted completely. I fear that it
takes years of being steeped in deception and infamy to recognize the possibility for both."

Ulrich patted Honeybee's neck, and she sighed. Ulrich nodded at the mounts, at their own equipage. At the moment he

and Karal were wearing only the plainest of their robes for travel. "As we are, with a single escort—yes, we are dressed well, and clearly Priests from a foreign land, but we could be from *any* foreign land. Unless we have the misfortune to come across someone who has seen a Sun-priest, we should meet with no one who will recognize our robes or our medals. Valdemar is awash with foreigners these days, many of them being escorted to Haven even as we. I think that we shall not draw undue attention to ourselves."

Karal did not answer his mentor, but in this case, he thought privately that, for once, Ulrich might be wrong. He took another covert look at the Valdemaran guards, compared the Sun-priest with them, and came up with an entirely different answer than Ulrich's.

They were both dressed with relative modesty, compared to the magnificent garments they would don once they were in the capital city and the Palace, but there were still a myriad of ways that anyone who had ever seen a Karsite would know who and what they were.

They both wore their Vkandis-medals on gold chains, first of all, round gold disks blazoned with a sun-in-glory—and how many people of moderate importance ever wore that much gold? For that matter, *was* there another sect that used that particular blazon? Their garments had a cut peculiar to Karse; certainly Karal had never seen any foreigner attending Her Holiness who wore anything like the Karsite costume. And if they were of moderate importance, why send an escort at all?

Oh, I suppose I worry too much. Ulrich is right; if what we have heard is true, there are foreigners arriving daily who are so outlandish that we shall not even attract a second glance.

Ulrich was certainly not particularly remarkable; many novices passed him by every day, thinking him a Priest of no particular importance. He was, in fact, utterly ordinary in looks and demeanor—of middling height, neither very young nor very old, neither handsome nor hideous, neither muscular nor a weakling. His gray hair and beard and perpetually mild expression belied the sharpness of his eyes, and his expression could change in a moment from bemused and kindly to implacable. These Valdemarans seemed to be of no particular physical type; one of the guards was lean and brown, the other muscular and blond. Not so with the two Karsites, for both were typical of anyone from their land; Ulrich could easily have been Karal's hawk-faced father; they were two from the same mold, dark-haired, dark-eyed, sharp-featured.

Perhaps that was all to the good, too. Outsiders might assume that they *were* related. Better and better, in fact, since Karal doubted anyone outside Karse knew that the Sunpriests were *not* required to be celibate or chaste, though many of them swore such oaths for various reasons. So if he and Ulrich appeared to be father and son—it might be that no one would think they were priests of any kind.

Karal rubbed his temple; all this thinking was giving him a headache. Ulrich patted his shoulder with sympathy as the guards continued to ignore them.

"Don't worry about it too much, young one," the Sunpriest said, with a kindly gleam in his black eyes. "Try to get used to the new land first, before you devote any time to learning about intrigue and hidden dangers. There will be enough that is strange to you, I think, for some few days."

The Sun-priest—the Red-robe who was once one of the feared and deadly *Black*-robe priests of the Sunlord, a wielder of terrible power and commander of demons—looked back down the road they had come and sighed. "You have seen so many changes already in your short lifetime, I should think you will cope better with this new place than I. To you, this must seem like a grand new adventure."

Karal choked back a reply to *that*; little as he wanted to be sent off into this voluntary exile, he wanted still less to be sent home in disgrace. But he did *not* think of this as a "grand new adventure," nor any kind of an adventure; at heart, he was a homebody. His notion of a good life meant achieving some success as a scholar, perhaps finding a suitable partner among the ranks of the female Priests, growing older, wiser, and rich in children and grandchildren. Yes, he had seen changes aplenty since he had been taken from his own family at nine, and being subject to having his world turned upside down before he was twelve had not made him any readier for having it turn again at thirteen, fourteen, fifteen, or now, at sixteen.

In fact, most of the time lately he was just plain bewildered, and there were moments when the stress was so great that he feared it was visible to anyone who looked at him.

Is there not some barbarian curse that wishes your life be interesting? If so, then he should find the barbarian who had visited such a curse on him and persuade him to remove it! He found excitement enough in books for anyone's lifetime.

At nine, he had been his father's apprentice; a horseboy and stable sweeper, and supremely content with his position and the world. He loved horses, loved everything about them, and looked forward to rising to take his father's job when he was old enough. He had three sisters, two older and one younger, to tease and torment as any small boy would, and a little brother who toddled after him at every opportunity with a look of adoration on his chubby face. There was always food enough on the table, and if it was plain fare, well, there were folk enough who had not even that, and he knew it even then. He had been *happy* as he was. He had not wanted any changes that he could not foresee.

By now he had seen enough of other families to know how idyllic, in many ways, his own had been. Both his parents were as ready to praise as to reprimand, and no matter what mischief he had been into, he could count on forgiveness following repentance. His Father was proud of him, and was teaching him everything *he* knew about horses and horseflesh. His world was full of things and people he loved; what more did any boy need?

There was only one cloud in all their lives—the annual Feast of the Children, when parents were ordered to bring their children to the Temple to be inspected by the Sunpriests. The examinations began when a child was five, and ended when he was thirteen. The Feast always brought suppressed terror to every parent in the town, but it was especially hard on Karal's father and mother, for both of them had had siblings who were taken away by the Priests, and were subsequently burned for the heresy of harboring "witch-powers." There was always the fear that one of their children might be taken—and worse still, might be given to the Fires. Even those who were not thrown to the Fires never saw their homes and families again, for that was the way of the Sun-priests. So it had "always" been.

For four years, the Priests had passed Karal over, and his father and mother had begun to lose a little of their fear, at least for his sake, if not for the sake of his younger siblings. Even he began to feel a cocky certainty that the Feast would never mean more to him than an occasion to claim a double handful of spun-sugar Vkandis Flames from the Priest's servants when the inspection was over.

But then, the year he was nine, his world and his certainty shattered.

A new Priest came to the Feast; a new Priest in black robes, rather than red, a Priest who watched him with narrowed eyes—

—and claimed him for the Sunlord.

One moment he had been standing with the others in a neat line; the next, a heavy hand came down on his shoulder, and two servants seized him before he could react, ushering him into the Temple, pushing him past the altar into the rooms beyond, where the townsfolk were never permitted, only those belonging to the Temple.

He didn't remember much of that day, or even of the following week, which might have been due to shock, or to the potion the Priest gave him to drink when he launched into hysterical tantrums. He had been the only child chosen from his town, and there was no one else he knew to share his ordeal and his exile. He vaguely remembered a long ride inside a dark wagon, which paused now and again so that another blank-eyed, stranger-child could join him on the bench. No spun-sugar for him or for them; only a bitter cup, a long period of shadow-haunted daze, and then the awakening in a strange and hostile place—the so-called Children's Cloister, where he and the others would live and study until they were accepted as novices or given duties as Servants.

Or until someone said they had witch-powers. He shuddered, cold creeping over him for a moment, as if the sun had lost its power to warm him.

In time, Karal came to accept what he could not change. He was told that he would never see his family again; that he was reborn into a new and greater family, the Kin of Vkandis.

They allowed him time to rebel, one chance to *attempt* to run away. This was unsuccessful, as were all such attempts as far as he ever learned. A terrible creature of flame caught him at the gate, and chased him back to the Cloister. *He* never made a second attempt, though he heard that others did; he resigned himself to his fate.

Then began the lessons, hour after hour of them.

Most of the children did not master much more than the barest skills of reading and writing; those were sent, at ten, to become Servants. Some, a fraction of the rest, were taken off by the Priests for "special training" that had nothing to do with scholarly pursuits.

Some few of *those* were given to the Flames, later, as witches. Karal and the rest were required to attend the burnings, and he was told that the ashes were returned to their families as a mark of the disgrace to their bloodline. The three burnings he had witnessed still gave him nightmares.

For some reason, Karal did well in scholastic pursuits and did not again attract the attention of those who meted out "special training." He found a pure pleasure in learning that was as great as his pleasure in anything he had ever experienced. He soon outstripped most of the others who had originally been "collected for Vkandis" with him. This gained him admission to another group of young pupils—the offspring of nobles and the well-to-do, sent as their parents' tithe to Vkandis, children who had the advantage of tutoring from an early age. These had never before been forced to share teachers or quarters with those of the lower classes . . . they resented this new development in their lives, and needed someone to take their displeasure out on.

And that had opened him to a new series of torments—not overt, but covert. He pleased his teachers, and the young nobles could not cause him trouble in his classes, but *outside* those classes, he was fair game for any prank they could invent that would not call down the wrath of their Keeper on them.

He shook his head, driving away the unpleasant memories for now. *None of that mattered, then or now. I have to remember that.* What mattered was that he had graduated into the ranks of the novices with high honors, despite the opposition of the other students, and when the time came to be taken by a mentor, he was selected by that *same* Black-robed Priest who had singled him out at the Feast of the Children.

Only now he *knew* what those ebony robes meant. His new mentor was a Priest-mage, a user of magic in Vkandis' name, and a summoner of demons.

He would have been terrified, if Ulrich hadn't immediately shown his kindly nature. And every morning since that day, he had offered up a paean of gratitude with his other prayers that it had been Ulrich who had chosen him. His Master had rank enough that not one of his fellow novices dared to torment him further, though they could, and did, shut him out socially.

Not that he cared. His Master was a scholar, and set him scholarly tasks that suited his nature. When his Master learned of his background and his love of horses, he suggested he find himself a mount early enough that the horses and mules were not all picked over. Ulrich *made certain* he had time out, every day, to spend at least a mark or two with his beloved gelding, Trenor. For a week or two, everything was well; he thought for certain that the future was again predictable.

He had already suffered two upheavals in his life—being torn from his family and being shoved, will-he, nill-he, into the ranks of those born far, far above his station. Now he suffered the third, but this time, the entire Kin of Vkandis "suffered" along with him.

Vkandis—the God Himself—selected a *woman* to be the Son of the Sun, in a fashion that brooked no denial of the validity of her claim to the position. That woman, High Priest Solaris, proceeded to set the entire established hierarchy on its side, declaring things that *had* been established orthodoxy for generations to be perversions of Vkandis' Word and Will.

And Ulrich not only approved, he was in the thick of it all, as one of Solaris' most trusted aides and assistants. So, perforce, was his protégé.

Not that I was unhappy about that initially—not when one of the first things she did was to order that all novices and under-novices were to be permitted the same contact with their families that Army recruits had! Until that moment, no one taken by the Priests was ever permitted any contact with his family, even the most casual. Now he was able to write to them, even visit them twice a year, something that would have been unthinkable under the old Rules. In fact, when Solaris appointed Ulrich as her special envoy to Valdemar, she had taken the effort to order that Karal also take a week of special leave to see his family before he left with his Master. And when had a Son of the Sun ever concerned himself with something as trivial as the needs of a mere novice?

He stroked Trenor's neck soothingly, smiling to himself. The very first time he had gone home, the entire fortnight had been a wonderful visit. His mother had been so proud of him—and his father had been beside himself with pleasure. *His* son was secretary to a powerful Priest! *His* son was privy to all the secrets of the high and privileged! *His* son would see people and situations his father could only dream about.

But that had come later; no sooner had Solaris staged her internal revolution and he had returned from his first Familial Visit, than Karse acquired a new enemy, in the person of King Ancar of Hardorn. Ancar staged a major attack on the border; not in living memory had there been anything in the way of a concerted attack from Hardorn. The shock of the attack had reverberated throughout the entire country; to be honest, most Karsites were used to scoring small covert victories and raids against Hardorn and Valdemar, not having a concerted attack staged on their own borderlands.

The skirmishing had become all-out war, with Karse very much the weaker of the two. Not even the Black-robe Priests and their magic could counter Ancar, his army, and his mages.

Solaris had predicted this. Very few had believed her. *Now*, with her star in the ascendant, she made the most unprecedented move of all.

She recruited a new ally; one not even Ulrich could have predicted.

Valdemar. Valdemar, home of the White Demons and their Hellhorses. Valdemar, land of Hellspawn, land that had given shelter to the heretic Holderkin, sworn enemies of Vkandis and all he stood for.

And once again, Vkandis showed by signs that could not be counterfeited that He approved.

Suddenly, by decree of Solaris and Vkandis Himself, Valdemar had become the abode of the slightly misguided, but noble-minded allies of Karse. It was nothing short of a miracle that Solaris managed to get just enough cooperation out of her own folk to rush the alliance through. It was just in time, just barely in time to keep Ancar of Hardorn from squashing Solaris and Selenay like a couple of insects, and their lands and peoples with them.

As Ulrich's secretary, Karal had been in the midst of everything, from the initial plan to the complex negotiations to the investiture of a woman from Valdemar as a Vkandis Priest. It left him breathless, and so bewildered before it was all over that all he could do was to hold onto his sanity with both hands and watch with wide and often confused eyes. Now, with the advent of peace, it was harder than ever to encompass the notion that the Evil Ones were now to be Karse's best friends. . . .

"I believe our escort is here," Ulrich said, breaking into Karal's thoughts.

He looked up, shading his eyes with his hand, staring past the gate and the two Guards to the roadway beyond. For a moment, he saw nothing against the glare of the sun on the dust of the road. Then he caught a glimpse of movement; his focus sharpened, and he spotted a rider coming around a far-off bend in the road.

The man could hardly be missed even against the sun glare; he was clad all in white, with a horse as white as the clouds in the sky above him.

This was no ordinary traveler; the quality of his clothing was very high—white garments were expensive to keep pristine. The garments he wore had the feeling of a uniform about them; Karal knew that the colors of Valdemar were silver, blue, and white. Was this Royal livery of some sort? As the man drew nearer still, Karal noted the extreme quality of his tack, specially dyed and constructed, of the same colors of silver and blue that the Guards wore. The Guards themselves were waiting for the man with a deference they had not shown the two Karsites, which in itself was interesting. Did this mean their escort was of higher rank than an envoy, or did it mean that no one had told these two Guards anything at all about Ulrich and his young secretary, not even that they were Solaris' envoys?

Well, it probably didn't matter at this point.

The man paused at the Gate, but he did not dismount; instead, he leaned over the neck of his mount to talk to the two Guards. Now Karal stole a moment to admire the horse he rode. The head was quite broad across the forehead, which argued for high intelligence. Aside from that—which some might consider a flaw, though Karal would not agree with them—the beast was breathtakingly beautiful. He had never seen a horse so perfectly white as this one, which gleamed as if someone had just washed it—and how on earth did the Valdemaran manage to get that silver sheen to the horse's hooves? Not paint, surely—paint would damage the hoof and deform it. No one but a fool would paint the hooves of a horse like this one.

As the rider spoke with the Guards, the horse shifted slightly, as if to watch the two Karsites. Its movements were as graceful as the horse itself was beautiful; it arched its neck so that its flowing mane fell just *so,* for all the world as if it knew how stunning it was.

Perfect. That was Karal's thought, and he reveled in the fact that he would be spending the next several days in the company of such a beast.

After a brief consultation with the Guards, the man in white beckoned to them. Now that he'd had his fill of watching the horse from afar, Karal was perfectly willing to mount Trenor and rein in behind Ulrich; he'd had enough waiting around to last him for quite a while!

It probably isn't going to be the last time I have to stand around and wait, though.

The escort had blond hair going to gray at the temples, a good, square jaw, deep-set, frank, hazel-colored eyes, and a nose that had obviously been broken more than once in the past. He sat his horse rather stiffly, which struck an odd note, given the grace of the horse itself.

The man hesitated for a moment, then held out his hand to Ulrich as they approached the gate. "Envoy Ulrich?" he said, as his horse stood rock-steady beneath him, showing no more inclination to shy away from strange beasts than if the horse were carved of pure alabaster. "I am your escort. Call me Rubrik, if you will."

It has blue eyes, Karal saw, with a surge of disappointment. Most blue-eyed, white creatures were stone deaf. Was this the flaw in this otherwise perfect mount? Certainly deafness would account for the horse's apparent calm.

Ulrich took the man's hand and shook it, as Honeybee eyed the blue-eyed white horse dubiously, probably expecting a nip or a kick from it.

The man's Karsite was excellent; much better than Karal's Valdemaran. He had very little accent, and when he spoke, there was no sense that he was stopping to translate mentally before saying anything.

"You speak our language very well, sir," Ulrich replied with grave courtesy, "and I hope you will accept my apology for not returning the compliment, but the truth is, I am nowhere near as fluent in your tongue as you seem to be in ours. This is my secretary, Karal."

The man held out his hand to Karal, who followed his mentor's example and shook it. Rubrik's clasp was firm and warm, without being a "test." Karal decided cautiously that he liked this Valdemaran.

Rubrik squinted up at the sun once he had released Karal's hand. "You have come a long way, and as I am sure you realize, there is a longer journey still ahead of you, Envoy," he told Ulrich. "Weather in Valdemar is still not so settled that I'd care to wager on clear skies for more than a day. I'd like to make as much distance as we can while the weather holds, if you've no objection."

Ulrich shook his head. "No objection whatsoever," he replied. "You are limited only to the number of leagues our two beasts are able to travel in a day; my secretary and I are good riders, and have no trouble spending dawn to dusk in the saddle, if you like."

Karal winced at that; *he* was not so sure of his endurance as Ulrich seemed to be. Hopefully, the man would not take him at his word.

Rubrik smiled warmly. "Your High Priest Solaris has chosen her envoy well, my lord," was his only reply. "If you would follow me?"

The trio passed the silent Guards, went through the open gate, and for the first time in his life, Karal entered a foreign land.

Karal had expected to feel—something—once he was across the border and in a new land. Some kind of difference in the air, or in himself. He'd expected that this alien place would *look* different from Karse somehow, that the grass and trees would be some odd color, that the people would be vastly different. There was no reason to have expected anything of the sort, of course—

—but emotions don't respond well to logic, I suppose.

As they rode northward all the rest of the day, there was literally no way of telling that they were not in Karse. The hills were virtually identical to the ones they had just traversed; covered with the same trees, the same grass. The scents in the air were the same; sun-warmed dust, the occasional perfume of briar-roses blooming beside the road.

The few people that they encountered were not really all that different either, except that it was obvious they were *not* Karsite. Their clothing was different; plain in the extreme, severely styled, in muted grays, browns, and tans. Mud-colors, really; no Karsite would ever wear such nothing-colors unless he were too abysmally poor to afford anything else, or unless he intended to do some truly filthy task and didn't want his proper clothing ruined. Even for work in the fields most Karsites wore good, strong saffrons and indigos—but not these folk.

They passed a number of folk cutting hay, one herding swine and another with a flock of geese, a few weeding fields of cabbages or other vegetables. The animals turned to watch the trio pass; the people themselves blatantly ignored the travelers, turning away from the road, in fact, in stiff and disapproving attitudes that bordered on rudeness. "Holderkin," Rubrik said, after the third or fourth time that someone deliberately turned his face from them. The escort sighed and shook his head. "I'm sorry about this. They don't like those of us who represent the Queen, much—hardly more than they like you Karsites. I do believe that if there was any way to manage it, they'd create their own little country here, build a high wall around it, and shut Valdemar *and* Karse outside forever and aye."

Ulrich laughed at that, and his eyes crinkled up at the corners with sympathetic good humor. "In that case, sir, I think my land well rid of them. I am marginally familiar with them, in a purely historical sense. They seem to have made themselves something of a thorn in your side."

Rubrik shrugged ruefully and rubbed the side of his nose. "I can't say that *no* good has come from them—the Queen's Own, Lady Talia, is of Holderkin breeding. But aside from that, they are a damned unpleasant people, and I've had occasion more than once to wish them somewhere far, far away."

Karal kept silent through this exchange, watching their escort, and trying to deduce why the man rode so stiffly. How was it that someone who seemed to be such a clumsy rider had such a fine mount? How was it that the mount was so used to the rider that the horse itself actually accommodated the rider?

Finally, as Rubrik turned to point out a wedge of geese flying overhead, pursued by a goshawk, the answer to all those questions came to him.

Rubrik's right arm moved stiffly; he could not seem to raise it above his shoulder. There was a "dead" quality to the right side of his face. And although his *right* knee stuck out woodenly, his left leg showed the perfect form of an experienced rider.

Rubrik was injured somehow—or he'd had some kind of brainstorm. He was partially paralyzed; the stiffness of his right side and the little tic in the corner of his right eye were the last clues that Karal needed.

Rubrik would have to have such a mount, one trained to compensate for *his* weakness, if he was to be at all mobile. Now Karal's admiration for the stunning horse increased a hundredfold, for a horse so trained must be as intelligent as one of the legendary Shin'a'in beasts.

His admiration turned to more surprise when he realized that Rubrik's horse was not a gelding as he had assumed, but a full stallion. A full stallion—one which showed no interest in Honeybee who, although a mule, was still a mare? What kind of training could ever give a horse that kind of self-control?

He would have asked just that question if Ulrich had not engaged their escort's attention completely, asking about some complex situation at the Valdemaran Court. A good half of the names Ulrich bandied about so casually completely eluded his secretary, although Karal recognized most of the rest from all the correspondence he had handled over the past few weeks.

I guess there was a lot more going on in those private conferences than Ulrich led me to believe. Not that *that* should surprise him!

He suppressed his own curiosity and simply listened to the two men talk, for this, too, was part of his job—to learn as much as he could by listening.

Eventually, either Ulrich tired of asking questions, or the envoy decided that he wanted to think about what he had learned before he asked anything more. By this time, the last of the farmlands were behind them; if anyone used the hills on either side of the road for anything, it was probably to harvest timber and for grazing. Silence fell on the party, broken only by the sounds of wildlife out in the forested hills, and by the sound of the hooves of their mounts.

That was when Karal noticed something else. While Trenor and Honeybee had perfectly normal, dull, clopping hoofbeats, the sounds of the white horse's hooves striking the ground had a bell-like tone to them.

Maybe the Valdemarans *did* treat the beast's hooves in some way; how else could they be silver and have such a musical sound to them?

The road they were on generally followed the contour of the land itself, staying pretty much in the valleys between the hills. Once in a while Karal caught a whiff of he-goat musk, or spotted the white blobs of grazing sheep among the trees. Forest rose on either side of the road; tall trees that had been growing for decades at least. In places the limestone bones of these hills showed through the thin soil; the trees themselves were mostly goldenoak with a sprinkling of pine or other conifers, and the occasional beech or larch.

What the forest lacked in human inhabitants, it made up for in animals. Squirrels scolded them as they passed, and songbirds called off in the distance, their voices filtering through the leaves. Jays and crows followed them with rowdy catcalls, telling all the world that *interlopers* were passing through. Once a hawk stooped on something right at the edge of the road, and lumbered up out of the way just as they reached the spot, with a snake squirming in its talons.

The road met the path of a wide river as the sun westered and sank below the level of the treetops. Karal caught glimpses of the water through the screening of trees, reflecting the light in shiny bursts through the brush.

By this time, despite his master's assertion that the two of them could stay in the saddle as long as need be, he was getting saddle sore and stiff. His buttocks ached; his back and shoulders were in knots. He began to wonder just when this Rubrik intended to stop—or did he want to ride all night?

There was no sign of a town or village, though, so there didn't seem to be any place they *could* stop. *I don't mind camping out—but Ulrich is too old for that sort of thing,* he thought, a bit resentfully, but telling himself that concern for his master was more important than his own aches and pains. *We don't have tents, we don't even have proper blanket rolls. Surely this man isn't going to expect the envoy of the Son of the Sun to sleep in leaves, rolled up in his own cloak like a vagabond!*

"There's a village I expect to reach just after sundown," Rubrik said, startling Karal. It was almost as if the man had just read his own thoughts! "If you don't think you can make it that far, please tell me, but I've made arrangements there for a private suite for you two." He made an apologetic grimace. "I hope this doesn't seem boorish, but I would rather that no one know your exact origin or your mission here until we reach Haven, and the best way to keep quiet is to keep the two of you away from people who might be a bit too curious about visitors to Valdemar."

Ulrich waved away any apologies. "Those are my thoughts, precisely," he replied. "The fewer folk who even know there are two Priests traveling here, the better. That was why I requested that Queen Selenay send only a single escort. But I must confess, I am not as confident of my stamina as I was when we met you." He shook his head at his own weakness, then shrugged. "We are used to riding most of the day, but I have just begun to realize that 'most' of the day is not the same as 'all' of the day."

"If it helps any, I have requested that a hot dinner be served in the suite as soon as you arrive," Rubrik answered with an engaging smile. "And hot baths to follow."

"I wouldn't say no to a bottle of horse-liniment as well, sir," Karal ventured, a little shy at inserting himself into the conversation.

"That I can supply myself—muscle-salve, and not horse-liniment, young sir," the escort said, turning to look at him, as if surprised that he was back behind his master. Perhaps Rubrik had forgotten him?

Karal was far more pleased than offended, for if that was what had happened, it meant that he had achieved his end of being "invisible." Ulrich had told him that a good secretary would develop the knack of vanishing into the background; that would make him less intrusive, especially to people who might be nervous about a third party being present at a delicate negotiation.

"That would be very much appreciated, my lord Rubrik," Karal replied, ducking his head in an approximation of a bow.

But Rubrik shook an admonishing finger at Karal. "Not 'my lord,' youngling," he chided gently. "Just 'Rubrik.' Among Heralds, there are no titles—with the sole exception of the Lady Elspeth, the Queen's daughter. My father—was something of a landowner, a kind of farmer."

"Ah?" That clearly caught his master's attention. "And what did he farm, if I may ask?"

"Root crops, mostly, though he had some herds as well," was the ready answer. That set the two of them off on a discussion of the condition of farms and farmers in both Valdemar and Karse, and it was Rubrik's turn for questions, mostly about the weather, and whether or not it had affected the Karsites as badly as it had their Valdemaran counterparts.

Karal wondered if Rubrik realized how much information *he* was giving with the way he phrased his questions.

The moon rose, silvering the road before them. Karal listened and made mental notes for later. If all that Rubrik told them was true, Valdemar had been suffering from truly horrible weather until very recently—storms and disturbances out of season that were somehow connected with the magics Ancar of Karse had been working.

"But now that we've got a few mages doing weather-working, things are getting back to normal. In time to save the harvests, we hope," Rubrik concluded.

If he hoped for a similar statement from Ulrich, he was not going to get one. "Vkandis has always cared personally for the welfare of His people," Ulrich replied, and Karal was very glad that it was dark enough that he did not have to hide a smile. *That* was certainly a double-edged statement, and quite entirely the truth as well! It could be taken by an outsider as the simple pious mouthings of a Priest—but the bare fact was that Vkandis *did* care *personally* for the welfare of His people. What His Priests could not deal with, using the powers of magic He had granted them, He might very well take care of Himself. Karse had not suffered more than inconvenience from what Ulrich called "wizard weather," precisely because Priests who could control the weather had been sent out to make certain that people, crops, and property were safeguarded properly.

If Rubrik was taken aback by this bland statement, he said nothing. Instead, he described some of the damage that had occurred in Hardorn, which was evidently much worse than that in Valdemar or what had been prevented in Karse.

Ulrich had taught his pupil that unshielded use of powerful magic disrupted the weather, but Karal had never had that lesson demonstrated for him. Now he *heard* what had happened, and he was appalled at the level of destruction that had taken place. And Ancar had done *nothing* to prevent it.

"Ah, look!" Rubrik said, pointing ahead of them. Karal squinted against the darkness and thought he saw lights. "There's our inn at last. We'll be there in less than a mark!"

"And it won't be too soon for me," Ulrich sighed, with feeling.

Nor for me, Karal added silently. His behind hurt so much he was sure that he had saddle-sores, something that hadn't happened since he was a child. The lights in the distance grew brighter and more welcoming with every moment, and the aches in his legs and back grew more persistent. No one had ever warned him that being the secretary to an envoy was going to involve *this* kind of work! *I hope this is the last time I ever have to ride like this for as long as I live!*

Rubrik

4

Karal didn't get his wish, of course. He did, however, get possession of a bottle of muscle-salve that had such near-miraculous properties that he suspected magic, or the talents of a Healer-Priest in preparing it. When he woke the next morning, his aches were mostly gone, and the little pain that was left eased as he rubbed in a new application of the salve. It had a sharp scent somewhat like watercress, not unpleasant, but nothing he recognized. Ulrich helped himself shamelessly to the potion as well, leaving the jar half empty.

They met in the courtyard of the inn, in the thin gray light of false dawn. Rubrik was already waiting, his cloud-white horse saddled and ready to ride. Rubrik himself looked quite disgustingly rested. One sleepy stableboy presented them with their mounts, already saddled, and a cook's helper, powdered with flour, came out from the kitchen with a tray of buttered rolls and mugs of hot tea. Karal was glad he'd used that salve after he helped Rubrik to mount and climbed aboard Trenor. "Stiff" simply wasn't an adequate description for how he felt when he tried to actually make his muscles do some work. That reminded him of how little salve was left in the jar in *his* saddlebag—between himself and Ulrich, it wasn't going to last more than another day or two.

The kitchen helper reappeared with a pair of cloth bags, and handed them to Rubrik, who slung them over his saddlebags. "Our noon meal," their escort explained. "I hope you don't mind eating on the road, but I want to make as much time as possible."

Lovely. Which means we'll probably be riding even longer

today. Somehow he managed not to groan. "Excuse me, sir," he said instead, anxiously. "But that salve you gave me last night worked very well—so well I don't have much left. And—"

"And there's more where that came from, young man," Rubrik replied with a wink. "It's very common in Valdemar; I have more, and I can make sure to *get* more when we stop for the night."

"I can tell already that we both will require it," Ulrich put in, with a rueful smile. "I purloined some of it myself. Perhaps you are used to riding all day, but we are not as sturdy as you. I fear the scholars' life has left both of us ill prepared for this situation."

Karal smiled at his mentor, grateful for Ulrich's little comment. It made *him* look like less of a weakling. After all, how did it look, that a man who was half-crippled could ride longer and harder than a fellow half his age?

They left with the rising sun, completely avoiding any of the other guests at the inn by leaving before anyone else woke up. They didn't stop until late morning, and by that time Karal and his master were both ready for another application of salve. How Rubrik managed such a pace, Karal could *not* fathom. Once they had stopped last night, he'd demonstrated his own physical weakness by needing help to dismount. On the ground, he had limped along with the help of a cane, his bad leg frozen with the knee locked, so that he had to swing it around from the hip, stiffly, in order to use it at all.

This morning he'd needed help to mount as well—help that Karal had provided, since the stableboy had vanished as soon as the lad brought their horses to them. Rubrik's horse had also helped on both occasions, much to Karal's surprise, by lying down so that Rubrik could get his bad leg swung over the saddle with a very little assistance. Karal bit his lip to keep from commenting or asking questions, since this went far beyond any horse training he had ever seen. Rubrik saw his expression, though, and simply smiled, without offering any explanation or inviting any inquiry, so Karal said nothing.

Once the sun actually rose, it looked as if (despite Rubrik's warnings) they were going to have another day of good weather. The sky held dark clouds to the east, but not many were close. It would probably be fairly warm later in the day, but the cool of morning was still in the air and riding would be very pleasant.

Provided my calves aren't tying themselves into knots by the time we stop next.

The second day was a repeat of the first; steady riding with brief stops to stretch, relieve themselves, and eat something. By the afternoon of this second day, the steep and forested hills gradually changed to gentler slopes; the fields beside the road showed signs of agriculture. They began to meet greater numbers of people, both on the road or working in the fields beside it; none of which looked anything like the surly Holderkin of the first day. These people, at least, wore clothing of bright and varied colors, and most were cautiously polite, waving or calling out a greeting as the three of them rode past.

There was curiosity in their expressions, but they kept their distance when Rubrik did not stop or encourage any closer approach. No one seemed terribly concerned or alarmed over their appearance, which eased at least one of Karal's anxieties. He was not anxious to be driven out of Valdemar by that mob of angry peasants he had envisioned. He'd had uneasy moments yesterday, when the Holderkin turned to stare with open hostility, just before averting their faces just as pointedly.

As some of his anxieties disappeared, more surfaced, however. All his life he had heard stories about the Hellspawn of Valdemar, the White Demons and the Hellhorses they rode. Did Rubrik wear white, and ride a white horse, as an honor to the White Demons? Surely all those tales had not been made up out of whole cloth. Certain Karsites—the Black-robe Priests in particular—had enough experience with real demons to know them when they saw them! So where *were* the creatures out of the tales his mother and every other mother told her children? Where were the demons that would *get him* if he wasn't good?

Magic isn't stopped by borders or boundaries, he thought, watching Rubrik's back cautiously. *Our Black-robe Priests could control demons, so it stands to reason that the people here have mages who can, too. So where are they? If this escort of ours intends to impress us with the power of Valdemar and the Queen's mages, now would be the time to trot out a few horrors. He wouldn't want to frighten anyone in a really populated area, after all. He'd want to make sure we were the only witnesses to his private show.*

But they rode up to yet another inn after sundown, tired to the bone, without any sign of horrors, monsters, or, truly, any magic at work at all. So now, were they being insulted by not being shown any magic at all?

By the time they reached the promised inn, Karal was so bone tired that it was all he could do to stay awake. The hot bath waiting for them *did* help the aches and cramped muscles, but once he'd climbed out of the tub and rubbed more of that salve into himself, he could barely keep his eyes open. He ate, but only because he was starving as well as exhausted. He helped his master Ulrich to bed, but he didn't recall falling into his own cot at all. He simply woke there to the sound of knocking on the door.

Once again, they rose before sunrise, leaving the inn behind them still shrouded in darkness. This time the breakfast included fresh berries as well as bread and whipped butter, but otherwise the routine was the same.

Ulrich didn't seem upset by what seemed to Karal to be unseemly haste in getting them north, so Karal held his peace as they ate their meal in the saddle and set out into the gray of predawn. It did occur to him that if it was Rubrik's intention to keep their very existence a secret without going to extreme lengths, such as riding at night and sleeping by day in hiding places, this was a good way to accomplish that intention. Certainly they hadn't had a chance to speak to anyone in the two days they'd been in this land! They arrived so late at their inns last night and the night before that no one would think twice when they ate in their rooms and went straight to sleep without going to the taproom to socialize with the rest of the guests.

And if it was Rubrik's plan to keep them from noticing pertinent military details about Valdemar—well, Karal, for one, was too tired by now to take note of much of anything. He wasn't likely to have known how to tell if something was strategic or not. Ulrich was exactly what he appeared to be, a scholar. The Priest had spent his life in studying magic and the Writ and Rules of Vkandis; Karal was at the beginning of those very same, intense studies, and the very thought of having *time* to study military strategy as well made Karal want to laugh.

Then again, how could Rubrik possibly be sure of that? True, he was only sixteen, but that was the age many young men were commissioned as officers in the Army. He *could* be a military spy; a successful spy presumably would look like something harmless.

Like some Priest's rather young, green, and confused secretary, I suppose.

He knuckled his foggy eyes and stifled a yawn, while Trenor walked briskly behind Honeybee. What was truly mortifying was that Ulrich, who *should* have been in worse shape than he was, actually seemed fresh and alert after his night's sleep. He talked at length with Rubrik, in Valdemaran this time, supposedly in order to refresh his memory and increase his proficiency. Karal listened while their escort rattled on about the people who lived along this road, what crops they grew, what beasts they herded. Pretty boring stuff, but it did sharpen *his* Valdemaran. And for the first time in any language study, they *did* have a reason to ask "how far to the Palace?"

The landscape gradually flattened until, by afternoon, there was nothing on either side of the road but farm country, and the terrain had turned to gentle, rolling hills. Trees lined each side of the road as a windbreak, and more trees were planted in windrows between each plowed or fallow field. A warm breeze crossed their path; warm enough to make him sleepy all over again. He caught himself nodding more than once, jerking awake as he started to lose his seat.

They couldn't avoid people now; every time they stopped to rest, there would be some curious farmer or passing merchant who wondered who they were and what their business was. Rubrik was friendly, but close-mouthed, describing them only as "foreigners." For most people, that seemed to be enough of an explanation.

"Been a mort'o foreigners, lately," said one old man, as he

drew water from his well for their horses. Rubrik agreed and did not elaborate, so the old man's curiosity went unsatisfied. Karal and Ulrich politely pretended that they had not understood him.

But Karal watched their escort closely all during the afternoon after that. He set himself a mental exercise to keep himself awake, trying to determine what choosing *this* man as their escort meant to their status, and hence, their ongoing mission. Of course, this was not technically anything he needed to worry about, but Ulrich would probably be asking him questions, sooner or later, to see what he had reasoned out for himself.

So while Ulrich talked in Valdemaran about the weather, the corn harvest, the other "foreigners" that had been in Valdemar because of the war, Karal watched and listened and thought.

While "crippled" Rubrik might look unsuited to this position, he was certainly bearing up under all this hard riding better than the two "able-bodied" people he was escorting. He didn't need all that much help, really; just what Karal or the occasional common horseboy could provide. His white mount took care of the rest. His command of Karsite was excellent, as Ulrich had already noted; how many people *were* there in Valdemar who were fluent in Karsite? There couldn't be many.

Rubrik was well-versed enough in the current situation in the Valdemaran Court that he had been able to answer most of Ulrich's questions so far. This business of hurrying them on their way could be a very clever means of making certain they didn't do anything really impolite—or politically unfortunate. Limit the contact, and you limit the chance of mistakes. After all, they were the first envoys from Karse to Valdemar in hundreds of years—and no one in Valdemar had any idea how they were likely to react.

We could just as easily be two of the "old sticks" that Solaris complains to Ulrich about; stiff-necked and stubborn and ready to make a stupid fuss about anything that might possibly be considered heresy—fighting the things she has restored to the Writ and Rules because there've never been Rules like that in their *lifetime. Someone like that would*

*probably cause an incident as soon as he got even half an ex-
cuse to do so, just out of sheer spite. He can't be sure yet that
we aren't like that, and the Valdemaran Court would plan
on it if they have any foresight.*

Rubrik probably *was* the best man for this job.

This third day out, Karal found himself warming to the
man. Rubrik *could* have been sitting around wallowing in
self-pity, recounting past glories to uninterested passersby on
Temple steps somewhere; instead, he was performing an important duty, perhaps freeing someone more able-bodied for
some other task, certainly seeing to it that he and Ulrich had
someone in charge of their journey who was not only competent, but fluent in their language, and at least marginally
friendly.

As the sun sank on their third day of travel, it also occurred
to Karal that finding someone who fit the criteria of "competent, fluent, and friendly" in the case of a former enemy must
be a rather difficult task. Perhaps, rather than trying to figure
out if the choice of Rubrik had been meant as an insult, he
should assume it was a compliment and should be *grateful*
that they had him!

Exhaustion impaired his reasoning fairly quickly after that.
As the lights of the next village neared, Karal found himself
thinking of nothing more than the bed he expected to fall
into.

*Soft bed, clean sheets, a hot bath . . . sleep. Not in that or-
der, of course. Food. Lots of fat feather pillows. Sleep. Some
more of that salve. Sleep.*

They rode into the courtyard of the inn Rubrik had chosen.
The courtyard was lit with lanterns and torches, the windows
glowed from the candles within, and wonderful aromas of
cooking meat and baking bread drifted out through the open
door.

A stableboy helped Rubrik dismount, then moved to hold
Honeybee and Trenor as Rubrik limped into the inn to
arrange for their lodging.

But he hurried right back out again, a serving-boy hovering
at his elbow, just as Karal helped his master dismount, and
the stormy look on his face made Karal's heart sink. Rubrik

was angry, and was keeping his temper carefully in check. Something must have gone wrong here.

Is it us? Has someone recognized that we're Karsite, and refused to grant us shelter? It was a real possibility—and the opening for a potentially damaging incident before their mission had even begun!

"I'm afraid this place is already full up," their escort said apologetically, while Ulrich steadied himself with one hand on Honeybee's shoulder. The flickering light from the torches did nothing to mask his chagrin and annoyance, and Karal felt his own face fall, but Ulrich seemed undisturbed. "This idiot of a landlord claims that he misunderstood the day; it's not a deliberate insult, I insisted on seeing the register, and they really have let out all the rooms. They can give you dinner while I see about some alternate arrangements, if you don't mind waiting for me to manage something."

"I do not see that we have much choice in the matter," Ulrich replied, with a philosophical shrug. "Personally, I simply can't ride any farther. No journey ever proceeds exactly as planned, and after all, the world does not arrange itself to suit our particular whims."

Rubrik grimaced, the torchlight turning his face into an ugly mask for a moment. "In this case, it should have," he said, annoyance overcoming his chagrin, "since I specifically stopped here on my way to the border to arrange rooms for us on this date. I—well, it doesn't matter. I managed to throw a good fright into the innkeeper himself, and he'd rather slit his own wrists now than inconvenience us further. I *do* have a private parlor for you to dine in, and I threw out the dice game some of the innkeeper's cronies were playing to get it, too. If you'll follow the boy, he'll see that you're served, and I'll see what I can arrange for the night."

Ulrich nodded as graciously as if this were all his idea, and put Honeybee's reins into the hands of the stableboy. He brushed off his riding robes, shook out a few wrinkles, and followed the serving-boy inside.

Karal trailed along in Ulrich's shadow, through the door into the inn itself, and crossed the crowded taproom.

Across the *very* crowded taproom. Every bench was full, every table loaded with full and empty plates and tankards.

The floor underfoot was sticky with spilled drink, and there was just enough room for the servers to squeeze in between the patrons. He was just as glad they weren't going to eat in here; the room was hot and stuffy, and his nose was assaulted with far too many odors at once to make his stomach happy. On top of that, it was noisy, and the babble was all in Valdemaran; it made him feel three times the foreigner, and between the confusion and his exhaustion, he found his grasp of the language slipping away.

The boy brought them to a door on the other side of the crowded room, opened it quickly, and motioned them inside. Even if he had tried to say something, he could not have been heard above the babble. Ulrich went in first; Karal followed on his heels.

The very first thing he noticed was the relative silence as the boy closed the door behind them. His ears rang for just a moment. The walls must have been incredibly thick for that much of a difference in the noise level.

The "private parlor" was a smaller version of the larger room, without the noisy crowd or the heat. The table in the middle of the room showed signs of the dice game Rubrik had presumably disrupted; a scattering of gaming counters and a few empty cups, which the boy swept aside as he gestured anxiously for them to take their seats. He produced a pitcher and a pair of cups, and poured cold fresh ale for both of them before vanishing out the door.

He returned in moments with two girls behind him, both of them bearing laden trays of food. At this point, Karal would have eaten the scraps usually thrown to the dogs, but it looked as if Rubrik must have given this innkeeper a stout piece of his mind, for the repast the two girls spread out on the table was a fine one, and there was enough there for half a dozen people. Platters steamed temptingly as the servers uncovered them, watching the faces of the two Karsites anxiously for a hint of approval.

Karal approved of it all, and couldn't wait to tuck into it. A tasty broth, thick with barley and vegetables began the meal, and a berry tart with a pitcher of heavy cream concluded it. Karal didn't realize *how* hungry he was until he wiped up the last of his berry-flavored cream with a bit of crust, and looked

up to see that he and Ulrich had done a pretty fair job of deci-
mating a meal he had *thought* would serve six.

He hadn't been paying any attention to anything except the
food in front of him. Now he looked around the room, following Ulrich's faintly ironic gaze.

There were no windows in the plastered white walls; this
room must have been in the very center of the building. There
was plenty of light, though, from a series of lanterns around the
walls, in addition to the candles on the table. There was no fire
in the cold fireplace, but it was hardly needed in this warm
weather.

Besides the table and half a dozen stiff-backed, wooden
chairs, there were three couches upholstered in brown leather
placed on three sides of the room, couches of an odd shape.
They had no backs, and only one fat, high arm.

"I think perhaps this room is used for other games than dic-
ing," Ulrich said quietly, still wearing that ironic little smile.
Karal blinked at him for a moment, then stared at one of the
couches again—

And blushed, the blood rushing to his face and making him
feel as if he was sunburned. He was *not* the naive horseboy
he'd been when he was first taken from his parents. Between
what he'd learned among the other novices, and the odds and
ends he'd picked up while serving Ulrich, he had an amaz-
ingly broad education in worldly matters. Oh, he knew what
those couches were for, now that Ulrich had pointed it out.

Still, a couch was a couch, and Rubrik still wasn't back. He
shoved away from the table, the chair legs scraping on the
polished wooden floor, and got up.

"I don't think anybody's going to bother us until Rubrik re-
turns, Master Ulrich," he said, gesturing to the couch nearest
the table. "I think you ought to get a little rest while we wait.
I certainly intend to."

Ulrich's smile widened a little, and he rose, a bit stiffly,
from his own chair. He took the couch that Karal indicated,
lowering himself down onto it with a grimace, and took a
more comfortable, reclining position. Karal waited until his
master looked settled, then chose one of the other two
couches and sat gingerly down on it.

The cushions were certainly soft enough, and a faint,

musky perfume rising from them as he lay down confirmed his guess as to the purpose they usually served. Small wonder they were covered in smooth leather; that kind of leather was easy to clean, easier than fabric.

On the other hand, he was *not* going to sit around on one of those straight-backed wooden chairs until their escort returned, while there was something a lot more comfortable in the very same room.

Besides, while he and his master were in here, the careless innkeeper was *not* able to use the room for any other purpose. Karal found himself almost hoping that Rubrik would not be able to make any other arrangements. These couches would not make the most comfortable beds in the world—unless you were accustomed to sleeping in certain positions—but they weren't the floor, or a pile of hay, or the ground under a tree. They certainly were softer than the pallet he'd been given in the Children's Cloister.

He didn't think he dared sleep, though, much as his body cried out for rest. They were alone and unarmed, and it could be presumed that the innkeeper was not altogether happy with their presence here, whether or not he knew anything about who or what they were. So Karal decided that this very moment was a good one to review his Valdemaran vocabulary, including all the tenses of all the verbs, in alphabetical order.

He had gotten as far as the third letter of the alphabet when Rubrik returned. His arrival woke Ulrich, who had been dozing. The priest sat up slowly and moved more stiffly than he had when he went to sleep. Karal frowned; that was not a good sign. Not only because it meant his master was very, very tired, but because Ulrich generally suffered from stiff and aching joints when the weather was about to change for the worse.

"I have good news of a sort," Rubrik began. "I have excellent accommodations for you—the problem is that you might wish to decline them. Your host—is actually a hostess. She is the local Commander of the Guard; as it happens, this village is her home, she has her command-post here, and she has offered her guest room to you."

Ulrich considered this for a moment, as Karal blinked, and

tried to imagine a *woman* in a position of military command. Women were not even permitted to serve with the Karsite army as Healer-Priests; only men could serve with soldiers. The *old* laws said that women who took on the "habit and guise" of men were demons, to be controlled or destroyed—whichever came soonest. Female mercenaries captured by the Karsite Army had fared rather badly, historically, something that Ulrich had never tried to conceal from his pupil.

For that matter, in Karse, the law still forbade women to hold property on their own; all property, whether it be land or goods, must be owned by a male. By Karsite standards, this Commander was doubly shocking.

On the other hand, Her Holiness had been making it clear that the days of laws forbidding women to do anything were numbered. Vkandis had made His will clear on the subject.

I guess that eventually we'll even have women fighters in our Army, given the way that things are going. Somehow, he did not find that as horrifying as he should have. Maybe he was just tired.

Maybe being around Her Holiness Solaris had taught him he'd better *never* underestimate the competence of a woman.

"If the lady in question is not offended by us, I fail to see why we should take offense at her offer of hospitality," Ulrich said, finally. "I would be very pleased to meet our hostess. I have never met a female warrior face-to-face before. I believe the experience will be enlightening."

He rose carefully and smoothed out the front of his riding robe with both hands. Karal scrambled to his feet, realizing belatedly that Ulrich had just accepted the unknown woman's invitation.

"I *did* tell her precisely who and what you are," Rubrik replied, with a twitch of his lips. "Since she is the local Commander, I had to inform her anyway. She said something similar about you, sir."

"No doubt," Ulrich replied dryly, but followed their guide out the door, through the taproom (which was still just as noisy and crowded as it had been when they entered), and back into the night, with Karal trailing along behind.

Evidently someone had already seen to their mounts, either stabling them at the inn or bringing them on ahead, and

Rubrik had (correctly) judged that, weary as they were, neither Ulrich nor his secretary were ready to climb back into a saddle again. Instead, they left the courtyard of the inn, turned into the street, and walked the short distance along a row of shops and homes to the large house at the end. The narrow two-storied buildings seemed abnormally tall and thin to Karal; each had a workshop or store on the ground floor, and living quarters above. The house at the end of the street differed in all ways from those lining it; this building had no commercial aspect to it, and it was as broad as three of the others.

It wasn't as big as the homes of several high-born nobles that Karal had seen, nor even as large as the inn, but it was quite sizable compared to its modest neighbors. The main door was right on the cobblestone street, with a single slab of stone as a step beneath it. Torches had been lit and placed in holders outside the white-painted door to light their way, and a servant opened the door before Rubrik could knock on it.

The servant ushered them into a wood-paneled hallway, lit by candlelamps. It was less of an entryway, and more of a waiting-room. They were not left to wait for the lady on the benches however; as soon as the servant shut the door, he directed them to follow him down the wide, white-painted hall to a room at the end.

Karal expected a lady's solar, or a reception room of some kind, but what the servant revealed when he opened the door was an office; businesslike, with no "feminine" fripperies about it. Their hostess was hard at work behind a plain wooden desk covered with papers; she nodded at the servant, who saluted and left. Rubrik gestured to them to go in, following and closing the door behind them.

The lady set her papers aside, and looked them both over with a frank and measuring gaze. Karal flushed a little under such an open appraisal, but Ulrich only seemed amused by her attitude. If she was as high an officer as Rubrik had indicated, there was nothing of that about her costume, at least not as Karal recognized rank-signs. Their hostess wore the same Guard uniform that they had seen before, with perhaps a bit more in the way of silver decoration.

Personally, she was quite attractive, and could have been

any age from late twenties to early fifties. She had the kind of face that remained handsome no matter the number of her years, a slim and athletic build, and an aura of complete confidence. This was someone in complete authority; someone who *knew* that she was good at her work, and did not bother to hide that fact. Karal was intimidated by her, and he realized it immediately. The only other woman who had ever had that effect on him was Solaris, and the Son of the Sun was relatively sexless compared to this Valdemaran commander. He was very glad that *he* was not the one that most of her attention was centered on.

"Well," she said, slowly, lacing her fingers together. "I've faced your lot across the battlefield, my lord Priest, but never across a desk. I hope you'll understand me when I say that I find our situation a great improvement."

"I, too," Ulrich replied smoothly. "Few Valdemarans would have such understanding, however, I think. Or is it forgiveness?"

"Huh." She smiled, though, and nodded. "I don't know about your Vkandis, sir Priest, but my particular set of gods tells me that past battles are just that; past. I am something of an amateur historian, actually. I like to know the causes of things. Some day, I expect, I'll have the leisure to sit down with one of your scholars and find out just what started this particularly senseless war between us in the first place. For now—" she waved one hand at the door, presumably indicating the house beyond it, "—allow me to do my part to cement the peace by offering hospitality." Her brow wrinkled for a moment, then she recited, in heavily accented and badly pronounced Karsite, "To the hearth, the board, the bed, be welcome. My fires burn to warm you, my board is laden to nourish you, my beds soft to rest you. We will share bread and be brothers."

Karal's jaw dropped. The very last thing he had ever expected to hear from this woman was the traditional invocation of peace between feuding hill families!

She smiled broadly at his open-mouthed reaction but said nothing.

Ulrich, for his part, remained unperturbed, although Karal thought he saw his mentor's lips twitch just a little. "For the hospitality, our thanks. Our blades are sharp to guard you, our horses strong to bear you, our torches burn to light your path. Let there be peace between us, and those of our kin." He then added to the traditional answer, "And I do mean 'kin' in the broadest possible sense."

"I know that," she replied. "If I hadn't, I wouldn't have offered you the blessing." She nodded, as if she had found Ulrich very satisfactory in some way. "Well, I think I've kept you standing here like a couple of raw recruits long enough. You've covered a fair amount of ground today, and I won't keep you from your baths or beds any longer. You'll find both waiting in your room, and my servant will show you the way."

And with that, the servant opened the door again, and she nodded in what was clearly a dismissal.

It occurred to Karal that a real diplomat might have been offended at her blunt speech and curt manner, but he was just too tired to try to act like a "real diplomat."

Then again, anyone who would be annoyed at a soldier acting like a soldier is an idiot. No, she didn't mean anything more or less than she said.

Instead of trying to analyze the encounter, he followed the servant, who led them to another room on the same floor, but on a different hallway.

It was tiled, floor and walls, with white ceramic, and contained two tubs, one a permanent fixture, and one smaller one obviously brought in so that Karal would not have to wait for his bath, both with steam rising from them. He and Ulrich had shared bathhouses often enough; they both shed clothing with no further ado. The servant came to collect their clothes as soon as they had both gotten into the tubs, indicating by pantomime that their beds lay in the next room.

Karal soaked his sore muscles, then wrapped himself in one of the towels and followed Ulrich into the bedroom. Valdemaran sleeping robes were laid out for them, a nice touch, he thought. He found his baggage, rubbed in his salve, and fell into the cot in the next room in a complete fog. Once his head touched the pillow, the fog became total darkness that did not lift until the servant woke them in the morning.

Solaris

5

After three days of what could only be described as endurance riding, Karal was finally getting used to the pace. He was also getting used to Rubrik, and it seemed that their escort was getting accustomed to them as well. His formal manner loosened a bit, and during the fourth day of travel, he began to talk with Karal directly.

At that point, Karal had to revise his opinion of their escort sharply upward, for Rubrik was even more of a scholar than he had guessed. He spoke four languages besides his own, and his rattling on about the geography, husbandry, and economics of the places they passed was no mere prattling to fill empty ears. He knew this area and the conditions in it as well as its own overlords did.

And that only made Karal more curious than before. Who *was* this man, that he had so much information at his very fingertips? Surely he had not memorized it just to impress or occupy them.

When they left the home of the lady Guard Commander, clad in riding gear that had been freshly washed and cleaned by the lady's servants, gray skies threatened rain. The rain did not actually materialize in the morning or even the early afternoon, but toward late afternoon the clouds thickened, and the wind picked up. Ulrich's joints hurt him quite a bit at that point, so they actually stopped *early* for once, at least two marks before sunset.

Their stopping place was yet another inn, this one with a courtyard surrounded on three sides by the inn itself, and on the fourth by the stable. A gate in the middle of the stable led into the courtyard, and this arrangement cut the wind completely. Ulrich descended from his saddle with a gasp of pain, and Rubrik was concerned enough to ask the Priest if he thought he would require the services of a Healer.

"Not unless your Healer can give me the body of a man three decades my junior," Ulrich replied with a ghost of a smile. "No, this is simply the result of old age. I shall retire to my bed with a hot brick and some of your salve, and with luck, this rain will move on so that we can follow suit as soon as possible."

But the rain didn't move on; in fact, no sooner had Karal seen his master settled into a warming bed than it began to drizzle.

The taproom of the inn was mostly empty; the miserable weather was probably convincing people to stay by their own hearths tonight. There was a good fire in the fireplace, though, quite enough to take the chill out of the air, and on the whole it was a pleasant place, all of age-and smoke-blackened wood. Heavy beams supported the ceiling, and below their shelter, gently curved tables and benches polished to satin smoothness were arranged in an arc around the fire. As the drizzle turned into a real thunderstorm, Karal found a perch at a window-seat table and watched the lightning dance toward the inn through the tiny panes of a leaded window.

"Impressive, isn't it?"

The eyes of Rubrik's reflection met his in the dark and bubbly window glass. The man smiled, and Karal smiled tentatively back.

"Would you prefer I left you to your meditations?" Rubrik asked politely.

Karal shook his head. "Not really," he replied. "You can join me, if you like. I've always been fascinated by storms; when I was a boy at an inn like this one, I used to sneak away and hide in the hayloft to watch them move in."

"And let me guess—you used, as an excuse to go to the stable in the first place, that the horses were frightened by the thunder and needed soothing, no doubt," Rubrik hazarded, and grinned, taking the seat on the other side of the table. "My father never believed that one, either, but his stableman was always on my side and backed me up with specious tales of how I had kept the prize mounts from hurting themselves in a panic."

Karal realized that at last their escort had just let something fall about his own past. Up until now Rubrik had been very closemouthed about anything of a personal nature. *His father's stableman. So that means he comes from a well-to-do family, if not of noble blood. So his father was no mere farmer as he implied.* He responded in kind. "My father never minded too much; there's less work at an inn during bad weather. It's a lot easier for people to stay at home, watch their own fires, and drink their own beer. And of course, once the few travelers who wanted to try and beat the storm got in, no one else would arrive until it was over, so we stableboys didn't have much to do either after we'd dealt with their beasts." There. It was out. If Rubrik was going to be offended by his low birth—

"That's probably the *only* time you didn't have much to do," Rubrik said, with a conspiratorial grin. "I've always felt a little sorry for inn folk during wonderful weather. They never get a holiday like the rest of us do. It hardly seems fair, does it, that in the very best of weather, when everyone else is out enjoying themselves, people in an inn have to work three times as hard tending to the holiday-makers? I would guess that storm watching was the closest thing to a holiday you ever got."

Karal chuckled and brightened. "I never thought about it, actually. It wasn't as bad as you might think, so long as you like horses. Father never made it easier on me than it was for the other horseboys, but he was a good and just taskmaster." He clasped his hands together on the tabletop and stared out at the rain. "I never really saw the heavy work, when it came to that; I wasn't old enough for anything other than light chores, like grooming. The Sun-priests took me at the Feast of the Children when I was nine, so I was never big enough to do heavy work."

Rubrik looked at Karal for a moment, then stared out at the lightning. The silence between them grew heavy, and Karal sensed that he was about to ask something that he thought might be sensitive.

Probably something about us, about Karse and the Sun-

priests. That's not a problem; Ulrich already told me what I can't say. No reason to avoid his questions, especially not if the information he wants is common knowledge at home. I think he's been looking for an excuse to talk to me alone, figuring that I will be less wary than Ulrich. He felt himself tense a little. He would have to be very canny with this man. It would be easy to trust him; hard to remember to watch what he said.

Rubrik coughed politely. "I—ah—suppose you realize we have all kinds of stories, probably ridiculous, about the reasons why the Sun-priests took Karsite children—and what they did with them afterward—"

Karal only sighed, then rested his chin in his hand. "The stories probably aren't any worse than the truth," he said at last.

Rubrik nodded and waited for him to go on. Encouraged, Karal told him all about his own childhood, what there was of it—how the Priests had taken him, how he had been educated, and how, finally, Ulrich had singled him out as his protégé. He told their escort about the Fires, too, and caught an odd expression on his face, as if what Karal had told him only confirmed something horrible that he already knew.

"The children taken are either extremely intelligent, intelligence that would be wasted in a menial position, or are children with the God-granted ability to use magic, of course. Ulrich told me later that I had both qualifications, but my ability to use magic is only a potential, rather than an active thing. He called me a 'channel,' but I've never found out what that means, exactly. I was absolutely terrified that at some point I'd start showing witch-powers like my uncles did, and a Black-robe Priest would come for me and that I'd end up going to the Fires," he concluded. "But I never did—though in one sense, I suppose, a Black-robe Priest *did* come for me."

Rubrik waited for him to say something; out of pure mischief he held his peace. Finally the man gave up. "Well?" he said. "What's that supposed to mean?"

Karal grinned; at least this would be one thing he could surprise the man with. "Ulrich was a Black-robe—that is to say, a Demon-Summoner—before Her Holiness Solaris made the Black-robe nothing more than a rank. And now, of course, there *aren't* any Fires. The Cleansing ceremony has gone back to what it *used* to be. Ulrich and I found the original Rite in one of the ancient Litany Books." He didn't make Rubrik ask for the answer this time. "It's a Rite of Passage, that's what it originally was, before it was perverted; children who are about to become adult bring something symbolic of their childhood to be burned as a sign that they are ready to take on adult responsibilities. Ulrich says it's easy to change holidays and rituals to suit a purpose, since they're usually subjective anyway. Harvest festivals and fertility rites are coming back, too, the way they were a long time ago."

Rubrik took all this in thoughtfully. "Solaris has made many changes, then?"

"Her Holiness certainly has! Mostly she has reversed changes that had been made by corrupt Priests seeking nothing more than power," Karal corrected. He wasn't certain why, but for some reason he felt that point needed to be absolutely clear. Solaris was not some kind of wild-eyed revolutionary, despite what her critics claimed; what she had done in the Temple thus far was restoration, not revolution. "Ulrich is not precisely certain how long things have been wrong, but we know that it has been several centuries at the least. True miracles ceased, and the illusions of miracles were substituted. The God-granted power of magic that *should* have been devoted to the well-being of Vkandis' people and to His glory was perverted into the use of that power to bring temporal power and wealth to the temple and the Priests. And Vkandis is very real, not an imaginary God like some people have!"

Rubrik smiled, but not mockingly. "I know."

Oddly enough, Karal believed him. "Ulrich believes we will know the date the corruption started when we learn just when the rank of Black-robe Priests was created. They were the heart and soul of the corruption."

Lightning lashed the top of a tree not too far away; Karal winced at the thunder but enjoyed the atavistic thrill it sent up his spine. *And I am glad to be in here, and not out there.*

"I thought you said that Ulrich was a Black-robe," Rubrik replied, slowly. "Your robes are *still* black, in fact."

"He was," Karal agreed. "His duty in the former days, according to the Writ and Rule, was to summon demons on the orders of the Son of the Sun and send them against the enemies of Karse. It was not a duty he took any pleasure in. He also frequently brought danger down on himself by refusing to counterfeit miracles." He turned his head a little so that his eyes met Rubrik's. "He showed me every counterfeit he knew, so that I would not be taken in by the tricks of the higher-ranked Priests," he told the man, whose eyes widened at his serious tone. "And that alone might have gotten him burned had I betrayed him. Some of the tricks were so simple anyone who paid attention could have seen through them—but that's the power of belief."

He turned his attention back to the storm. There were other things Rubrik might do well to learn about Ulrich, but Karal would rather that it was his master who told the Valdemaran.

Besides, how could I tell him about the times that Ulrich returned from a summoning, troubled and heartsore—how he hinted that the definition of "enemies of Karse" was becoming broader and broader? No, that should come from my master and not from me. I do not want this Valdemaran to think that I am in the habit of betraying my mentor's confidences.

"You said something about Solaris changing all that," Rubrik ventured, after several long moments filled only by the boom of thunder and the pounding of rain on the roof. "Was that when she became the head of Vkandis' religion?"

Karal nodded, and smiled a little. *This* was the part of the tale he really enjoyed. "That was what gave her the office, in fact. It was a miracle—a *real* one, and no fakery. I was there, I saw it myself. For that matter, so was Ulrich, and *he* is certainly an expert at spotting something that was not a God-produced miracle. I do not believe that there is any kind of fakery, either slight-of-hand and illusion, or magic masquerading as a miracle, that he cannot detect."

It had been a very strange day to begin with; the day of the Fire Kindling Ceremony at Midwinter, when all the fires of Karse were relit from the ones ignited on the altars of Vkandis. It should have been bitter cold—

"It was the strangest Midwinter Day I have ever seen," he

said slowly. "Hot—terribly hot and dry. Hot enough that the Priests had all taken out their summer robes for the Fire Kindling Ceremony. There was not a single cloud in the sky above the city, but outside the city the sky was covered with dull gray clouds, from horizon to horizon. Ulrich and I were at the front of the Processional; Solaris was no more than three people away from Ulrich." He closed his eyes for a moment, picturing it, and chose his words carefully, trying to set the scene for his listener. "We Priests and novices surrounded the High Altar in a semicircle; the beam of sunlight—called the Lance of Hope—shining through the Eye in the ceiling above us slowly moved toward the pile of fragrant woods and incense on the Altar. The golden statue of Vkandis-In-Glory, wearing the Crown of Prophecy, shone like the sun itself behind the Altar, and Lastern—the False Son—stood beside it, ready to kindle the flames by magic if the sunlight didn't do the trick promptly enough."

Rubrik nodded. "I take it that this was a fairly common practice?"

Karal snorted with disgust. "I never once saw the False Son bring forth a single true miracle. For that matter, he was so feeble in magic that the most he could do was to kindle flame in very dry, oily tinder. Well, that day, he never got the chance for his deceptions."

He turned toward Rubrik, and lowered his voice like a true storyteller. "Imagine it for yourself—the crowd of worshipers filling the temple, the golden statue of Vkandis shining behind the Altar and the False Son standing beside it like a fat, black spider. The Processional ended just as the beam of sunlight crept up to the Altar platform; Solaris was no more than five paces away, watching, not the False Son, but the beam of light, her face mirroring her ecstasy."

Was that a little too florid? No, I don't think so.

"Most of the important Priests only looked bored, though, on what *should* be an important day for them, the Holiest of all of Vkandis' Holy Days. They couldn't wait to get back to the Cloister and the feast that waited there for them." Ulrich and a great many of the low-ranked Priests avoided the feast when they could. It was little more than an occasion for those in favor with the Son of the Sun to lord it over those who were not. Hardly Ulrich's choice of a way to spend a Holy Day. He preferred to spend his rare free time reading.

"The beam of sunlight slowly moved onto the Altar itself, while the Children's Choir sang. I saw the False Son's hands moving as he prepared to trigger the fire-starting spell if the wood didn't catch. Then, just before the beam touched the kindling in the middle of the Altar—"

As if he had triggered it himself, a tremendous bolt of lightning lanced down right beside the inn, and as they both jumped and Karal squeaked, the thunder deafened them and everyone else inside the inn.

He sat there for a moment, waiting for his ears to clear, and very grateful that he had not been looking out the window at that moment. If he had, he'd have been blinded!

Rubrik laughed shakily. "Next time, tell me when you are going to produce a surprise to liven up your tale!"

"I'm *not* responsible for that one!" Karal retorted, with a shaky chuckle of his own. "Perhaps you ought to ask Vkandis if He has widened His lands to include Valdemar! Because that was precisely what happened in the Temple—a bolt of lightning shot down through the opening in the Temple's roof, out of the cloudless sky, and completely evaporated the False Son of the Sun."

Rubrik stared at him skeptically, as if he suspected that this was just more tale-telling.

But Karal shook his head emphatically. "I promise you, I was there, and so was Ulrich. He'll corroborate what I've said. There was literally nothing left but the man's smoking vestments and boots, too—I've never seen anything like it, and neither had anyone else. But that wasn't the end of the miracle, it was only the *beginning!*"

"What next?" Rubrik asked, his tone conveying that even if he was not quite convinced, he was certain that Karal was telling the truth as he saw it.

"Next, was that when we could see again, every stone column in the Temple had been turned upside down, and since they all had carvings on them, it was pretty obvious that they'd been inverted. We didn't know it at the time, but we found out later that every cloud vanished from over the whole of Karse, and the First Fires on every Altar blazed up and burned for a full week without any additional fuel." He left out the other, smaller miracles—about the children waiting to be burned who had vanished from the hands of the Black-robes, only to be discovered long afterward, hidden in the homes of their families. He eliminated the story of the Priest's Staffs—how some of the staffs turned brittle and disintegrated at a touch, while others put out green branches covered with flowers.

And the Staffs that turned to dust were the ones that belonged to the False Son's favorites and cronies, and those Black-robes who had truly enjoyed the demon-summoning and the burnings. . . . He himself had held Ulrich's Staff, which had so many tiny red flowers covering the branches at the top that the wood could scarcely be seen. It had remained that way for a week, the flowers sending out a heady perfume. Ulrich and every other possessor of a flowering Staff had planted their Staffs in the various Temple meditation gardens, where they remained as flowering bushes, living reminders of the day of the miracles.

"But none of that would have gotten Solaris made Son of the Sun," he continued. "No woman had *ever* been named Son of the Sun, the very idea was absurd. No, if that had been all that happened, the Priests would have convened and elected a new Son, perhaps one a *little* more pious than the old one, but still—"

"It would have been business as usual," Rubrik supplied, his ironic nod showing that he understood the situation all too well. "So what *did* happen?"

"Another miracle. The last, and greatest of all. Silence hung over the entire Temple, for the worshipers were too stunned to cry out or even move. Then, before anyone could recover enough to say or do anything to break that silence, the golden statue of Vkandis began to move." He closed his eyes to picture it again in his mind, and described the vivid memory as best he could. "It moved exactly like a living man—there was nothing stilted or jerky about the way that it looked about, then stepped slowly down out of the niche behind the Altar. That convinced me it couldn't be some mechanical thing substituted for the real statue. I remember staring up at it, and thinking how *much* like a man it was;

the skin moved properly over the muscles; the muscles rippled as it stepped over the Altar and stopped in front of Solaris. *She* was staring up at it, with that same enraptured expression on her face, even though most of the Priests were groveling and babbling out a litany of every sin they'd ever committed."

That had been rather funny, actually. For some reason, it never occurred to him to be *afraid* of the image, and there were a few more, like Solaris and Ulrich, who actually seemed to be in a trance of ecstasy as they gazed upon it. The face of the statue wore a look of complete serenity, as it always had—yet there seemed to be a hint of good humor in the eyes, a ghost of a smile about the lips, as if Vkandis found the groveling Priests just as funny as Karal did.

"The statue took the Crown of Prophecy off its own head; once the Crown was in its hands, it *shrank*. It dwindled until it was small enough to fit a human. Then the statue bent down and placed the Crown on Solaris' head."

The eyes of the image and of Solaris had met and locked. *Something* passed between them; Karal didn't know what it was, and on the whole, he would really rather not find out. *I'm just not ready for the personal attentions of Vkandis. I would be very happy to stay with Ulrich and work researching the old Rites and never have Him notice me.*

"Then the image went back to the pedestal behind the Altar; that was when the fire there on the Altar in front of it blazed up so quickly and so high we thought another lightning bolt had hit it. When the flames died down so we could see the niche again, the statue was exactly as it had been, *except* that it wasn't wearing the Crown anymore. Solaris was."

"And you're sure that there was no trickery involved?" Rubrik persisted.

Karal nodded. "Absolutely. It wasn't an illusion, or how would Solaris have gotten the Crown? It wasn't a mechanical device, because no mechanical could have moved as the statue did. And besides that, how would a mechanical creature make the Crown shrink like that? And Ulrich says it definitely wasn't human magic, or he would have known immediately; even without summoning demons, he's still one of the most powerful mages in the Priesthood. None of us have ever seen Solaris work *any* magic, before or since, except for the demon-summoning she was required to perform because she was a Black-robe. Ulrich says he doesn't see how any mage could have delivered a lightning strike like that, animate the statue, and light the First Fire and still be standing afterward. Even if she or a confederate, or even a number of conspirators, *could* have done all that with magic, there's still one question—*how* would she have gotten the Crown off the statue, and shrunk it down to fit her? The Crown wasn't just some piece of jewelry that had been made to fit the statue—it was *part* of the statue, part of the original casting. The Crown is part of the statue's head. It was deliberately cast that way to discourage thieves."

"Huh." Rubrik stared at the rain which was coming down in a solid sheet. Karal watched his expression very carefully, trying to guess his thoughts. "Well," he said, very slowly, "I would have said that I didn't believe in miracles, if I hadn't seen one or two lately with my own eyes. Smallish ones, mind, compared to your moving statues and shrinking Crowns, but they definitely qualified." He paused, and Karal had the sense that he was choosing his words with the utmost care. "The Lady-Goddess of the Hawkbrothers and Shin'a'in seems to intervene now and then on behalf of her own people, so why not the Sunlord, right?"

Karal nodded cautiously. He wasn't entirely certain he ought to be agreeing to anything that compared Vkandis with some outlandish heathen Goddess—but Rubrik *said* he'd seen this Goddess working miracles. . . .

Vkandis was supposed to have a Goddess-Consort in the oldest records, but she seemed to have gotten misplaced somewhere far back in the past. Or had the Priests in that far past been right to eliminate her?

This was getting more confusing by the moment. "Goddess?" he replied weakly. "What Goddess?"

Rubrik shook his head, and chuckled. "Oh, this theology business is too much for a simple soul like me! Let me order us some dinner, and you tell me just what Solaris did once she had that crown on her head, all right?"

Karal agreed to that with relief. Rubrik summoned a serving-girl, who eyed Karal in a way that made him blush and wish secretly that he wasn't sharing a room with his master. *He* was only a novice; he hadn't taken any oaths yet, much less oaths of celibacy and chastity. . . .

Rubrik must have ordered something that the kitchen already had prepared, for the girl returned with laden platters in short order. Karal's stomach growled as the aroma of hot sausage pie hit his nose. The scent was unfamiliar, as unfamiliar as most of the Valdemaran food, but even if he hadn't been starving, it would have been enticing. He felt ready to eat the pie and the plate it was baked in.

Rubrik dug into his own portion without hesitation. "So," he said, gesturing with a fork, "what did your Solaris do next?"

"There was no question of naming anyone else the Son of the Sun, of course," Karal replied, around a mouthful of sausage and crust. He swallowed; the pie was wonderful, and the spices weren't *too* different from the ones used at home. "Everyone who would have protested was there for the Miracles, and they were terrified that any more miracles would target *them.* Solaris was invested right then and there with the White Robes—she already had a Crown—and the acolytes swept what was left of the False Son out with the ashes of last year's Fire. The next day she called a convocation, and told everyone that the duties of the Black-robes would change from that moment. She ordered that Black-robes would retain their rank, but they would serve exactly the same duties as the Red-robe Priests. Demon-summoning was declared anathema, forbidden, and the texts that taught the means of summoning the creatures were to be burned."

"That's a good start, though normally I don't hold with burning books," Rubrik observed. "But destroying something so open to misuse instead of burning innocent people was a pretty good way of beginning her rule."

Karal nodded enthusiastically and had another couple of bites before continuing. "She said that she had been having visions for some time now, and that the event in the Temple merely confirmed that her visions had been from Vkandis and not mere dreaming and vainglory. She told us all that she had been shown that the ways of the Writ and Rule were not the ancient and true ways of worship."

"I'd hardly expect her to say anything else," Rubrik pointed out dryly. "If she was going to establish herself as an authority, she would have to shake up things in your Temple right from the beginning. First day."

Karal bit his tongue to keep from making a sharp retort, and took a little time eating before continuing, lest he say something he shouldn't. No matter what Solaris was, one thing she *wasn't* was a mere political creature. Yes, she understood politics, but it was only to take them into account. When politics didn't agree with what she was going to do, she worked around them.

"She made quite a few changes in the first week," he told the Valdemaran, "And later, when Ulrich and I were doing research into the older ways, we found out that the changes she had made *were* nothing more than a reestablishment of those ancient paths. 'The Sunlord has always been a God of life, not destruction,' she said. 'His Fire is the life-giving Fire of the Sun, not the Fires that eat the lives of children.' She decreed an end to the Cleansing Ceremonies as we knew them. She declared the Feast of the Children to be a time of testing youngsters for their powers and intelligence, but ordered that no child was to be dragged away from its family; children must come to the Temple by consent of their families and their own will." He answered Rubrik's slightly raised eyebrow with a sardonic smile of his own. "She also pointed out that in families with many children and limited resources, telling the child and its parents that from now on the Priesthood would feed and clothe it would get them to at least give the Cloisters a try. I have to admit that I was fed and housed better than my parents could afford when I was in the Cloisters, and on the whole I had less work to do. I'm told now that children sometimes cry when they *aren't* taken, instead of crying when they are."

"Ah," Rubrik said, with a twitch of his lips. "As we say in Valdemar, presenting the apple instead of the stick."

"Precisely." He finished off his portion of pie and took a long swallow of ale. "The changes she made with the children and the novices were that they were to be allowed full contact with their families and annual leave to visit them if they wished, just as if they were recruits in the Army. But that all came later; it was part of the changes she made that were really restorations of the old ways."

"The old ways . . ." Rubrik finished his own food thoughtfully. "So, just how did she come to know all these 'old ways'? More visions?"

Karal laughed. "Oh, no, not at all! She appointed a number of friends of hers among the former Black-robes to find them in the archives!"

"Don't tell me—" Rubrik said quickly, holding up his free hand. "One of the places where she used to spend a lot of her free time was the archives, right? And I already know that she is a linguist and a scholar and can read all the oldest records for herself. So that was how she just happened to know that the 'old ways' weren't exactly the same as your current— what did you call it?"

"The Writ and Rule." Karal shrugged. "I don't know, but does it really matter? The point is that she knew that there was a record of the old ways in the archives, and everything we found confirmed or added to what she had already declared. Ulrich was one of the former Black-robes she assigned to the archives, and since I was his secretary, I worked beside him."

The serving-girl came to clear away their empty plates, refill their cups, and bring them a dessert of fruit and cheese. Rubrik said nothing while she was there, and spent some time carefully cutting up an apple without continuing the conversation. "None of this ever got to Valdemar," he said at last. "We only heard that there had been some disturbance, and that suddenly the ruler of Karse was a woman. Then we learned nothing at all for a year or two." He looked up from his apple dissection, and cocked an eyebrow at Karal. "Is there any connection between your Solaris and the other woman that called herself 'the Prophet of Vkandis' about ten or fifteen years ago? The one that decided she was going to be the head of your army and damn near got herself a big chunk of Menmellith?"

Karal shook his head. "No—and in fact, that woman is the reason the original Crown of Prophecy went missing. It was lost with her when she vanished."

No point in getting into that; the story was much too complicated. And if Rubrik did not know the part of Solaris' story that his own countrywoman Talia figured so prominently in—he wasn't as well-informed as Karal had thought.

Rubrik ate his apple thoughtfully. "I can't imagine that the rest of your priesthood just rolled over like cowed dogs and let Solaris rule as she wanted."

Indeed they didn't, Karal thought quietly. But this was one of the subjects Ulrich had instructed him to say nothing about. There had been a great deal of opposition to Solaris' new Writ and Rules, and to her decrees as well. Not only from the Priests, either.

There had been plenty of people in Karse who liked the corrupt ways very much indeed. A number of the highly born resented the intrusion of the Priests into areas of governance they had always considered their private preserve. There had been a kind of understanding between the Priests and some of the nobles that certain—excesses—would be ignored if gifts "to the Temple" were valuable enough. There had been Priests who were as corrupt as some of those nobles; they had shared in those excesses.

Solaris put an end to those "understandings." And an end to the slave trade, to a profitable market in deadly intoxicants, and a number of other unsavory trades that had been ignored or even given tacit sanction by the Priests.

This did not earn her friends in some quarters.

There were Priests and the favorites of Priests who lost prestige and position with the change in stature of the Blackrobes—those who were no longer permitted to call demons did not inspire the same fear. This didn't earn her any goodwill from those factions, either.

There were even those at the borders who *wanted* the demon-summoners back. At least when demons roamed the night, the bandits stayed hidden, and conducted their raids only by day, when it was somewhat easier to see them coming and to fight them. There were plenty of border dwellers who feared the Rethwellans, the Valdemarans, and the Hardornens on the other side of those borders, and wanted the demons and their summoners to keep the "foreigners" away.

The two years that followed the Miracle were not easy

ones, and Solaris had fought a grim and mostly-silent battle against a number of enemies. But Karal was not going to tell Rubrik any of that. If the Valdemaran spies weren't good enough for their Queen to have learned *that* much, too bad. And if no one had bothered to inform this agent of the Queen of these things, that was not Karal's problem.

"So, at some point after Ancar stole his father's throne, he decided that Karse was an easy target, hmm?" Rubrik took the hint, restarting the conversation with something obvious.

Karal shrugged. "I suppose so. I've never talked to anyone from Hardorn. Those who were trying to escape went across your borders. I suppose they didn't want to chance the demons; they had no reason to know there weren't any demons anymore. All I know is that suddenly we had an army trying to run over the top of us. Solaris was very good at picking brilliant generals, but good generals were obviously not going to be enough. Ancar's fighters didn't seem—human."

"They weren't, exactly, anymore," Rubrik replied, and it was obvious from his expression that *he* was not going to elaborate on this point. Well, fine. So they both had things they weren't supposed to share.

"You should know the rest," Karal continued. "Solaris retreated to the Sun Tower and came back down with a new decree from the mouth of Vkandis Himself."

"Truce with Valdemar." That was a statement, not a question, but Karal nodded anyway.

And if the situation hadn't been so bad, that would have been the end of Solaris. As it was, Ancar's fighters and mages committed so many outrages that even her worst enemies were convinced that she was right. There hadn't been a single family in all of Karse that didn't know of *someone* who'd been affected. Torture and rapine were the least of the vile deeds Ancar's followers had perpetrated, although they in themselves were quite bad enough.

Rubrik shook his head with an expression of wry sympathy. "You know, when your messengers reached our people, and we were finally convinced that Solaris meant what she said, there were some of us who thought the world had surely come to an end. I mean, truce with *Karse!* How much crazier could things get? And most people were certain it wouldn't last."

A flicker of expression on Rubrik's face, quickly suppressed, told Karal that this man was in the group of those in Valdemar who had felt that way. "I don't imagine your people were terribly happy about the idea, especially anyone in your Guard."

Rubrik grimaced. "Well, when those Priest-mages of yours came north and helped hold Ancar's armies to a crawl, it pretty well convinced even the most skeptical that you meant to hold by the spirit of the truce and alliance as well as the letter of it. At this point, we've got acceptance—if a grudging acceptance—of the situation. There are still people who can't keep up with the changes in the land, though. So much has changed so quickly inside Valdemar—and outside her borders—that probably half of the population is in a whirl."

Karal sighed, and then caught himself in a yawn. How late was it, anyway? "I suppose you could say the same about us," he replied. "Except for two groups, that is."

Rubrik raised an eyebrow.

"Those who support Solaris without reservation, like Ulrich, purely because she *is* the Son of the Sun by Vkandis' Own hand," Karal said, "And those who are simply too young to have fought Valdemar personally, and so have no personal grudges to bear. When you're young enough, the world is new every day."

"Ah." Rubrik considered this for a moment—perhaps noting that Karal did not say which group *he* belonged in—and straightened a bit in his seat, stretching and flexing his shoulders. "And on that optimistic note, I suggest we both find a nice warm bed," he said.

Optimistic? Well, I suppose so—if you consider that he means that eventually all the old fossils will die and the new generation, presumably without the prejudices of the old, will take over. "That sounds like a good idea to me," Karal agreed. "And forgive me if I hope that your bad weather holds long enough to prevent us from leaving until the sun is properly *above* the horizon!"

Rubrik only laughed. "I won't promise anything," he

replied. "But I think this is a wizard-storm, and if it is, it will be cleared up before midnight at the latest."

Karal sighed.

Ulrich was still awake when Karal came in, and Karal reported the whole conversation faithfully. As Ulrich's secretary, he had learned how to memorize long conversations verbatim, when they had been in a situation where taking notes would have been impolite or impolitic. Ulrich listened without comment, then nodded approval.

"You did very well," he told his protégé. "You told him nothing he should not know—and perhaps, having been told of the Miracles by an eyewitness, he will be reporting them as fact rather than hearsay to his superiors."

Karal stretched his knotted muscles and grimaced. "Master, I have to tell you that although I do enjoy this man's company, I had almost rather be facing an armed enemy than have another of these conversations with him. He is *very* good, very subtle. I think that if he tried, he could probably have gotten much more out of me than I intended to tell him. I believe he was hoping for just this sort of opportunity to catch me alone and question me. He knows what will be good for Valdemar to know of Karse now, but if I spent too much more time in his presence I think it might be that I would tell him too much—or something he would misinterpret."

Ulrich considered this for a moment, staring into the fire in the tiny fireplace in their room. "I think you are probably right," he replied, his expression thoughtful, though not at all apprehensive. "It was probably not coincidental that he began asking all these questions of you at the moment when I was out of reach and earshot. I think that the next such conversation should include me."

Karal heaved a sigh of relief at that. He had been concentrating so hard on telling only the truth, and yet not *all* the truth, that he had not realized how tense he had been under Rubrik's scrutiny until he got back to the room he shared with his mentor. Now, he found he had to go through every stretching and relaxing exercise he knew just to get himself unknotted enough to sleep!

This Rubrik was subtle, very subtle. And although he had

not consciously been aware of the fact, something instinctive had reacted to that. Among the Priests, "subtle" frequently meant "dangerous."

And among the Priests, "subtle" *always* meant that the man must never be underestimated.

But as Karal blew out the candle and climbed into his own bed, he found himself hoping only one thing—that in this case, "subtle" did not mean "treacherous" as well.

Ulrich

6

Regrettably, Rubrik was right about the weather. A tap on their door at an absolutely unholy hour proved that the storm *had* cleared, before dawn, if not by midnight. Karal pried himself out of his warm cocoon of blankets with a groan of regret that was only slightly softened by the fact that the servants who woke them also brought breakfast along with wash water and a candle. A *real* breakfast this time, not just bread and drink.

I might be able to face the day, he decided, after a decent meal of eggs and bacon, hot bread and sweet honey-butter, with plenty of freshly pressed cider to wash it all down. The hastily-snatched meals on horseback tended to wear very thin, long before Rubrik would decree a halt for further food.

"I think that our escort has probably forgotten how much a young man needs to eat," Ulrich observed with an amused smile, as he watched Karal devour the remains of his mentor's breakfast as well as his own. "I shall remind him."

"Thank you, Master Ulrich," Karal said with real gratitude. "It's not as if he hasn't been very reasonable, but—"

"But he is probably as many years removed from the age at which one devours one's weight in food every day as I am," Ulrich replied. "One forgets."

Karal only smiled, and washed his hands and face clean of the sticky honey he had devoured so greedily. If there was one thing he had a weakness for, it was sweets.

Which means I'd better never take a real scholar's position, or I'll soon resemble Vkandis' own seat cushion.

"Are you sure you can ride?" he asked his mentor anxiously. Ulrich had been moving with the slow, deliberate care that meant his joints were still stiff. Karal had more than a duty to Ulrich as his mentor, he was under *orders* to make certain Ulrich remained healthy during his tenure as Karse's envoy.

He was fairly certain Ulrich was not aware of this, however.

Solaris had called Karal into her Presence just before they left, to make him promise he would take particular care of his mentor. One session with that formidable lady's will concentrated on him and him alone was more than enough. He could not imagine that the Eye of Vkandis Himself would concentrate any more force than did His earthly representative's. Karal did *not* ever want to report to her that Ulrich had come to any kind of grief.

"Oh, I shall live," the Priest said, sighing. Then he smiled wanly. "Don't be too concerned, Karal. These joint aches are not a sign of anything dangerous."

But Karal continued to stare at his mentor with a frown of worry on his face until Ulrich grimaced. "I swear to you that I will ask our escort to stop for the day if I need rest. Will that suit you?"

"I suppose it will have to," Karal told him, trying to sound as severe as one of his own instructors had, when *he* had tried to avoid making pledges. "Since I doubt I'm going to get anything more reasonable out of you."

But Ulrich only raised a quelling eyebrow at him. "Don't try to sound like Ophela, child; it doesn't suit either your years or your personality."

Suitably rebuked, Karal flushed with embarrassment and quickly turned his attention to his packing. Not that there was much to pack—most of what they would be needing at the Court had been sent on ahead with a merchant pack train, and should arrive shortly before they did. Ulrich had not wanted to attract attention by traveling with the number of wagons they would need to maintain their proper state as Officials of the Court. Wagons would mean armed guards, and guards would imply importance or value—and they would end up with the same problem that a large escort would have caused them.

By way of simultaneously showing his contrition and his rebellion, he packed up Ulrich's gear as well, before his mentor could get to it himself. Ulrich only raised his eyebrow even higher at this implication that he was too feeble to deal with it on his own.

With packs assembled, Karal shouldered both, and stepped aside for his master to lead the way out to the courtyard.

As usual, Rubrik was already there, waiting for them in the gray light of false dawn, this time already astride his lovely white horse. Karal fastened the packs behind Honeybee's saddle first, then Trenor's, and swung quickly up onto Trenor's back so that he could watch while Ulrich mounted.

At least Ulrich didn't seem to be in any great difficulty. Maybe he *was* overreacting.

And maybe I really don't ever want to have to face Her Holiness and confess to carelessness. Better safe than sorry, as the saying goes.

They were some few leagues down the road, when Rubrik pulled up his mount beside Ulrich, and motioned to Karal that he should stay abreast of them as well. "I had a rather interesting conversation with your young secretary last night," he said, and waited for Ulrich's reply.

"I know," Ulrich said calmly. "He told me."

"I rather thought he might," came Rubrik's amused response. "You and your leader have chosen well. If I may venture a guess, he told me *exactly* what he was permitted to—no lies, but nothing more and nothing less than what he had been granted leave to reveal."

Ulrich laughed out loud. "*Very* good, friend! And now, since your appetite—or that of whomever it is you are reporting to—has been whetted, you are coming to me for more information than you think he is allowed to give, in the hopes that I have permission to tell you more. And knowing that young Karal would not have been permitted to tell you *anything* if we had not intended for you to come to me."

Rubrik made a slight bow from the saddle, full of amused irony. "Now that we have both agreed that we are too clever for the usual diplomatic half-truths, if you will allow me to give you a starting point, perhaps you can tell me how the Karsites reacted to the alliance with Valdemar, especially after we got rid of Ancar. Do feel free to ignore anything *you* haven't got leave to answer."

"I shall," the Priest replied with urbane courtesy. Then Ulrich nodded, as if to himself, and while the steady sound of hoofbeats filled the silence, spent a moment in thought. "Many of the Karsites felt the alliance would not endure past that moment," he replied. "There was a sizable number, though not a majority, who believed that the alliance had *never* been a good idea. But then the army of the Empire appeared, already well into Hardorn, and heading for Karse and Valdemar."

Rubrik snorted mirthlessly. "Indeed. An unpleasant surprise for all concerned."

The sky to the east showed a hint of color; sunrise would be spectacular—which did not presage a very pleasant ride today. A colorful sunrise, at least in Karse, meant that there would be storms during the day. There was no reason to think that the weather had changed just because he was across a border.

"We knew of the Empire, of course, but probably no more than you," Ulrich said after a moment. "Some had even dismissed the power of the Emperor and the size of the armies he controlled as nothing more than myth or exaggeration. But then—there he was, or rather, there his army was, even bigger than all the stories had claimed. Suddenly there was nothing standing between us and an Empire fabled for gobbling up entire countries. We had nothing that could stop them—except, perhaps, our own resourcefulness, our God—and that insignificant, inconvenient little alliance with Valdemar."

"Which probably didn't seem so insignificant or *nearly* so inconvenient, all things considered, when troop estimates came in," Rubrik replied. And if there was a hint of smugness in his voice, well, Karal could hardly blame him.

"There was another side to all of this that you probably had no hint of," Ulrich said, after another moment of thought. "And that is what the appearance of the Empire did for Her Holiness' credibility."

Ulrich nodded at his secretary, and Karal couldn't resist the invitation to have a word of his own in the discussion. "She'd been saying all along that Vkandis was warning her of an even greater peril to come," he offered proudly. "There weren't too many people who believed her, Son of the Sun or not, except Ulrich and a few other Priests."

He stopped then, afraid he might have overstepped himself, but the look Ulrich gave him was approving rather than the opposite. "Precisely. *Now* she showed that she was a true prophet, for no one could have predicted that the Empire would take an interest in Hardorn—and everything beyond it, one presumes. There is not a soul in Karse who doubts her now."

Well, that wasn't quite true, but it was near enough.

"Now our people as a whole are somewhat—bewildered," Ulrich concluded. "They are having some difficulty with the various changes she has decreed, but it is obvious even to the worst of her detractors that she *knows*, in the broadest sense of the word, what must be done to save us. It is very clear that if her instructions—or rather, the instructions of Vkandis, as passed to her—are not followed, Karse will not survive the attentions of the Empire. For the people, it is a difficult time. For those of us who believed in Solaris and in our land and God, it is a time of vindication."

"Interesting," Rubrik replied, softly. "I hope you won't mind if I think all this over for a while."

"Be my guest," Ulrich told him, with a hint of a smile. "I believe you might be having just as much difficulty with some of this as some Karsites I could mention."

Rubrik gave him an oblique look but did not reply. Karal felt immensely cheered. It looked as if his mentor had given the Valdemaran more to chew on than he had reckoned possible. Karal had the feeling that the Valdemaran, for the first time, actually believed that Solaris truly was the Son of the Sun, and not just another power-hungry Priest. The Valdemarans would have been perfectly willing to deal with another False Son—provided he (or she) set policies that benefited Valdemar. Karal was not so naive as to think otherwise. But a ruler with the *true* power of the One God behind her— now *that* was another proposition altogether.

Seeing Vkandis as something other than an empty vessel or a puppet for the Priests to manipulate was something Karal guessed Rubrik had not been prepared to deal with.

One point scored for us, he thought with satisfaction, and settled into the ride.

Rubrik inevitably came back with more questions, of course, but they were not about the political situation in Karse, but rather, about Ulrich himself. Gradually Karal came to see the pattern to those questions. Rubrik was trying to discover what the envoy *himself* was made of, the kind of man that the Valdemaran government would be dealing with—and just how much trust Solaris placed in the hands of that envoy.

It was sometimes hard to tell what Rubrik was thinking, but Karal judged that on the whole he was satisfied—and rather surprised to *be* satisfied. Whatever he had been expecting, it had not been a pair like Karal and his master.

Karal found it amusing to speculate on what he *might* have been expecting. An oily, professional politician like the last False Son had been, interested only in power and prestige? An ascetic, like Ophela, with no personal interests whatsoever, blind and deaf to anything other than God and Karse?

Throughout the morning, storm clouds had threatened to unleash another torrent; by the time they stopped at an inn for a meal at noon, it was obvious that they were going to ride right down the throat of another storm like the one yesterday.

This time their escort had found them a decent inn, which had its own share of travelers, and none of them paid any attention to a pair of black-clad clergy and their white-liveried escort. Most seemed too concerned with eating and getting on their way again to waste any time in idle curiosity about other travelers. While Karal and his master lingered over a final cup of ale, Rubrik went out to the courtyard, brooded over the state of the weather, then stared at his horse's head for a long time.

Finally he signaled to the stableboy to come and take his horse, Honeybee, and Trenor to the shelter of the stables, then limped back to the inn. "There's no use going any farther today," he said, clearly annoyed, but not with them. "This storm reaches from here past the inn where I intended us to stop. I wish that Elspeth had a few more Herald-Mages to go around. It seems that this so-called 'wizard-weather' is getting worse, not better."

Now how did he know all that? Karal wondered. He hadn't spoken to anyone. Then again, he was very familiar with this area, as he had already demonstrated more than once. Maybe he could tell what the weather was doing by looking for clues too subtle for Karal to catch.

"I can't speak for your situation here," Ulrich replied carefully, "but I can tell you that in magic, sometimes things do have to get worse before they get better."

"*Not* the sort of thing that your escort cares to hear, my friend," Rubrik replied with a weary laugh as he turned to look at the lowering clouds. He shook his head for, if anything, they were darker and thicker than before. Even Karal could tell they were in for a blow. "I was hoping to make up some time—"

"Not today, friend," Ulrich said with regret. "If we do not stop here, we would *have* to stop soon. I'm afraid that my old bones are not dealing well with this weather of yours."

Inwardly Karal cheered. At least Ulrich was going to keep his promise!

Rubrik looked around for the innkeeper. "Well, I might as well bespeak some chambers. At least we are well ahead of anyone else."

So it seemed, for he returned to them in a much more cheerful frame of mind, just as the stableboy brought up their packs from the stable. "I think you'll enjoy this stay. This may make up for the fool who sold our rooms out from under us," he said—then told the boy, "Bard Cottage."

The horseboy led them around to a door at the rear of the inn, which seemed a little odd to Karal. Such doors were normally used only at night, by servants, and he could not begin to imagine why the boy had taken them this way.

Then the boy led them outside, and there, connected to the inn by a covered walkway, was a neat little building standing all by itself. It was *probably* supposed to look like a farmer's cottage, but no farmer had ever built anything like this. Toy-like, cheerfully painted, and far too perfect; if Karal was any judge, it had probably cost more than any three real cottages put together. *It's more like the way a highborn would think a farmer's cottage looks,* Karal decided, regarding the ginger-bread carvings, the window boxes full of flowers, and the freshly-painted, spotless exterior with a jaundiced eye.

"This place is usually taken," Rubrik said with satisfaction. "It's very popular with those with the silver for absolute privacy. There's a small bedroom for each of us, beds fit for a prince, cozy little parlor, private bathing room, and they'll bring dinner over from the inn. If we're going to have to wait out a storm, this is the way to do it."

The rooms were tiny, but the beds were as soft as promised; Karal had the absurd feeling that he was sequestered in a doll house, but the place was comfortable, no doubt about that. The cottage would be hideously confining for a long stay, especially for three adults who did not know each other very well.

By the time they'd each taken a turn at soaking in the huge bathtub, however, Karal was quite prepared to agree with Rubrik's earlier statement. For waiting out a storm, this was the best of all possible venues. He was the last to take his bath, and when he got out, the smell of fresh muffins and hot tea greeted his nose.

He followed his nose to the parlor, where a servant from the inn had just set a tray on the table. Ulrich looked up at his entrance and chuckled at his expression. "Evidently our innkeeper has several young men of your age," the Priest told him. "His cook sent this over before I could even ask Rubrik to find a servant to get you a snack."

Rubrik turned around in his chair and grinned at Karal's expression. "Your master reminded me that young men your age are always hungry, and I pointed out this simple fact to our host. He is good at taking hints."

Karal entered the parlor and took the third chair in front of the newly-lit fire just as the storm broke outside. A crash of thunder shook the cottage, and rain lashed the roof in a sudden torrent, making Karal very glad that they were all inside, and not out on the road.

The windows in this pseudo-cottage were small, and not very satisfactory for storm watching, so Karal contented himself with listening to the thunder and the rain pouring down on the roof, as he helped himself to muffins and tea. He'd always enjoyed watching flames dance in a fireplace, anyway. It would be nice to spend a couple of nights here, if it came to that. Ulrich could use the rest, and he had some papers Ulrich had suggested he study that he hadn't had the time for.

But Rubrik is never going to wait that long, he decided, listening to the conversation with one ear. *He wants us in Haven as soon as possible. I wonder what could be so urgent?*

Ulrich had turned the tables on their escort, and was asking personal questions of *him*. Rubrik didn't seem at all reluctant to answer them now, although he had not been so forthcoming before this. Perhaps he had decided that not only was Ulrich worthy of trust as an envoy, he was to be trusted with other things as well.

Ulrich had just asked him—with the Priest's customary tact and delicacy—how he had come to be injured. Karal stopped listening to the rain outside, and devoted his full attention to the conversation.

"That is—an interesting question," the envoy replied measuringly.

"I hope you'll forgive such impertinence," Ulrich told him, with sincerity that was obvious, "but I couldn't help but think, since from the scar it is a recent injury, that it occurred in the war with Ancar. I thought perhaps it might have a bearing on why *you* are our escort, and not—someone else. And I wondered if something in that tale might account for your astonishingly good command of our tongue."

"It's not all that impertinent. I find stares a great deal ruder. And oddly enough, it does have something to do with why I am here—and why I know Karsite so well," the Valdemaran said, after a pause to examine Ulrich searchingly, as if he was trying to ferret out some hidden motive in asking such a question. "It happened while I was trying to protect one of your fellow Priests of Vkandis."

Ulrich nodded gravely. "You did seem to know a bit too much about us." He raised his mug of tea and sipped. "More than could be accounted for by your presumed acquaintance with a certain Master of Weaponry that we both know is in your Queen's employ."

"Correct." Rubrik smiled crookedly. "Your fellow Priest

was not particularly happy to have *me* guarding him, at the time. Not that I can blame him, since at the time *I* was not particularly happy to be there. We had something of a cautious truce, but neither of us really trusted the other."

Why does that not surprise me? Karal thought, with heavy irony.

Rubrik closed his eyes briefly and set his cup down. "We went through several encounters without much trouble, but then our lot got hit hard, by a company of Ancar's troops that not only included *a* mage, but *several* mages. Good ones, at that. He agreed to hold the rear in a retreat—damned brave of him, I thought—counting on me to keep him from getting hurt while he set up the magic that would take care of that. He got wrapped up in working some complex bit of magery, and couldn't move—"

"Tranced," Ulrich replied succinctly. "Many of the young Priests cannot work magic without being entranced."

Rubrik coughed, picked up his cup again, and sipped his own tea. "Yes, well, the line moved back, and we didn't move with it, and no one noticed for a long, critical moment. And since I'd been assigned to guard him, well, I did."

"And?"

He coughed again. "There were several of them, and only two of us, Laylan and me. I'm not a bad fighter, but I'm no Kerowyn. One of the biggest got through my guard, and I went down, right about the time *his* magic finally started working. That was when someone behind us noticed we weren't with the group anymore, and came back to get us."

Ulrich tilted his head to one side. "A glancing blow? But obviously one that did a great deal of damage."

Rubrik shivered, in spite of the warmth of the fire. "It was closer than *I* ever want to come again. I will say the Priest stood by me until the others got to us, right along with Layla. And he was touchingly grateful, and dragged another one of your Priests over to Heal me as soon as we were hauled back to safety, since there wasn't one of our Healers around that could handle a wound like this one. I'm told that's why the only lasting effect of what could have killed me is this bit of stiffness and an uncooperative leg. Your Healer-Priest was a damned fine human being, treated me as if I was Karsite—and your other lad not only thanked me when I woke up, but acted like he *believed* in the alliance from then on. That's when my view of your lot changed to something a bit more charitable."

Ulrich refilled his mug from the teapot and nodded. "As his did of you Valdemarans, I expect."

Rubrik chuckled. "I won't say we became the greatest of friends, but we got along just fine after that. He did express a great deal of surprise that a White Demon would take a life-threatening injury to save him, and that the Hellhorse would then proceed to guard both of us."

Karal paled a bit. White Demon? Hellhorse? Rubrik?

Ulrich grinned broadly. "I daresay. Perhaps some good came out of the bad, then—"

"I just wish it hadn't happened to *me*." Rubrik sighed. "Ah well, the life of a Herald is not supposed to be an easy one. I could count myself lucky that the ax went a bit to the left. To end the story, that's why I'm your escort, and not someone like—oh, Lady Elspeth. I was impressed enough with the way that stiffnecked youngster turned around, and with the Healer-Priest that helped me, that I specifically requested assignment to any missions dealing with Sun-Priests. I wanted whoever met you two to be someone who would at least treat you like human beings."

Herald? White Demon? Hellhorse? Oh, glorious God—

Rubrik was a Herald. A White Demon. And that beautiful horse that Karal had admired so much was no horse at all.

He stared into the fire, stunned, quite unable to move. It was a good thing he wasn't holding anything, or he'd have dropped it, his hands were so numb. He didn't even realize that Rubrik had excused himself and gone back to the inn for something, until the door closed behind him.

"Child, you look as if someone smacked you with a board," Ulrich observed dispassionately. "Are you all right?"

Karal rose to his feet, somewhat unsteadily, and stared at his mentor, trembling from head to foot in mingled shock and fear. "Didn't you hear what he said?" Karal spluttered. "He's one of *them*! Demonspawn! The—"

"I know, I know," Ulrich replied, with a yawn. "I've known all along. If that 'here I am, shoot me now,' white livery of theirs wasn't a dead giveaway, the Companion certainly *is*."

"But you didn't say anything!" Karal wailed, feeling as if he'd been betrayed.

"I thought you knew," Ulrich told him, a hint of stern rebuke in his voice. "We *are* in Valdemar. We *are* envoys from Her Holiness. The Heralds *are* the most important representatives of their Queen, and the only ones she trusts fully to accomplish delicate tasks. We've always called them *White* Demons. It should have been logical."

Karal just stared at him.

"Then again," Ulrich said, after a moment of thought, "I apologize. I should have told you, you're correct. I suppose I shouldn't be so surprised that you didn't recognize our friend for what he is—you've only had those ridiculous descriptions in the Chronicles to go on. I should have said something."

"But—" Karal began, wildly. "He—"

"—is the same man he was a few moments ago, before you realized what his position in Valdemar was," Ulrich pointed out, sipping his tea. "*He* is still the same. You are still the same. The only thing that has changed is how you see him, which is not accurate."

Karal tried to get a breath and couldn't. "But—"

"Does he eat babies for breakfast?" Ulrich asked, with a hint of a grim smile.

Karal was forced to shake his head. "No, but—"

"Do he or his mount shoot fire from their nostrils, or leave smoking, blackened footprints behind them?" Ulrich was definitely enjoying this.

Karal wasn't. "No, but—"

"Has he been *anything* other than kind and courteous to either of us?" Ulrich continued inexorably.

"No," Karal replied weakly. "But—" He sat back down in his chair with a *thud*. "I don't understand—"

Ulrich picked up Karal's tea mug and leaned over to put it back in his hands. "Child," he said softly, "he has heard the same stories of us that we have heard of the Heralds. The trouble is—I fear that the stories about us were partly true. We *did* have the Fires of Cleansing. We *did* summon demons to do terrible things, often to people who were innocent of wrongdoing. And yet he has the greatness of heart to assume that you and I, personally, never did any such things. What does that say to you?"

"That—he's the same man whose company I enjoyed this morning," Karal finally said, with a little difficulty. His mind felt thick. His thoughts moved as though they were weighted. And yet he could not deny the truth of what Ulrich had just said.

"I suggest that you relax and continue to enjoy his company," Ulrich replied, leaning back in his chair. "I certainly am, and I intend to go on doing so. In fact, after hearing his story, I am inclined to trust him to live up to every good thing that Her Holiness told me about Heralds."

But— Karal's thought froze right there, and he clasped his mug and stared down into the steaming tea as if he would somehow find his answers there. Ulrich was right; nothing had changed except for the single word.

Herald. Not such a terrible word. Just a word, after all. A name—and Karal had, in his own time, been called plenty of names.

That never made me into anything that they called me.

Yes, well, the word "Herald" in and of itself was nothing terrible either. What word really was?

Ulrich was right about the rest of it, too. *He* had never seen a Hellsp—

A Herald.

Right. He had never seen a *Herald* in all his life. The descriptions in the Chronicles were infantile, really—composed of all the horrors mothers used to frighten little children into obedience, rolled into one and put into a white shroud. Not a neat uniform, a livery like Rubrik's, but a tattered, ichor-dripping shroud of death. And no matter what other things he'd learned that had been *wrong* about their former enemies, somehow he had still expected Heralds to be monsters.

If you want to make your enemy into something you can hate, you first remove his humanity. . . . Had Ulrich said that at one point, or had that been something he'd heard during one of Solaris' speeches? It was true, whoever had said it, and the Chronicles had certainly tried to remove all vestige of humanity from these Heralds. *Make them only icons. When they are seen as a type, and not as individuals, they are easy for a fanatical mind to grasp—and hate.*

Karal didn't *think* he was fanatically-minded, but then again, what fanatic ever did? It was going to take a while to get used to this.

"I think I'm going to go—ah—meditate for a while," he said to Ulrich, who was staring into the fire with every evidence of utter contentment. The Priest waved a lazy hand at him.

"Go right ahead," his master said. "I believe you ought to. You've just had a shock, and you need to think about it. I'm sure your nose will tell you when dinner arrives, if your stomach doesn't demand it first."

Karal put down his mug and retired to his room, flushing in confusion, and wondered how things in his life had managed to become more complicated than he had ever dreamed possible.

And how was he ever going to make all the scattered pieces of it fit again?

He still hadn't quite wrapped his mind around the concept of "Rubrik-as-Hellspawn, Hellspawn-as-Herald" by the time dinner arrived. He ate quickly and quietly, listening, but not participating in the conversation at all. Ulrich and their escort continued their chat as blithely as if nothing whatsoever had changed, although Rubrik did ask, with some concern, if Karal was feeling all right.

"You look pale," he observed, as Karal bolted the last of his dinner. "If you're getting sick, please tell me—this is a good-sized town, and there are real Healers here. Healer-Priests, too, and there may even be one of the splinter Sunlord Temples here—"

"Ah, I meant to ask you about that," Ulrich interjected. "Later, that is."

"It's nothing, sir, my master already knows about it," Karal said hoarsely, taking the proffered excuse for what might be considered rude behavior. "It's just a headache. I—I think I'll go to my room, and sleep it off."

Karal fled before Rubrik could ask anything else. His dinner lay in his stomach like a ball of cold, damp clay. It had probably been excellent; he'd bolted it so fast he hadn't really noticed.

He spent part of the night staring sleeplessly at the ceiling, the murmurs of conversation in the next room scarcely audible over the pounding rain. He wasn't able to make out what the other two were saying, and he wasn't sure he wanted to. He just couldn't handle this. How could he act normally around Rubrik ever again?

But the soft, comfortable bed and the rhythmic pounding of the rain overhead seduced him into a dreamless sleep, and in the morning his anxiety seemed pretty stupid. He lay there in his bed, sheepishly wondering why the "revelation" had seemed so terrible last night. Ulrich was right; Rubrik was still the same man—and Heralds, as Karsite myth painted them, couldn't possibly have been anything like the reality. After all, there were plenty of things that had "always been True" or had been "the Will of Vkandis" that Solaris had proven were lies. So why should anything the False Ones taught about the Heralds be true?

He rose and went into the parlor, to find Ulrich already there and in high good humor, which meant his joints no longer pained him. The doors and windows were standing open wide to a wonderful warm breeze, there was a meal waiting on the table for him, and Rubrik was nowhere in sight. This storm had swept through cleanly last night, leaving behind a morning like a new-minted coin, the air washed so clean and pure that it was a pleasure to breathe. Rubrik had *not* sent servants to wake them up, and had let them sleep until after the sun rose. After a truly excellent breakfast, they joined their escort in the courtyard of the inn beneath an absolutely cloudless blue sky.

"Headache better?" Rubrik asked, as the horse-boy led Trenor up to Karal and held him so that Karal could mount easily.

"Yes, sir, thank you," Karal was able to reply, with a smile.

"Good. I get a touch of one myself in these wizard-storms. They say most people with any hint of mind-magic do." He gazed searchingly at Karal, who had no idea of what he was talking about. Karal shrugged his incomprehension.

"Yes, but how does that explain my poor, aching joints?"

Ulrich put in, with a faint smile. "I certainly do not hear thoughts with my knees!"

Rubrik laughed heartily. "A good question, and one that probably proves that, as always, the nebulous 'they' are probably as foolish as the things 'they' are reputed to say!"

On that cheerful note, he led them out to the road, heading north again, under a brilliant sun.

That seemed a good enough omen to start, and as the morning wore on, Karal managed to dismiss the rest of his lingering fears as absolutely groundless. The Herald and Ulrich must have shared a great deal of personal information after Karal went to bed, for now they acted like a pair of real friends.

Huh, he thought, with astonishment, for Ulrich had never been *friends* with anyone that Karal had ever noticed. But there it was, as they rode side by side, there was an easiness between them that could not be anything but friendship. *Ulrich respected him as soon as we met—and after that, there was a kind of—fellowship, maybe? Something like that, anyway; like he'd have with, oh, one of the Army Captains. Someone who deserved respect and was an interesting and intelligent person, a man he had things in common with. But this is different. I'm not sure how, but it's different. Ulrich seems happier, more open, and the tone of his voice is warmer than it usually is around other people.*

He found that Rubrik was taking pains to see that Karal was included in conversation as the day wore on. And somewhat to his astonishment, he realized that he had begun to actually relax around the Herald. If anything, Rubrik reminded him of his favorite uncle, the one who'd been a guard with a merchant caravan and had a wealth of tales about strange places and the wonderful things he had seen.

Rubrik was evidently in the mood to tell some of his own tales this morning, for he began to describe some of the other "foreigners" that they would meet once they reached the capital of Haven and the Court of Queen Selenay. Some of them, Karal would not have believed under any other circumstances, but Rubrik had absolutely no reason to lie and every reason to tell them the whole and complete truth.

But if he *was* telling the whole and complete truth—some of the other envoys weren't human at all. . . .

Ulrich didn't act at all surprised, though, as the Herald described some of the strangest creatures Karal had ever heard of. The Hawkbrothers were bad enough, with their white hair, intelligent birds, and outlandish clothing. But then he described the gryphons—Treyvan, Hydona, and their two youngsters. It was the little ones that made Karal decide that the Herald was *not* trying to play some kind of elaborate trick on them. Why make up that kind of detail if it was only a jest? The adult gryphons would have been more than enough.

"I'd been warned," Ulrich said laconically, when Rubrik ended his description. "After all, several of our Priests actually worked with these gryphons. Including one young lady who learned a valuable lesson in—hmm—"

"Cooperation?" Rubrik suggested with a wry smile.

"I was thinking, humility, but that will do." Ulrich's eyes actually twinkled. "Karal, you'll remember her, you were schooled with her. Gisell."

Karal's mouth dropped open with astonishment. "Gisell? *Humility?*" The two simply did *not* go together! Gisell had been one of the most stiffnecked little highborn bitches he'd ever had the misfortune to meet. Nothing could induce her to forget her lofty pedigree or her many important relatives.

Rubrik laughed heartily, and his smile reached and warmed his eyes. "Oh, a gryphon can bite you in two and have your legs shredded while your top half watches. When he tells you that you *will* work with the son of a pigkeeper and *like* it, you learn to be humble very quickly."

"If Gisell can learn to be humble, then I *can* believe in gryphons," Karal said firmly, provoking another burst of laughter, both from the Herald and from his master.

"Gryphons are just as real as my Companion Laylan, I promise you," Rubrik assured him. "And no more a monster than he is."

Now that triggered another thought, one that had sat in the back of his mind, pushed aside by the pressing dilemma of Rubrik-as-Herald. His horse—or rather, his Companion. Karsite legend had plenty to say about the creatures that Heralds rode, too! And now his behavior, which had seemed to be "only" remarkable training, had an explanation.

Laylan wasn't a horse. Obviously. *"No more a monster than he is"* he said—*but he isn't, can't be, even a magical horse like the Hawkbrothers' birds. Even if back home they'd call him a Hellhorse. So what is he if he isn't a horse?*

He held the question back, but it irritated him like an insect bite he couldn't scratch. Laylan himself seemed to know that it was tormenting him, too, because he kept *looking back* at him, and now he saw what his assumption that he was an animal had not let him see before. He *watched* him, watched Ulrich, and he had the sense that he was somehow participating in the conversation, even if he couldn't say anything in words.

Finally he couldn't stand it anymore. "Sir? Your—Laylan—what *is* he?"

Rubrik blinked, taken quite by surprise by the breathless question. "I suppose you *wouldn't* know, would you," he said, finally, turning in his saddle and squinting against the bright sunlight. "Ah—the best explanation we have is that Companions are a benign spirit in a mortal body. In some ways, rather like gryphons, except that they deliberately ally themselves with Heralds in order to help us help our land. They choose to look like horses, we believe, because horses pass without notice practically everywhere."

"Ah!" Ulrich's exclamation of delighted understanding made both of them turn toward the Priest. "That is the *best* explanation I have heard yet; I never had heard any reason why your Companions should have that particular form. It seems an inconvenient one."

Rubrik snorted, and so did Laylan. "Say that some time when you see him in full charge! This is several stone of muscle and *very* sharp hooves, my friend, and he knows how to use both to advantage! I'd rather have him in a fight than twenty armsmen, and that's a fact." He tilted his head to one side and added, as if it had never occurred to him before, "Odd though, that you Karsites don't seem to have anything like Companions, with your Vkandis being so—"

He flushed, and cut the sentence off, but Ulrich chuckled. "So much of a divine busybody in our lives, is that what you were going to say?" Rubrik winced, but the Priest only grinned. "Oh, don't apologize, even Her Holiness has been known to comment on that from time to time. Actually, though, Vkandis *does* have two supernatural manifestations that ordinary Priests—which are the closest thing we have to your Heralds—can experience. The sad part is that one of those was and is tragically easy to feign."

Ulrich gave Karal a prompting look.

"The Voice of Flame?" Karal asked with interest, taking the look to mean that Ulrich meant him to supply the correct answer.

Ulrich nodded. "Good, you recall what I told you." He turned back to the Herald. "The Voice of Flame is a source-less nimbus of fire; it appears above the head of a Priest and speaks through him. It is, by far, the most common manifestation of Vkandis' Will. Since we Priests are often mages as well as clergy, I'm sure you can see how easy this particular manifestation of the Will was to counterfeit."

Rubrik made a sour face. "Not a chance you could counterfeit a Companion—" he began.

"Ah, but this is what is interesting," Ulrich interrupted eagerly. "There was, traditionally, *another* manifestation that was impossible to counterfeit—and it was one that had not been seen in so long that it had fallen almost into myth. Until recently, that is. And it seems to me that the Firecats are *very* like your Companions."

"Firecats?" Rubrik shook his head. "I've never heard of them."

"Not likely anyone has, outside of Karse," Karal put in. "In fact, until one showed up with Solaris, I'd say most of the Priests didn't believe in them anymore, either!"

"A cat?" Rubrik's skepticism was quite clear. "How could an ordinary cat—"

"No more an *ordinary* cat than your Laylan is an ordinary horse, my friend," Ulrich told him gleefully. "First of all, there is the color—Firecats are unique. They are a pale cream in color, with red ears, facial mask, paws, and tail. And like your Companions, they have blue eyes. Then there is the *size*—they are as tall as mastiffs. And they talk."

"Talk?" Rubrik was incredulous for just a split second. "Wait—you mean, in Mindspeech?"

"Mind-to-mind, yes," Ulrich agreed. "They can, and do, speak to whomever they choose, however, and I believe your Companions speak only to their selected Heralds?"

Rubrik nodded, and Ulrich went on.

"Firecats historically appeared at significant times to offer advice, not only to the Son of the Sun, but often to anyone else who was of crucial importance. In ancient times, the Son of the Sun was always accompanied by at least one, and often two Cats." Ulrich shrugged. "Now, the Cats stopped appearing, I believe, about the time that the Fires of Cleansing were begun; I also believe that there has not been a genuine manifestation of the Voice since that same period, at least not among the Priests in the capital and the larger cities. Until recently."

Rubrik sat as bolt upright in his saddle as his infirmity would allow. "Are you telling me that—"

"I, myself, have seen Her Holiness speak with what I believe to be the genuine Voice," Ulrich told him. "But far more important, Solaris has a Firecat. He calls himself 'Hansa'— and that *is* the name of one of the most ancient Sons of the Sun, a name not even a demon would claim with impunity— he is not only seen sitting beside her, but he actually appeared *shortly after Vkandis struck down the False Son.*" He nodded as Rubrik's eyes narrowed in speculation. "His appearance served to further confirm her in the eyes and minds of the populace. But if you have any doubt, I have heard it from her own lips—and from Hansa's mind—that *he* is the one who advised her to make Herald Talia an honorary Sunpriest to cement our alliance."

Rubrik's mouth formed into a silent "o", but Ulrich wasn't quite finished yet.

"All the Firecats have traditionally referred to themselves by names of former Sons of the Sun. We have always believed that they *are* the spirits of former Sons who have taken on a material form in order to guide and advise us." He cast a significant glance down at Laylan, who looked up at him blandly and actually batted his eyelashes at him. "Obviously, they are exactly like your Companions, except that there are fewer of them. I assume that is because there are fewer deceased Sons than there are deceased Heralds."

Now it was Rubrik's turn to look as if someone had hit him in the back of the head with a board. And there was a whicker from Laylan that sounded suspiciously like a snicker.

"Of course—" Rubrik replied weakly. "Obviously." As if it wasn't obvious at all, and the thought had *never once crossed his mind.*

Rubrik's astonishment was so total, and so blatant, that Karal came very near to disgracing himself completely by blurting out the question, *"Do you mean that hadn't ever occurred to you?"* He stopped himself just in time.

In the first place, such a question would be twenty leagues beyond rude, and Ulrich would be completely within his rights—even his duty—to send him back in disgrace on the spot. One did not ask questions like that if one was a diplomat.

In the second place—

It's possible that the Companions actually have been keeping Heralds from even thinking just that. The Firecats were known to be what they were *only* to the Priests—the rest of the Karsite populace simply regarded them as signs of Vkandis' favor. Most ordinary folk were not even aware that the Cats spoke to the Priests; after all, the Priests had the Voice, what did they need with a talking feline?

I can think of several reasons why Companions would not want it known that they had once been Heralds, Karal decided, rather grimly, after a moment of silence that gave him plenty of time to really examine the idea. For instance, there had been one infamous attempt to destroy a Firecat by the traitor who had brought about the assassination of the Son of the Sun whose name the Firecat bore.

Not that that worked. Firecats can protect themselves very nicely. The assassin made a lovely bonfire, so the story goes. But surely, there were people who would be very unhappy if certain Heralds were to reappear after their demise—and Companions, unlike the Cats, *could* be killed.

And even a Karsite knows that if you kill the Hellhorse— the Companion—you'll probably kill the Herald.

There could be emotional conflicts among the Heralds as

well. *How* would a loved one feel, knowing that the beloved ex-Herald *could return if he chose*, even if in a rather—inconvenient—form? It would be devastating if he *did*, and nearly as bad if he *didn't*.

As he was mulling all this over, he caught sight of Laylan staring back at him over his shoulder—and when he caught his eye, he nodded as if he had been following his very thoughts.

As if—like Hansa—she can see what is in my mind—

Once again, he sat frozen in place, stunned. *Like Hansa. The Cats* are *like Companions—*

Once again, he nodded; gravely, but unmistakably.

Only one thought floated up out of the shock.

If the Cats are like the Companions, then we are not so different from our ancient enemies after all.

And he could not for the life of him decide if that realization was a reassuring one.

An'desha

7

An'desha stared unhappily out the window of his provisional home. Late afternoon sunset streamed through the branches of the trees around Firesong's *ekele*, and left patches of gilding on the grass beyond the windows. The silence that must surely be outside was not mirrored within. The indoor garden was full of laughter and talk, even to the point where the burbling of the waterfalls and fountains was overwhelmed by human chatter.

An'desha sat on a rock ledge in the farthest corner of the hot pool, dangling his feet in the water and trying not to sulk. He could not suppress his bitter unhappiness, though, and by the gods, he wasn't sure he wanted to! Firesong had *not* consulted him on this; he hadn't even been warned that there were visitors coming this afternoon. Firesong had simply showed up with all of them in tow, some of whom An'desha had never even met before. It was rude, it was unfair, and he was not in a mood to make the best of it.

This was *supposèd* to be his retreat away from all the strangeness of Valdemar—so why did Firesong have to bring half of Valdemar into the retreat and spoil it?

Well, maybe not half of Valdemar, but it certainly sounded like it. The garden *felt* overcrowded, and the fragile peace he had been trying to cultivate was shattered.

An'desha had not had a very good day today; not that everything had gone wrong, but nothing had quite gone *right*. Firesong kept telling him that he needed to get out and interact with other people, to *meet* some of these foreigners, so today he he had gritted his teeth and made an attempt, hoping for Firesong's approval. Hoping for *some* success to show him, however small that was.

He'd gone off on his own this afternoon while Firesong taught the young mages. A few days ago he had volunteered to help a group of those youngsters who wore the rust, blue, or gray clothing with one of their lessons in Shin'a'in, and their teacher had gladly accepted his offer. Today was to have been the first of those lessons, and An'desha had some vague idea that he might socialize with them after the lesson. Wasn't that what these strange children did? First have lessons, then socialize?

The lesson had gone on all right, but afterward, when they accepted his hesitant suggestion that they could ask him questions and he would try to answer them, he'd retreated in bewildered confusion within a few stammered sentences. They were just too—weird. They weren't anything like the Shin'a'in of his Clan; they seemed avidly, greedily curious about everything, at least to him, and they asked things he considered terribly callous and horribly intrusive. Of course it was possible that they had no idea that they were being so intrusive—and it was possible that with their limited grasp of Shin'a'in they simply didn't know what they were asking, but why ask him all those prying questions about Firesong? And what in the name of the Star-Eyed was a "Tayledras mating circle?"

Rudeness was bad enough, but they were also shallow, or at least their questions pointed in that direction. To him they seemed selfish and preoccupied with trivialities. He found himself getting angry at them for being so cavalier and carefree, then was appalled at himself for being angry with them simply for acting like children.

A Shin'a'in child was an adult the day he (or she) could ride out on the horse he had trained from a colt, and survive on his own on the Plains for one week. That could be any age from nine up. These Valdemarans, raised in cities, had no such measuring stick for maturity. They *were* children—more to the point, for all that they were not all that much younger than his apparent age, they were sheltered, protected children. He gathered that most of them had never personally been touched by the war that had threatened their land, and certainly none of them could ever even imagine, in their worst nightmares, the kinds of things *he* had gone through. How could he fault them for being what they were?

But they not only had nothing in common with him, they were so very different from him that they might just as well have been gryphons or *kyree*. For that matter, he had more in common with the perpetually ebullient Rris than he did with any of *them!* At least he understood why Rris was always asking questions; he was a historian, and he wanted not only the facts, but the feelings and reasoning that brought the facts about. *Kyree* oral histories took these factors into account; they were important parts of the tale. These children had no such excuses for *their* greedy curiosity.

So he returned in confusion and some distress to the only shelter he had anymore—only to find that Firesong had led an invasion of Valdemar into the place where he sought tranquillity, an invasion planned without his knowledge or consent.

Oh, granted, there were only half a dozen of the strangers, but it seemed like more, three times more. They poured into his garden and inserted themselves into his heated pool, barely stopping long enough in their ongoing conversation to greet him. And if he sequestered himself upstairs, Firesong would want to know why and probably be disgusted with him for not even trying to be polite and sociable. So he stayed and found himself virtually excluded from the conversation anyway, simply because he had no idea what was going on or what they were talking about.

To his right were Elspeth and Darkwind; well, at least he knew them. Elspeth was the daughter of the ruler of this place, and a Herald—she had a spirit-creature called a "Companion" that looked something like a horse and spoke in the mind. A lithe and lively young woman, her dark hair was now more silver than sable, and her eyes a soft blue-gray, turned that way by her use of the node-energy from the Heartstone beneath her mother's palace. She was that unique creature among humans, strong *and* beautiful, and perfectly self-confident, if rather headstrong. Darkwind was another Hawkbrother, an Adept, though not the equal of Firesong, with the raptoral features of most Tayledras, and the pure silver hair and blue eyes all Tayledras grew into eventually, simply by living around Heartstones. Both Elspeth and Dark- wind knew Firesong long before An'desha had met any of them; he got the impression that Firesong had been their teacher at one point.

Beyond them, up to their necks in hot water, were a tall blonde woman they called "Kero" and a man whose name An'desha hadn't even caught. It had sounded something like "elder" and that surely couldn't be right. Both of them were older than anyone else here, but An'desha wouldn't have challenged either of them to a fight. Their muscles and the way they moved told him that they were a lot more danger- ous than they looked. The clothing that the man had shed was of the white kind worn by the Heralds, and though the woman had been wearing dark leather gear, they both seemed to have those same kind of spirit-beasts that Elspeth part- nered.

Beyond them was Firesong, holding court, and beyond him, the Shin'a'in envoy and some mage or other this "Kero" knew who looked to have a lot of Shin'a'in blood in him. He was a little younger than Kero was, and although he had the dark hair and golden skin of a man of the Plains, he had emerald green eyes. Besides, he was definitely a mage, and An'desha knew from personal experience that no Shin'a'in could be a mage, unless he was a shaman as well. He seemed comfort- able in this strange gathering, anyway. A lot more comfort- able than An'desha, who *belonged* here.

Not a huge group, after all—only six, eight if you counted An'desha and Firesong, but they were all such vivid personal- ities that An'desha felt smothered, ignored, or both. They were all chattering away like old friends, which they probably *were*, but they seemed to have forgotten that An'desha didn't know any of them, really.

This invasion of his private preserve, coming at the end of an uncomfortable afternoon, made him want to throw a very childish tantrum. He wanted to be alone with Firesong—no matter how hard it was to reconcile his feelings about the young mage, at least Firesong was one person he could *under- stand*. Firesong would make excuses for him and help find answers! An'desha wanted the music of falling water, not insistent chatter. Or, if there must be talk, he wanted to talk to Firesong about his difficulties with these strange, intrusive people of Valdemar. They were nice enough, but *nosey*.

He would have said that he wanted to go home, except that he had no home, and this was the closest he was likely to get. Now these strangers had just proved that it wasn't *his* home, and never would be, simply by being here.

He didn't want to share Firesong *or* his place with the group of laughing, splashing invaders.

They were talking like mad things in three languages, only two of which he understood at all well; his own Shin'a'in and Tayledras. They chattered about *more* people and doings he knew nothing about.

That was not all that upset him. There was something about this gathering that set his nerves on edge, something intangible that had nothing to do with the invasion of his place. There was a frenetic, feverish quality to the conversation he sensed, but couldn't fathom. They acted as if they were trying to drive something unpleasant away by sheer volume of talk.

And as if that wasn't bad enough, it was becoming increasingly clear to him by the moment that Firesong was *flirting* with Darkwind. In front of everyone!

Was Firesong *trying* to humiliate him?

He pulled his feet out of the water in a fit of sullen fury, and snatched up a towel and his clothing. Furious, he began to dry himself off, ignored by the others. Ignored even by Firesong, who was engrossed in his flirtation.

Oh, gods. How could he not have guessed that something like this would happen? Weren't the Hawkbrothers supposed to be as light-in-love as their feathered companions?

But must Firesong take on a new conquest in front of him and everyone else? And why Darkwind?

Well, naturally, they are both Tayledras Adepts, and Darkwind is attractive and clever and mature, and I'm a half-Shin'a'in freak with more problems than twenty sane people. I'm a cowardly fool who doesn't understand most of what Firesong tries to show me.

". . . and now that you're properly silver-haired, as an Adept should be, with a *decent* wardrobe, you're actually a credit to k'Sheyna instead of a disgrace," Firesong teased, while An'desha struggled into his shirt and breeches; a difficult proposition with still-wet skin. "I don't know how Elspeth was ever attracted to you, with your hair dyed the color of mud and full of bark. You looked like a mad hermit, not a proper Hawk-brother."

"Oh?" Darkwind arched his eyebrows and grinned, then splashed Firesong with a handful of water. "Really? And *who* was it told Elspeth he wanted to braid feathers into my hair? I thought perhaps you liked the rustic look. You might have found me challenging."

"Hmph." Firesong sent the droplets flying back at Darkwind with a flicker of magic. "If I did tell her something like that, it was because I was *hoping* to induce some sense of proper grooming into you."

Darkwind pouted. "And here all the time I thought you *wanted* me!"

"We-ell, now that you look like a civilized human being and not a patch of brush—" Firesong fluttered long, silver eyelashes at the lean and muscular k'Sheyna Adept, who smirked and fluttered right back at him.

An'desha stared, aghast, embarrassed, humiliated. Oh, he *knew* that the Hawkbrothers were free enough with their favors, but—

—but how could they carry on like this! And *right in front of him!* They *were* trying to hurt him! He hadn't done anything to deserve treatment like this!

He felt his skin grow cold, then hot; his throat choked, and his stomach knotted. As he struggled to control himself, astonishment turned to something darker, in the blink of an eye.

He flushed again, hotter this time. From "how could they," the thought turned to another.

How dare they!

His hands knotted into fists; his stomach cramped. He clenched his jaw so hard he thought his teeth would shatter. He choked back an exclamation of pain and outrage.

Firesong continued to flirt, without a single glance at him.

His heart pounded until he shook with the rhythm and blood roared in his ears. His jaw ached as he clenched it tight.

Firesong leaned closer to Darkwind and murmured something that made the other Adept laugh aloud, throwing his head back and showing a fine set of white teeth. Firesong laid one elegant hand on Darkwind's shoulder.

Rage flared, fed by jealousy, into an all-consuming conflagration which left room for only one thought.

I'll—I'll eviscerate him! Though which "him," he couldn't at that moment say. He struggled with his numb, impotent anger, fought with the feelings that threatened to bind him where he stood.

Something dark uncoiled like a newly-awakened snake, deep inside him. It oozed through his veins and tingled along his nerves.

For a brief moment, his rage lacked a target, torn as it was between Firesong and Darkwind equally. But then, as Darkwind made to snatch at a feather from his bondbird's tail to give to Firesong, it all turned against the interloper.

How dare he!

And suddenly, as soon as he *had* the target, his anger was no longer impotent.

The darkness filled him, burned his fingers, longing to be unleashed. He felt power rising in him, rushing to his summons eagerly, flowing into him, all too familiar from the anger-fueled mage-attacks of Mornelithe Falconsbane; power that was poised to tear the guts right out of Darkwind's treacherous body and fling them back in the bastard's face—

—tear the guts from—

—tear—

Realization froze him in place, just before he let the power loose to turn the interloper inside out.

What am I doing!

He stopped himself, appalled, before the power got away from him; hauled it back and quashed it; dispersed it, let it drain out of him in a rush that left him trembling, this time not with anger, but with horror.

I nearly killed him—

—nearly—

—oh, gods—

Rage turned inward and ate itself, and with a strangled sob of terror, he whirled and fled the garden.

He dashed up the stairs to the second story, blinded with panic, with fear, and with tears of shame. There was only one thought in his mind.

I could have killed him. I could have. I almost did.

Panic gave his stumbling feet the strength his body lacked. He had to get away, away from everyone else, before something worse happened. What was he? What had he become?

Worse yet—*what was he still*?

A monster. I'm a monster. I'm the Beast. . . .

Falconsbane was alive and well, and living inside *him*. Waiting for a chance to get out, or better still, looking for a way to make An'desha into the kind of sadistic, perverted, twisted horror he had been.

He heard the running footsteps of someone following him, and turned at the top of the stairs, intending to send whoever it was away, far away from him—away from one irrevocably contaminated with the lurking shadow of Mornelithe Falconsbane. He wasn't thinking any more clearly than that; he only knew that no one should be near him.

But he didn't get a chance to say anything, for it was Elspeth who had followed him, hard on his heels. He had been misled by the soft sound of her bare feet into thinking she was farther behind him. She didn't stop when he did; she ran up the last three stairs and caught him up in her arms and in an impulsive embrace as soon as he turned and faced her, ignoring the fact that she was dripping wet and so was the brief tunic she wore. That simple embrace undid him completely.

Oh, gods. . . .

He collapsed against her without a thought and began to weep, hopelessly; she held him against her damp shoulder, and stroked his hair as if he had been a very small child caught up in a nightmare. In a moment, it didn't matter that her tunic was wet; tears of pain and panic burned their way down his face and into the sodden cloth, and his throat ached with the effort of holding his hysterical sobs back. He simply clung to her, a shelter, a sure refuge, and she supported him.

"An'desha, it's all right," she said quietly, over his strangled sobbing. "Dearheart, it wasn't what you thought it was! Darkwind and I are bonded and Firesong knows it, and Darkwind knows how Firesong feels about *you!* They were only teasing each other, dear, truly, and they would never, ever have done that if they had any idea how hurt you were just now. We just all thought you were tired and wanted to be left alone, and Firesong's had mischief in him all day."

"But you—" he got out, through the tears. "You—"

How she knew he was trying to ask why she had followed him, he had no idea—but she knew, or guessed right, and gave him the answer.

"I was the only one close enough to see your face, *ke'chara*. It was only play, and now they're teasing Kero. You were so quiet that we all assumed you'd join in after you revived a little. No one else knows you ran off. You mustn't let things like this bother you so much!" She held him very tightly for a moment, and he felt the warmth of her concern flowing over him. He *wanted* it to help; he wanted to feel comforted.

It did nothing to thaw the frozen center of his fear.

Worse, she only thought he'd fled, like some stupid jilted lover, like an idiot in a ballad. She hadn't a clue why he was falling apart like this.

He had to tell her. She had to know. It might be her life he threatened next. *Would* be, if Falconsbane got loose.

"That's not—" He fought the tears back as they threatened to choke him into incoherence. "Els-peth, it wasn't *that*—didn't you feel it? I was angry, and power just—took over and I almost struck Darkwind! I almost killed him!" He pulled away from her, afraid that he would somehow contaminate her as well. "It's Falconsbane!" he choked out. "He's still—here, he *must* be, he's still controlling me and I—I—"

He began to shake, trembling with absolute terror. How could he have done that? How could it not have been the Beast within?

Yet she did not draw away from him as he was certain she must, and when she pulled him back against her shoulder he did not resist.

"Is there somewhere up here we can go to sit for a while?" she asked quietly, as the tears began again. He waved vaguely to the right, and she supported him as she steered him away from the staircase and into the sitting room with its view from among the tree branches. She helped him down onto a cushion and sat beside him, still holding him, until his shaking stopped.

"Let's start over," she said quietly as the sun set somewhere beyond the trees, and thick, blue dusk gathered about them. "You were obviously tired, out-of-sorts, and we thoughtlessly came trampling in to destroy what little peace and quiet you had. That put you further out-of-sorts, right?"

He nodded, his stomach churning, only half of his mind on what she was saying. How could any of this matter now?

"Then, already unhappy and angry with us, you *thought* that Firesong was trying to seduce Darkwind. What you really saw was just Firesong teasing someone who is a good enough friend to tease back." He heard a definite tone of wry amusement in her voice. "I was told by a—a Shin'a'in friend that Hawkbrother teasing usually involves a lot of innuendo and flirtation. She told me that I might as well get used to it, since it's as stupid to get upset over something *they* grow up with as it would be to become upset because birds fly. So—I got used to it, and I've been known to give as good as I get."

"S-s-so I've got no choice but to get used to it, too?" he said, with a touch of anger getting past the tears, momentarily distracted from his deeper and weightier fears.

He felt her shrug. "If you don't, you're only setting yourself up for more pain," she replied logically. "An'desha, I don't know if you've ever felt strongly about anyone before, but there is one thing you had better get into your head right now. You *don't* go into a pairing intending to try and change someone to suit you. They were themselves long before you came along. You *do* go into a pairing ready to compromise."

He shook his head numbly, his entire soul rebelling at the idea that she thought his troubles were no more serious than simple hurt feelings, and once again she divined what he meant though he could not say it.

"Huh . . . it's not that?"

He nodded, then shook his head helplessly.

"It's not that, and it's more than that?"

He sniffed, and nodded.

She paused for a moment, and thought, her brows creased. "All right. I'll start with what's simplest. Now, listen to me and *believe* me. Darkwind and I are lovers, partners, and friends; there isn't much that is going to come between us, and Firesong *knows* that. He also knows that I am not Tayledras, and that I would be very, very hurt if what you saw and heard was anything other than friendly teasing. So does Darkwind. That's one of the compromises *we've* made." Then she laughed dryly. "More than that, he knows that there is a very real possibility that *he* would be very, very hurt as well— physically! I have quite a few faults, An'desha, and I have a very bad temper. I do *not* care to share Darkwind with anyone, and I will *not* be humiliated, especially in front of others. If I thought that was going to happen, well, someone would need a bandage or splint."

"Oh," was all he could say.

"So—for the answer to the situation that made you angry in the first place and triggered all this, if I don't have a reason to feel jealous or humiliated, and I'm the most jealous wench in Valdemar, certainly *you* don't!"

Uncertainly, he rubbed at his burning eyes with the back of his hand and coughed. A certain Shin'a'in proverb sprang immediately to mind. Not a flattering one, either. "But they say that the—"

"The lady is always the last to know." She snorted, a most unladylike sound. "Yes, but 'they' don't reckon on bondbirds and Companions, both of whom would tell tales, I promise you. Vree doesn't much care for Firesong's bird Aya, and he likes me and Gwena both; he'd babble like a scarlet jay either to me or to her if Darkwind got up to something with Firesong that I didn't know about."

An'desha wiped his eyes again. It certainly sounded logical. "But—"

"But that's giving Firesong no credit whatsoever for any kind of feelings, honor, or decency; that's assuming that he *is* as shallow and light-minded as he would like us to think. That is not fair to him, and you know better. For that matter, so do I." She took his chin in two fingers, and angled his face towards hers so that he had to look into her eyes. "*Ke'chara*, he is a *Healing Adept*. Don't you realize what that means? Of all people, you should. For all that he seems light-minded on the outside, he *cares*, more than anyone I have ever seen. He cares for *you*, and I think he has surprised himself by how much he cares for you. He has put a great deal of himself into the Healing of *you*, and he will literally empty himself for you if you let him, right down to the dregs. He is as decent and honorable as any Herald I know, and that is the greatest compliment I could give anyone."

An'desha swallowed slowly past the great lump in his throat. "I—"

"He has his faults, plenty of them, but failing to care about you and what happens to you is not one of them. He and I are rather alike when it comes to matters of the heart. Maybe it's the blood we share, I don't know." She looked very stern, and he was forcefully reminded of Need. "Give the man some credit. He has the capacity for great love, and he's not going to risk great love for something trivial. It was nothing more than a game. He would never, ever jeopardize anything having to do with you."

He had to believe her. *She* knew; she knew people, and she knew Firesong and Darkwind. He blinked, his eyes feeling gritty and sore, and nodded. Then his fear rose in him again, worse than before, when he realized what he could have done *for no cause*. Somehow that made it all worse.

"But Fal—" he began, with a wail of despair.

She cut him off with a look and a finger placed against his lips. "Falconsbane had nothing to do with the way you reacted. Being far too ready to think yourself hurt *did*, but not Falconsbane. He is gone, and good riddance."

"No," he replied, with heat. "This time *you* don't understand! Even if he's gone, he's still a part of me, he's corrupted me, he's gotten into the way I think and react and—"

"Hell, no," she said firmly. "Horseturds. For one thing, I doubt that Mornelithe Falconsbane ever cared enough about anything or anyone to *ever* feel jealousy! In order to become jealous, you have to care for and value something besides yourself, you know."

That took him aback; it was something that had never even entered his mind. He had to nod cautiously. Falconsbane had certainly never cared for anyone—only valued them as prizes.

She smiled grimly. "As for your own reaction and how strong and irrational it was—perfectly ordinary people have moments of jealousy as terrible as anything you just experienced. It happens all the time." Her smile turned into a grimace of pain. "Unfortunately, Heralds see the aftermath of that kind of jealousy all the time, too."

"I'm *not* ordinary," he began.

"No," she agreed readily. "You aren't. Ordinary people do not have the ability to rend people limb from limb with little more than a thought. But ordinary people *do* have the ability to rend other people limb from limb, period, if they are angry enough. It just takes a little more effort on their part, and as I said, Heralds see the aftermath of those episodes of jealousy and rage all the time. The gods know that in this city alone there are plenty of beatings and knifings and other kinds of mayhem inflicted every day to prove that perfectly ordinary people can be driven to kill over jealousy. The only difference between them and you is that they will use perfectly ordinary physical means against the object of their rage." She coughed and rubbed her nose. "It's horrible, it's tragic, but there it is."

"But my point—" he tried to interject.

"What makes you *different* from those stupid, ordinary people," she continued inexorably, "is that you stopped yourself from acting. You *controlled yourself*. You were horrified by the very idea you could have hurt Darkwind, even though *you* were already hurt *by* him."

"But I might not have!" he cried, panicking again.

"But you *did*," she replied with emphasis. "You did, even when you didn't know it was a game and meant nothing. You did control yourself, when you thought you had every reason to strike back. *Now* you know what the silly teasing-game looks like between two very good friends, and you won't make that mistake again. You know how much *we* value you, and that we would never knowingly hurt you, and I hope that you will *ask* one of us before you jump to any conclusions."

"I—"

He stopped and never completed the sentence, because he frankly did not know what to say. She *had* an answer for every one of his fears and his arguments. She could even be right. He had no way of knowing.

She waited patiently for him to say something, then shrugged. "Right now I think we ought to do something to salvage this situation. I don't think you want anyone else to know that you came running up here, hurt. If I were you, I wouldn't."

Well, he had to agree completely with that, anyway. He felt enough like a fool; the last thing he wanted was for everyone else in the gathering to *know* he was a fool.

"In that case, we need to think of some logical reason for both of us to have come up here." She nibbled a fingernail for a moment, deep in thought. "Food, maybe? Or something to drink? Do you two keep those things here?"

"Yes," he replied, nearly speechless with gratitude at her quick thinking. "And surely everyone is thirsty by now."

"Good. Let's go get some drink and bring it down to them; maybe something in the way of a snack as well." She rose to her feet and gave him her hand. He took it and she helped him to his. She was a lot stronger than she looked.

Her brief tunic had dried, and so had her hair; it curled around her face in a wispy silver-streaked cloud. He wondered how it was that she could be so earthy and so unearthly, all at the same time.

"Lead the way, *ke'chara*. I'm not a lot of good as cook, but I can carry a tray with the best of them." She winked at him, and he found himself smiling back at her as he led the way to the tiny kitchen where he prepared meals from time to time.

They assembled enough food and drink to have accounted for their absence, and she used a damp, cold cloth to erase any lingering traces of his hysteria. He allowed her to persuade him to rejoin them all by promising that she would make *certain* he was not left out of things from now on.

But he did not go back down those stairs without an invisible load of misgivings along with his other burdens. She was very likely right when it came to her assertions about Darkwind and Firesong—but when it came to himself, he was not so sure.

And despite Elspeth's kind words, Falconsbane *had* left traces inside him, in the form of knowledge and memories. Even if he was able to control his emotions forevermore, there were things he could never have faith in again. There were too many things he could not blindly believe in now, after hosting a madman in his body. No, when it came to the future, he could not seem to muster Elspeth's level of hope. There was no blind optimism left in him, no confidence that he'd control his rage next time, and he was very much afraid of that uncertainty.

There was more than one way for a madman to be born.

8

Horses were never suited to traveling by night, especially moonless nights. Karal was a good rider, and the gelding's tension communicated itself to him through a hundred physical signals he felt in his hands and his legs; the horse was nervous as well as tired, and all of his nervousness stemmed from the fact that he couldn't *see.*

Trenor stumbled on the uneven road, and Karal steadied him with hand and voice. The gelding whickered wearily, and Karal wondered if he ought to tell Herald Rubrik he was going to have to dismount and lead the poor horse before he took a tumble and ruined his knees.

"We're almost there. Just over the next rise, Karal, you'll see it in a minute," Rubrik's voice floated back through the moonless dark. He could have been a disembodied spirit or hundreds of paces ahead; there was no way of telling. "Or rather, you'll see the lights. Once your horse can see where he's going, he'll have an easier time of it."

"I'm not foundering Trenor," he replied stubbornly. "I'm not going to ride him to exhaustion, and I'm not going to let him take a fall with me on his back. One more stumble, and I'm walking him in."

A white shape loomed up in front of him, and he realized that Rubrik and Ulrich had pulled up on the road verge to wait for him. "No one is asking you to hurt Trenor, lad," the Herald said in a tired voice. "I'd spare you both if I could, but there's nowhere to stay but hedges between here and Haven, and once we reach Haven we might as well go to the Palace. I'm sorry I had to push you like this, but I had word there's more wizard-weather coming in, and that last bridge was about to go."

He's repeating himself; that's the third time he's told me that. He's pretending to be in a lot better shape than he really is. I'll bet he's in a lot more pain than he's letting on, too.

Since they'd passed that last bridge right at sunset, and Karal had been able to see for himself just how shaky the structure was, he hadn't argued with going on at the time, and didn't now. And since he had also seen the remains of the huge tree that had caused the damage to that bridge mere hours before they had reached it, he also didn't ask why such an important bridge hadn't yet been repaired.

Thinking back on it, he recalled something else he hadn't paid a lot of attention to at the time. That tree, which had a trunk as big around as two men could reach with their arms, had been torn up by the roots. It hadn't simply washed down into the river, it had been torn up and flung there. He really didn't want to think about the kind of weather that tore up trees by the roots and sent large rivers into flood in a matter of hours.

Once they'd crossed the bridge, they'd found there were no rooms to be had at any of the inns. Everything was full up, in no small part due to the effect the weather was having in disrupting travel during the heaviest months for trade in the year.

So they had pressed on, knowing that once they reached Haven, at least there would be rooms and meals waiting for all of them. But once the sun set, the going had gotten a lot rougher than Karal had thought it would. It was a moonless night, and heavy clouds obscured the stars; that might not trouble a Companion, but poor little Trenor found it rough going, and so, probably, did Honeybee. A couple of handfuls of grain and some grass snatched as they rested was not a satisfactory substitute for his dinner and a good rest in a stall.

Karal's mood matched his horse's, even if he knew the reasons why they were moving on through the middle of the night. At least it was better for Ulrich to ride than to rest beside the road, perverse as it might sound. Honeybee had carried him on all-night rides in worse conditions than this, and while he was riding, his joints stayed warm and flexible because they were being exercised. If they stopped beside the road to rest until the sun came up, he'd be too stiff to move after a night without shelter.

The thick darkness smothered sounds because there were so few visual reference points; even the insects by the side of the road sounded as if they were chirping behind a wall.

"I promise, I've sent messages on ahead of us," Rubrik continued. Karal believed him, even though there was no way *he* knew of that messages could be racing ahead of them. Except magic, of course, there was always that possibility. Ulrich had been taking it for granted that their escort was reporting regularly to his superiors *somehow*, so it must be by magic. "There are servants waiting for us, and the Queen's own farrier will be taking care of your gelding as soon as we reach the Palace."

Karal patted Trenor's neck without replying. Tired as the gelding was, he wasn't winded or strained yet. For all of his stumbling, he hadn't actually taken a fall or an injury. A good hot mash inside him, a good blanket covering him, and a warm stall to sleep in, and Trenor should be all right in the morning.

For that matter, I wouldn't turn down a hot mash, a good blanket, and a nice thick bed of straw right now.

"Thank you," he said at last. "I'd rather take care of him myself—but I'm as tired as he is, and I'd do something stupid, like let him drink too much or too fast."

I'm babbling. I'm too tired, and I'm babbling. It's a good thing Rubrik's probably too tired to notice, or he could get anything he wanted out of me right now, just by starting a conversation and letting me run on. Ulrich is too tired to pay any attention to anything I say.

"This is the last rise," Rubrik promised. "It's a long slope downhill from here."

Well, I hope so. Or I will get off and walk.

Rubrik's promise was good; a few moments later, from his vantage point in Trenor's saddle, the lights of Haven appeared as they crested the long hill they'd been climbing for the past half mark and more. There weren't many of those lights, late as it was, but it was obvious from how spread out they were that Haven was a good-sized city. It was possible to guess the general shape and size from here, in fact.

Large. Quite large.

A few years ago, Karal might have been gaping with amazement, but that was before he'd been taken to Sunhame, the capital of Karse and the site of the first and biggest Temple, as was proper for the Throne of Vkandis. Sunhame was at least the size of Haven, and might even be bigger. So he wasn't impressed, except by the fact that the city was closer than he had thought.

"Not long now," Rubrik repeated. "We're almost at the outskirts. With no traffic, we should make excellent time through the city streets once we're within the walls."

Trenor lifted his head and sniffed; he must have liked what he scented because he arched his neck tiredly and picked up his pace a little. Beside him, Honeybee did the same, though her call was not a soft whicker but an asthmatic bray.

"They probably smell the other horses, and possibly the river down there," Ulrich murmured to himself, clearly not even aware that he had spoken aloud.

He's babbling, too. Well, good, if he's that tired, he won't be up first thing in the morning. I may get a chance to sleep in.

The first building that could properly be said to belong to the city appeared on the right; it was too dark to make out what it was, but from the scent of cold, damp clay, smoke, and heated brick, Karal guessed it might belong to a large-scale pot maker or something of the sort.

That, too, was similar to the way that Sunhame was set up; a lot of tradesfolk on the outskirts, warehouses, even mills and the like. Smiths and manufactories. Not too many people wanted to have their houses where there was noise from people going about their trades, so those trades tended to get shoved to the outskirts of the city.

Other buildings appeared soon after, mostly just unlit shapeless bulks against the sky on either side of the road. One or two candles or lamps burned behind curtains, but not enough to cast any kind of light. The hooves of their beasts echoed dully in the silence, a silence broken only by the occasional bark of a dog or creak of wood from an unseen sign swaying in the scant breeze. A few insects called, but no birds, and no other animals. They might have been riding in a city of the dead.

Karal shivered; he did *not* like that particular image at all.

A few more lights appeared up ahead, lights which proved to be lanterns mounted on posts outside closely-shuttered shops. There were still more of these lanterns up ahead, evidently placed along the road at regular intervals. As they passed the third set, Karal finally saw a living, waking person approaching—a young man leading a small donkey laden with a pair of stoppered pots and a short ladder.

Now what is that all about?

Karal's question was soon answered. The man took the ladder down off the donkey's back just as they neared him, and propped it against the lantern-post. He waved as soon as he spotted them.

"Evening, Herald!" the man called in a soft, but cheerful voice, without pausing in his climb up to the lantern.

"And a fine evening to you, sir lamptender," Rubrik called back. "They told me wizard-weather is coming in tonight—"

"So I was told, so I was told. I'll be finishing here in a candlemark, I hope. I'd like to be indoors when it hits." The man lifted the pierced metal screen that shielded the lamp wick from wind, and carefully trimmed it, then filled the base of the lamp from a smaller jug at his hip. "This is like to be a nasty storm, the mages say. At least we've got warning now, though they don't seem to be able to do much about it. More's the pity."

Huh. Well, maybe that's why everything is so quiet; everybody's shut their houses up, waiting for the blow. They passed the man as he started down his ladder. He waved farewell to them, but was clearly anxious to finish his job for the night.

Why can't the Valdemaran mages do something about the weather? We can. . . .

"Too much to do, and not enough mages," Rubrik said, his shoulders sagging. "For some reason, weather-working seems to be one of the abilities *we* don't see often. Weather-witches, the people that can predict weather, we have in plenty now that we know how to train them, but not too many that can fix problems without making them worse elsewhere."

"We have something of a surplus of weather-workers," Ulrich said, very carefully. "It seems to be a talent we Karsites have in abundance. Perhaps it is because our climate would be so uncertain without them."

"I know," Rubrik replied, his voice so tired that Karal couldn't read anything into it at all. "That is one of the first things that Selenay wants to discuss with you. We thought that we would have everything under control once Ancar stopped mucking about with unshielded magic, but things are getting worse, not better. You saw the bridge—"

"Hmm." Ulrich said nothing more, but Karal knew what he was thinking. Aside from all other considerations, Valdemar was a wealthy land by Karsite standards—in the only real wealth that counted, arable land. Karse was hilly, with thin soil that was full of rocks. Valdemar had always had a surplus of grain, meat, animal products. Karse would not be at all displeased to acquire some of that surplus in return for the service of a few weather-workers. *That* sort of thing hadn't come up in the truce negotiations, and the tentative arrangements for the alliance that followed.

That sort of thing was why he and Ulrich were here now.

That sort of negotiation would be impossible if it weren't for the presence of the Empire looming in the East, an Empire whose magics were legendary.

Not even for food would some of those stiff-necked old sticks be willing to negotiate anything with the Demon-spawn. Only Vkandis and the threat of complete annihilation managed to get them to agree. Well, if we start getting these little incidental negotiations through, perhaps by the time the threat is disposed of, either the old sticks will be dead, or they'll be so used to having deals with the "Demon-spawn" that it won't matter to them anymore.

Still, it seemed odd that Valdemar should be having *more* magically-induced problems, not less. They had Adept-level mages enough to teach the proper ways of handling and containing magic, and now that Ancar wasn't spreading his sorcerous contamination everywhere, things *should* have been settling down. Shouldn't they?

Unless there was something else stirring things up.

"I wonder if the Empire has anything to do with this," he

wondered aloud, not thinking about what he was saying before he said it.

"To do with what?" Rubrik asked sharply.

Karal flushed hotly, glad that the darkness hid his embarrassment. Stupid; that was twice in a row, and he was going to have to watch himself. And school himself not to talk when he was so tired—his thoughts went straight to his lips without getting examined first. "The—this bad weather, sir," he replied. "The Empire is full of mages, so they say. Could they be sending bad weather at you, to soften you up as a target?"

"It's possible—it's more than possible. I just didn't know something like that could be done at such long distances." Rubrik cursed quietly for a moment. Then he stiffened, stifling a gasp, and Karal realized that the man must still be in a tremendous amount of pain. This business of pressing on was as hard on him as it was on any of them, for all that his Companion seemed as fresh as when he started out this morning.

"It can be done in theory, though no one in Karse ever tried that I know of," Ulrich told him. "There's some mention of such things in older texts on magic, but using magically-induced or steered weather as a weapon is generally considered too unreliable to count on, since it is too easy to counter."

"Unless, of course, your enemy is known for *not* using magic." Rubrik cursed again. "The Empire's spies surely picked that up, at the very least. They must be laughing up their sleeves at us, if this *is* their doing. I'll make sure and mention it, just so that someone considers the idea."

"Even if it's sent-weather, a reliable weather-worker can deal with it," Ulrich offered. "The worker doesn't even need to be particularly powerful. I can't tell you if your 'wizard-weather' is sent or created myself; at least not at the moment. I'm too tired, and the probable distance between us and any Empire mages is too great. But if it is something the Empire is causing, that very distance works for us far more than it does the Empire. As far away as they'd be working, they wouldn't be able to stop a minimally-talented weather-worker from getting rid of anything they could send at us. In fact, a *minimally* talented worker, casting close to the target, can disperse the sendings of someone much more powerful than he is."

"That is good to know." For all his weariness, Rubrik sounded grateful. "Please, in case I forgot to tell this to someone, make sure you do."

"Take note, Karal," Ulrich told his aide, who filed it carefully away in his memory. He would, some time within the next two days or so, make certain that this whole bit of conversation was included in the notes that Ulrich would take into a discussion with Valdemar's leaders.

"What is *that*?" Ulrich asked, as Karal repeated everything to himself once, just to be certain he had it all. Karal looked up; there seemed to be something awfully large across their path, and it was much too big to be a building. There were lights across the top of it, lights that might be torches or lanterns. How high was it? Several stories, at least. Well, *this* part of Haven rated some admiration, at least.

"The old city walls," Rubrik replied, with relief in his voice. "They mark the boundary of the original city of Haven. We are almost home."

The walls *were* impressive; quite thick, as demonstrated by the tunnel beneath them with gates at either end.

And manned by competent, alert Guards, as demonstrated by the ones that stopped them. They were detained at the gate long enough for the Guard Captain to look through a set of papers, scratch something with a stick of graphite, and wave them through.

"Efficient," Ulrich noted. Rubrik only nodded.

Looks as if they really were waiting for us—

By now the lights along the side of the road were frequent enough that neither they nor their mounts had any trouble seeing, and once inside the walls, there were further signs of life. Taverns were still open; music and the sound of voices came from windows open to whatever breeze might happen by. Here and there an industrious tradesman burned candles to finish a task. The scent of baking bread told Karal that bakers in Haven were no different from those in Sunhame; they did most of their work late at night, when it was cooler. Here and there they even crossed paths with a huge, heavy cart hitched to a team of four or more enormous draft-horses, hauling wagonloads of barrels and huge crates about that could not be transported during the heavy traffic of full day.

The streets here were paved, covered with something smooth that didn't resemble cobblestones or any other form of pavement Karal recognized. Rubrik looked around at the fronts of the buildings, though, and frowned.

"This storm is likely to be worse than I was told," he said, after a moment or two. "Look how all the shutters are up, and I think they've been latched on the inside."

Karal nodded, finally realizing why the place had seemed so dead and so quiet. Most windows *were* firmly shuttered against whatever weather was coming; shutters that would shut out light and sound from within as well as weather from without. "Is that unusual at this time of year?" he asked.

"Very," Rubrik said shortly.

Well, if they are expecting the kind of storm that ripped a huge tree up by the roots, if I lived here, I'd shutter my windows too. Better a night spent behind shutters than to have a window blown in—or worse, find something storm-flung coming through it.

It seemed to Karal that they were spending a lot of time winding back and forth; far more time than was necessary. He started looking around, craning his neck, trying to see if there was a shorter way to the Palace anywhere. Great Light, he hadn't even *seen* the Palace, and if this was Sunhame, they'd be looking right down the Grand Boulevard straight *at* it!

"Haven wasn't built like Sunhame," Ulrich said in a low voice, as he continued to search for some sign that they were nearing their goal. "It was built on strictly defensive lines. I'm told that the Palace was originally a true fortress, that it's not a great deal taller than many of the homes of the high-ranked and the wealthy. And the streets here were planned to make invasion difficult, even if an army penetrated the outer walls. The streets all wind around and around the city; there is no direct way to the Palace or to any other important building."

Where Sunhame was built as a place of worship first; the Temple is the center of the city, the Palace of the Son of the Sun a part of the Temple, and all roads lead directly there.

Sunhame was planned as a stylized solar disk, in fact; the main buildings were placed in a circle in the center of the city, and the main streets all radiated from that circle. He could only hope that the minds of these Valdemarans were not as twisted and indirect as their streets.

At least the quality of shops and houses was steadily increasing, which was a good sign that they *were* nearing their goal.

Eventually the shops and taverns vanished altogether, leaving only the walled homes of the great and wealthy. Finally, just when he thought for sure that Rubrik was leading them in a circle, that they were hopelessly lost in this maze and that they would never find their way out again, they came to another wall.

This one was much shorter than the first, a bare two stories tall. If it was manned, Karal saw no signs of guards, although there were lanterns hung high on iron brackets. They were high enough to be above the heads of any riders who followed the street beside the wall, and seemed easily within the reach of someone walking along the top to service them.

There was a large building on the other side. Before Karal could ask anything, however, they came to a small gate—so *very* small that he could easily have passed right by it.

"Heyla, Rubrik!" a cheerful young man in a livery of lighter blue than any Karal had seen before hailed their escort. "What, bringing the envoy in by the kitchen entrance? *That's* hardly the way to treat an ally!"

Karal stiffened at the implied insult, but Rubrik just aimed a kick at the Guard. "You insolent idiot! This isn't the kitchen entrance, it's the Privy Gate, and well you know it, Adem! What are you trying to do, start another war with Karse for me?"

Karal relaxed. The Guard just laughed and unlocked the gate. "Come now, those stiff-necked fellows probably don't speak a word of our—"

"Oh, I speak your tongue well enough to know that you mean no harm, but you ought to learn to mind your manners, young lad," Ulrich said in a casual tone. "With so many foreigners coming to your Queen, you should learn *never* to assume they are ignorant of your language, and guard your tongue accordingly."

The Guard whirled, turning as pale as the bleached stone of the wall, and started to stammer an apology.

But Rubrik interrupted him, turning in his saddle to look fully at Ulrich. "Well, my Lord Priest? It was you who he insulted by his cavalier manner, so I leave it to you to decide how many weeks he is suspended."

He spoke in his own tongue so that there could be no misunderstanding by the Guard. Ulrich pondered the question for a moment and answered in the same language. "I believe you should report him—but do not repeat his exact words," the Priest said, very carefully. "Say only that he was not—ah—professional, and that he acted that way on the assumption that we did not know your language. He means no harm, I think, but such behavior *could* be construed as an insult. In fact, I believe that the *best* punishment to recommend would be that he must learn the rudiments of *our* tongue!"

Rubrik looked down at the trembling Guard, who Karal now saw was certainly no older than *he* was. "You heard him, Adem. You'll be on report in the morning, and they'll probably put you on stable duty for a fortnight, but that's less than you deserve. You represent the Queen at this post, whether or not it's the dead of night and you never see anyone, and you had better remember that."

The Guard saluted smartly, and pushed the gate open for them, standing aside and keeping his eyes straight ahead. "Yes, sir!" he said, his voice still shaky, but relief obvious in his eyes. "Absolutely, sir!"

Rubrik went through the gate first, followed by Ulrich. The Guard looked up as the Priest passed.

"Thank you, sir," he said, very softly.

Ulrich nodded, and allowed a ghost of a smile to cross his lips as he nudged Honeybee through the gate.

Karal followed, and the Guard closed and locked the gate behind them with a creak of iron hinges and the clatter of a key in a massive lock. Ahead of them was a long, stone-surfaced path that led to the enormous building Karal had glimpsed above the wall. This structure was illuminated on the outside by carefully placed lanterns.

Very carefully placed lanterns; guards on patrol would be able to see every corner of the outside, there would be no place to hide. And they don't blend in with the exterior—I wonder if the Queen has had some unpleasant visitors in the recent past!

It was apparent now that the area enclosed by the wall was far larger than he had supposed. It was huge, in fact—it looked even bigger than the city itself. There even seemed to be a forest of some kind off to the left—

But it was to the right that his attention was drawn, to the multistoried, gray stone building there, and the group of people coming up the path to meet them.

At least four of these were servants, but there were two men dressed in rich clothing, and two more in the white uniforms that Karal now knew meant they were Heralds.

Rubrik turned to Ulrich as the group approached. "Thank you for your understanding, sir. Young Adem is well-intentioned, and as you surmised he meant no harm, but he's also known me since he was a babe, and he's highborn and inclined to be very cavalier about rank. He volunteered for the Guards, but I'm afraid he still thinks things like sentry duty are something of a joke."

Ulrich shrugged, but Karal could tell that he wasn't displeased. "Well, really, one can afford to be cavalier about rank when one has it, true? If he's going to be mucking out stables for a fortnight, I think that's likely to teach him all he needs to learn from this little experience."

Rubrik nodded, and the Companion tossed his head and uttered what sounded a lot like a laugh. "I'll be leaving you here, sir. It has been a pleasure escorting you. I hope we will be able to meet socially in the future."

"I have enjoyed your company, and I shall make a point of meeting you when leisure permits," Ulrich said with emphasis, then turned toward the group approaching them.

Rubrik straightened in his saddle as best he could; the group stopped just beyond his Companion's nose. Karal noted that he didn't dismount, and neither did Ulrich—but it didn't appear that anyone expected them to. "My Lord Priest Ulrich, Envoy of Her Holiness of Karse, Son of the Sun Solaris, the

Prophet of Vkandis, may I present to you Lord Palinor, Seneschal of Valdemar and the Seneschal's Herald, Kyril—"

The two older men bowed; the Seneschal was marginally younger than his Herald, a trifle taller, and a bit less in shape. And every bit the diplomat. In body type he was neither thin nor fat, nor was he either exceptionally handsome or ugly. The grandeur of his robes made up for his otherwise unremarkable exterior. The Herald, on the other side, was as memorable a person as Karal had ever seen; from his erect carriage to his iron-gray hair, his chiseled features to his direct way of gazing straight into the eyes of the person he spoke to. Karal did not think too many people ever had the temerity to lie to this man.

"I am gratified that you meet me in person, my lords," Ulrich said, his own demeanor as professional and diplomatic as that of the Seneschal. "In fact, I am flattered, on my own behalf and on that of my ruler. It is *very* late, and—" he paused to gaze significantly upward, "—I am given to understand that there is unpleasant weather expected at any moment."

"Too damned true," muttered the other man in the Heraldic uniform. Then, despite the rising wind he stepped forward and bowed. Rubrik raised his eyebrows in shocked surprise.

He recovered quickly. "And the ah—entirely accurate gentleman, is Prince-Consort Daren, Queen Selenay's personal representative."

This was the Prince? In Herald livery? Karal was too well-schooled to gape with shock, but he very nearly bit his tongue. Rubrik had clearly not expected any of the royals to meet them out here, or he surely would have warned them. Karal was all too conscious of how shabby and unkempt he and his master must look after riding since dawn.

Prince Daren smiled, and echoed his gesture. "You are most welcome and well-come, my Lord Priest Ulrich. I was afraid that if I did *not* come in person, this initial meeting might degenerate into a minor diplomatic event, and if you will forgive my being as blunt as the soldier that I am—"

A chill wind screamed up out of nowhere, whipping their cloaks and making even the tired horse and mule dance and shy. Leaves torn from the nearby trees, and dust and sand pelted them. A growl of thunder in the distance warned that the storm was at hand; a flash of lightning told it was coming on as fast as the wind could blow it.

Thank Vkandis for the Prince! He's the only one here with rank enough to override diplomatic protocol without making it an insult, and he knows it!

"—that 'weather' you mentioned is going to drench us all if we *don't* get you under cover!" Prince Daren shouted over the howling of the wind.

Neither Ulrich nor Karal needed any further prompting; they dismounted as quickly as Ulrich's aged bones and Karal's weary ones permitted, surrendering their mounts into the hands of the servants. Then, as fat, icy drops of rain splattered onto the path, they surrendered all pretense of dignity, gathered their robes and cloaks around them, and *all* ran for the shelter of the Palace.

Prince Daren proved to be a far more graceful politician than he claimed; he cut through protocol with a smile and an eye to their comfort, sacrificing his own dignity to preserve Ulrich's. "I'm just a blunt soldier, and I don't hold with a lot of this political dancing about," were words that were often on his lips, and neither Karal nor his master believed them for a moment—but paying lip service to those words made it possible to retain the respect due to their office while at the same time getting things done with dispatch. By common consent, proper diplomatic maneuvering was deferred to the next day. Prince Daren showed them personally to their suite, and left them there after demonstrating the system of bells that summoned servants.

"It's late. You need food and rest in that order, my lords," he said as he departed. "And your proper reception will take place at *your* convenience. Selenay and I will make certain that one of us is free for you to make the appropriate presentation of your credentials tomorrow. When *you* are ready, send word. This alliance is very important to us, and it is equally important that everything be done properly so the quibblers have less to wag their tongues about."

All things considered, it was an auspicious beginning for continued relations.

The suite of rooms they had been granted, on the second story of the Palace and in the section reserved for other ambassadors, was far above anything that Karal had experienced, even as Ulrich's secretary. It was composed of a total of five rooms. They had their own bathing room with an indoor water closet, two private bedrooms, a casual sitting room, and a reception room quite elegantly appointed. The suite was arranged in an odd pattern; they entered at the reception room, which led to the sitting room to the right. Then came the bedrooms, with the bathing room between them. The reception room and the sitting room were rather longer than they were wide, which might prove useful. Someone had pulled the shutters closed over the windows, so there was no way to tell what kind of view they had—if any—but from the hideous noise of hail pounding the wooden shutters, Karal was just as glad. There was a fine five-course meal waiting for them in the sitting room, and a servant who spoke some rudimentary Karsite to serve them, a young man, strongly built, with a thatch of thick, black hair and a pair of bushy eyebrows as thick as Karal's ring-finger.

They settled into chairs on either side of a small table, and the servant filled their plates, then excused himself to draw a hot bath for his guests' comfort.

Karal was hungry enough to have eaten the plates along with the savory roast chicken and succulent steamed roots. Ulrich barely picked at his meal, though, which told Karal that his master needed that hot bath *very* badly, and bed just as much. He always lost his appetite when his joints pained him.

"Don't bother with that, sir," Karal said, as Ulrich brought the same forkful of food to his mouth and laid it back down for the third time. "Go get into the bath; I'll fix one of those little bread pockets for you, mix up your medicine, and bring both to you."

Ulrich did not even argue which told Karal that his master was in more pain than he had thought. He allowed the servant to guide him into the bathing room, help him disrobe, and get into the bath.

The servant took himself into the master bedroom; Karal ate in silence for a little longer, then, when he reckoned that

Ulrich had warmed and relaxed enough for his appetite to return, cut a slice of breast meat and laid it inside a sliced-open roll. A trickle of the white sauce followed it, and some thin slices of roots. Their saddlebags had arrived by that point, and before the servant took them to the proper rooms, he got Ulrich's medicines, poured a glass of sweet, white wine, and mixed the powders into it.

He brought both to Ulrich, who lay back in the bath with the lines of pain and strain slowly easing from his face. His master looked up at his footsteps, and managed a smile.

"Food first," Karal told him. "If you drink this, you might fall asleep before you manage to eat."

"Especially on an empty stomach." Ulrich accepted the bread pocket and managed to eat all of it, which surprised and gratified Karal. When Ulrich was truly exhausted, he often lost all semblance of appetite, and had to be reminded that he *had* to eat. When the last crumb was gone, the Priest held out his hand for the wine glass, and downed it in a single gulp.

"Be a good lad and call that servant to help me out now, would you?" his master said, when the last of the potion was gone. "You go finish your meal—and mine, if you've a mind to. I'll be going straight to bed, I think."

Karal went to the sitting room to do just that. "The Envoy needs some help getting to bed, please," he said in careful Valdemaran. "He's not young, and he has just had medicine that will make him sleepy."

The servant nodded. "Yes, sir," the young man replied. "Ah, I believe you should know that we servants assigned to you and your master are not precisely ordinary. We're Heraldic trainees."

Karal raised an eyebrow himself at that, but nodded, slowly. So, that explained why this young man's clothing, though gray, looked very much like the livery that Rubrik wore. "Well, neither of us is likely to offend any of you by being unreasonable or demanding; frankly, I'm more used to serving than being served, and my master is a Priest and does not usually have any servant other than myself."

Let him make what he will of that. It can't do any harm to be thought ascetic. It might make people think twice about trying to bribe us; a true Priest is as hard to sway by material offerings as the statue of Vkandis.

The young man smiled shyly. "My name is Arnod, sir. I'll be on night duty. Day duty will be either Johen or Lysle. Would you like a Healer to look at your master?"

Karal gave it a moment of thought, then shook his head. "No, he'll be all right once he gets into bed. It was just a very long ride, and this storm isn't helping matters any."

As if to emphasize that, the wind shook the shutters, a violent rattle that sounded for all the world as if an angry giant had seized them and was tugging on them.

"Let me get the Envoy into his bed, then, and I'll return to see if there's anything you need." With a glance at the shutters, Arnod left Karal alone with the half-finished meal.

Karal quickly made certain that it became a *finished* meal, although he ignored the rest of the wine in favor of water. He knew what would happen if, as tired as he was now, he drank wine.

I'll sleep for two days and wake up with the world's worst headache.

The sitting room was as well-appointed as it was comfortable; two chairs, a couch for lounging, the table, a desk, and a fireplace shared with the reception room on the other side of the wall. Hard to tell in the soft light from the candles, but he thought it had all been decorated in neutral tones of gray and cream. There were no rushes on the floor, but the hard wood was softened by attractive rugs with geometric designs woven into them.

It was interesting that Heralds-in-training should be assigned instead of Palace servants, however. That might be a good sign.

It might also be a sign that the authorities did not trust the servants around a pair of Karsites. Or these almost-Heralds could be a not-so-subtle way of keeping an eye on the Envoys, and an ear in their midst.

It is also possible that they are doing us some kind of honor, he mused. *It is hard to say.* The only thing he could be sure of was that this Arnod fellow—who was perhaps seventeen—seemed to be a likable enough chap on the surface, not at all put out by being made into a servant. That would make things easier on all of them. Arnod could make things uncomfortable for them if he resented his current position.

Arnod reappeared about the time Karal polished off the remains of Ulrich's custard. "The Envoy fell asleep as soon as I got him into the bed," the young man said, his black brows furrowing together with concern. "Is that right? Should he have done that?"

Karal mentally reckoned up the effect of the medicines when taken with Ulrich's exhaustion, and nodded. "It's mostly that we had been riding since before dawn; we've been almost twenty marks in the saddle, and that's hard on him."

Arnod winced. "It's a good thing you didn't stop, though, if you'll forgive my saying so. We got word that the bridge at Loden is out; if you'd waited there tonight, you'd have had to go clear up to Poldara to cross in the morning. You'd have been another week getting here." His brows knitted. "I'm not being too forward, am I? Tell me if I am, please—I'm not used to this serving business, but they thought you and I might have a bit in common, since my da raised horses."

Karal laughed, a little startled at the young man's open, easy manner, and Arnod gave him a tentative grin. "Oh, just be as respectful to Lord Ulrich as you would to any Priest that you honor, and I think it will be fine. Like I told you, I am *not* used to having a servant around, or to being served by anyone. The reverse, in fact." He shared a conspiratorial grin with Arnod. "You see, *my* father was the stablemaster at an inn."

It was a very good thing that he and Ulrich had a chance to practice their Valdemaran with Rubrik on the journey up here; Arnod's Karsite was barely adequate to manage simple requests. A conversation like this one would have been impossible.

The wind pounded on the shutters again, and sent hail pounding against it in a futile effort to get through. Karal felt more relaxed than he had been in a long time.

Unless these "servants" are far, far more subtle than anyone I've ever heard of before, they're probably nothing more than they seem. They certainly are not accustomed to the kinds of intriguing I've seen in Ulrich's service. No, I think that while they certainly will be reporting what we say and

*do to their leaders, Ulrich and I can assume they are not ex-
pert spies.*

That was a relief, a great relief. So great a relief that he relaxed enough to yawn.

"Oh—I drew you a bath, sir—" Arnod began.

"Karal. Just Karal," Karal corrected. "My master is 'sir,' or
'my lord.' I'm just a novice, I haven't taken any vows, and I'm
not highborn, so I'm just plain 'Karal.' "

Arnod nodded, earnestly. "Right—I drew you a bath, Karal,
I figured you'd want it when you finished eating. Can I get
you anything else, or shall I just clear the plates away and let
you get that bath and some sleep?" He hesitated a moment,
then added, "We have a pair of guards stationed on this corridor, outside your doors. Not just for your benefit, but all the
ambassadors. You won't have to worry about your safety."

*Oh, and by the way, don't try to get out to prowl around.
Right, well, that's the last thing on my mind. If Solaris
wanted spies here, she'd have sent someone other than us.*

"Bath and sleep," Karal said firmly—or he would have, if he
hadn't had to yawn right in the middle of the sentence. Arnod
chuckled and began picking up the dishes even as Karal got
up to go find that hot bath.

He was impressed all over again by the bathing chamber;
tiled in clean white ceramic, it contained a tub large enough
to relax in, supplied by heated water from some system of
pipes and a wood-fired copper boiler. It also contained an indoor, water-flow privy, an amenity Karal had come to appreciate after living with Ulrich. *Especially* on a night like this
one. Going out to a privy, or even to a jakes on the outside
wall, would have required more courage than he thought he
had. The mere idea of that cold, hail-laden wind coming at
one's tenderest parts. . . .

*Wouldn't need to take a vow of chastity after that. I
wouldn't have anything left to be unchaste with.*

When he returned, warm and dry and relaxed in every muscle, Arnod and the remains of dinner were both gone, and all
but one of the candles in the sitting room had been blown
out. Karal made his way across the chamber to his own room,
smaller than Ulrich's, and with one wall on the outer hallway
where the guards supposedly prowled. His room would pre-

sumably shield his master's from any intrusive sounds from
the hall—and any sounds from the hall would wake *him* up
so that he could defend his master if need be. Of course, this
meant that he had no window in his room, but tonight he
didn't want one. The howling of the wind and the roar of rain
on the shutters was *quite* clear enough.

Candles had been left burning in his room, and a set of bed-
clothes had been laid out for him—a sign that their luggage
had arrived safely. Thanks be to Vkandis, indeed. If they did
not have the appropriate clothing, they could not be formally
presented without disgracing themselves and their ruler.

And besides, there were a dozen books in there he'd been
wanting to read.

Good. One less thing to worry about.

He dropped the towel he had wrapped around himself and
pulled the soft, loose shirt and breeches on, blowing out all
the candles but one and climbing into bed. The bed had
been warmed, a welcome, if unexpected touch, and the candle nearest the bed gave off a delicate fragrance as well as
light.

I could get used to living like this, he decided. It was a far
cry from sleeping in the stable, or the hard pallets in the Children's Cloister. There was a lot to be said for the life of an envoy. He blew out the bedside candle, and lay back in the
warm embrace of what had to be a real featherbed.

*This is beginning to feel like undeserved luxury, actually. I
haven't done a thing yet to earn all this.*

On the other hand, the real work was about to begin—not
physical labor, but mental. Tomorrow, in addition to his
work as a secretary, Ulrich would begin asking him to watch
certain people, or take note of situations, and he would be expected to make accurate observations. When they were presented formally to the Valdemaran Court, it would be his job
to remember the names, the faces, the positions, and the
identifying characteristics. Then there would be long diplomatic meetings, during which he would be taking mental
notes—and later, transcribing those notes into an accurate
copy of what was actually said.

No, this was not unearned luxury after all, now that he
thought it all over. He could foresee, without recourse to a

mage-mirror or a scrying crystal, that there would be days when he would not see this bed until well past the midnight hour.

Then again—in some ways, everything in this world is paid for, in the end. . . .

But before he could ponder that any further, he fell asleep.

"Watch the Heralds," Ulrich said, just before they left their suite the next morning. Only that, but it was all the direction that Karal needed. Ulrich had trained his secretary well; Karal did not need to be told the rest of his job.

Ulrich would be watching the Prince and the other officials of Valdemar during this first day of introductions and preliminary negotiations. He wanted Karal to keep a covert eye on the other power in this land, the power that never quite revealed itself openly but had a hand in literally everything.

The Heralds. Even a Karsite knew *that* much.

He was the perfect person to perform that particular task; it was not likely that anyone would pay a great deal of attention to *him*. He was only the secretary, after all, of no importance, and furthermore, no older than the callow lads who had been assigned to serve them. *He* could not possibly be hiding anything.

Well, he *wasn't*. He doubted that he could ever successfully conceal the fact that he knew something, if anyone ever entrusted him with a real secret. But he didn't have to hide anything; all he had to do was *watch* passively.

They rose late—for Ulrich, at least, who was used to rising at dawn. A new young man, who introduced himself as "Johen" but otherwise was as silent as Arnod had been talkative, brought them their breakfast and took away Ulrich's request for the formal presentation.

He returned with the word that it would be agreeable to everyone if that presentation could be made at the regular Court session in a mark. Or "candlemark," as the Valdemarans reckoned time. Easy enough to judge, since the candle that had been left burning all night was a time-candle—marked off at regular intervals. As near as Karal could judge, the Valdemaran "candlemark" and the Karsite "mark" as reckoned by water-clock were about the same length.

Since immediate reception was precisely what Ulrich had hoped for, they sent Johen off with word of their agreement. They both dressed with care for the occasion; fine velvet robes that had been especially created for their roles as both Priest and Novice, and Envoy and Secretary. There was a great deal more gold and embroidery than Karal personally felt comfortable with; he rather liked the simple, short black woolen robes, sashes, and breeches that those who served Vkandis normally wore. But he was a representative of Her Holiness—it was right and proper that he should *look* like a representative of Her Holiness.

Besides, Ulrich was laden with three times the gold braid and embroidery that *he* had to endure. He didn't even want to *think* about the amount of ecclesiastical jewelry Ulrich was carrying; it was enough to make his shoulders ache just looking at it.

Johen brought a young Guard to serve as their escort to the Court chamber, or whatever it was that the Valdemarans called it. The Throne Room, Karal had thought he'd heard Johen say. This second Herald-in-training spoke a lot faster than Arnod, and it was harder to follow him.

The Guard left them at the door, which was wide open, and they simply took their places among the other people gathered there. They stood out among the Valdemaran courtiers like a pair of crows in an aviary of exotic birds. As they waited their turn to be summoned before Queen Selenay, there was a little space around them, a degree of separation from the rest of the Court that clearly showed that most Valdemarans were still not altogether sure of their new allies.

Watch the Heralds, Ulrich had said. Karal kept his eyes humbly down, but he watched the people around him through his lashes. There were not too many Heralds out here among the courtiers—one, standing beside a man who *looked* like a soldier, and a second, female Herald in a very *strange* and exotic white outfit, chatting with the first. There were three up on the dais with the Queen—well, five, if you counted the Queen and her Consort as well. Another surprise, that—the Queen wore a variation on the white livery, as well as the Prince. One Herald he already recognized; that was Talia, who had come to Karse herself as the representa-

tive of Selenay. Not a bad idea, really, although there were
Guards in their blue and silver uniforms everywhere in this
room, standing at rigid attention along the walls.

The last two he dismissed, at least temporarily. If they
were standing there in any capacity other than as guards, it
was probably to do the same task that Ulrich had assigned to
him—*watch*. He would learn nothing from their faces which
would wear the same receptive blankness that his would.

No, he would concentrate on Talia and the other two, the
man who shadowed the richly-dressed warrior, and the fascinating, peculiar white-clad woman.

He would have watched the latter just out of sheer curiosity. If he was a gilded crow in this aviary, *she* was the exotic
bird-of-prey. For all her fancy plumage, the deliberate way
that she moved and the implicit confidence of her carriage
warned him that she would be dangerous in any situation,
and that very little would ever escape her notice. She looked
far too young to have that mane of silvered hair, though; that
was strange.

Then he recalled his magic lessons, rudimentary as they
were. *Ah. She may be an Adept; handling node-magic
bleaches the hair and eyes.* Ulrich's hair had gone all to gray
and silver before he reached middle age, his master had told
him. So, if she was an Adept, who was she? There weren't
that many Adept-level mages in Valdemar, after all.

The reference points quickly fell together for him; the
exotic garb, the age, the deference with which she was
treated. . . .

*That's Lady Elspeth. The one the who went away to find
mage-training in far-off lands, and returned with more than
mere magic.*

There was some commotion at the door, and more people
entered; people . . . and *things*.

The sea of courtiers parted with respect tinged with just a
little fear, making way for an odd party indeed. There were
two men, both silver-haired, both dressed in costumes as foreign and elaborate as Lady Elspeth's. Neither of the costumes
was white, however, and compared to them, her outfit was
quite conservative. The younger and handsomer of the two
was the more flamboyant, in layered silks of a dozen different

shades of emerald green; the second contented himself with garments cut more closely to his body, in the colors of the deep forest.

But they paled beside the creatures that followed; a huge, wolflike gray beast the size of a newborn calf, and—

—a gryphon—

Oh, my. Oh, Lord Vkandis.

He stared, his heart racing, as he took in the near-mythical beast. He felt very much the same way as he had when he had first seen Hansa—except that the Firecat was nowhere near this *big*.

Even after the descriptions, Karal realized he had not been prepared for the reality. For one thing, this creature was *huge*, as tall as a draft horse, and its crest-feathers brushed the top of the sill as it passed through the double doors to the Throne Room. For another, it was unexpectedly beautiful. It was not, as he had imagined, some kind of put-together thing, a bit of cat, a handful of eagle. No, it was *itself*. If he hadn't known any better, he would have said it had been designed by the hand of an artist.

It had a head that was something like a raptor's, except for the greatly enlarged skull, with a wicked beak he would not have wanted to get in the way of; the tightly-folded wings would be enormous when unfurled. The four legs ended in formidable talons; he noted with slightly hysterical amusement that someone had constructed talon-sheaths, wooden-tipped and laced across the back, so that the ends didn't damage the wooden floor. In color it was a golden-brown, with shadings of pure metallic gold and darker sable. And when it turned and he caught its huge, golden eyes, he lost any last bit of doubt that this was a creature every bit as intelligent as he was. There was not just *intelligence* in those eyes, there was humor there as well, and a powerful personality. It looked him over, unblinking, then transferred its regard to his master, pupils expanding and contracting a little as it focused its gaze.

The entrance of this little cavalcade seemed to be all that anyone had been waiting for; Court proceeded briskly from then on.

He and Ulrich were evidently the center point of this session of Court; there was some ordinary enough business, dealt with efficiently and quickly, and then the major-domo beside the dais called them forward.

Karal followed behind his master, keeping his mind blank and receptive. He already knew what Ulrich would be doing; there were documents to present, authorizations, copies of the existing treaties. Ulrich would be telling the Queen, in a suitably flowery and elaborate speech, just how much Solaris welcomed the opportunity to change the truce into a true alliance. The Queen would respond in the same way.

This time, at least, there would be truth behind the speeches, at least on the Karsite side of the equation.

Maybe on the Valdemaran, given that storm last night, and the Prince's assurances. From the damage he'd seen to the gardens from their window, the storm had been fully powerful enough to make people concerned. There had been at least one uprooted tree, and many thick branches broken and tossed about like wood chips. It appeared that Karse, in the form of its weather-mages, had something Valdemar needed very badly.

So, there would be truth enough on the Queen's part as well. Enough to overcome centuries of hatred?

From the thoughtful look on Herald Talia's face—yes. There, if anywhere, was the proof of sincerity. Talia was of Holderkin stock, and had grown up on the border with Karse. If she could forgive Karsite depredations enough to become an honorary member of their very religion, it was possible that anyone could, given enough incentive.

Ulrich made his graceful speech, the Queen made hers; Karal didn't pay much attention. He was watching Talia closely. *She* was paying no attention to Ulrich after the first few moments of his speech. Instead, her eyes wandered over the envoy's head, for all the world as if assessing the temper of the rest of the courtiers.

There wasn't much to read in her thoughtful expression, however; it seemed to be just as carefully blank as his own.

"If you have no objection, my Lord Priest," the Queen was saying as he pulled his attention back to the work at hand, "I should like to take this opportunity to present you to the other dignitaries of this Court, and the representatives of our other allies and friends."

So that's why the gryphon and the rest showed up! As Ulrich accepted—after all, this was precisely what the Priest had hoped would take place—the crowd of courtiers reshuffled itself, and Karal found himself standing at Ulrich's elbow in a formal receiving line.

Now I earn my good dinner and soft bed! Ulrich would be depending on his trained memory to keep track of everyone introduced to them. Well, that was why he was here.

The full Council paraded by first, beginning with the Seneschal, Lord Palinor, whom they had met last night. Then came the Lord Marshal, who proved to be the military-looking fellow that Lady Elspeth had been speaking with. He was followed by a horsey woman, Lady Cathan, who represented the Guilds, and she in her turn was followed by a relatively young cleric, Father Ricard, who turned out to be the Lord Patriarch, the putative leader of *all* religious organizations in Valdemar.

Huh. I'll believe that when I see it! Never yet saw two priests of two different religions able to agree on anything, not even that the sun was shining!

But it was not his duty to pass judgment; just to remember who these people were.

There were more representatives from the four "quarters" of the country, then came the other Powers. The Heralds—the ones with offices.

Kyril, the Seneschal's Herald. A man who appeared to be Talia's age, tall, and strongly built, named (oddly enough) Griffon, who was the Lord Marshal's Herald. Another older man, Herald Teren, Dean of the Collegium (whatever that was). Lady Elspeth, "Herald to the Outlanders," which was a title just as puzzling; he could not imagine why she was not titled "princess" or "heir." Another *very* formidable woman, tall, and blond, who carried herself with completely unconscious authority, Herald Captain Kerowyn, a woman he had heard so many tales of he could not even count them all. Names he knew of from his briefings, and his discussions with Rubrik, names he could now put faces to.

Then the other envoys and ambassadors—from Rethwellan, J'katha and Ruvan, from the Hardorn court in exile (what there was of it), from the Outland Guilds, from the Mercenary's Guild, from the White Winds and Blue Mountain mage-schools—

And the most exotic. A hawk-faced woman, blue-eyed and ebony-haired with golden skin, dressed in deep blue trews and wrapped jacket, Querna shena Tale'sedrin, envoy from the wild Shin'a'in of the Dhorisha Plains. Behind her, the flamboyant, silver-haired beauty of a man in the emerald-green costume, who proved to be one Firesong k'Treva, Adept and Envoy of the Tayledras.

The wolflike creature was also an envoy—Rris, who represented not only his own species, the *kyree*, but others, *tervardi*, *hertasi*, and *dyheli*. Ulrich nodded, as if he knew precisely what those creatures might be, but Karal knew he'd be doing some quick scuttling about, to ferret out descriptions and, hopefully, pictures later.

And last of all of the ambassadors, the gryphon.

The magnificent creature bent his head to acknowledge Ulrich's bow of respect, and opened a beak quite sufficient to take the envoy's head off. "I am Trrreyvan," the creature said in Valdemaran, and Karal could have sworn that it smiled. "I am mosssst pleasssed to make yourrr acquaintance. I believe we have a mutual frrriend? A Red-robe Priesst called Sssig-frrrid?"

Ulrich's mask of polite geniality turned into a real smile. "Indeed we do," he replied warmly. "I had hoped to find someone here who worked with him, sir gryphon, but I did not expect it to be you!"

The gryphon *did* smile. "We ssshall trrrade talesss and trrrack down Sssigfrrrid, laterrr, I think," he said, and bowed again.

The gryphon moved off gracefully, leaving only the courtiers to be presented. None of these were especially interesting; Karal simply memorized names and faces as they moved past.

Finally, it was over. The Queen dismissed the Court and departed with her entourage, after inviting Ulrich to present himself to her privately after the noon meal. By then, the exotics had dispersed, leaving no one that Ulrich wanted or needed to speak with.

As the courtiers filed out of the Throne Room, Ulrich finally looked over at his young protégé. "I've had enough for an hour or two, at least," he said in Karsite. "Would it shatter your heart if we had our meal in our room, rather than with the Queen and Court?"

Karal thought of all those eyes, curious, occasionally hostile; thought of trying to choke down a meal with all of them watching him, and shuddered. This position was far more public than he had thought. Ulrich chuckled. "I will take that as a 'no,' and leave the arrangements up to you," he said. "Meanwhile, I will go consult with Herald Talia and discover if this is to be an informal or a formal meeting."

"I'll see to it," Karal said, taking that as his dismissal. Evidently they no longer required a Guard; he was allowed to leave the Throne Room and return to their suite without one.

After he rang the bell for the servant, he went to the desk in the sitting room, where he had just this morning laid out pen and paper. By the time the servant arrived, Karal had already begun on the list of dignitaries they had just met. He ordered a meal to be served in the room with all the absentminded confidence of someone who was actually used to having a servant at his beck and call, and it wasn't until after the young man disappeared that he realized what he had just done.

The thought made him stop in his tracks. For just a moment, he was stunned. He had only been in this land a few short days, and already it was changing him.

He could not help but wonder where the changes would lead.

Darkwind and Firesong

9

Ulrich returned to their rooms about the same time lunch arrived. He ignored the food for a moment to fetch a brown-leather document case from his room; Karal took just long enough to bolt his portion, then returned to his frantic note-taking. Ulrich watched him for a moment, then said, "If you would be so kind as to take a change in direction, I'd like your notes on the business of offering the skills of our weather-workers as a trade measure, and please tell me any observations you made on Herald Talia. The meeting is to be an informal and closed one, and I was specifically asked to come alone."

Karal stopped writing, his pen poised above the paper. "Do you think they believe me to be a spy? Do you think my function offends them?" he asked.

Ulrich shrugged. "I am not certain; remember, these people are more familiar with mind-magic than with true-magic, and as a consequence might believe that you are actually somehow speaking mind-to-mind with an agent outside. I shall attempt to determine what it is they think you do; in the meantime, complete your notes on the Court dignitaries, then relax until I return." He smiled. "I saw some of your books; I do not think you will have any trouble passing the time."

Karal flushed, because fully half of his books had been nothing more enlightening than popular romances and tales of high adventure. Ulrich chuckled.

"Please, Karal," he chided, "A young man who buries himself in scholastic tomes is learning nothing of life—and a young man who knows nothing of life will find ordinary people baffling. We can't have that, can we?"

"No, sir," Karal replied, still flushing. He turned quickly to his work and took out a fresh sheet of paper, making neat notes in the short version of Karsite hieratic script. It would be enough for Ulrich to use as a guide; he just wished that he was going to be there for this initial conversation. He would have to make notes based on whatever Ulrich remembered.

As he completed the page of notes and dusted it with sand to dry the ink, he looked up at his mentor. Ulrich was standing with his back to the room, looking out the window at the gardens below.

"A copper for your thoughts, Karal," his mentor said, without turning back to face his aide.

He looked at his list, remembering all the conversations they had shared with Rubrik. "Not very original, master," he replied. "Only that, even though we are so very different from these Valdemarans, there are fundamental things we have in common. And some of them I never expected—the Companions being like Firecats, for instance."

"Yes, although personally I am just as glad that the Cats are fewer in number than the Companions," Ulrich said with a chuckle, as he turned away from the window. "I am not certain I would care to share as much of my life and inner thoughts with any creature, as Solaris shares with Hansa."

Karal had nothing whatsoever to say to that; he knew that Ulrich had been a good friend to Solaris before she became the Son of the Sun, but he had not known that she continued to speak as informally with him as his comment just implied.

How important is he, then? Karal wondered. From the sound of it, Ulrich might well be the one person in all of Karse that Solaris trusted to speak authoritatively with her voice. So the elaborate robes and badges of rank actually *meant* something. Did the Valdemarans know this?

"I was hoping you would be thinking along those lines by now," Ulrich continued, going to the mage-sealed case he had placed on the table. "I have something for you to read besides those old books of law you brought with you."

He unsealed the case with a whisper of invocation and a touch of his finger. The seal glowed briefly, then parted; he reached inside and brought out a handful of small, dusty books. The bindings had all faded to a mottled brown with age, and the edges of the pages were yellowed. He opened each of them, glancing at the first pages, and selected three, replacing the rest in the case and sealing it up again.

"I think you are ready for these, now," he said, placing them beside Karal on the desk. "Let me know if there is anything in them you want to discuss. I suspect there will be quite a bit."

And with that, serenely ignoring Karal's surprise, he gathered up the pages of notes his protégé had penned for him and left the room, allowing the door to close behind him with a quiet *click*.

Karal could not restrain his curiosity and snatched up one of the books as the door closed behind his mentor. To his vast disappointment, it was handwritten in very archaic Karsite, and difficult to puzzle out. The other two were similar, and it was quite clear that reading these things was going to require a lot of hard work on his part.

It was also going to take a great deal of time, and he did not have it to spare. With regret, he put the books aside and turned his attention back to his list of dignitaries. Duty must come before pleasure, or even curiosity, and his duty was to complete that list.

Several pages later, he put down the pen, feeling virtuous and ready for a little recreation. He thought about the adventure tales still buried in his luggage, but somehow the three dusty volumes still on his desk had more allure than the sword play and sorcery of "The Tale of Gregori."

He took the first of the books and moved over to the couch, curling up so that he got the full benefit of the sunlight.

A few moments later, he knew he had made the right decision. Not only was this a very old book, it was a copy of something that was much older, the personal journal of a Vkandis Priest.

With a shock of excitement that made his fingertips tingle, he spelled out the name of the Priest who had written the journal.

Hansa.

If what Ulrich believed was true, and the Firecat who sat at

Solaris' side at this very moment had once been a Son of the Sun himself, then *this* book had been written by the same entity. And from the look of it, the Journal had been started when Hansa was a man no older than he, right after he took his vows as a Priest and long before he became the Son of the Sun. Was this very book where Ulrich and Solaris had found some of their revolutionary ideas? If so, how much more was in here that they had not yet revealed?

"The Tale of Gregori" could *wait!*

Several marks later, he put down the volume and rubbed his tired eyes. This was no scribe-made copy, but someone's handwritten version. The writing was tiny, crabbed, and barely legible in places; the archaic language more difficult to work through than he had thought. He hadn't read more than two pages so far, and he'd been forced to take notes in order to get that done.

On the other hand, there was still a thrill of excitement as he contemplated the closely-written pages of the book. It was definitely going to be worth working through this. The things he had already gleaned about the Priesthood back in those long-ago days were enough to widen his eyes. *When* had the order of the Priests of the Goddess Kalanel—the consort of Vkandis—disappeared, for instance? And when had Her statue vanished from its place beside Vkandis' in the Temples?

The door opened, and Ulrich walked in as Karal put down the book with a slightly guilty start. His master only dropped his gaze to the little volume in his hands and smiled.

"I see you have been putting your time to some good use," he said. "But before you wear out your eyes, I have some other duties for you to attend to, while I am at private meetings."

He must have looked disappointed, for Ulrich only chuckled. "Don't fret, they have little or nothing to do with negotiations. I'm going to meet with Lady Elspeth and Darkwind on a regular basis to analyze our various magics. I'll be doing the same with the representatives of the White Winds and Blue Mountain mage-schools. *You* would find all that very boring, and there would be nothing you could record that would be at all useful."

Karal sighed but nodded his agreement. His own mage-craft was minimal; barely enough to light a fire, and that only if he happened to be particularly hard-pressed. In ordinary circumstances, he would be well advised to keep a firestriker on his person. "Yes, sir," he said with obedient docility. "What is it you wish me to do?"

"Attend classes," came the surprising reply. "I wish you to become as fluent in Valdemaran as you are in our tongue. There may be shades of meaning in our negotiations that I may miss otherwise. I do not have the time to spare for this, and you do."

Well, that was reasonable enough. He and Arnod had been able to make conversation last night, but it had been stilted and rudimentary, and both of them had paused often to search for words. Someone needed to be able to understand all the talk going on around them. For that matter, he could pick up a lot of information from idle conversation if no one realized that he was exceptionally fluent in Valdemaran.

He nodded, but Ulrich wasn't finished yet. "You are going to spend far too much time sitting at a desk," he continued. "You need exercise, and more than that, you need to learn how to defend yourself. *I* can hold off an enemy with magic, but if you were ambushed by someone, what would you do?"

Karal opened his mouth to reply, then thought better of it and closed it again. Ulrich was right; what had served him at the inn and the Children's Cloister would do him no good here. He was no longer just another child, and anyone who intended to attack him *here* was likely to be trained and practiced, perhaps even an assassin. Yes, the Valdemarans had provided guards, but anyone who had weathered the war with Ancar knew that guards were not always enough. For that matter, there were probably plenty of people in the Valdemaran ranks who would like to see him dead as a means of starting hostilities again.

"I've arranged for Johen to come and take you to your weaponry teacher in a few moments," Ulrich said. "So you ought to change into something like your riding gear; something you can sweat and tumble about in, and do it before he arrives."

"Yes, sir," Karal replied and stood up quickly. He was all

the way to the door of his room when he thought to ask a question.

"Who is going to be teaching me these things, sir, do you know?" he asked, as he looked for a clean set of riding clothes in the chest at the foot of his bed. In a way, he was hoping to hear that Rubrik was to be his language teacher. It made sense, and Rubrik was the one friendly, familiar face here.

"Well, there's only one person who is equally fluent in Valdemaran and Karsite," came the easy reply. "Herald Alberich, the Weaponsmaster. He's already agreed to the idea."

Clothing dropped from Karal's numb hands, and he felt as if his stomach had dropped right out of his body.

Alberich? *The* Alberich? The Great Traitor? The man whose very name was used as a synonym for traitor back home?

The man whose intimate knowledge of the Karsite Army and the Karsite Border had prevented Karse from gaining so much as a grain of sand or a word of reliable intelligence for twenty years and more?

The man who was the first that Solaris approached to arrange the truce, he reminded himself. *The man she trusted to keep his word when she sent her agents in to negotiate for a Valdemaran envoy. He is not, cannot be, the enemy I was always told he was; if he was, Solaris would never have gone to him. She values honor above all else, except devotion to Vkandis. I have never heard the truth about him, nor why he deserted his post, all those years ago.*

But still—Alberich? The very idea turned his blood to dust.

"As for your weaponswork," Ulrich continued, blithely unaware of Karal's shock and dismay, since he could not see Karal from his seat in the next room. "I had a volunteer before I even asked for one. Herald Captain Kerowyn."

Karal dropped his clothes again.

"Karal?" Ulrich called, when he said nothing.

Karal tried to move, forcing his shaking hands to reach for his riding clothes. It took him three tries to pick them up, and when he put them back down on the bed, it took him an eternity to get the fastenings undone on his Court robes.

"Karal, there is nothing to worry about," Ulrich said into the silence, finally divining the fact that Karal was disturbed by these revelations. "She is not going to drive you the way she does the young Heralds-in-training. She knows that you are never going to have to do more than defend yourself in an emergency."

But she is eight feet tall, his mind babbled, ignoring the fact that he had already *seen* her just this morning, and she was nothing like the creature that reputation painted. *She eats babies for breakfast, and washes them down with nettles and wolves' milk! She can break warriors in half with one hand! She—*

"At any rate, she's waiting for you now," Ulrich said cheerfully, as Karal fumbled his breeches on. "I'm really very flattered; she doesn't take individual pupils very often."

I'm not! I'd rather have some nice, quiet little under-trainer—

Oh, calm down, Karal. It could be worse.

It could be Alberich!

He pulled his shirt on over his head, and came out into the sitting room. Ulrich had his back to him, examining some papers, as Johen tapped diffidently on the door and entered.

Ulrich looked up to see who it was, then waved absently at them, returning his attention to the papers. "Off you go, then. I'll see you later, Karal. Try not to get too bruised; we'll be taking our dinner with the Court, and I'll need you to be presentable. I'll get a bad reputation if it looks as if I beat my secretary on a regular basis."

Karal staggered after the silent Johen, incoherent with nerves.

Try not to get too bruised! Oh, lovely, I shall. . . .

Johen led the way down a set of stairs and out into the gardens. Under other circumstances, Karal would have enjoyed the impromptu tour, for the Palace gardens were nothing like similar gardens at home, and were full of trees and plants he didn't even recognize. But he was too numb to pay a great deal of attention, and it was *far* too soon for his peace of mind that Johen brought him to a large wooden building, standing very much apart from the rest of the Palace complex.

It didn't resemble any building Karal had ever seen before—but then, he had never had any occasion to find himself inside one of the army training halls. The windows were right up near the edge of the roof, which seemed very strange to him. He couldn't imagine the reason for such an odd arrangement.

But he got no chance to ask Johen about it, for the young man hurried on ahead of him as if he could not get his escort duty discharged quickly enough. Arnod might be friendly, but this young man certainly was not.

He followed Johen into the building; once inside, it proved to house, in the main, one huge room. The closest comparison he could come up with was that it was like an indoor riding area with a sanded wooden floor; with mirrors lining the walls, and benches placed in between the mirrors, pushed up against the walls. The fourth wall held racks of wooden practice weapons, and those benches were laden with what even Karal recognized as protective padding. He sniffed; the place held the mingled odors of sweat and sawdust, leather oil and dust. At the moment, it was empty of everything else.

A door at the back of the room opened, and Herald Captain Kerowyn stepped out into the room. She was not wearing that white livery that every other Herald wore, which seemed very odd to Karal; there was no way of telling that she was a Herald without that white uniform, since her Companion wasn't with her.

Huh. Maybe that's the point?

She was, however, dressed in a way that would have scandalized most good Karsites and not just because she was wearing "men's clothing." No one could ever mistake her for a man, in a brown leather tunic and breeches, both so tight-fitting that they showed every curve and muscle of a quite spectacular figure.

Karal swallowed, hard; she might be old enough to be his mother, maybe older, but there was no sign of those years on her body or in the way that she moved. There was also no question but that she was just as attractive as she was dangerous. He was very glad that his own tunic was long enough to hide his inevitable reaction, but he flushed anyway.

Then he paled, and his body lost interest, as she shifted her weight in a way that reminded him of her profession and her history. This was *Kerowyn*, Captain of the Skybolts, mercenary fighter long before she became a Herald. If she didn't eat babies for breakfast, she certainly had a reputation for devouring certain parts of the conquered as a battlefield trophy feast!

She stood with her feet slightly apart, hands on hips, and studied him. Johen simply made a gesture toward him and left without a word. She tilted her head to one side, and he hoped that his trembling wasn't as visible as he thought.

"Be steady, youngster," she said at last, in heavily-accented Karsite. "I be not going to eat you. Not without good sauce, anyway; you be too stringy for my liking."

He flushed again as he realized that she was laughing at him. She knew he was afraid of her, and she was laughing at him! But his fear was a lot stronger than his anger, and his good sense at least as strong.

Let her laugh—if it keeps her from pounding me into the ground like a tent peg!

She paced toward him, slowly and deliberately. He stood his ground—mostly because he wasn't able to move. His feet were frozen to the floor, and he couldn't look away from her.

She circled him, looking him over from every angle, as if he was a young horse she was considering for purchase. He flushed even harder; he wasn't used to being given that kind of scrutiny by a woman, or at least, not by a woman like this one. *Solaris* had given him that kind of detailed examination, but there was nothing remotely feminine about Her Holiness; when Solaris sat on the Sun Throne, she *was* the Son of the Sun, and that was all there was to say about it. Kerowyn was as female as she was formidable.

"Right," Kerowyn said at last, as if answering a question, though he had said nothing. "Come here, boy. I be wanting to be testing the strength of you."

For a moment he hesitated. What was she going to do, feel his legs and arms, as if he was a young racing colt and she the prospective buyer? But she beckoned peremptorily, and he followed her, not daring to do otherwise.

She brought him over to the corner of the room, to a series of ropes and pulleys. The corner looked like a setting for some kind of arcane torture, or worse. But it turned out that what she had in mind *(thank the God!)* were only tests of how much he could lift, pull, or push; the ropes could be loaded with weights, and she would watch him as he tried to raise them from various positions. When she was done, *he* was sweaty, and she looked satisfied.

"Be better than I be *thinking,*" she told him. "You be not spending all your time pushing paper around on desks. Now, here be what we be going to do. I not be making a fighter out of you, and I be not going to try. What I be going to do, is I be teaching you some things you be using to be defending yourself with, things that be buying you enough time for help to be getting to you. *Real* help, trained fighters."

"That makes good sense," he said slowly.

"Here be problem, that we be going to be making these things into ways that you be acting without thinking. And we be going to be making you stronger than you be already. So—" she waved at one of the things he had just been using, weights loaded onto ropes attached to pulleys, "—be doing what I be showing you, fifty more times, then we be working on the first move."

Not what he wanted to hear. . . .

By the time she was done with him, he was weak-kneed with exhaustion, and quite ready to drop, but he already had one move down well enough to use against an attacker who wasn't expecting it. The likeliest scenario, as Kerowyn postulated it, was that he would be attacked from behind by someone who intended to strangle him. She showed him how to use the attacker's rush and momentum to tumble forward, throwing the attacker over as he did so, then get to his feet and run.

With enough practice, he *would* do just that without thinking.

When she dismissed him and sent him out the door with the admonition to return at the same time the next day, he realized that there had been another effect of the lesson besides exhaustion. He had absolutely, positively, not a single drop of desire in his veins for her, despite the fact that they had been tumbling all over each other, often ending tangled in positions that would have caused her father to issue Karal an ultimatum to marry her—had they been in Karse.

He wasn't certain how that had come about, but there was no denying the effect. If she had stripped herself stark naked and posed for him like one of the street women, he would not have been able to perform with her. She overwhelmed him.

She was now, in his own mind, in the same class as Solaris, and therefore untouchable.

He was simply grateful to be allowed to escape.

He dragged himself back to his room; Ulrich was not there, but *someone* had had the foresight to fire up the copper boiler in the bathing room. Johen? If so, then perhaps that young man was not as unsympathetic as he had seemed.

After a hot bath, the world seemed a little friendlier, and he was ready to face Ulrich, the Court, and whatever else came up. And it was a very good thing that he *was* prepared for just that, for just as he finished dressing, there was a decisive knock on the door. Before he could answer it, the door opened.

There was a man standing there; a man wearing dark gray leather very like Kerowyn's except for the color. Tall, lean, and dark, Karal had never seen a human being who looked quite so much like a hungry wolf before. His hair was snow-white, and his face seamed with scars; he regarded Karal as measuringly as Kerowyn had, out of a pair of agate-gray eyes as expressionless as a pair of pebbles.

He was Karsite; his facial features and body type were as typical as Ulrich's and Karal's own. There was absolutely no doubt of that.

Which meant that there was only one person that he could be. Karal had forgotten that he was also scheduled for lessons in the Valdemaran tongue.

Karal swallowed, his mouth gone dry, and bowed. "H–herald Alberich, I–I–I am honored," he stuttered in his own tongue.

He rose from his bow; Alberich was smiling sardonically. "Honored? To be tutored by the Great Betrayer? I think not." The Herald strode into the room and closed the door behind him. "You are one of three things, boy—diplomatic, uninformed, or a liar. I hope it is the first."

Karal didn't know what to say, so he wisely kept his mouth shut. Alberich looked him over again, and the smile softened, just a little.

"The first, then. When you report, tell Solaris that I compliment her on her choice of personnel." He reached for a chair without looking at it, pulled it over to him, and turned it so that the back faced Karal. Then he sat down on it backward, resting his arms along the high back.

Karal took this as an invitation to sit, and took a chair for himself. He was weak in the knees again, but this time from the sheer force of the man's personality.

"First, we'll see just how much Valdemaran you really know," Alberich said—and then began a ruthless examination. Or rather, interrogation; he spouted off questions and waited for Karal to answer them. If Karal didn't understand or lacked the vocabulary to answer, he shook his head, and Alberich moved on to another question.

During this entire time, Alberich never once took those gray eyes off him, and whether or not it was by accident, the questions he asked revealed more about the man than Karal had ever expected to learn.

It was impossible to remember that this man was called the Great Traitor—no, not impossible to remember, but impossible to believe. Not when everything he said or did reinforced Karal's impression that Alberich lived, breathed, and worked beneath a code of honor as unbreakable as steel and as enduring as the mountains of his homeland.

"Come with me," Alberich said after about a mark's worth of this intensive questioning. He stood quickly and gracefully, and Karal scrambled to his own feet, feeling as awkward as a young colt and drained completely dry. "I'll get you some books to get you started."

He turned and led the way, Karal following behind him; eventually, after many turnings and twistings and sets of stairs leading both up and down, Alberich turned to open a pair of unguarded doors. Behind those doors—as far as Karal was concerned—lay Paradise.

Books. Floor to ceiling, and huge freestanding shelves full of them. The only other library Karal had ever seen to rival this one was the Temple library at home, and novices were never allowed in *there* alone. He stood in the door, gawking; he would never have known where to start, but Alberich seemed to know exactly where he was going. He went straight to the rear, and took down half a dozen small volumes, blowing the dust from them as he did so. He stalked back to where Karal was waiting for him, and handed them all to him.

"I don't think anyone has looked at these since I used them," he said, with another of those sardonic smiles. "There are a couple of Valdemaran-Karsite dictionaries, and a pair of advanced grammar books, and a history of the beginning of the war with Karse from the Valdemaran point of view, written by one of the Priests from the schismatic branch of the Sunlord. It's a little archaic, but it will give you some perspective and a good lesson in language at the same time. I'll question you on the first chapter or so tomorrow."

With that, he led Karal back to the suite; this time Karal tried to memorize the way, since he would certainly want to return to a library as impressive as that one, but for once his memory failed him. That was more than a disappointment; he *wanted* to be able to return there at will. He'd brought his own books largely because he was afraid he would not be permitted access to other books in the Palace, but there were no guards on that library door, which implied that residents in the Palace were free to come and go as they pleased.

If they could *find* the place, that is. Maybe the maze of corridors was enough to keep them out of it!

But Alberich might have been a reader of thoughts after all, for when he brought Karal back to the door of their suite and opened it for him, he paused.

"Any time you want to visit the royal library, ask a page to take you," he said. As Karal twitched reflexively in surprise, he added—again, with that peculiar softening of his normally sardonic expression, "I've seen book-hunger before, lad. There's nothing in there that's forbidden you, and you could do a great deal worse than learn how these people think from their own words. Feed your hunger and open your mind at the same time."

Then he turned on his heel and strode off down the hallway, leaving Karal clutching his books and staring after him.

Finally, Karal went inside and put his books down on his bed, then sat down beside them, wondering where he was going to find the energy to complete the day.

All this—and there was still the formal dinner with Selenay's Court to endure before he was allowed to collapse!

He'd never thought this was going to be an easy position to fill, but this was insane. How did Ulrich manage his schedule? It was at least as difficult as Karal's, probably much more so.

The same way he always tells me to take things, Karal decided. *One at a time. . . .*

One thing at a time—and right now, that meant finding and laying out another set of Court clothes for Ulrich. He got to his feet with an effort, and let momentum and habit take over.

One thing at a time.

For the first several days he thought he was going to collapse at any moment. There were never enough daylight hours to complete all of his tasks, and he and his mentor spent long candle-lit sessions after dinner trying to catch up. Sometimes he attended meetings with Ulrich, but often Ulrich scheduled meetings during his lessons with Kerowyn and Alberich, probably a tactful way of excluding him without needing to manufacture an excuse. Ulrich was a diplomat, after all. Karal gave up trying to understand why the Valdemarans were so worried about *him* being present; it really didn't matter in the long run. And on the positive side, it *was* one less duty in a schedule that was already too full.

There were endless pages of notes to turn into something legible, Ulrich's postings back to Karse to write out properly from *his* hastily dictated notes, more pages of notes to transcribe from Ulrich's private meetings, preliminary drafts of agreements to put together; the work seemed never-ending. For a while, Karal despaired of ever getting any time to himself. It seemed as if the only time he was anywhere without a mindbending task in front of him was when he was in the bathtub!

Yet, after the first rush of activity, things *did* slow down. Initial agreements were drawn up, agreed to by Ulrich and the Queen's representative—usually Prince-Consort Daren—then sent off to Karse. The initial stage of setting up diplomatic relations was over; now it must all be approved by Solaris and then by the Queen's Council. Solaris would ponder Ulrich's suggestions long and hard before deciding on them, then make her own changes; the Valdemaran Council was like every ruling body Karal had ever heard of and must debate things endlessly before agreeing to them. Work for Karal slowed to a mere trickle; work for Ulrich was in getting to know those in power on a personal basis. That meant more meetings, informal ones this time, just between Ulrich and one or two of the people in power—meetings Karal didn't attend.

Karal found himself alone in the suite more and more of-ten, with nothing to do but read his recreational books, study Valdemaran, and puzzle out the journals that Ulrich had given him. At first he welcomed the respite, but his own books were soon devoured, studying Valdemaran was *work*, and trying to make his way through the journals no less so.

He went out looking for company on several occasions, but the search didn't bring him any success. When he encoun-tered the highborn offspring of Selenay's courtiers that were his own age, they ignored his presence as if he was another statue or a plant in the garden. Wherever he met them, they looked right past or even through him, and no one ever replied to his cautious greetings. The Heralds-in-training seemed mostly afraid of him and avoided his presence en-tirely; Arnod was the only exception to that, and Arnod was on duty only late at night.

He finally found himself sitting and staring out the window down into the gardens one afternoon, burdened by what could only be "homesickness." Whatever it was, it left him de-pressed and profoundly unhappy; aching with the need for something, anything that was familiar, and so enervated he found it hard to even think. He wasn't tired, but he couldn't find the energy to move, either. What he *wanted* was to be home, back in his familiar little cubicle near Ulrich's rooms; back in the Temple library, helping Ulrich track down a par-ticular book, or copying out designated text. Oh, this place was very luxurious, but he would have traded every rich and exotic dish for an honest Karsite barley-cake. He would have traded his soft bed and private room for a breath of mountain air, every sweet, cream-rich cake and pudding for a mouthful of fruit-ice, and all their spiced wine for a good, strong cup of *kava*.

There was nothing about this land that was quite the same as in Karse, not the food, the scents, the plants that grew in the gardens, or the furniture. *Everything* had some tinge of the foreign to it; he couldn't even sleep without being reminded that he was not at home, for the herbs used to scent the linens were not the ones he knew, no bed he had ever slept in had been so thick that you were enveloped in it, and there were no familiar night-bird songs to thread through the darkness and lull you to sleep.

And there was no one he could confide in, either. Ulrich was too busy to be bothered with nonsense like this, and he would probably think him immature, unsuited for the duties he had been given. He was here to serve his master, not get in the way with his childish troubles.

I was able to talk to Rubrik—no. No, he has more important things to do than listen to some foreigner babble about how lonely he is. What would the point be, anyway? What could he say, "go home?" I was given this duty; there is no choice but to see it through.

Confiding in either Kerowyn or Alberich was absolutely out of the question. They would lose what little respect they had for him. They, too, would think that he was acting and reacting like a child. He was supposed to be a man, filling a man's duty—and furthermore, if they knew he was this unhappy, they would tell their superiors. This homesickness could be used against the mission; any weakness was a danger.

I knew what I was getting into when Ulrich told me where we were going, he told himself, as he stared out at the garden, wishing that he could make the bowers and winding pathways take on the mathematical radial precision of a Karsite garden. *I knew how alone I was going to be, and I knew that I was going where there were no signs of home.*

But *had* he known, really? As miserable and lonely as his years in the Children's Cloister had been, they were still years spent among people who spoke the same language as he did, who ate the same foods, swore by the same God. Here the only two people who even knew his tongue as native speakers were both men so many years his senior, and so high above him in social position, that there was no point in even thinking of confessing his unhappiness to them. Neither his master nor Alberich were appropriate confidants.

This was a marvelous place, full of fascinating things, a place where he had more freedom than he had ever enjoyed in his life—but it was not home.

It would never be home. And he despaired of ever finding anyone here he could simply *talk* to, without worrying if something that he might say could be misconstrued and turned into a diplomatic incident—or just used as a weapon of leverage against the mission.

If he couldn't have home—he needed a friend. He'd never really had one, but he needed one now.

He continued to stare out the window, feeling lassitude overcome him more and more with every passing moment. He was too depressed, too lonely, even to think about rereading one of his books.

This is getting me nowhere. If I don't do something soon, I might not be able to do anything before long. He'd just sit there until someone came along and found him, and then he'd be in trouble. Ulrich would want to know what was wrong, people would think he was sick, and he'd just stir up a world of trouble.

I don't think the Healers can do anything about homesickness. Not even here.

There was a section of the gardens, a place where kitchen-herbs were grown in neatly sectioned-off beds, that reminded him marginally of the gardens at the Temple. It had no rosebeds, no great billows of romantic flowers, no secluded bowers, so it was not visited much by people his age. Perhaps if he got out into the sun, he would cheer up. Maybe all this gloom was only due to being cooped up indoors for too long.

And maybe fish would fly—but it was worth trying. Anything was better than sitting here, feeling ready to drown himself in his own despair.

Feeling sorry for myself isn't going to fix anything either.

He managed to get himself up out of his chair; that was the hard part. Once he had a destination, momentum got him there. The kitchen gardens were deserted, as he had thought—with the sole exception of one very old Priest of some group that wore yellow robes. The old man sat and dreamed in the sun, just like any of the old Red-robes in the Temple meditation gardens; his presence almost made the place seem homelike.

With a bit of searching, Karal found a sheltered spot, a stone bench partially hidden by baybushes and barberry-bushes. He moved into their shade, and slumped down on the cool stone.

The depression didn't even fade, not the tiniest bit. Now that he was out here, the bright sunshine didn't seem to make any real difference to how he felt.

He closed his eyes and a lump began to fill his throat; his chest tightened and ached, and so did his stomach. Why had he come here? Why didn't he find a reason not to go? Why hadn't he let someone older, more experienced, come with Ulrich? He could have found a new mentor, couldn't he? And even if the new Priest wasn't as kindhearted as Ulrich, wouldn't dealing with a new mentor have been better than being this lonely? Did it matter that Ulrich was the only person who had ever been kind to him since he'd been taken away from his family? He had survived indifference and even unkindness before—and at least he would have been home! He would not have been stranded in a strange land, where everyone was a potential enemy.

"And lo, I was a stranger, and in a strange realm, and no man knew me. Every man's heart was set against me, and every man's hand empty to me."

He jumped, stifling an undignified squeak; he opened his eyes involuntarily. Who could be quoting from the Writ of Vkandis, and with such a *terrible* accent?

For a moment he did not recognize the woman who stood just in front of him, smiling slightly; she was dressed in a leather tunic and breeches like Kerowyn wore, though not so tight, and of white leather rather than brown.

A mature woman, rather than a girl, he guessed she was somewhere around thirty years old. She wasn't very tall; in fact, she would probably come up to his chin at best; her abundant and curly chestnut hair had just a few strands of silver in it, and her eyes were somewhere between green and brown in color. She gave an oddly contradictory impression of both fragility and strength.

Then his mind cleared, and his memory returned; he had been fooled by her clothing. He had never seen this particular Herald in anything other than formal Court costume before. Talia—the Queen's Own Herald.

Granted, she *was* a Sun-priest, but how had she learned the Writ? Why had she bothered? There was no real need for her to have done so; the office was only honorary.

"Thought I wouldn't take my office as Priest of Vkandis seriously, did you?" she said, with a smile that was full of mischief. "Maybe Solaris only meant the title to be honorary, but it seemed to me I ought to give the honor its due respect, and learn something about the one I was supposed to be representing."

"Oh," he said, feeling very stupid and slow-witted. But then he realized that she was speaking in his tongue, and as bad as her accent was, the words soaked into him like rain into dry ground. He wanted to hear more; he needed to hear more.

"I thought that particular quote seemed awfully apt, given how you looked when I came up," she continued. "Not at all happy, actually. Of course, it *could* just be indigestion—"

She cocked her head to the side, as if inviting his confidences. He hesitated. She seemed friendly enough, but how much difficulty could he get himself into by talking to her?

On the other hand, she's not only a Herald, she's one of the Kin of Vkandis. If she did hurt one of the Kin, wouldn't the Sunlord do something about that?

She waited a moment more, then her smile widened a trifle. She had wonderful, kind eyes. "Or perhaps it's a peculiar kind of indigestion," she suggested impishly. "You've swallowed a great huge lump of Valdemar, and it isn't going down easily."

He had to laugh at that, it was so unexpected, and so vivid an image. "I suppose that's as appropriate an explanation as any," he replied, relaxing marginally. He had longed for someone he could talk to—and here was someone offering herself, someone it might even be safe to unburden himself to. What *did* he know about this woman? She was some kind of special advisor to the Queen—Solaris had spent an awful lot of time in her company—but there was something more, something important.

Hansa trusted her. That was it; he had the memory now. The Firecat had definitely trusted her; it was Hansa who had suggested she be made an honorary Priestess, if what Ulrich had told him was true.

She nodded at him in a friendly manner, and she did not seem inclined to move off despite his hesitation. Interestingly, she also made no attempt to intrude on him by sitting down on his bench uninvited. "I felt the same way when I first came here," she told him, as she shifted her weight from one foot to the other. "I was from a place so unlike this that it might as well have been on the other side of the world. You may find this difficult to believe, but my people kept their children very isolated from anything outside their farms. I had *no* idea what Heralds or Companions really were, other than the few things I'd been able to pick up from a bit of reading. I thought when Rolan Chose me that I had simply found a lost Companion. I thought I was supposed to bring him back to his owners, like returning a strayed horse!"

He had to laugh at that one with her; at least he knew a little more than she had! Rubrik had described the business of being "Chosen" by a Companion, that it was rather like being picked out for a Firecat's particular attentions. Hard to believe that anyone in Valdemar could have been unaware of a Companion's real nature.

On the other hand, it was easy enough to control a child, as she had pointed out. But being Chosen was supposed to be rather dramatic—he could well imagine someone trying to deny such a selection, for being Chosen would definitely put an end to any other plans one had for one's life, but Talia must have been unique in her ignorance of what being Chosen meant.

"Seriously, though, I was as out-of-place here as you are feeling now; I think you must have gone through Holderkin lands to get here—well, that's where I'm from." She smiled as he nodded, very cautiously. "They swear they escaped from Karse, but I'd be more willing to believe that your people threw them out; there can't be a more intransigent group of stoneheads in all the world. Personally, I think they're more trouble to deal with than they're worth."

"I don't know one way or the other," he confessed. "I never studied them, so I couldn't venture an opinion. But I can see how you would be feeling very—ah—foreign, when you arrived here. It was obviously very different here than among your own people. You probably *were* as foreign to Haven as I am." There. That was diplomatic enough.

She studied her fingertips, then looked back up at him. "I've heard you haven't been able to make any friends here, though, and that's where our circumstances differ. Of course, you are laboring under a double handicap," she pointed out. "You are with the envoy, which makes you dangerous to know, and you are from our former enemy, from a Priesthood known to be able to call up very powerful magic forces, which makes you *personally* rather dangerous to know. There's a Shin'a'in saying, 'It is wise to be remote in the presence of one who conjures demons.' Hard to make friends when people you meet are afraid you're going to turn them into broiled cutlets if you get annoyed with them."

"Ah—interesting," he replied, to buy himself time. It had not occurred to him that he might be frightening away would-be acquaintances; he never considered himself to be any threat to anyone. "I never thought of that."

"Yes, well, our younglings can be a rather timid and conservative lot," she said casually. "At least the children of the courtiers can. At the moment, I don't know of anyone in the younger set who would deliberately be rude or hostile to you. On the other hand, they've had a rather unsettled time of it; that can make even the boldest youngling into a mouse. Most of the youngsters here have lost at least one family member to the conflicts with Ancar, and there are a few who went from being fifth- or sixth-born to being second or third heir to their parents' holdings within the space of a few weeks. Many of them don't even have parents anymore; they're under the guardianship of older siblings. They don't like to think of any of that; to escape from their memories they tend to concentrate on some fairly shallow interests. The trouble is, no one has put you into the set that's actually doing something with their time—mostly because *they* are as busy as you."

That shocked him out of his own depression entirely. *How* many of the Valdemar elite had died in this war? Had Karse suffered as much at the hands of Ancar? Surely not, at least, not at first. Perhaps once the alliance had been made public—

"I'm sorry to hear that," he said at last, hoping his tone conveyed the fact that he really *was* sorry. "I don't believe we had nearly that much trouble with him."

"No, you didn't, not at first," Talia agreed. She ran her hand through her hair in what looked to be a gesture of habit. "For one thing, he really didn't want Karse all that badly, and for another, he was under the rather mistaken impression for some time that Solaris was male." She shrugged, and spread her open hands. "Once he learned she was female, it was only a matter of time before he included her in his vendetta against women. We guessed that was why Solaris sent messengers to Alberich, looking for a truce."

Then she smiled again. "But this gloomy talk is not why I stopped here! I saw you looking unhappy, and I hoped I could cheer you up. I don't think war-talk is going to achieve that, do you?"

"Probably not," he agreed.

"I did want you to know that once people realize that you aren't going to call up demons to avenge imaginary slights, they'll probably be more friendly," she continued. "I think I can count on at least a few of them being curious enough to start asking you questions. You certainly are not the most exotic creature gracing our Court, or even the most formidable; they'll get over their nerves soon enough."

He thought of the gryphons and found himself chuckling. "At least I walk on two legs," he offered. "And I am afraid that my ability at magic is very overrated. Not only can I *not* conjure a demon—even if Solaris hadn't forbidden the practice—but I can't even light a fire. Candles, yes; fires, no. My master Ulrich *is* a mage, but he didn't choose me for my magical abilities, he chose me for my scholastic bent. Your people are safe around me."

He meant it as a joke, but she took the joke a step further. "I wouldn't go so far as to say that," she replied, and if he thought he'd imagined a sly twinkle in her eye, he knew now it wasn't imagination. "You'd be a very handsome young man if you just didn't look as if you were about to deliver a sermon on Moral Life at any moment. If you smiled more often, I wouldn't wager on *any* of our young women being safe around you!"

Belatedly he remembered that if she knew enough to quote the Writ correctly, she also knew that Priests of Vkandis took no vows of celibacy and only a modified vow of chastity. Which meant she knew that he was as free to pay court to young women as anyone here. He guessed she was encouraging him to do just that, and blushed.

Still, he found her very easy to talk to, and more so with every moment. She invited confidences and made it easy to give them to her; a lot like his own mother, in fact. *Mother used to adopt every stray that happened by the inn, from motherless horseboys to kittens. Talia must be like my mother—that's why she stopped when she thought I looked unhappy.*

She chuckled at his flush and his slow smile. "I hope you don't mind my teasing," she said, then added wryly, "we aren't as far apart in age as you might think. It wasn't all *that* long ago that I was your age, and if I wasn't happily wedded and very much in love with Dirk—" She laughed and wrinkled her nose at him. "Well, consider my reaction representative of what the young women of the Court are probably thinking about you."

His cheeks heated, and he blinked. Her reaction? She considered him attractive? No female, girl *or* woman, had ever told him that!

She shook her head. "Listen to me—'if I was your age'—I sound like I think I'm an old crone! My, motherhood certainly has taken the ginger out of *me!*"

He had to laugh at that. "My mother says the same thing," he told her. "She swears that we each added five years to her age with every prank we pulled!"

"Some days I would agree with her," Talia replied, and sighed. "I don't remember littles being this much trouble to *my* parents! You have brothers and sisters?"

"One brother and several sisters," he told her, then found himself talking about his family while she simply stood there and listened to him with no evidence of boredom. She even asked him questions that proved she had really been listening, and not just pretending to pay attention. .

He progressed from telling her about his family, to finally confessing his own depression and loneliness. It seemed natural, after the way she listened to him about everything else. After all, if Hansa trusted her, why shouldn't he?

"I don't even know where they took Trenor," he sighed, after talking for what seemed to be the better part of a mark. "He's Karsite, too, after all . . . and horses have always been as much my friends as people. I'd love to go riding, but I don't know where I would be allowed to go, even if I *could* find him, and I don't know what people would think if I asked for the stables." He shrugged. "They might think I was some kind of spy, looking for a way off the grounds to pass messages on, when all I want to do is ride my horse."

She brightened at that. "Havens, at least *that* is one thing I can help you with," she told him. "I certainly know where the stables are, and there are riding paths all through Companion's Field; there's no reason why you can't ride your gelding in there. Plenty of people ride their Companions on the paths. I can't imagine why anyone would forbid you riding Trenor in there. Would you like me to show you where the stables are right now, and get you acquainted with the stablemaster? Once he knows who you are, he can have Trenor set up for a daily ride for you, if you'd like."

He stared at her for a moment; this was the last thing he had expected, and the one thing that would help! He had a little trouble replying, until he got his wits back about him. "Thank you!" he exclaimed. "Oh, that is exactly what I *do* want! Thank you so much!"

But she waved away his thanks. "Not to worry, Karal. I'm glad that there is at least one remedy I can give you for your homesickness that will work right now. Time, I fear, is the only other remedy." She laughed at his grimace. "I know, I know, the one thing a young man hates to hear is that the only cure for *anything* is time! It can't be helped, though; it's a cliché precisely because it's so often true. When problems are big, it's usually because they're swallowing up everything else you would be thinking about. When you have some time, new things come up, and make the old problems seem smaller when you look back at them. So let some time pass, do a few things you really enjoy, and let your mind rest."

He stood up quickly as she gestured for him to follow her, and she led him off at a brisk pace, pointing out exactly where they were and what places they were passing. "Here's the rose garden, the maze is just through there; if you look through the rose trees you can just see the end of the Courtier's Wing of the Palace. That's where your suite is, though most Courtiers don't live here, they have their own manors outside the walls—" That helped him orient himself, and he began to suspect that Alberich had led him in circles that first day, when he had taken Karal to the library. Perhaps it had not been deliberate; perhaps it was simply in the man's cautious nature to attempt to confuse. Perhaps there had been work going on that required they make some elaborate detours. But from the outside, at least, the Palace and the buildings around it were laid out in a logical fashion. He knew that the library was on the first floor of the wing that contained most of the other rooms used for "official" purposes, and that wing lay directly across from his, according to Talia.

But she was pointing out other buildings now, buildings that were separate from the Palace. "That's Healer's Collegium, and that's Bardic—look, there are the stables, you can see them from here, just on the other side of those trees."

But it was not the stables that caught his attention, but the huge wooded field to their right. It *seemed* to be full of horses.

Then he realized why his mind had phrased it that way, for the "horses" were all white. There wasn't another color of four-legged beast to be seen. Which meant, surely—

Talia saw where he was looking; she squinted against the sun in that direction. "That's Companion's Field. Do you want to go look over the fence for a moment?"

As well ask him if he wanted to fly! Of course he did—and at the same time, the idea terrified him. Companions! The beautiful creatures that Rubrik had so eloquently praised, and the Hellhorses of Karsite stories. His *head* knew that they were not the monsters from his childhood, but his stomach lurched at the idea of so many of them concentrated here. Still, he nodded numbly.

She must have guessed something of his thoughts from his expression, or lack of it. "You do realize that they aren't demons, don't you?" she asked, a little nervously. "Your escort surely explained what Heralds and Companions really are—didn't he?"

I must look as tense as a cocked crossbow. "Yes," he told her, "Our escort and my mentor had a number of conversations about the Companions. I think Ulrich plans to come out here one day when he isn't busy chasing diplomatic rabbits down holes." He moved closer to the fence, until at last he was leaning right up against it, staring at the beautiful creatures in their Field.

Not demons, he reminded himself; orthodox theology held that demons could be as beautiful as they pleased, but he still did not have to remind himself too forcefully. Now that he was here, watching them, his stomach settled again, deciding that maybe his head was right after all. There was something about the Companions that was so completely innocent that the idea of their being demons was absurd.

Not horses, either. He could see how they would excite lust in the heart of any horsebreeder, though. If only one could achieve lines like that with horses! They were easily the most elegant creatures he had ever seen; Rubrik's Companion was no isolated case. Well, rumor said that the Shin'a'in had bred horses to equal Companions, but who knew? Rumor also had it that the Shin'a'in rode naked and painted themselves blue, and he rather doubted either was true.

For one thing, riding naked is damned uncomfortable. You can get yourself such a set of blisters if you have a saddle, and such a rash if you don't. . . .

"Well," he said at last, shaking himself out of the reverie the field full of Companions induced in him. "Your time is precious, even if I'm at leisure at the moment. And I am selfishly devouring it. So, if you can spare me a few moments more to take me to the stables—"

"I can spare you as much time as you need," Talia said firmly. "Come on, and I'll introduce you to the stablemaster."

Talia was no out-of-shape courtier; she set out again at a stiff walk, and he was glad he'd been working out with Kerowyn. The stable was huge, which was only to be expected; their luck was in, though, for Trenor was in the third stall from the door, and whickered as soon as he caught Karal's scent.

Karal let himself into the gelding's stall, while Talia went looking for the stablemaster. Trenor was overjoyed to see him and whuffled his hair and chest with such enthusiasm that he left damps spots all over Karal's clothing. When Karal looked him over carefully, he saw no signs of neglect, much less any of ill-use. That eased most of his worries; these Valdemarans were taking very good care of his "baby."

The stablemaster arrived while Karal was examining Trenor's feet and hocks. He was clearly pleased by the way Karal carefully examined his gelding, rather than being offended at the implication that the stable staff had been neglecting the horse.

"You know horses," the man said—a statement, rather than a question—as Karal finished his examination and stood up to be introduced. Karal nodded anyway, and the man turned and spoke to Talia in a dialect of some kind, too heavily accented and rapid for Karal to follow.

Then he turned away and went back to the work they'd taken him away from; shoeing a pretty little mare. It rather surprised Karal that the stablemaster himself would tend to a task like that, instead of assigning it to underlings. On the other hand—the mare had the delicate lines of a very highly-bred palfrey, and the nervous air of a horse that had been brought up to be high-strung. Better that the stablemaster handle a beast like that; that was what Karal's father would have said.

"Tahk says that you obviously are a good horseman, and that he'll arrange for Trenor to be readied for you for a daily ride if that's what you want. He also offered another option; if you prefer, he'll simply leave orders with the stableboys that when you show up, they're to fetch your tack." Talia scratched Trenor's neck, just along the crest, and laughed when the gelding leaned into her scratching. "I told him I thought you'd probably prefer to make less fuss than the highborns, and would take care of your own saddling, and he simply repeated that you were a *good* horseman."

"I would, and thank you," Karal replied sincerely. "I'd rather not have Trenor saddled up at any specific time, since I don't always know exactly when Ulrich will need me."

"Thought so." She moved her scratching to under Trenor's halter, and the gelding sighed with bliss. "You know, you could combine your lessons with Alberich with a daily ride; he has to make sure his Companion gets some exercise, and neither of them are anything but stiff first thing in the morning, which is when they *have* been going out." She tilted her head to one side, as if sensing his apprehension at trying to approach the formidable Alberich with any kind of a request. "Want me to suggest it? I can tell him it was my idea."

"Oh, would you?" He was appallingly grateful. "By the Light, I seem to be getting deeper and deeper in debt to you."

Once again she waved away any suggestion that he might "owe" her anything. "Don't mention it. I really just want you to be happier than you are. *That* would make a big difference to me, and if you're happier, your work will go smoother."

"And if the work goes smoother, my master will be likelier to be in a good mood, and if he's in a good mood, he'll make concessions, hmm?" He chuckled, and she joined in. "That I can understand! Everyone here is a diplomat."

Though why my being happier would make a big difference to her in particular I can't fathom. . . .

"We'd better be going," he said, reluctant to leave Trenor, but feeling better than he had in days. "His blanket's damp, so they've obviously had him out for a good workout today, and from tomorrow on I can take over his exercise."

"I—I had one more thought," Talia said, hesitantly. "You were saying that you wished you could make some friends here, right?"

He hadn't *said* anything of the sort, but he'd certainly *thought* it, so he nodded.

She licked her lips. "There's another person here I would really like you to meet. He's in a similar position to yours, but without even the authority of being a secretary to an envoy. I know that he is very lonely, and even though you don't have anything at all in common in the way of background, you are still both from places that are so different from Valdemar that you are alike in your reactions."

He turned to stare fully at her, because he sensed that she was not even telling him a fraction of what she knew about this person—that describing this person as coming from a place that is "different" from Valdemar just might be the understatement of the millennium.

"What exactly . . . ?" he asked. "What do you mean?"

She made a face of frustration. "I'm really not certain what I can and cannot tell you about him. His situation is—well, nothing short of what you would read about in a legend, and even then you would probably not believe it. The thing that the two of you have in common is that you're both—bewildered, I suppose is the right word. Bewildered and quite foreign to Valdemar. He *does* need a friend, and he is terribly shy. He is also very reserved, and tends to think of questions as being intrusive, which makes him unhappy when he is around our younger Heralds-in-training."

Karal nodded, grimacing. He had met one or two besides Arnod who hadn't been afraid of him—but both of those *children* had been full of questions that in Karse would have been considered dreadfully rude. He had answered them anyway, because they *were* clearly children and hadn't meant anything offensive by their questions.

"I will meet this person, if you like," he offered, feeling that he had to offer her *something* after all the help she had given him today. "I cannot promise anything after that. We might immediately hate one another, after all."

"Oh, I don't think that is very likely," she replied, looking quite satisfied. "I usually manage to find people who are going to enjoy each other's company, rather than the reverse." Then she bit her lip, as if something had just occurred to her "There is just one thing—"

Karal looked at her sharply. "Which is, what?"

"Do you recall the Tayledras envoy? Firesong, the Hawkbrother Mage?"

Of course he recalled Firesong. Even if he did not have a secretary's trained memory, he could hardly have forgotten *that* flamboyant young man. He nodded.

Talia sucked at her lower lip, and her brow creased a little.

"An'desha is with him, but he isn't exactly Tayledras, even though he looks like he is. Technically, he's Shin'a'in. And he's a lot younger than he looks, literally. He's really about your age, maybe a year or two older."

"Ah." Karal nodded again, even though that was more confusing than it was enlightening. That phrase though, "An'desha is with him. . . ." Was she implying what he thought?

Could be. Then again, maybe not. There are probably those who think Ulrich is more than just my master and mentor.

In any case, did it matter? Despite the fact that such a liaison was supposed to be against the Will of Vkandis, there were plenty of situations, pairings like that in the Priesthood, something which had been made very clear to him and every other novice once they graduated from the Children's Cloister.

It was also made very clear to the entire Priesthood once Solaris came to power that *nonconsensual* liaisons, whether they be of opposite or same sex partners, were Anathema, right up there with demon-summoning. *You shall force no one,* seemed to be the whole of the law as far as Solaris was concerned.

And as for Karal—as long as this An'desha wasn't looking for a—

"He's devoted to Firesong," Talia said, as if she could read his mind. "He's going to be a very powerful mage, and Firesong is teaching him. I thought you ought to know about that, too."

Karal thought about any number of responses, and finally settled on a shrug. She might be implying what he thought, and she might not. It hardly mattered.

I have had so many things in my life turned upside down, why not this one as well?

"Good enough," Talia responded, looking cheerful again. "Come on, then, and I'll tell you more about him. If you thought *your* life was strange, you haven't heard anything yet!"

The Compass Rose

10

An'desha might not yet be even half the mage that Falconsbane had been, but he knew an Empath when he saw one, at least. He readily recognized that Gift in the Herald who came up the path to the *ekele*, black-clad stranger in tow. He thought he recognized the woman, vaguely, though he could not remember her name. Oh, Falconsbane would have *loved* to get his hands on a female like this one! That was one Gift he had been unable to simulate, and no real Empath would serve Falconsbane of his own free will.

No point in trying to force an Empath to serve, either. It's a Gift that can't be coerced, though Falconsbane certainly tried often enough.

He wondered if these were more of Firesong's friends, and at first he was put out at the prospect of yet another invasion of his home. He left his seat in the garden and went outside to meet them, torn between a desire to be polite and irritation at Firesong for bringing more strangers in without consulting him.

But the Herald brightened when she saw him, and approached with the young man a step or two behind her. "An'desha?" she said (and she gave his name the correct pronunciation, which was a wonder). "You don't know me, but I am Elspeth's friend, Herald Talia. She's told me a great deal about you—and to be honest, I *am* an Empath, and you haven't exactly been shielding yourself from me, so I've been learning a bit about you from that as well."

He started; he had not been aware that his emotions had been carrying that far. And when he thought about his predominant feelings since arriving here, he flushed. Mostly tension, unhappiness, even despair—he would not have wished that on *any* Empath.

But she was going on. "Elspeth said something about you spending a great deal of time alone out here, and what I picked up from you—well, it seemed to me you might like to try a little company. I thought that you and this young fellow probably have a great deal in common."

She turned to the young man. "An'desha shena Jor'ethan, this is Karal Austreben, secretary to the envoy from Karse. Karal, this is An'desha, who is an associate of the envoy from the Hawkbrothers." Not only was she an Empath, but she was a skillful one; he felt her exerting her powers to soothe him, and at this point, he was intrigued enough to let her do so.

He knew who she was, once she introduced herself to him. This Talia was the person Elspeth trusted most in the whole world, even above and beyond Darkwind. An'desha was more than ready to be soothed at the moment; he had tried once again to socialize with the Valdemarans yesterday, and once again had met with failure. Here, though, was an Empath, bringing someone she *wanted* him to meet. It stood to reason, given her Gift and her expertise, that she just might have found someone he *could* get along with.

"I thought you two ought to at least meet," she said to the handsome, dark-eyed, black-haired young man. She spoke slowly and carefully so that he—and presumably, Karal—could pick out every syllable. "I can't imagine two people who have less in common with most of Valdemar. Even Firesong knows more about us and feels more comfortable with us than you two do. I'm sorry I waited this long to introduce you—in fact, I'm sorry I waited this long to introduce myself to you—but I wanted to make certain your mutual vocabularies in our tongue had gotten beyond the basics."

An'desha had to laugh at that. "That was a good idea. You are probably right, that I feel less at home here than even Firesong," he said, just as carefully. "Although I do not think I would ever *fit in* with any place or person."

Just a cautious warning—*I hope she isn't expecting us to be instant friends.*

Talia shrugged. "You're probably right, An'desha, but at least Karal is familiar with magic, and he's not afraid of it. That makes him better company for you than most of my people; many of the—how shall I put this?—more reticent folk are afraid of both of you and your magics. Those who are not, or who pretend they are not, tend to be too forward. Oh, let me be blunt—they are *obnoxious*. They want to know everything about you, and they want to know it *now*. At least magic is hardly a novelty to the two of you."

An'desha's eyebrows raised at that. Karal nodded. "My master Ulrich is a powerful mage as well as a Priest," the young man said diffidently. "He *was* one of those who summoned demons, until the Son of the Sun, Her Holiness Solaris, forbade the practice."

"Demon-summoning?" Excitement thrilled along his nerves. Perhaps Talia had more in mind than simply introducing two lonely strangers. If *anyone* was likely to understand his dilemma, it would be one who was familiar with demons and their ilk.

"He never cared to practice that skill," was all Karal said, but An'desha sensed a great deal behind that statement that Karal did *not* say. "I, personally, have no magic to speak of. My skills lie elsewhere."

All the better, so far as An'desha was concerned; the last thing he wanted at the moment was another would-be "teacher." Firesong was quite enough in that department.

"It often causes more problems than it solves," An'desha offered tentatively. Talia watched both of them with a slight smile on her face.

Then Karal smiled himself. "That sounds like something my master would say," he replied warmly. "The people here do *not* seem to understand that, they keep wanting to know what magics can be done to cure this or that—" He stopped himself and shrugged. "Well, I suspect you know."

"I do," An'desha replied. The corners of his mouth lifted along with his heart; this Talia was right, he and Karal *did* have a great deal in common, even though their backgrounds were probably utterly opposite.

An'desha had not realized how hungry he was for a *friend* until this moment. An Empath as strong as Talia would have to have sensed the need even though he had not voiced it to her—sensed it even past the stronger and darker emotions that his fears for the future had been calling up in him. The fact that she had brought Karal here indicated that she had sensed that same need in him as well.

This was a good thing; one of the first unreservedly good things that had happened since he entered the Gate to this land.

"Well, I wasn't able to tell Karal a lot about you, because I didn't want to take liberties that I was not entitled to take, An'desha," Talia told him. "So why don't you explain your situation? Who you are, how you came here, that sort of thing."

An'desha groaned. "I am *not* so fluent in your tongue!" he exclaimed, in mock protest.

But Talia wouldn't hear any excuses. "You are better than you think," she said, as she nodded at the open door to the *ekele* garden, then raised an eyebrow in silent inquiry.

Well, if Firesong could invite people in, so could he! He asked them both into the garden, and described how it had been built—partially to buy himself time, and partially as a way of feeling Karal out. He was more than pleased; Karal's questions were as discreet and nonintrusive as those of the young Heralds had *not* been.

Talia quietly absented herself a few moments later, and he and Karal sat down next to the waterfall in the garden. He noticed only because he sensed the absence of her soothing "spell." He doubted that Karal had any idea that she was gone. The gentle gurgling of the waterfall created an atmosphere of peace and privacy; an ideal place to talk.

By then, Karal was describing his own background. An'desha listened with fascination—sometimes horrified fascination—as Karal explained what the Vkandis Priests had once done to the children, and to the enemies, of their land. While Karal's descriptions were no match for the things that Falconsbane had done, An'desha guessed that at least *some* of the Vkandis Priests had been well on their way to becoming twins of An-car of Hardorn, and all under the guise of religion. The only thing they had not done was to poison and drain their own land for further power.

And given time, they might well have done that, too.

"That is over now," Karal concluded. "Solaris has decreed the Cleansing Fires and the summoning of demons to be Anathema—that is, completely forbidden, unholy. So, here we are, Ulrich and I, trying to forge an alliance with people we were once at war with. It is—rather unsettling. I was brought up to believe that the people and especially the Heralds of Valdemar were beasts of utter evil and depravity, and now I find that they are—just people." He shrugged. "I have seen so many changes in my lifetime, though, that I expect I will get used to this change as well. What of you?"

An'desha struggled to find the words to describe his own situation, and decided on the simplest possible explanation. "I was Shin'a'in," he said at last. "Longer ago, I think, than you realize, my body is older in years than it looks. I am—was—linked by descent to an ancient mage, an Adept. A very *evil* man, as evil as any of your demons. Because of that, he was able to—" *What to say?* "—to steal my body."

"Ah!" Karal nodded with complete understanding, the very first time he had seen that statement met with anything other than blank incomprehension. "Possession. That's what we call it. That was one of the powers the demons had, to be able to put on the body of a person as if it was a garment. The Black-robes used that power for ill. But Vkandis also has that power, and can use it with the Priests and sometimes with very holy lay people for good. It is called 'the Voice of Flame,' and Vkandis can use the voice of the person to deliver prophecy. But this Fal-cons-bane must have been a very strong demon to displace you; only the strongest and most evil of the demons had that power." Karal's voice and expression were quite sober. "You are a very lucky person, An'desha. Most people do not survive the touch of a demon upon their souls. *You* must be very strong as well."

"You *do* understand! Though I think it was luck that let me survive." For *once* he was talking to someone who didn't look at him as if he was half an idiot and all mad. "Strong," "evil," and "demonic" were certainly all words that could have been used to describe Mornelithe. "He had lived in many other bodies, and I still am not certain how I remained alive after he took mine. Perhaps it was because I was a coward and tried to flee instead of fighting him."

"Perhaps he had grown careless," Karal suggested shrewdly. "Demons are known for their pride, and great pride makes for carelessness. So he stole your body. Then what occurred?"

"He did great evil with my body, and I could not stop him," An'desha continued, the words tumbling out of him now. "Then he sought to bring harm to my people, and to the Hawkbrothers, and these Valdemarans, all at once. But he was damaged by some of what he had done, and my Goddess sent to me two of her—" Now what Valdemaran word could he use to describe the Avatars? "—two of her spirit-beings. They helped me, a mage called 'Need' helped me, and Elspeth and Darkwind and Firesong helped me, and Falconsbane was cast out after much battle. When it was all over, the Goddess made me look the age I had been when he first stole my body, or nearly, returning to me the years he had stolen from me."

Well, it was oversimplified but fundamentally correct. Karal was looking at him with a sober expression on his face, and biting his lip as if he had something he wanted to say but was not certain how it would be accepted.

"Possession is a great evil, if it is not the Voice of Flame," he said finally. "I think it is a greater evil than even you know, and you were possessed in truth."

"How do you mean?" An'desha asked, hoping that perhaps, just perhaps, this Karal might have some real answers for him. He might be the only person in this whole country who truly *did* understand, completely, what had been done to him.

"Possession can hurt the one possessed," Karal told him earnestly, leaning forward with the intensity of a greyhound about to be loosed for the chase. "It can make deep wounds, unseen wounds to the spirit. It is wounds like these, though they are invisible, that are harder to heal than *any* physical wounding. Evil corrupts, like the touch of any foul thing; it corrodes, like acid. It can etch the shape of itself into a spirit."

That was exactly what the Avatars had said! An'desha nodded, not bothering to hide his astonishment. But Karal was still not through.

"I do not know you well, An'desha," he said, diffidently. "You are not of my faith, you do not swear by the Sunlord, and yet when the Voice of Flame possessed Solaris, Vkandis Himself laid the duty upon all of us to bring the breath of healing to *any* who needed it. '*He who does good in the name of another god, does it for Vkandis,*' He said, '*and he who does ill in the name of Vkandis does it for the darkest demons in hell. Let those of good will bring succor to one another, and dispense with the naming of Names.*'" Karal took a deep breath, and An'desha held his, every muscle tight, every nerve singing with tension. "Healing hurts to the spirit is something of what my training is about," he continued. "My master Ulrich knows far, far more than I. There are many who were hurt in this way by the Black-robes that my master and others have later helped."

He paused, and An'desha nodded, unable to speak. Karal took that as license to continue.

"I think that you are still in pain and fear, An'desha," he said, as somber as any shaman. "I cannot see you in pain and not offer to help. If it is your will, my master or I can try to help you." He smiled shyly when An'desha did not immediately reject the offer or turn away. "I do not know *if* we can help you, but I know that we would try. This—healing does not require that you swear by Vkandis; it only requires that you be willing to have it done. Even if we can do nothing, perhaps we can give you the direction to help you heal yourself."

For a moment, hardly more than the blink of an eye, young Karal was surrounded by a soft, golden glow—as if he sat in the midst of warm summer sunshine. But the waterfall was in shadow—

An'desha blinked, as he realized that there was something more about this young stranger that he had sensed but had not understood. After his own brush with the Avatars, he had become far more sensitive to those the shaman would call "god-touched." It did not even matter that the god in question was not his own Star-Eyed Lady. There was something about this Karal—a color, or a sense of Light about him—that was a great deal like the feeling he had when the Avatars were near, though it was much weaker. And now—this glow about him was clearly a confirmation of what he had felt. He had sensed similar Light about the Shin'a'in envoy, although he had been far too shy to approach her; she was sworn to the Goddess, marked so by her dark apparel, and he had not had the courage to speak with her after the way he had run off from his own Clan, so long ago. And this feeling Karal called up in him was also identical to the kind of feeling he had when he was around a Companion. . . .

Whoever, whatever he is, he hasn't made this offer frivolously, or because he wants to impress me. He has *something that can help. And Firesong doesn't understand me when I try to tell him what's wrong with me. . . .*

If there is *any hint of Falconsbane around me, surely someone like Karal or his master can banish it! And he talks as if he understands the horrible things I've been feeling and the terrible things I've almost done!*

He flushed with embarrassment and ducked his head a little. "Yes," he said softly. "Please. I don't know why you have offered, but—"

Karal patted his hand, that he had unconsciously clenched into a fist on his knee. "I have offered because it is my—my job? I suppose that is right. It is something I must do, as flying is something that a bird must do. I think I know now why Herald Talia brought me to meet you; if it was not of her will, it might well have been of the will of Vkandis. She *is* a Priest, and He can work through her, if He chooses."

"That may well be," An'desha began. *After everything I have seen, I am not about to say that there is anything a god may or may not do!* "And—"

Bells from the Collegium marked the hour, chiming clearly over the sound of the waterfall, and the young man started as he counted them. He said a word that An'desha did not recognize, though he *did* recognize the tone of annoyance easily enough. "Of all the times—" He shrugged helplessly. "I must go to attend my master at a Council session. Pah! I would gladly have it be some other day, but I have no choice."

"I understand," An'desha said quickly, and then he grinned. "Council sessions do not wait on the needs of such as you and I!"

"No, we are only poor underlings to dance to the bells." But Karal's answering smile took any hint of sourness out of those words. "I will return, I pledge you, and I will see what I can do for you then. I will send word when I may come, if that is well with you?"

"Very well, and I cannot begin to thank you," An'desha replied, rising to escort him to the door. Karal ran off with a backward wave, soon vanishing among the trees and bushes screening the trail; An'desha watched him go with a much lighter heart than he had ever expected to have.

I have a friend. And there was one other thing, small in the light of all that Karal had offered, but in its way just as comforting. *I did not—desire him, except as a friend.* He had been afraid that his desire for Firesong was yet another example of how Falconsbane had warped his spirit. In fact, now that he thought about it, he had found Talia rather comely . . . and Elspeth as well, though she was as intimidating as she was attractive.

What I feel for Firesong is not of Falconsbane's doing.

Yes, in a way, that was the most comforting of all.

Karal ran down the trail that led back to the Palace; his feet and heart felt as strong and light as the hero Gregori's on his way back from the Ice Mountain. He had not known what to expect from the silver-haired, gray-eyed young man that Talia had brought him to meet, and at first he had mostly been grateful that this An'desha was dressed *far* more conservatively than his friend Firesong. But then, as they talked, something unexpected had happened.

He found himself really liking the quiet man, so unlike anyone he had ever met before. This was very much akin to the liking he had felt for Rubrik, and yet it was different from that. His feeling for Rubrik had been in part because he had admired the man; they were too different in age and personality to be true friends. But for An'desha—there was the interest of kindred personalities. As they spoke, he realized they had much in common, from a love of learning, to a liking for the same kinds of music. But there was something more to it than that, as well, and although he did not understand it, he waited for the moment when the feeling would be explained.

Then An'desha had revealed that he had been possessed— and there was the explanation.

Ulrich had told him, all of his teachers had told him, that when he came upon a spirit that needed his help, he would feel that need and would respond to it. He was of the Kin of Vkandis, and Vkandis would guide him to those in need. *Now* he knew what they had meant.

If I cannot help him, surely Ulrich can, he thought as he ran. *Now I understand how Healer Priests feel, when someone nearby is wounded or ill, though they cannot see the person. There is a hunger to help, a hunger as strong as the hunger for nourishment. Yes, we can and will help him.*

He broke through the trees and began the sprint to the Palace buildings in the distance. Fortunately, he had heard the bells that gave him a half-mark of warning *before* the meeting. It would take him a quarter-mark to reach the Palace and get his note-taking supplies; that should give him enough time to catch his breath so that he didn't make an unseemly entrance.

Ulrich would much rather work the magics of healing the soul-sick than do any other kind of magic. He has said as much to me more times than I can count. Surely Vkandis moved subtly through Herald Talia today, to bring the two of us together.

There was a stile that went over the fence around the Field, and he headed for that instead of the gate, since it was nearer the Palace. He leapt from the top of the stile as if he was trying to fly and hit the ground running; a few of the gray-clad youngsters stared at him as he ran past them, but that was probably because they didn't recognize him. He only stopped at the outer door to wait for the guard there to acknowledge him and open it for him, then he was off again, running down the hall to the staircase. A few moments later, he burst into the suite, half expecting to see Ulrich there.

He was faintly disappointed to find the rooms empty. Still, nothing could be discussed until after that meeting anyway, and he put his impatience and his news aside.

Business first. An'desha has waited this long, a few marks or even a few days more will not matter a great deal. Patience. Isn't that what Ulrich always tells me?

Given that he had a few more moments than he had anticipated, he took just long enough to peel off his tunic and pull on another, more presentable one. Then he snatched up his pouch of paper and pens and headed for the Council chamber, walking slowly and taking deep breaths to ease his panting, so he would *not* look as if he had been running a quarter-mark ago. *Appearances. Always appearances. Something no foreign envoy can ever forget.*

He had been to this great Council Chamber several times before, but this was the first meeting he had been permitted to attend that would include all the envoys of all the allies. That meant, among other things, that one or both of the gryphons would be there.

He had not seen a gryphon since the formal presentation, although he suspected that Ulrich had spoken more than once with the male, Treyvan. The idea of seeing them again, closely, made him shiver with excitement. There were no magical creatures in Karse—unless one counted the Firecats, of course—and calling them simply "magical" seemed rather blasphemous. Gregori had rid the land of the last of the ice-drakes, and although there was a skull of a basilisk in the Temple, there had not been a living one in even the most inaccessible swamps since long before the first battle with Valdemar.

And ice-drakes and basilisks are evil creatures; Treyvan and his mate are anything but evil. I have seen gryphons listed in the Writ, among other creatures that Vkandis is said to love—sunhawks, snowhorns, scaled ones. They are said in the Writ to be special, "created without guile;" no one could ever tell me just what that was supposed to mean, but perhaps I will be able to ask them some time soon for myself.

Daydreaming aside, there were other good reasons to be here that had nothing to do with his duty to his master. *I will see a bit more of Firesong here, which will be a good thing. If I am to help An'desha, I must know something of the one he is "with."*

He got to the door of the Council Chamber to find that he was actually the first one to arrive; there were only a pair of guards and a young page on duty.

Well, that was convenient. He would have a chance to impress, not only his master, but the other dignitaries, with the diligence of those from Karse. Anything that could show Karsites in a good light was definitely to be pursued.

He had the page inside the chamber show him where Ulrich's seat was, and took the lesser one beside it. He opened his pouch and took out everything in it, sharpening his pens, making certain the ink was mixed, readying all his materials so that there would be no unseemly fumbling with pouch, pen, and papers when the meeting began.

Just as he completed his arrangements, the rest of those who were to attend the meeting began to filter in. He recognized all of the Councilors, of course, though they paid him no attention whatsoever. *Both* gryphons arrived with Firesong between them, and they took a place behind him, since they obviously would never fit at the table itself. The Shin'a'in envoy arrived as well, and with her, Ulrich.

Well, *that* was certainly interesting. Had Ulrich been engaged in a private discussion with her before this meeting? The way they were talking suggested that he had been. But Ulrich's seat was at one end of the horseshoe-shaped table, and the Shin'a'in's seat was at the other, next to Firesong.

Ah, I see—they have us grouped by geography—those who live near each other are seated next to each other. That's useful, and practical as well.

Ulrich sat down next to Karal with a smile of approval for his preparations: Karal was not the only secretary attending this meeting, but he was clearly the best organized of the lot. The others were fumbling out their supplies and trying to be unobtrusive at the same time, and it wasn't working.

The envoy from Rethwellan was supposed to sit next to Ulrich, but to Karal's astonishment, which he quickly cloaked, it was the Prince-Consort who took the chair there. A solemn-faced young man in sober blue took the seat next to Daren's, and prepared to take his own set of notes on behalf of the Prince.

So the Prince-Consort also plans to act as the Rethwellan envoy? That's just a little irregular, isn't it? But no one else seemed to mind, and only the Shin'a'in envoy raised an eyebrow. On the other hand, Daren had once been his brother's Lord Martial, and presumably could still speak with authority on military matters within Rethwellan. Perhaps he was the best choice for this meeting.

Eventually the Queen herself arrived with very little fanfare. Talia came quietly along behind her, and took up a special seat that Karal had *thought* was for the Prince Consort.

Evidently not. He studied the Queen's Own, wondering just what the basis for her position was here. Clearly she was some kind of advisor, but what did she do? *I'm going to have to ask someone some time soon.* These Valdemarans were so surprising that they might even tell him the truth!

When everyone attending the meeting was seated, and all the underlings had their papers and supplies in order, the Queen stood. Selenay wore only a circlet of gold on her head to denote her rank; otherwise her clothing was nothing more than a richer version of the Herald's livery. That in itself was fascinating, because Solaris of all of the Sons of the Sun in living memory was doing precisely the same thing with *her* robes of office. She seldom wore the Crown of Prophecy except when the Voice was going to possess her; as for the rest, the sole symbol of her office was the special Sundisk pectoral that only the Son of the Sun wore, a neckpiece as ancient as Karse itself. Her robes were the same as any other Priest; save only that the cloth was a little softer, of a slightly finer weave. This was very effective, as it made her seem much more approachable than any of her predecessors. Had she taken her cue from the Queen of Valdemar, or had she contrived the notion herself?

"The forces of the Eastern Empire are currently not moving forward through Hardorn," the Queen began, as soon as the murmur of talk was replaced by silence. It was odd, but she looked a lot calmer than Karal would have been in identical circumstances. He made note of that; impressions could be useful. "We have taken this opportunity to gather intelligence information, and we have called this Council to present it to the representatives of all of our allies at once. Much of this will be new even to me."

Ah. So she isn't using the royal plural; when she says "we," at least in this Council, she is talking about more people than just herself. Also useful to know.

And with that, she sat down and gestured to the first of a series of underlings to come forward and make his report.

Karal took copious notes. The first was a basic report on how much territory the Empire had already annexed, and the current situation with what was left of a government in that portion of Hardorn still held by loyalists.

The news wasn't good. The Empire held roughly half of Hardorn at this point. There was resistance, which became more organized with every passing day, but the question in the minds of those who had written this report was whether or not it would become well-organized enough in time to actually stop the Empire short of the Valdemar border.

"The current government consists of a Special Council," the clerk read, as Karal wondered who had been intrepid enough to ferret out all this information. It *had* to have been obtained at firsthand. "There are thirty surviving nobles, the heads of the Guilds, and someone who claims that he speaks for all the mages who are left. It is the opinion of those who have watched this Special Council in action that they are still disordered and demoralized, and a single leader has yet to emerge from the chaos."

The clerk presented his papers to the Queen and bowed himself out. She looked straight at Ulrich as she accepted them, but she waited until the clerk was gone before saying anything. "My Lord Ulrich," Selenay said smoothly, "has your leader any interest in this situation while it remains on the opposite side of her borders?"

Karal fully expected Ulrich to say nothing, but once again, his master surprised him. "I would be lying, and we both know it, if I said that this was *not* a very tempting situation for us, your Highness," he replied, just as smoothly. "The secular advisors to Her Holiness would like nothing better than to annex a bit of Hardorn while the situation is so very unstable, and they have, in fact, so advised her. We might already have done so—but for one insurmountable barrier." He raised his eyebrow. "The Voice of Flame spoke through Her Holiness and made His Will quite plain, to the public in general, and again to Her Holiness in her private meditations. Vkandis Sunlord does *not* approve of the notion of increasing Karse beyond the present border, and will make His displeasure clear to anyone who flouts His holy Will. Since that displeasure has been known to be fatal, no one has suggested any more annexations."

One of the Valdemar Councilors snorted in derision, but it was not Ulrich who answered that clear expression of disbelief.

"I do assure you, my lord," the Shin'a'in envoy said, in a tone of voice that put frost on the rim of every glass in the room, "while deities are not known for personally manifesting Their wrath inside your realm, we who live outside are quite accustomed to hearing our gods *and* obeying them. It is more than faith that governs us, it is *fact.*"

The Councilor in question flushed a painful scarlet and mumbled an apology in Ulrich's direction. The Priest bowed slightly in acknowledgment and acceptance, and the Queen took the floor again.

"It is just as tempting for Valdemar to act during this period of confusion," Selenay said gravely. "We are overcrowded with Hardornen refugees, for one thing. It would be very convenient for us to send them back into their own land again, under Valdemaran supervision. Sending military advisors, perhaps?"

The Councilor for the East asked for the floor. "We *have* been encouraging them to go back to Hardorn and take back their own land again, but it's very difficult to convince them to do so when *we* can promise them no help. Ancar drained his land dry, and times would be very hard there without an army of occupation holding half the country. They simply cannot do anything against the Empire without substantial aid."

"But if we offer them aid, we open up another bag of troubles entirely," the Lord Marshal said instantly. "At the moment, Hardorn is still a buffer between us and the Empire, and the Emperor seems in no great hurry to take the rest of the country. If the Emperor decided that offering aid to Hardorn was a direct act of aggression, he *could* escalate his occupation in order to get at us. Frankly, he can move more troops and resources faster than we can respond. I don't advise any kind of intervention, no matter what words or titles we cloak it in." His mouth twitched in a grimace of chagrin.

"I may be a military man, but I know my facts. Fact one—we don't have the resources to take on the Empire. Fact two—we can't afford to antagonize them. We have no choice."

"What *is* the Empire doing right now?" Prince Daren asked. In answer, Selenay gestured to Kerowyn, who stood up with a sheaf of papers in her hand.

"I have an intelligence report on precisely that right here," Kerowyn said, her voice carrying easily to all parts of the room. "In essence, they've stopped moving forward. My agents say that there is a new commander in charge of the entire operation, someone reporting directly to Emperor Charliss. This new commander seems to have decreed a halt to further conquest while he builds a supporting infrastructure behind his lines. How long that will take—I can't tell you. They have more resources than we do, and anybody with a lot of resources can do quite a bit very quickly, barring bad luck and acts of nature or gods."

"Granted." Prince Daren nodded. "Then what happens?"

"Once that is in place," Kerowyn continued, "chances are he will order another push forward, then halt to build, and repeat that pattern until he has the entire country. It's my opinion that he'll hold to that pattern as long as there is little or no organized resistance."

"What will he do when he reaches the Valdemar border and the Karsite border?" the Guild representative, Lady Cathal, asked in a tone of quiet tension.

Kerowyn shrugged. "Frankly, he's got a big enough army that if I were in his shoes, I wouldn't stop. I'd keep right on going as long as losses were acceptable. And don't ask me what 'acceptable losses' are for him; the entire population of all our peoples could be less than a regional garrison to them. I don't know what counts as 'acceptable,' because he hasn't yet met with any resistance that's given him any palpable losses at all. I haven't been able to see the conditions that make his commanders pull back. For Ancar, *any* losses were acceptable as long as he took ground. For us—we're more inclined to retreat than lose lives. He could follow either pattern, but chances are he'll be somewhere in the middle. I can tell you this; 'acceptable losses' will be a percentage of his troops, rather than a hard number. One percent of *his* strength is a lot more in real numbers of men than one percent of *ours.*"

"And our land is worn out from the conflict with Ancar," the Lord Marshal pointed out glumly. "We could mount some resistance, but how could it be enough to discourage an army like the Eastern Empire can field?"

"Karse is not in much better shape than Valdemar, although we took little direct damage," Ulrich added. "Indirectly—we did lose troops to Ancar, and mages that we sent up here to you."

"And speaking of mages," Kerowyn put in, taking over the floor again, "the Empire seems to have mages that do things differently than ours do. Many of you have heard Elspeth describe how the Imperial Ambassador to Hardorn created a Gate without any physical counterpart, and our mages have all reacted to *that* bit of news with dropped jaws. Maybe these mages are better than ours, and maybe they aren't. It hardly matters; they're *different,* and that's a problem. Vastly different approaches to mage-craft make it quite likely that they can hit us with something we would never expect in a hundred years."

"And there are," Firesong added smoothly, "many, many *more* mages in the Empire than the entire Alliance can currently supply. Again, that is a real fact. Herald Captain Kerowyn asked me to look at the section of her intelligence report that deals with magic. It is evident to me that much of Imperial infrastructure depends very heavily on mages. I would judge, from the descriptions in the report, that they use mages for communication, construction, and transportation, making their conventional supply-lines much different from what we would use. In layman's terms, I believe that all of their supplies come from deep within the Empire itself by means of Gates. If they can afford to use mages for tasks where we would use carts, workers, and messengers, what kind of offensive magics can they muster?"

"I'm not sure I want to think about it," someone muttered grimly, as shocked silence fell around the table.

Kerowyn is a good commander who does not shrink away from the truth, however unpleasant, Karal decided, and wrote exactly that down. *She has a talent for stating baldly the things that no one else truly wants to consider.*

Finally the Lord Patriarch cleared his throat, making no few of those sitting around the table start. "Well," he said, unsteadily, "What *are* our options, with such a force levied against us? It begins to look as if the only one we have is to pray!"

The Shin'a'in envoy looked at Firesong, and he nodded, deferring to her. She stood up, took a pointer from a page, and went to the great map inlaid on the wall.

"The Shin'a'in and the Tayledras have agreed to establish safeholds in the west, in this line," she said, pointing out a line that began at the southern rim of Lake Evendim and continued down to the Dhorisha Plains. "We will hold a safe path of retreat at all times, just as we did during the war with Ancar. We can also receive some of your Hardornen refugees that are willing to take a chance on making new homes in the west, and we hope that this will take some of the strain from the resources of Valdemar."

She sat down again, and Firesong took up where she had left off. "I must admit to you all, however, that as reinforcements, both of our peoples are fairly useless. We are equipped to wage very small-scale battles at the best. The Shin'a'in excel as individual warriors, but they have no organization or structure above the Clan hunting party. The Tayledras have better organization among our scouts, but again, we field very small units. We can offer a place of retreat, we can offer some support, but as *armies* go—" his expression was rueful, "—we can't manage much that is going to be useful to you."

"What about mages?" The Guild representative called.

"Ah, mages." Firesong nodded. "First of all, the Shin'a'in do *not* have mages. However, the Kaled'a'in—that is an offshoot tribe of both our peoples—do practice magic, and the Star-Eyed has given them leave to use it up here, am I correct?" He glanced back at the gryphon called Treyvan, who chuckled.

"Betterrr sssay that Ssshe hasss given them theirrr marrrching ordersss," the gryphon said, with a glance over at the fellow who had expressed scorn over Vkandis' implied power. "Asss sssomeone elsssse herrre pointed out, therrre arrre sssome of usss who arrre usssed to hearrring dirrrectly from ourrr godsss."

"So, that's one group—and I have to admit that even I am not certain what these magic-users can and cannot do. They have been separated from us for a very long time, and casually use things that we had long considered lost arts. We, the Tayledras, are also prepared to strip the Vales of mages and bring them here. We will not endanger our Vales, but there are many projects that can wait a little longer while we aid you."

"White Winds, Blue Mountain, and any other school we can contact will be doing the same," the White Winds representative put in. *Quenten, I think. A friend of Kerowyn.* Karal noted that they appeared to be about the same age. "If the Empire moves this far west, we freelance mages cannot afford to stand by idly. The Empire will annex *us,* or destroy us. That has been their policy in the past, and it is what they are doing now in Hardorn."

Firesong nodded. "I did say that there is no way that we can even begin to equal the sheer number of mages that the Empire can bring to bear—and I still mean that. However, the fact that the Empire works in a different tradition from us can work against them as well. If we don't know what *they* can do, the reverse is true for them. Right now, absolutely the best thing we can concentrate on is to learn everything we can about the Empire and its mages."

"True, and we're working on that," Kerowyn replied, "but don't forget they'll be doing the same thing about us."

Karal was taking notes furiously, while fighting his wish to gawk at the rest of the table. Firesong was as flamboyant as the last time Karal had seen him, though this time his color of choice was scarlet with touches of bright blue; the Shin'a'in envoy was sleekly exotic, as quiet and deadly as one of her arrows.

Then there were the gryphons. Once again, hearing an intelligible, intelligent sentence emerge from those beaks gave him something of a start. If he had not seen the Firecat Hansa conferring with Solaris with his own eyes, he would have been even more startled—and inclined to suspect trickery, some kind of magic to make it *look* as if the "beast" was speaking.

Ulrich stood up, and all eyes went to him. "I am inclined to agree with the Herald Captain in principle," he said, carefully, "But there is another factor involved here. The Empire is enormous, very old, and has probably never met with serious opposition in a very long time. They are likely to be used to these favorable conditions. They may very well dismiss all of us as 'barbarians' and inconsequential. They may not pursue their own intelligence-gathering operations as vigorously as they should. We cannot *count* on this, of course—" he added, as Kerowyn looked ready to protest such hubris, "—but we should be watching for patterns that indicate this. In fact, I believe that we should pursue the notion of planting information that we are as disorganized on this side of the border as the poor Hardornens are, and as paralyzed with terror. If we see the attitude of complacence developing, we will then be poised to take instant advantage of it."

Kerowyn smiled broadly at that, and bowed a little in acknowledgment of Ulrich's cleverness. He returned the ironic little salute as he regained his seat.

"What about the mages of Valdemar?" Prince Daren asked into the silence.

Now it was Elspeth's turn, and she rose to her feet. "The obvious answer is that we should train as many, and as quickly, as we can—which we are doing. The second obvious answer is that we should also recruit as many freelance mages from the south as possible, just as we did during the last conflict with Ancar. The problem with that second obvious answer is that other than mages from the Kaled'a'in and Tayledras, and those coming from schools and teachers personally known to Quenten, we *have* to suspect that at least some of the mages we might recruit from the south are agents of the Empire. Most of the mages that Quenten knows and can vouch for are already up here. That leaves us with the first answer. We're training our own—but there are only so many of them."

"Whoa, wait a moment," Kerowyn interrupted, a look of concentration on her face. "I just thought of something. Why make so hard a push for mages at all?"

"But—!" someone cried, triggering a storm of protest from around the table; she waved the protests away.

"No, I'm serious. What put the idea in everyone's head that mages were the answer to everything?" she asked.

Well that certainly put a fox among the hens. Stunned silence reigned for a moment, until Kerowyn broke it.

"Yes, we *needed* them desperately when we were fighting Ancar, but that was because without them there were things he could field that we simply couldn't fight. But that's not the case now." More protests erupted; she waved for further silence. "Wait, hear me out!"

The Queen herself ordered silence when it was obvious Kerowyn was not going to command it herself. From the looks of suppressed panic around the table, unless Kerowyn made her point very well, the silence was not going to last very long.

"Look," Kerowyn said earnestly, leaning over the table to emphasize her point. "The things that the Empire is simply not prepared for are the factors that make Karse and Valdemar absolutely unique in their experience. In Karse—it's something *we* aren't even prepared for, the fact that Vkandis Sunlord can, will, and *does* intervene with and guide His people directly. For all I know, if the Empire penetrates the borders of Karse, He might even decide to lob a few firebolts at some select Imperial generals!"

"It would take more than simply penetrating our border to cause Him to do so," Ulrich murmured gently, as she looked at him with expectation, "but it is possible He could choose to intervene selectively."

"Yes, well, miracles do happen with predictable regularity in Karse," she retorted.

Ulrich simply smiled very, very slightly.

"That's going to make it difficult, if not impossible, for the Empire to attack successfully in that direction. And meanwhile, I'll bet your Sunlord is doing something else the Empire isn't prepared for. I'll bet He's feeding Solaris with better information than any of my agents can get," Kerowyn stated baldly, then smiled at Ulrich's cautious nod. "Well, I've got some good news for you and your people. As far as my spies have been able to determine, the people of the Empire have a state religion that venerates the current Emperor, his predecessors, and all his ancestors. I'm sure that's very nice for Charliss, but I've got no evidence that he has any special power that an Adept couldn't duplicate, which means that the Sunlord isn't going to be squaring off against another deity if He does decide to throw firebolts around."

Karal scribbled all this down furiously.

"Ah," Ulrich said, brightening. "That does put the likelihood of intervention, at least within the Karsite borders, much higher."

"Thought so," Kerowyn said, with an even bigger smile. "All right, then. In Valdemar, one thing that the Empire is not prepared for is the simple existence of the Heralds and Companions. We have brought mind-magic to a high art here; I don't think there's another place north of Ceejay that has people using mind-magic so—scientifically. For that matter, I don't know that there's anyone using it this way *south* of Ceejay either."

Quenten shrugged. "Not that I've ever heard of."

Kerowyn nodded. "That's what I thought. We had to do without magic from the time of Vanyel; we found ways to deal with problems that didn't require magic. *They* put a tremendous emphasis on magic—you all heard the report, they do things with magic we wouldn't dream of, but that makes them very vulnerable if they expect us to do the same and plan their magical attacks accordingly."

Firesong nodded vigorously, Ulrich cautiously; Elspeth simply looked thoughtful. "That sounds good for a working premise," Elspeth said at last.

"So, this time we have one thing that we didn't have when we were fighting off Ancar—we have time, while they're busy eating Hardorn a gulp at a time." Kerowyn shrugged. "I know it sounds cold-hearted, but just at the moment I can't recommend helping the Hardornens directly. My recommendation is that we study the Empire, we make diplomatic overtures to them to buy time, and we find out how we can counter their magic *without* using magic of our own—or with using mind-magic instead. We use what we can apply with confidence to the absolute limit, because they simply will not be expecting that."

More nods around the table, as Karal caught up with everything that had been said so far. He was *very* glad now for all those lessons from Alberich; without them, he'd have been lost long before this.

Prince Daren spoke up next.

"The Empire waited decades—maybe longer—before they moved on Hardorn," he pointed out. "They actually *attacked* only when they could do so with an absolute minimum of resistance. We know they had an agent at the highest levels to feed them accurate intelligence—we should assume that they have had agents there all along. If we convince them that it would be too expensive to take us, they may decide not to."

"We can hope for that," Selenay said. "We can work toward convincing them of that. But we cannot risk *assuming* that."

"Agreed," rumbled the Lord Marshal.

There was more discussion, a few more pertinent comments and additions, but on the whole the real work of the meeting was over at that point. When people had begun repeating what had already been stated, Selenay called a halt to it all, and declared the meeting closed.

It was not too soon for Karal; his fingers were beginning to cramp.

And none of this had driven An'desha and An'desha's plight out of his mind. He could not wait to get Ulrich alone, and see what his mentor had to offer.

"You're very quiet tonight," Firesong observed, as An'desha stared at lamplight reflected in the waterfall. "Are you well?"

"Just tired," An'desha replied truthfully. "I did some work in the garden, and then repeated all the mage-exercises you showed me until my control felt uncertain; then I quit."

Firesong looked pleased, and An'desha relaxed. He had made the conscious decision to keep this new friendship with the Karsite a secret from Firesong for at least a little while. That was partly because he was not certain how Firesong would react to such a revelation. Granted, Firesong had been encouraging him to be more sociable, but An'desha was not altogether sure what he would do if he learned that An'desha had made *a,* singular, friend. Especially when he found that friend was male.

It had occurred to him that under those circumstances, Firesong was very likely to come to the erroneous conclusion that his friendship with Karal was based on physical attraction, not mental attraction, and that it might go beyond mere "friendship" before too long.

No, it would be a good thing to keep his meetings with Karal between the two of them—unless Karal brought his master, Lord Priest Ulrich, along. Then it should be safe enough to reveal.

The oddest thing is, he'd never make the same assumption if my friend was female, and it would be far more likely that I'd—ah—get involved with a female than with another man.

"Any more of those premonitions of doom?" Firesong asked, a little teasingly. "They might be useful, actually; it seems that the mages in the Empire—"

Premonitions of doom—

An'desha gasped, as the ground seemed to drop out from underneath him, and Firesong's voice faded into a roar that filled his ears. He clutched at the rock he was sitting on, but his fingers didn't work. Darkness assaulted him—then blinding light. Then darkness again, filled with the twisting snakes of red An'desha always saw after a bright light. He tried to scream and couldn't. He couldn't even feel his jaws opening.

Then light, striking him in concentric circles. It was almost as if something had picked him up and was shaking him, waving him as a maiden might wave a scarf in the Rainbird Dance. And everywhere, everywhere, was terrible fear, filling him with icy paralysis. Then the darkness again, and then less light than before, then darkness.

Then it was over, as swiftly and without warning as it had begun. He found himself falling backward, still on his stone, Firesong clutching his shoulders and staring into his eyes, while *his* hands held to the rock underneath him, spasmed into rigidity.

"What—?" he choked out.

"You were in a trance," Firesong said, testing An'desha's forehead with the back of his hand for fever. "You cried out once, and grabbed for the stone—I saw how your eyes looked, and sensed power about you, and knew you were in a trance. You looked terrified."

"I was. Am." An'desha gulped. "It was terrible, horrible, yet there was nothing that I can describe. Light and dark in waves, disorientation."

Firesong looked into his eyes, and frowned. "It happened when I asked if you were still troubled by premonitions. This seems too well-timed a response to be simple coincidence."

Numbly, An'desha nodded. If anything, his sense of dread, his tension, had *increased* now.

"Listen, and I will tell you what was related at the Council," Firesong said at last. "Mornelithe Falconsbane was not given to prescience—but *you* are not he, and there is no reason why you should not have that Gift. For that matter, *She* might well have granted it to you; as we were reminded at the Council, there are more hands than the merely human working in this stewpot now."

I wouldn't be too sure that I am not Falconsbane, An'desha thought bleakly, but he listened quietly while Firesong recited what had transpired at the meeting.

"Did anything I spoke of wake a resonance with you?" he asked, when he was done. An'desha had to shake his head.

"Nothing," he said sadly. "You might as well have been telling me facts concerning cattle or sheep. It meant nothing."

Firesong tugged at a lock of silver hair, frowning. "I am at a loss," he said finally. "It would seem to me that our great enemy is at hand—that the Empire and all the Empire's mages should be the source of your fears, and yet—"

"It is not the Empire, peacock!" An'desha retorted, losing his temper. "I have been *trying* to tell you that! It is something else, something we have not even dreamed of! And I think—" he gulped and felt his skin turn cold and clammy as he voiced what he feared he must do, "—I think there is some key to it among the memories that the Great Beast left with me."

Firesong winced, but a moment later placed one hand comfortingly over An'desha's clenched fist. "Then we must examine those memories," he replied, with more gentleness than An'desha would ever have credited him with. "You and

I. I have been remiss in forcing you to walk those paths alone, An'desha. I had been so certain that I knew what the answer to your fears was." An'desha stared at him, startled at this new and unwonted humility. "I do not know. Captain Kerowyn made it very clear to me in ways I could not ignore after the Council meeting that these Imperial mages were so very different from anything I have ever experienced that it was wildly unlikely I would be able to counter anything they brought to bear on us effectively." Then a ghost of his old self came back for a moment. "Or at least, it would be unlikely the *first* time they unleashed something upon us. I daresay once I had seen it, I could deal with it."

Then even that bit of arrogance faded. "Still, they need only keep changing their weaponry—and the Captain pointed out that what I cannot anticipate, I cannot *personally* guard against, either." His own face grew paler as he looked solemnly into An'desha's eyes. "For the first time in my life, I cannot be sure that I can guard *myself* from harm. That is— very unsettling. Even when wrestling the power of a renegade Heartstone I did not have such a sense of mortality as I do now. It makes me unsure."

Oh, most lovely. Now what?

"But if that is true, then it is also true that things I had assumed—things regarding you—might also be incorrect." He sighed. "So, now, at long last, I *am* listening to you. And I am asking you; what do *you* think we, together, should do?"

Run away! his cowardly inner self said. But he swallowed, took a steadying breath, and said, a bit shakily, "You must help me with those memories of lives that Falconsbane had before he took my body. We must go farther than I have dared to."

If only the Avatars would come again, he thought, stifling fear, as Firesong nodded his agreement. *They knew what it is I am floundering about in search of—*

Or did they? In all their warnings, they had seemed to bear a sense of frustration that they could not explain themselves clearly. Perhaps even *they* did not know. They were very near to the flesh-and-blood bodies they had once worn, after all, and in fact, Tre'valen and Dawnfire were not technically "dead" at all as they had explained it to him. That was *why* they had been able to help him, so far from the Plains and the Hills, and out of the range of the Star-Eyed's influence.

They are likely back where they might do some good, doing—whatever it is that Avatars do. Perhaps they are aiding the Kal'enedral, the Swordsworn. I do not think they have the power to aid me now.

But Firesong did. As frightening and as perilous as it might be to invoke *anything* connected with the creature that had once possessed his body, An'desha could not in conscience see any other choice.

"Perhaps we should begin tonight?" he suggested timidly.

Firesong nodded gravely. "I think it would be best, *ke'chara.* Before we both lose our nerve."

Ah, but mine is already lost, An'desha thought, yet he did not protest as Firesong helped him to his feet, and led him to their heavily-shielded circle in the garden where all An'desha's fumblings at magic took place. *But perhaps—perhaps now I can find new bravery. . . .*

Natoli

11

"So—there was *nothing* left of the False One?" An'desha had listened, completely enthralled, to Karal's tale of how the Son of the Sun came to power. There was something oddly comforting in the notion that there were other peoples whose deities tended to express themselves as directly as the Star-Eyed did. More directly, in fact, although An'desha could not even begin to envision how a false prophet could ever set himself up as sole authority to the Shin'a'in, much less how an entire succession of them could have. The Star-Eyed would have been much more likely to have arranged for the first fool to be eaten by something large and predatory before he ever became a problem.

"Nothing. Just a pile of smoldering ashes." Karal nodded. "It was quite—ah—daunting. It made me certain that I never wanted to find myself receiving the Sunlord's direct regard. I will be quite *happy* to remain in obscurity!"

"I can well understand that," An'desha replied. "The Star-Eyed is—a little more subtle." *That may be the understatement of the century. Kal'enel is not inclined to strike people dead with lightning even at Her angriest.*

The serene little indoor garden had become their meeting place; they were reasonably certain of being left alone there, and since An'desha and Firesong already practiced all magic there, it was one place where An'desha felt relatively confident. And no matter what the weather—which continued to be uncertain—it was always balmy summer in this miniature Vale.

He noted that Karal was no longer wincing whenever he

mentioned the Shin'a'in Goddess, and his dark eyes no longer clouded with unease. *Poor Karal. He was so shocked at first to learn that Vkandis might not be the One True God.*

"But then again," An'desha continued with a shrug. "She and He are both gods, so who are we to say what they will and will not do? For all that I was touched by the Star-Eyed's own hand, I am still hardly qualified to judge Her or Her probable actions."

Karal coughed politely. An'desha took the hint.

"Speaking of probable actions—I spoke with Ulrich about you." Karal waited for An'desha's reaction.

His reaction would have been enthusiastic enough to satisfy anyone. Excitement sent a chill along his arms. "Will he come? Has he time? Does he think he can help?" An'desha had spent enough time delving back into the memories of Falconsbane's previous lives to feel as if the already uncertain ground beneath him had become a quagmire. He couldn't help thinking that only extreme good fortune had kept him from stepping into a bottomless pit that would swallow him up before he could cry out for help. He'd had a particularly hag-ridden nightmare last night, after yet another stroll through the memory-fragments of the past. He'd spent the rest of the night huddled into a blanket in a fearful ball of misery, and finally Firesong had thrown his hands up and lost patience with him after failing to calm him. Firesong had gone off to the garden to sleep, leaving An'desha to watch out the last of the night by himself.

I knew that he was right, that it had only been a nightmare, but what could such nightmares lead to? What if I fell into one and never came out again? That was what held me so terrified that he could not comfort me. I don't know how many more nights like that I can go through.

Karal nodded solemnly. "He said he would try to come this afternoon, unless I came to tell him otherwise. Shall I go see if he is free?"

"Please!" An'desha replied, with more force than he had intended. He made himself relax, though Karal gave no sign that he was alarmed by the violent response. "Please. Things are—I would truly like to speak with him."

"He'll come. I'll go find him now." Karal knew An'desha

well enough by now to take him seriously. He got up and trotted off without another word, leaving An'desha alone in the garden again. Although An'desha was not normally given to pacing, he did so now. After all this time—someone who understood his pain and his peril, who was willing to help him—

What would this Ulrich be like? *Let him not be like the shaman of my Clan . . . that would leave matters worse than they are now!* He could not bear that—to have someone deliver a lecture to him on his own moral weakness, on how he should be showing some spine instead of cowering like a child afraid of monsters in the tent shadows. He *was* doing his best, he *was!* Even if Firesong didn't think so—

Now that the moment was at hand, he was rapidly tangling into a knot of tension.

"Here we are. I found him on the very path," said Karal cheerfully, from the door. An'desha spun about to see his friend entering through the doorway, with a much older man beside him, a man who walked carefully and a little stiffly.

As they neared, An'desha noted the calm expression on the older man's face—a face, thin and intelligent, with a sharp and prominent nose and matching chin. He and Karal were very much of a "type," as Shin'a'in, Kaled'a'in and Tayledras were of a "type." Interesting, since Valdemarans were as mixed in "type" as a litter of mongrel puppies.

The priest had probably seen some fifty summers or so; his silver hair had a few black threads in it, but not many. But more important to An'desha than his years was his expression; there was none of the querulous impatience An'desha remembered the shaman wearing more often than not.

"An'desha." The man bowed a little in greeting to An'desha, rather than extending his hand to be clasped as Valdemarans did. "Karal has told me something of you and your plight, but I would like to hear it all from your lips, as well." He smiled a little, and his eyes wrinkled at the corners. "Sometimes things can be garbled in the translation, as any diplomat will tell you."

The smile was enough to convince An'desha that, whatever Ulrich was, he was nothing like the shaman. The shaman had *never* smiled.

Ulrich listened to his history and his current fears with no sign of impatience, and even took him back over a few points to clarify them. As Ulrich questioned him, An'desha was reminded more and more of the spirit-sword Need, the blade that was now carried by Nyara. Need had coached him through his ordeal as he acted against Mornelithe Falconsbane from—literally—within. She had never promised more than a chance at his freedom; she had never given him pity or sympathy, only guidance.

Ulrich was of a similar mind. He did not want to hear excuses, and would not accept them if An'desha tried to make them—but as long as An'desha had clearly been doing his best, Ulrich would praise him for it, and make allowances for things that could not yet be helped.

He did spend quite a bit of time asking many questions about An'desha's experiences with the Avatars, after An'desha mentioned them. He had done so with extreme caution, remembering how shocked Karal had been at the intimation that there were more real deities in the world than his own. But to An'desha's relief and mild amusement, Ulrich was not only *not* shocked, he seemed to accept it as a matter of course.

"You do believe me, don't you?" he asked, when Ulrich fell silent. "I mean, you believe me about Dawnfire and Tre'valen, that they *are* Her Avatars, and not something I hallucinated, or something else."

Ulrich took a moment to think before replying. "I admit that such an explanation had occurred to me, when you first mentioned them," he said at last, steepling his fingers together. "You hardly qualified as sane under normal definitions. But after all you have told me, I am quite certain that they are exactly what you claim. And that your 'Star-Eyed' is what you claim Her to be."

Karal made a small sound, something like a strangled cough; An'desha glanced aside and saw him turning a fascinating color.

Ulrich chuckled and turned to his protégé. "What, surprised to hear me say that, young one?" he chided gently. "Did you think me so bound by the letter of the Writ? Here is another lesson for you. Most wise priests are well aware that the Light can take many forms, many names, and all are valid. It is there in the earliest copies of the Writ, for those who care to look."

He turned back to An'desha. "It is a man's deeds that define him," he said earnestly. "As I believe Karal has told you—Vkandis Himself has passed that stricture to us, that a good deed done in the name of the Dark is still done for the Light, but an evil one done in the name of the Light is still quite evil, and a soul could be condemned to Darkness for it."

An'desha nodded, as much relieved by those words as by anything else Ulrich could have said or done. The tradition-bound shaman of An'desha's Clan would never have said anything like *that*.

"I have always felt," Ulrich continued thoughtfully, "that before I passed judgment on any man because of the god he swore by, I would see how he comported himself with his fellows—what he did, and how he treated them. If he acted with honor and compassion, the Name he called upon was irrelevant."

All very well, An'desha thought, after a moment of silence, *And I am glad he feels this way—but what about me? What about the dreams, and—*

"However, that has nothing to do with your predicament, An'desha," Ulrich said, startling him. Could Ulrich read his mind? "You have some very real fears that need to be addressed. Let me start with the one closest to your heart—the fear that you are still possessed by that evil creature that called himself Bane-of-Falcons."

An'desha leaned forward eagerly, misgivings forgotten. Point by point, with careful detail, Ulrich proved to him that he knew what he was talking about—and that, as Firesong and everyone else had said, Falconsbane was *gone*.

What convinced him was that Ulrich had a reason—a sound, believable reason, for some of the things he'd been experiencing. "There really is a simple explanation. You are only now able to feel the physical effects of your emotions, after so many years existing only as a disembodied spirit, so to speak," Ulrich told him patiently. "For you, such things are as fresh and startling as regained sight for one who was blinded, or hearing restored to the deaf! Think of how such a former deaf man would react to a sudden noise—and then think how you are reacting to a sudden surge of emotion. Not only that, you are feeling the sweat of your palms, flushing of the skin or paleness that come with emotions, for the first time in a very long time. They must feel overwhelming to you, easy to interpret as signs of possession. Yet you now feel them with your own body, and not one taken over by an evil spirit."

An'desha nodded, very slowly. This made such good sense, he hardly knew what to think.

"I'm not—I cannot seem to deal with all this," he began hesitantly.

Ulrich smiled. "If you were handling all this well, *then* I would suspect another possessing spirit, for no sane human could be taking your situation *well* at this moment!"

Weakly, An'desha returned his smile. "I suppose you are right, when you put it that way—"

"An'desha, not every soul is suited to being a Priest, or a conquering hero, or a serene Healer. You blame yourself for being a coward, when in fact you show more bravery than anyone should expect of you. Judge yourself, not what others would think of you, and be content with what you can do. This does not excuse you from learning how to control your emotions," Ulrich warned. "The shadow of your demon still lurks there. His taint is that it is much, much easier for you to feel anger than joy, hatred than compassion. These are old, worn paths through your body, which will react according to long habit—and old, worn paths through your mind, which experienced what Falconsbane experienced. It is always easier to take the well-worn path than the new one. You must over-come that taint. The scars upon your soul can be smoothed away, but it will take not only time, but your own will, that you will prove to be nothing like him."

That, too, made sense, and An'desha nodded, more com-forted now than he could express. Granted, others—including Firesong—had said exactly the same things to him, though in different words, and with no explanations; but this time he felt he could believe them, since they came from an impartial source.

Perhaps Ulrich *was* a kind of Mind-Healer—or perhaps, a Spirit-Healer, if there was such a thing.

And who am I to say that there is not? Karal said so. I think that I must believe him.

"But this other—this great fear you have that there is danger for all of us that we cannot foresee—this troubles me," Ulrich continued. "This may be something you are sensitive to because of those ancient memories you carry; that would be *my* guess, at least." He chewed his bottom lip thoughtfully. "If you would like it put another way, part of you, the part of you that holds those ancient memories, *knows* what they contain, and knows that there is something going on at this moment that relates to those memories, or even matches them. But most of you does not want to face those terrible memories. So, that part of you that is aware and knowledgeable is trying to force the rest of you to become aware and knowledgeable." He cocked an eyebrow at An'desha. "Am I making sense to you, or is all this gibberish?"

"It is making sense," he replied dazedly. In fact, like the other explanation, it was making a little too much sense. He'd had a sense of being divided internally for some time now, but he had thought it was a sign of Falconsbane's continued presence. Now he had another explanation for the feeling, and it was one that did not cater to his fears and left him no excuse for inaction—

Which makes it more likely to be the right one.

"It is what the shaman called 'The Warrior Within.' The voice inside us that tells us what we must know," An'desha said slowly. "The source of all honor, faith, and prosperity under the Goddess is that voice, if we listen with wisdom, they say."

Ulrich studied his face as he sat there with all those powerful thoughts passing through his mind; at last the priest nodded, as if he was satisfied with what he read there. He raised an eyebrow at Karal.

"I have laid the foundation," he said to his protégé. "I think you can complete the work. Simply keep your mind as open as it has become, and I do not think you will misstep."

He turned back to An'desha. "The bulk of your solutions lie within you, I do think," Ulrich told him. "Karal will help you, but on the whole, you will be doing the real work to find them. I will do what I can, but there is nothing that I see in you now that requires my further help."

Which meant—what? That he *had* needed Ulrich's help until this moment?

"I would be the last person to assert that things cannot change, however," Ulrich continued. "If they do, I would be distressed if you did not come to me. Meanwhile, you may trust Karal. He is sensible, he has learned good judgment, he is not afraid of the strange or the powerful, and he has, most of all, a good heart."

Then, while Karal was still blushing a brilliant sunset-crimson, Ulrich got up and left the two of them alone again.

With Ulrich's encouragement, Karal spent as much of his free time as possible with An'desha. As the days passed, Karal became more and more convinced that Ulrich was right; the key to everything An'desha feared lay in those buried memories. Not only was there something in those recollections that was triggering An'desha's prescient episodes *and* his nightmares, but there were also things about An'desha himself that needed to be dealt with.

So Karal continued to work on the "foundation" that Ulrich had established; building An'desha's confidence, convincing him that he *had* passions and would make purely human mistakes, but that as long as he remembered to keep his *powers* under a tight rein, the mistakes he made would teach him how *not* to make other mistakes.

"Compassion and honor," he said, over and over again. "Those are what is important. So long as you have both, and act with both, you cannot make any mistake that will bring lasting harm."

"No?" An'desha replied with skepticism—a healthy sign, that he should respond with anything other than blind agreement. That meant he was thinking for himself. "But—"

"But good intentions count for something, else I'd have been condemned to Vkandis' coldest Hell long ago!" He grinned and hugged An'desha's shoulders. "If you have compassion and honor, and you made a mistake that harmed someone, must you not, out of compassion and honor, see that the mistake is *being* made and try to stop it?"

"Well, yes, I suppose," An'desha replied slowly.

"And having seen the effects of such a mistake, must you not also try to reverse them?" he continued, with purest logic. "Don't you see? Compassion and honor require that you *not* make excuses, nor allow yourself to say, 'nothing can be done.' So even if you make a mistake, you must fix it. You'll *want* to."

Perhaps because Karal had no great powers of his own, and yet was (relatively) fearless in the face of great powers, An'desha came to trust him, even as Ulrich claimed he would. And although An'desha was not told, Ulrich's interest went far beyond the one meeting. The priest questioned his protégé carefully every night, and asked Karal what his continuing plans were. He very seldom suggested any other course—Karal had the feeling that Ulrich was letting *him* make his own mistakes and rectify them as well—but it gave Karal a feeling of increased confidence to know that his mentor was keeping track of all this, though the progress came by infinitesimal increments.

But there was some measurable progress. An'desha *did* start looking at some of the older memories. He was already past the life of a strange creature that had called himself simply "Leareth" (which meant "Darkness" in the Hawkbrother tongue), a time that seemed to be several centuries ago.

And Firesong was a great deal happier with him, at least according to An'desha. An'desha carried some of his confidence back into his lessons with the Adept, and was making more and steadier progress toward using those powers he carried, instead of wishing them gone.

Success gave An'desha further courage to look farther and deeper into those dark memories, and to face what lay there.

And, just as important, An'desha was able to look at the terrible things in those memories and acknowledge, without flinching, that the hateful or jealous things *he* felt (and did not act on) could be considered a faint, far shadow of the dreadful things that the one who had been Falconsbane had done.

And Ulrich pointed out something that Karal had wondered about. The farther back those memories went, the *more* human, rather than less, that entity became. And the more "reasons" and excuses he made up to justify the unjustifiable.

Ulrich made no conclusions in Karal's hearing about the pattern, but it certainly left *him* wondering what it meant, and trying to come to a few conclusions of his own. He continued to read those ancient notebooks that Ulrich had given him, and found more than one place in the text that sounded familiar. Then he realized that Ulrich had been quoting extensively from these very texts when he had given An'desha that little speech about doing deeds in the name of the Light.

He was reading in his room, puzzling through another Valdemaran history that Alberich had recommended, when Ulrich cleared his throat from just outside his open door. He looked up, quickly, and sat straight up on his bed. His master wore an unusually serious expression, and his robes were not only immaculate, he was wearing one of his formal outfits, robes of heavy ebony silk that shone with full magnificence.

"I dislike ordering you out of your own room, Karal," his mentor said apologetically, "But I have only just arranged a meeting with someone very important, who wishes to discuss matters of a sensitive and theoretical nature. And if—"

"If I'm here, your important person won't talk, because I might overhear something. Yes, sir." Karal put a marker in his book and quickly got to his feet. "Since these discussions are theoretical, you won't need a record of them. I'm certain I can find something to occupy my time between now and— say—dinner? I'm already dressed for it, so I won't need to return."

"Excellent, and thank you." Ulrich stood aside to let him leave, with no further comment. Karal had been expecting something like this for the past few days; negotiations between his mentor and not only the Valdemaran government, but the Rethwellan government as well, had gotten to the point where some significant gains could be made. That meant private, one-to-one meetings, where both parties could discuss possibilities in total confidence and privacy.

As he walked down the wood-paneled hallway with a friendly nod to the guard patrolling there, he realized that he was, for once, completely at loose ends. An'desha would be with Firesong, in his magic-practices. There was no use going into the garden to be snubbed by the young nobles there—and it *was* snubbing, now; they had learned he was no noble, and saw no reason to treat him better than any other servant. The library, ordinarily enticing, was usually as full of young Heralds at this time of the afternoon as the gardens were full of young courtiers. *They* weren't snubbing him, but he wasn't in the mood for fending off questions and curious glances, either.

I'd ride, but I'm not exactly dressed for it, he thought wryly. Dressing for dinner early might not have been such a good idea. A pity; another workout wouldn't have hurt Trenor in the least. One simply did not go in to dinner with the Court smelling of horse, however.

That did give him an idea, though. He'd been passing through Companion's Field on a daily basis without gawking at the inhabitants, but he could spend whole marks watching real horses, so why not spend some time watching these not-horses? It might give him some insight into what they were.

With that in mind, he took himself down to the first door to the outside, and headed for the path that would take him to the Field.

While there were plenty of people about, none of them paid any attention to him. He leaned up against the fence and simply watched the graceful creatures, taking a completely aesthetic pleasure in the way they moved rather than consciously analyzing what they were doing. Within a very little time, though, he was aware that they did not act like horses at all. There was no sense of a "herd" at all; the closest to "herds" were small groups of foals playing together, with the mares standing or grazing nearby, very much like mothers keeping a careful eye on their toddlers while gossiping. There was no dominance-shoving or scuffling among the young stallions as there would have been in any other situation where there were mares present; rather, the young stallions were as calm as the mares, and the only way of telling one from the other was by the physical attributes. There *was* one stallion that every Companion there deferred to, but there was nothing of the submission to the dominant herd beast; they acted more like loyal courtiers with a genial and approachable monarch. It was rather fascinating, actually. Any person with a bit of knowledge of real horses would be well aware that this was not "normal" behavior. In fact, he had a disconcerting impression of a large group of people taking their ease in a park. . . .

"There have been times when I would have been pleased to have traded places with any of them," said a familiar voice behind him.

"I can certainly see why, Herald Rubrik," Karal replied, turning to greet their former guide with a smile. "Perhaps one day you will also be able to explain to me how a creature as large as your Companion can succeed in creeping up behind someone, while making no noise whatsoever!"

Rubrik shrugged, gazing down on Karal from his vantage point in his Companion's saddle. "I have no idea, but the gryphons are just as good at it. I've had the male come up behind me unexpectedly and scare the wits out of me; he didn't intend anything of the sort, and he was very apologetic about it, but I can't imagine how he managed to do it in the first place." The Herald eyed Karal speculatively. "Think you could spare a few moments to help me down?"

"Surely. Here, or at the barn?" he replied readily.

"The barn, if you would be so kind." Rubrik chuckled. "You aren't dressed for grooming, so I won't ask you to help me, but I'd appreciate some company while I take care of things."

"Actually, so would I," Karal admitted, as the Companion started off toward the gate at a sedate walk, and he took up a position at Rubrik's stirrup. "I found myself at loose ends, and I was just thinking how few people I really know here. Most of the ones I know by name, I do not know well enough to speak casually to."

"Ah." Rubrik nodded sagely. "I can see that. In part, I would suspect that is the burden of being a diplomat, if only by association. Whatever anyone says to you is likely to be scrutinized from every possible angle. And—I understand as a 'commoner' forced to operate socially with highly born folk with an exaggerated sense of the importance of bloodlines, things are not as pleasant for you as they could be. Your master is protected and given status by his rank as ambassador, but you are no more than a lowly secretary, completely beneath their notice. It is rather difficult to have an enlightening conversation under those circumstances."

Karal sighed, and fidgeted with his Vkandis-medal. "I could wish that was less accurate, sir."

"At least your Valdemaran has improved significantly," Rubrik observed as they reached the barn and crossed the threshold into the cool and shadowed interior.

Karal managed a smile. "If it had not, your own Herald Alberich would be having some irritated words with me. As I'm sure you are aware, his irritation is not an easy thing to bear!" He helped Rubrik from the saddle, then assisted with removing the tack and handing Rubrik grooming brushes while they talked.

Rubrik succeeded in drawing him out, as he had so many times in the past. It wasn't hard; Karal desperately wanted someone to talk to, and he realized before too long how much he had missed the older man's insights and quiet observations.

"I suppose I'm lonely," he said finally, with a sigh, as he leaned against the wall of a stall and watched Rubrik comb out his Companion's mane. "I was so much of a loner at home that I wasn't expecting to be lonely here, but it's harder than I thought, being so much a foreigner here. It's partly because in Karse, one of the Kin would feel at home in any holy place, and they were everywhere. But here, there is only one strange place after another."

"I think I might have a solution for you, rather than a handful of platitudes, for a change," Rubrik replied; a completely unexpected response. Karal stared at him as he patted his Companion and sent him on his way out the door, then turned back to him with a smile that hinted of plans behind Rubrik's eyes. "What if I found you someone about your own age to talk to? The Court is far from being *all* there is to this place, and even Herald's Collegium is not the center of the universe—though we'd like to think it is!"

Karal wasn't sure how to respond, so he just smiled weakly at this sally. Rubrik didn't take any offense at this lack of enthusiasm.

"There are quite a few young people your age here—far

more than either the Heraldic students or those conceited young nobles," he continued. "Would you care to meet people who are more concerned about your skills than your birth?"

"It sounds good, but I don't know, sir," Karal said carefully. "As you pointed out, I am a foreigner here and associated with the diplomatic mission. *They* might not care for *me*."

But Rubrik was not to be dissuaded, and put forth a number of convincing arguments. It sounded too good to be true, actually, and entirely too idealistic, but finally Karal allowed himself to be swayed by Rubrik's enthusiasm and agreed, keeping his reservations to himself.

Rubrik still had tack to clean, and was quite prepared to talk more, but time got away from them. As the warning bell rang to signal that dinner was imminent, he walked back to the Palace alone, wondering who this mysterious group of people *was*. He certainly hadn't seen any sign of them in all the time he'd been here. And why would they be any different from—say—the Heraldic trainees?

Oh, well, he decided, as he entered the Palace itself with a nod to the guards at the door, and sought the Great Hall, joining the thin but steady stream of courtiers heading that way from the gardens. *It is certainly worth a try. I have more time on my hands now than I expected to, and much less to fill it.*

Dinner was the usual controlled chaos of conversation and Karal was at his usual place at Ulrich's right hand; and as usual, Karal understood less than half of what was said around him. On the other hand, he didn't expect to need to understand what was said; he was watching what was done. The subtle languages of movement, expression, and eyes told him more than speech did, anyway. He paid very careful attention to Ulrich's dinner companion, the Lord Patriarch, since his mentor seemed to be having a particularly intense discussion with that worthy gentleman. It seemed to be an extension of an earlier conversation but was couched in very vague terms; Karal couldn't figure out exactly what they were talking about. He wondered if the Lord Patriarch was the person Ulrich had been meeting with this afternoon. There were offshoot Temples of Vkandis here in Valdemar, Temples whose members had defected from the Mother Temple when war

broke out with Karse, holding their allegiance to Valdemar—
or the older Writ—higher than their allegiance to the Son of
the Sun in Karse. Given all that Karal had learned about those
times, it could be they had placed their allegiance correctly!
But could Solaris be planning on bringing these strayed sheep
back into the fold? That would certainly cause a great deal of
upheaval in the offshoot Temples at least, and make for more
diplomatic incidents at the worst.

He wasn't too surprised when after dinner he found himself
alone again, excluded from the suite by more "confidential
conversations." But this time the library was empty, so that
was where he went.

And that was where Rubrik found him.

There was someone else with him; a young woman dressed
in a uniform very like that of the young Herald students, but
colored a light blue rather than gray. She was thin and earn-
est, with a nose that was a match for Karal's, deep-set brown
eyes, and short, straight brown hair—scandalously short, by
Karsite standards. She was not exactly pretty, but her face
was full of character and hinted at good humor.

"I thought I'd find you here," Rubrik said cheerfully, as he
limped up to the desk where Karal was leafing through an
illustrated book of Valdemaran birds. "This is the person
I wanted you to meet. Natoli, this is Karal; Karal, my daughter Natoli."

Daughter? Oh, no—is this some kind of matchmaking ploy?

His eyes widened involuntarily at the thought, and he frantically tried to marshal some kind of excuse to get away, but
Rubrik's next words collapsed that notion.

"She's one of what the Heraldic trainees call 'the Blues,' for
their uniforms," Rubrik continued. "What that means is that
they share classes with the trainees without being Heraldic,
Healer, or Bardic trainees themselves. Some of these students
are the children of nobles, but many are lowborn or of the
merchant classes, young people with high intelligence who
distinguished themselves enough to find patronage into the
ranks of the Blues. Most of Natoli's friends are mathematicians and crafters, like Natoli herself."

The girl nodded briskly, with no attempt at flirtation,
which relieved Karal immensely.

"I've asked her to give you a tour of the Palace and Collegia as a Blue would see it, then introduce you to some of her friends." Rubrik grinned. "You might be surprised. Some of them actually speak rudimentary Karsite."

Before Karal could stammer his thanks, Rubrik limped off, still chuckling to himself. His daughter examined Karal for a moment, with her arms crossed over her chest and her feet braced slightly apart.

Evidently she approved of what she saw. "Actually, Father doesn't really understand what I want to do," she said, with no attempt at making small talk. "I'm going to construct devices, *engines*, we call them, to do the work that several men or horses are needed for now."

"What, like wind and water mills?" Karal hazarded, and she grinned with delight.

"Exactly!" she replied. "And I want to build special bridges too, that would allow for the passage of masted ships and—well, that doesn't matter right at the moment. There's still some sunlight, would you like to take that tour now?"

She seemed friendly enough, even if she wasn't like any female Karal had ever encountered before. It occurred to him that he was meeting a great many women here in Valdemar who weren't like the females he knew at home. He nodded, and she motioned to him to get up and follow her. "You're in the Palace library, I'll show you the others, and the classrooms for the three Collegia first," she said—and proceeded to do just that, with a brisk efficiency that had his head spinning.

She pointed out things to him that he would never have had any interest in on his own—details of architecture and the mechanics that created the many comforts in the Palace itself. How the chimneys were structured so that the fireplaces in each room drew evenly for instance, or the arrangement of rainwater gutters and cisterns on the roof that put water in every bathing room. It was quite clear that she loved her avocation, and equally clear that flirtation was the farthest thing from her mind.

The sun set just as she completed her tour, and she marked the crimson glory with a nod of satisfaction. "The Compass

Rose should be just about filling now," she said, a non se-
quitur that caused him to knit his brows in puzzlement.

"Compass Rose?" he repeated.

"Oh, that's the place where all my friends and their teachers meet, just about every night," she replied airily. "Father
told me to introduce you around, so I figured that I'd take you
there tonight and get all the introductions over at once."

"Tavern?" he echoed. "Uh—tonight? You mean, right
now?" *I'm not sure I'm up to a strange tavern in a strange
city full of strange people. . . .*

"Of course," she said, and set off down the path that led to
the small gate in the wall he had first entered when he and
Ulrich arrived here, without waiting to see if he was going to
follow her. "That's much more logical than trying to track
them down tomorrow, one at a time. And much more efficient as well."

He had the feeling, as he trailed in her wake, that "logical
and efficient" played a very large part in how she regarded the
world. He could only wonder what some of his teachers back
at the Temple would have made of her.

The gate guards let them out without a comment, and they
made their way through the lamplit streets. Natoli threaded
her way through the traffic with the confidence of someone
who passed this way so often she could have done so blind-
folded. The tavern lay just beyond the ring of homes of the
highly born or wealthy, but Natoli knew shortcuts that
Rubrik apparently hadn't, little paths that led between garden
walls and across alleys he would never have guessed were
there. By the time the last sunset light had left the sky, they
were already at the door of the Compass Rose itself.

Karal knew what to look for in a good tavern, and he was
pleased to find all of it in this one; clean floors and tables,
enough servers to take care of the customers without rushing, decent lighting, and no odors of spoiled food or spilled
drink. In fact, in the matter of lighting, the Compass Rose
was as well-equipped as the Temple scriptorium, which
rather surprised him.

Most of the tables were full, or nearly, but Natoli knew exactly where she was going. "Come on," she told him, as she

peered across the room with her hand shading her eyes. "It looks as if everyone's here."

She started out across the crowded room, expertly dodging chairs and servers as she moved. "We form up in groups according to what we're interested in, and each group has its own tables," she explained over her shoulder, as he struggled through the crowd to keep up with her. "The teachers are all in the back room, of course—you know they've graduated you when they send you an invitation to join them. That's when you stop taking classes and start looking for work or a patron, or start teaching, yourself."

"Oh," he replied, which was really all he could say, for by that time she'd reached the table she wanted—a long affair surrounded by two dozen chairs at least, all but three of them filled with blue-garbed young men and a few young women, and covered not only with tankards and mugs, and platters of food, but with books and papers, water-stained and dotted with mug rings. Now the reason for the good lighting in here came to him. It looked as if these people were as accustomed to doing some of their work and reading here as in libraries or other quiet places! No few of the people who greeted Natoli were just as foreign-looking as Karal himself, though he was the only one wearing anything other than that ubiquitous blue uniform. They greeted her with varying degrees of enthusiasm, from boisterousness to carefully contained cheer.

"This is Karal," his guide said, when they'd finished. "He's with the Karsite ambassador. Secretary."

"Really?" One of the nearest, a young man with sharp, fox-like features and a wild shock of carrot-colored hair, raised his eyebrows in surprise. Then he grinned, and said in careful Karsite, "I would be grateful, good sir, if you could tell me the direction of the Temple."

"South, about four hundred *meiline* from here," Karal replied shortly in his own tongue, then continued in Valdemaran. "Your accent is really quite good, but you need to form your gutturals farther back in your throat, and they're like hoarse breathing, not like gargling."

"Ah! Alberich never could explain that properly, thank you!" the young man said, and he hooked the nearest empty chair with his foot, dragging it over. "Have a seat, won't you? Natoli, we need your help on the drawbridge project."

Karal took the proffered chair as Natoli helped herself to another, and was immediately engulfed in a technical discussion of which Karal understood perhaps half. The center of attention for the group was a huge piece of paper, covered with scribbles surrounding a drawing of a bridge, that they had placed in the middle of the table so that everyone could look at it at the same time. Someone got him a tankard of light ale, and someone else shoved a plateful of cheese-topped bread rounds at him, and everyone else at the table acted as if he *belonged* there, so he simply sat and listened while they thrashed out whatever the problem was. When the topic turned to other subjects—the problem of the drawbridge having been satisfactorily dealt with—on the occasions when he could contribute a word or two, he did.

To his pleasure, these people ignored what he looked like and where he came from in favor of what he thought and said. Granted, at the moment, that wasn't much—he was much more comfortable with simply listening to the others—but the few things he did say were treated with no more and no less respect than what anyone else said.

He drank his ale and kept his ears and his mind open, covering a great deal of astonishment by hiding his expression in his tankard. He had never before seen anyone with the kind of unbounded curiosity these young men and women shared. They talked and acted as if there was nothing that was impossible, from flying like birds to moving beneath the surface of the water without needing to breathe, like a fish. And they behaved as if there was nothing, no subject, that was "not meant for man to know."

He knew what *most* of his teachers would have said by now. At one point or another, every single one of the people sitting at this table uttered something that could be taken as blasphemous, and at least before Solaris' day, blasphemers met with the Fires.

By the time Natoli declared that they both needed to get some sleep and led him back out into the cold darkness, his head was swimming with so many conflicting ideas and emotions that it felt as if a hive of swarming bees had come to rest inside it. Excitement warred with nervous fear, and he was glad that the darkness hid his expression from Natoli as she led him back to the Palace. Her own excited monologue about some mathematical progression or other required only that he make vague noises in response from time to time and covered the fact that he *couldn't* have answered even if he'd known what it was she was talking about.

The guard at the gate knew her very well, it seemed, and shook his head when the two of them approached. "I don't know what I'm going to tell your father, young woman," he said, as soon as they came within earshot. "Out until near midnight, and with a young man!"

"Who is someone Father *told* me to introduce around, so you can curb your lurid thoughts," she replied smartly. "As for coming in late—if he doesn't ask, you don't have to tell him, do you?"

The guard continued to shake his head, but he opened the gate for them and locked it behind them without another word.

She left him on the path to the Palace, parting from him with a cheerful wave and a promise to meet him tomorrow. "I live in the dormitory with the Bardic students," she told him. "Most of the people you met tonight actually live in town, rather than on the Palace grounds, but since Father's a Herald, they let me live here. Will you be free right after lunch tomorrow?"

"Uh—yes," he said, responding before he could think.

"Good, then I'll meet you in the Palace library." And without giving him a chance to say anything else, she trotted off into the darkness.

He made his way back to the Palace in something of a dazed condition. The guards he encountered must have recognized him, since only two of them stopped him to ask who he was and where he was going. He managed to find his way back to the suite with a minimum of stumbling around in the dark, as most of the halls were lit by a minimum of lamps at this time of night.

He waved a silent greeting at the corridor guard, who grinned as if he had his own ideas about where Karal had been. The door was unlocked, and he pushed it open slowly, hoping that it wouldn't creak. The suite of rooms was dark but for a single candle burning in the night-lamp, and he made his way to his own room, stepping carefully to keep from waking Ulrich up.

He felt a certain amount of guilt at not leaving a note for his mentor. *I only hope Rubrik told him that Natoli carried me off . . . even if Rubrik didn't know where we were going.* He had the feeling that there was going to be a lot of explaining to be done in the morning.

At least he was used to staying up this late. When Ulrich didn't need his services, he generally read until just about midnight anyway. He didn't seem to need as much sleep as some people did, which was very useful, given the number of times Ulrich had needed multiple copies of documents at short notice.

He pushed open the door of his own room and closed it carefully behind him, heaving a sigh of relief as it shut with a minimum of sound. Only then did he turn around—

And froze.

There was someone waiting for him on his bed, a long, pale form that lay curled up against the pillows. It *wasn't* Ulrich, unless Ulrich had suddenly acquired a pair of green-gold eyes that glowed in the dark.

He gasped, and the lamp in the bracket beside the door lit itself with a little *puff* of sound.

As the lamplight steadied, a slender, cream-colored body uncurled itself gracefully from the place where it had been lying, near the head of the bed, cushioned by the pillows. The green-gold disks became the widened pupils of a pair of intensely blue eyes, surrounded by a brick-red mask. The otherwise pale-cream face was topped by a pair of brick-red ears, both of which were swiveled to face him. A red tail switched restlessly, curling up and curling down again, rather than *thudding* against the bed as a dog's would have.

:*Well, you certainly have been enjoying a night on the roof,*: the Firecat said in his mind. Its tone was amused, genial, and quite friendly.

It's a Firecat. A Firecat—in my room, on my bed, talking to me.

"I—uh—" He stared at the Cat with his mouth dropping open, unable to make his mind or his body work properly. What was a Firecat doing *here?* And why was it in *his* room?

:*Close your mouth, child, you look like a stranded fish,*: the Cat said, and purred with high good humor. :*I'm not here to drag you off to some kind of punishment. I've simply been sent here to give you some advice from time to time— advice your mentor wouldn't be able to grant you. That was what you wanted, wasn't it? Someone you could trust to advise you?*:

He was irresistibly reminded at that moment of an ancient proverb. "Be careful what you wish for—"

:*Indeed. "—you might get it." Quite true, which is why it's a proverb, but in the current situation it's not entirely apt. I'd have come here even if you hadn't wished for an advisor you could trust. This is an unstable situation, and you are in the middle of it. You are central to a number of complicated problems, the confidant to several key persons, and we simply couldn't have you walking about and chancing blunders without a little guidance.*:

"Oh," he said, weakly, and could not help wondering if he had already blundered somewhere?

:*Oh, Bright Flame, no! You've been doing just fine so far. And I'm not here to steer you into some kind of predestined future. Just at the moment, no one knows what may be coming, how this situation will resolve itself. No, not even the Sunlord Himself. The advice I am to give you will simply be based on a little more information than you have access to. If we are all very lucky, we will all work to bring this to a good conclusion.*:

The Cat tilted its head to the side, waiting for his response.

"If that's supposed to be comforting," he replied with more bravado than he felt, "it isn't."

:*Good. I'm not here to comfort you. I hope you're nervous; given what I know, you should be. Now, just shed those clothes and get into bed, you'll need the sleep.*: The Cat moved down to the foot of the bed and sat there, watching him, its bright blue eyes fixed on him in a way that suggested if he didn't hurry up and do what he'd been told, the Cat would—help.

Probably by shredding the clothes right off my body.

He quickly stripped off his clothing, and slipped into bed. The Cat arranged itself comfortably near his feet, without weighing him down, and gave its paws a quick wash. *:By the way,:* it said, as he put his head warily down on the pillow. *:That Herald with the limp did come by and tell Ulrich that his daughter had kidnapped you, and not to wait up. And my name is Altra.:*

Altra? But wasn't that the name of the Son of the Sun who—

He didn't even get a chance to finish the thought, for he fell asleep instantly.

Birdsong coming down his chimney woke him—which meant it must be a fair day, rather than a stormy one. Perhaps the Heralds had finally gotten their weather-magic working.

He stretched and yawned, without opening his eyes. *Odd. I dreamed that a Firecat was here last night. What a strange—*

He opened his eyes as his foot encountered a heavy weight at the foot of his bed. The Firecat raised his head and blinked at him.

:Good morning. As you see, I'm not a dream.: Altra yawned, showing a formidable set of teeth. *:You do have a very comfortable bed, and I am pleased to report that you neither toss nor snore.:*

"Uh, thank you." He racked his brain for something to say. *What do you say to an Avatar of your God?* "Hello, heard any good Sunlord jokes recently?" "Good morning, how may I worship you?" "Can I get you anything for breakfast? Uh—fish? Milk?"

:Nothing, thank you,: Altra replied loftily. *:Firecats are above such mundane considerations as eating.:*

Well that was something of a relief. If the Cat didn't eat, it didn't probably didn't eliminate either, which meant he wasn't going to have to find a box of sand somewhere—or would a Cat be able to use facilities made for humans?

Oh, this was too much to think about—but how was he going to explain the presence of a huge feline in his room, when he hadn't arrived with any such thing? "It followed me back from the tavern"? And how was he going to explain the presence of a Firecat to Ulrich, who *knew* what they were?

:*Don't be surprised if you don't see me very often*,: Altra continued, getting up and giving a full, nose-to-tail stretch. His claws were as formidable as his teeth. :*I have other business to worry about. Your master is as much in need of that bit of advice now and again as you are. I'll just drop in discreetly whenever you require the extra information I'm privy to—and if you think you really want it, I'll also give you—ah—"fatherly" advice, in the absence of your real father, if you feel too embarrassed to ask Ulrich.*: Altra actually winked slyly. :*Meanwhile, I shall be—invisible.*:

The door to his room opened of itself. The Firecat stretched again and jumped down off Karal's bed. There was a patch of bright sunlight just beyond the now-open door; Altra strolled casually out the door and into the sunlight.

And vanished.

Karal collapsed back against the pillows, not sure whether he should be elated or frightened out of his wits. He settled for a mixture of the two, with a healthy dose of panic.

Oh, Bright Flames, the last thing I need is the personal attentions of the Sunlord in my life! And a Firecat! *The Cats get into everything and anything—what if Vkandis finds out about all the strange things I've been learning here? What if He finds out about what goes on at the Compass Rose?*

Wait a moment. Vkandis was a god, all-knowing, all-powerful. How could He *not* know what Karal had been getting into?

Altra said I was doing the right things—so—

A visitation from an avatar, warning that the situation was unstable and about to become perilous, a hundred strange and possibly blasphemous things to think about that he'd heard last night—

—a powerful mage who was frightened of his own memories, unsure of himself—and called him "friend"—

—and a young woman, bright, intelligent, and competent, and disturbingly attractive—

—my head hurts.

All this before breakfast.

If I go back to sleep, will all this go away? No, probably not. He might as well get up and deal with it, then. It certainly wasn't going to get any better. *I just hope,* he thought glumly, as he climbed out of his bed and started looking for a clean set of clothing, *that it doesn't get worse.*

Tremane

12

Belief, however, is a fragile thing, when coupled with shock. By lunchtime, he had a hard time convincing himself that he had actually *seen* the Firecat; in the face of all of his everyday work and lessoning, the whole incident seemed more like something brought on by a little too much imagination—and ale—than anything real. Besides, it made no sense! After all, why would a Firecat come to *him*? How could *he* possibly be central to anything? Now—Ulrich, or even that Herald Talia, *that* he could believe, but there was no reason to even *dream* he'd get the attentions of a Firecat. He was nothing more important than a secretary; a good one, but no more than that. Oh, there was that mysterious business that Ulrich sometimes alluded to, that he was a "channel," which was presumably rare, but nothing ever seemed to come of it, and he doubted that anything would.

After a good, solid lunch of perfectly ordinary food, and when no further manifestations of the Sunlord's regard appeared in his path, he had just about put it all down to an extraordinarily vivid dream just before waking. When he returned to his room to change after his lesson and ride with Alberich, he had second and third thoughts. There were no celestial cat hairs on his bedspread, no glowing paw prints on the wooden floor of his room. There had never been a Firecat; it was all the fault of reading those notebooks. He'd had a vivid dream, then let his imagination take over, that was all.

Comforted by those thoughts, he headed for An'desha's home (his *ekele*, he reminded himself; An'desha was teaching him Tayledras to go along with his Valdemaran), with noth-

ing more on his mind than gratitude for the lovely, fair day.
Too many times of late he'd had to make his way across
Companion's Field through drizzle, or worse, a downpour,
just to visit his friend. Today, he might even be able to persuade An'desha to take their discussion outside. The young
mage spent far too much time cooped up inside.

He was planning just where he would like to go, when he
noticed that the Companions were not ignoring his presence
the way they usually did. In fact, they were moving in on him
from all directions, with a cheerful purposefulness to their
steps. Some of them even seemed to be trying to block his
path in a nonthreatening way. He stopped right where he
was, and they continued to move toward him—but still not
with any threat that *he* could detect. Rather, he got the impression of welcome, as if they had suddenly decided to play
the gracious hosts.

This was decidedly strange behavior, even if he *knew* they
weren't horses!

But before he could say anything to them—though he wasn't
sure what he *would* say—or make any move to retreat, they
took the initiative away from him.

They surrounded him completely, closing him inside a circle as they stood flank-to-flank. He couldn't possibly get past
them unless he pushed through them, and he knew from handling horses that if they didn't want him to pass, he wouldn't
be able to move them.

One of the nearest tossed its—his, it was definitely a young
stallion—head, and made a sound that closely resembled a
human clearing his throat. As Karal turned his attention to
that particular Companion, it blinked guileless blue eyes
at him.

:*Ah—you're Karal, as I understand,*: said a voice speaking
into his mind, exactly as Altra had. :*I hope you'll forgive the
informality of introducing myself. I'm Florian.*:

The "tone of voice" was as different from the Firecat's as a
young man's high and slightly nervous tenor would be from an
older man's confident and amused bass. But with no one else
anywhere around, it was pretty obvious that the "voice" was
coming from the Companion directly in front of him, the one
with deep blue eyes it would be incredibly easy to fall into—

Twice in one day! Twice in one day that uncanny crea-
tures decide they're going to speak in my mind!

Why now! And why me!

Karal shook his head to clear it, and wondered if he ought
to sit down. He coughed, tried to think of something clever to
say, and then settled for the first stupid thing that came into
his mind. "Ah—Florian? Are you a Companion?"

:Last time I looked, I was.: The one who must be Florian
switched his tail and cocked his head to one side. The other
Companions had broken their circle and were moving away
now, as if they were satisfied that Karal was not going to run
screaming out of the Field.

That was probably only because his knees were so shaky he
wasn't certain he could walk, much less run, screaming or
otherwise.

"Why—why are you talking to me?" he asked, inanely.

:Well, partly because of Altra,: Florian told him, dashing
his half-formed conviction that the Firecat had only been a
dream. *:He's a stranger here as much as you are, and he doesn't
know some of what we know. We're familiar with the entire
history of Valdemar, including a lot that isn't in the books.
We thought it was time you had someone around who could
answer your questions about this place, the Heralds, and all.
You never ask the questions that are in your mind; you keep
trying to find the answers in books.:* Florian snorted. *:That's
not always possible. People don't always write down important things.:*

Well, he had been a little reticent about asking questions.
He hadn't wanted to look like a complete idiot. . . .

*:You hardly need to worry about looking stupid in front of
a horse now, do you!:* Florian flipped his tail playfully, and
Karal got the impression that he was grinning.

"Well, couldn't An'desha have told me?" he replied, feeling
stubborn. He hadn't *asked* for this—or for Altra, for that matter! "Or—Natoli, *she's* from Valdemar! And her father's a
Herald, too!"

But Florian only stamped his hoof scornfully. *:Your friend
An'desha is just as much a stranger to this place as you are,
and while young Natoli is a very nice young lady, she doesn't
know anything at all about politics.:*

"And you do?" he responded dubiously.

Florian snorted. *:Not me alone. We do. We, the Companions as a whole. Remember, our Heralds are up to their ears in politics, and we share their thoughts. There isn't much at all about us in the books, either, nor Heralds; the details of our partnerships aren't the kinds of things that get written down. I can tell you all about that, whatever you want to know.:*

"All?" He wasn't sure he believed that, either.

:Well, if there's something I can't tell you, at least I won't lie to you, all right? I won't mislead you.: Florian's mood was as mercurial as anyone Karal had ever seen; now it seemed as if he was pleading with Karal. His ears went down a little, and his head sank a bit. *:Look, we just wanted to make certain that you knew where you could find someone to help you. Altra may be your guide, but you know cats. They show up when it suits them, and not necessarily when you need them. And they love secrets. He could withhold things from you just to appear mysterious. That happens all the time.:*

That did sound just like a cat, and he chuckled weakly in spite of his shock. "Still—I mean, I'm not a Valdemaran, I'm a Karsite. What's more, I'm sworn to Vkandis. Are you really, really sure this shouldn't this be left to Altra?"

Florian snorted. *:Altra doesn't know near enough about Heralds and Companions, things that you will need to know—but being a cat, he'll act as if he does, and make up what he doesn't know. Really, Karal, I'm honestly here to help you. If you'll let me, that is.:*

Karal hardly knew which way to turn; he could only remember one thing. According to Ulrich, Companions were "just like" Firecats. That made them, in effect, speakers for the Sunlord—

Or Whoever, he reminded himself.

:Well, remember what Ulrich told you,: Florian reminded him. *:Does it matter who I speak for? We're both on the same side. Karal, this is important. You need to accept me. Please, trust me in this.:*

Wonderful. Now something else wanted him to trust it.

On the other hand—

:You need me,: Florian repeated stubbornly.

He sighed. "All right," he said at last, with resignation. "I'll trust you. But mainly because it's a lot easier coming to you for answers than it is to go look them up—or try to, anyway."

:*Good!*: Florian tossed his head and pranced in place. :*Excellent! I told them you'd see reason! Now—since I happen to know that your friend An'desha is still with Firesong, and I also know you have a head* full *of questions you haven't asked yet—*: The Companion nudged him with his nose in the direction of the barn, :*—you can groom me while you're asking those questions. I haven't got a Herald, and no one spends any amount of time grooming Companions who don't have Heralds. I itch.*:

"I'm sure you do," Karal sighed. "I'm sure you do."

He headed obediently toward the barn; after all, he might as well do the Companion that little favor in return for getting an easy set of answers to all his questions, starting with, "just what *does* the Queen's Own do?"

But if anyone had asked him, among Natoli, Altra, and Florian, he was beginning to feel as if he was suffering from a spiritual concussion!

Some people are born to greatness, Grand Duke Tremane thought glumly. *Some people stumble into greatness. And some people get all the responsibilities without the acknowledgment.*

From the moment he had walked through the Gate into the headquarters of the Hardornen Campaign, he had been forced to improvise. The situation was a complete nightmare, the worst campaign he had ever seen or read about. The only good thing about the disaster was the headquarters itself; the fortified manor of some nobly-born Hardornen his men had taken intact. Not even the paintings on the walls were disturbed, nor more than a handful of jewels and other small objects looted. If he must be in a perilous situation, at least he would endure it in comfort. This was the privilege of command and control.

Normally when the Empire moved in on a country to conquer it, the conclusion was foregone from the moment the troops first crossed the border. The situation within the target nation was always in a state of turmoil; the central gov-

ernment would be in chaos thanks to the internal machina-
tions of Imperial agents, and generally the populace was in
revolt as disorganization allowed greedy nobles to take liberties. That made conquest little more than defeating the few
troops willing or able to oppose the Empire, and moving in.

Front-line Imperial shock troops always went in first to
take a *precisely* calculated amount of terrain. They would
take no more, and no less. At that point, they would stop and
hold a line; consolidation troops would follow to mop up
whatever weak resistance still remained. Once the commander was certain that the conquered territory was going to stay
conquered, holding troops moved in. Their task was one of
fortifying strongholds, establishing or repairing roads, mills,
and whatever industries existed or needed to be built.

They were followed in turn by administrators and policing
troops, whose *only* task was to maintain order and establish
Imperial Law. By this time, the populace was always so daz-
zled with the superiority of Imperial life that they welcomed
the establishment of Imperial Law and government with religious fervor.

And lastly, Imperial priests moved in, to establish worship
of the Emperor and all his predecessors alongside the worship
of whatever gods the barbarians kept.

With all that done, and a secure base behind him, the front-
line troops could leapfrog out again.

This strategy had never failed—until now.

Mages were always part of every phase of the invasion, of
course. None of this could be done without them. They were
better and more reliable than spies, enabled all commanders
to communicate with each other and with their general instantly, and their offensive magics usually terrified the enemy. Without the Portals they built, it would be impossible
to maintain troops in the field; with the Portals, fresh soldiers
and supplies were available at a moment's notice, and a general was able to return in person to the capital—or any other
place, for that matter.

The mages were the keystone that made it all work—
which was why every candidate for the Iron Throne must be
enough of a mage that other mages would not be able to trick

him by under- or over-stating their own abilities. Ideally, he would be First-Rank, but Second would do in a pinch.

Tremane himself was not only a First-Rank, but was a First-Rank Red; the only two degrees above him were Blue and Purple—and the only Rank higher than First was Adept. That was one reason why he considered himself the best choice for the Throne. And it was one reason why, after due reflection, he had decided that the conquest of Hardorn had simply been bungled by a general who did not understand how to utilize his mages properly.

He had discovered the instant he set foot on Hardornen soil that he had been completely wrong.

The conquest of Hardorn had begun with the usual Imperial efficiency. It should have continued that way. There was no reason—on paper—why everything should not have gone according to the plans.

Tremane rested his chin on his hands and glowered down at the map on the table before him. But not at Hardorn—at the land beyond its borders in the west.

Valdemar.

Valdemar was to blame; he knew it in his bones, although he could not prove it. There was only one agent inside Valdemar in a position to observe *anything* in the Court, and he was not terribly effective. He was not able to get close to anyone in the queen's councils, and as a commoner, he was excluded from anything but the most trivial of gossip. He had reported nothing in the way of aid from the Queen, but Tremane knew better.

The Valdemarans were, must be, offering covert support and organizing the resistance, no matter how much they might pretend otherwise. It was a situation that simply should never have occurred, and what was more, it made no sense. Until the moment of Ancar's death, Valdemar had been locked in war with Hardorn. That state of war should have continued, even with Ancar slain. Valdemar should have been grateful to see someone else trouncing their enemy. They should have been as happy to see the Imperial troops marching into Hardorn as the poor oppressed citizens of Hardorn itself.

It didn't, they weren't, and we're bemired. And I can't even prove it's Valdemar that's behind it all.

As had been reported, the conquest of Hardorn had slowed to a crawl, and it had become much more expensive in terms of men and material than had been projected. The situation was worse than he had expected. The Empire ran by close accounting; sometimes he suspected it was the accountants that actually ruled it. Every unexpected loss meant resources would have to be reshuffled from elsewhere.

He buried his face in his hands for a moment. He was tired, mortally tired. He'd spent every waking hour since he had arrived trying to staunch the hemorrhage this campaign had become, and he had been awake for far too many hours in the day. Now, at least, they were no longer losing men and supplies at the rate they *had* been, but the situation had turned into a stalemate. They could not go forward, but could not go back, either. They could not even move in the support troops, for the countryside that had been "taken" had not yet been pacified.

I have to make a decision, he realized wearily. *I can try to press on, as General Sheda did, or I can make this temporary halt more permanent, consolidate what we have, and try to figure out how to break the deadlock.*

He had already made far too many command decisions that he was going to have to justify later. There were spies in the ranks; he knew that, and he also did not know who all of them were. He came into this too late to put enough of his own men inside to be really effective at ferreting out who belonged to whom. Some of the agents in place were spies for his rivals, some for the Emperor, some spied only to sell information to the highest bidder. That was the problem with Imperial politics; if you served in any official capacity, you had to worry as much about enemies from within as enemies of the Empire.

I didn't expect to have to make decisions this risky the moment I took command. His stomach burned, and there was a sour taste in the back of his throat no amount of wine could wash away. *And how is it going to look to the Emperor when the first major order I give is for a retrenchment! He told me to conquer Hardorn, not sit on my heels and study it! I'll look weak, indecisive. Hardly the qualities for an Imperial Successor.*

"Uncomfortable" was an inadequate description for the situation, although that was how he had politely worded it in his first dispatch back to the Emperor.

He took his hands away from his burning eyes and studied the map again, this time ignoring the taunting shape of Valdemar. *Ignore them. Pretend for the moment that they do not exist. Now study the tactical display.*

It showed far too many hot spots behind his own lines, areas where there were still attacks on the troops, where there were pockets of resistance that melted away like snow in the summer whenever he brought troops in to crush them. This was *not* pacified territory. He could not and would not ask support troops to come into a situation like this one. It would not be a case of risking their lives, it would be a case of throwing their lives away.

I will have to retrench, he decided. He took up a pen, and studied the map again, then drew a line. *Here—to here.* The Imperial troops would retreat until they were all behind the line he drew on the map. Most of the resistance was on the other side of that line; such pockets of trouble as still remained could *probably* be dealt with in an efficient manner.

I hope, he thought glumly, writing up his orders and ringing for his aide to take them to his mage. A great weight lifted from his shoulders the moment the boy took the rolled paper, although a new set of worries descended on him in its wake.

It was done; there was no turning back. In a few moments, the mage would have magical duplicates of the orders in the hands of the mages attached to every one of his commanders, and the retreat would begin.

He rang for another aide as soon as the first had left. "Bring me the battle reports again," he told the boy. "This time just for Sector Four. And set up the table for me. Leave the reports on it."

The boy bowed, and took himself out. When Tremane finally gathered enough strength to rise and go out into the strategy room, the reports were waiting, and the plotting table had been set up with the map of Sector Four and the

counters representing Commander Jaman's troops were waiting along the side of the table, off the map.

At least he had this thick-walled, stone manor as a command post, and not the tent he had brought with him. The
weather around here was foul—no, it was worse than foul.
Out of every five days, it stormed on three. Outside the windows, a storm raged at this moment, lashing the thick, bubbly glass with so much rain it looked as if the manor stood in
the heart of a waterfall. It would have been impossible to do
anything in a tent right now, except hope it didn't blow over.

These people knew how to build a proper fireplace, and a
sound chimney, which edged them a little more into the
ranks of the civilized so far as Tremane was concerned. One
of those well-built fireplaces was in every room of the suite
he had chosen for himself. A good fire crackled cheerfully at
his back as he lined up the counters and began to replicate
the movement described in the battle reports.

He had chosen Sector Four because it was typical of what
had been happening all along the front lines, and because Jaman wrote exceptionally clear and detailed reports. But this
time, he did not put any of the counters representing the enemy on the table; Jaman had not been able to *really* count the
enemy troops, and everything he wrote in those reports about
enemy numbers was, by his own admission, a guess. Instead,
Tremane laid out only the Imperial counters, and dispassionately observed what happened to them.

By the time he had played out the reports right up to today's, he *knew* why the Imperial army, trained and strictly
disciplined, was failing. It was there for anyone to see, if they
simply observed what was happening, rather than insisting it
couldn't happen.

The Imperial troops were failing *because* they were trained
and strictly disciplined.

If there was any organization in the enemy resistance at all,
it was a loose one, and one which allowed all the individual
commanders complete autonomy in what they did. The enemy struck at targets of opportunity, and only when there
was a chance that their losses would be slim. The Empire was
not fighting real troops—even demoralized ones. It was fight-

ing against people who weren't soldiers but who knew their own land.

Disciplined troops couldn't cope with an enemy that wouldn't make a stand, who wouldn't hold a line and fight, who melted away as soon as a counter-attack began. They couldn't deal with an enemy who attacked out of nowhere, in defiance of convention, and faded away into the countryside without pressing his gains. The Hardornens were waging a war of attrition, and it was working.

How could the army even begin to deal with an enemy who lurked *behind* the lines, in places supposed to be pacified and safe? The farmer who sold the Imperial cooks turnips this morning might well be taking information to the resistance about how many turnips were sold, why, and where they were going! And he could just as easily be one of the men with soot-darkened faces who burst upon the encampment the very same night, stealing provisions and weapons, running off mounts, and burning supply wagons.

And as for the enemy mages—*his* mages were convinced there weren't any. They found no sign of magic concealing troop-movements, of magical weapons, or even of scrying to determine what *their* moves might be. But he had analyzed their reports as well, and he had come to a very different conclusion.

The enemy mages are concentrating on only one thing— keeping the movements of the resistance troops an absolute secret. That was the only way to explain the fact that none, *none* of his mages had ever been able to predict a single attack.

They weren't keeping those movements a secret by the "conventional" means of trying to make their troops invisible, either. They didn't have to—the countryside did that for them. There were no columns of men, no bivouacs for Tremane's mages to find, no signs of real troops at all for FarSeeing mages to locate. That meant it was up to the Forescryers to predict when the enemy would attack.

And they could not, for the enemy's mages were flooding the front lines with hundreds of entirely specious visions of troop movements. By the time the Imperial mages figured out which were the false visions and which were the reality, it was too late; the attack was usually over.

In a way, he had to admire the mind that was behind *that* particular plan. There was nothing easier to create than an illusion which existed nowhere except in the mind. It was an extremely efficient use of limited resources—and an effective one as well.

Whoever he is, I wish he was on my side.

The only way of combating such a tactic was to keep the entire army in a combat-ready state at all times, day or night.

And that is impossible, as my enemy surely knows.

Try to keep troops in that state, day after day, when nothing whatsoever happened, and before long they lost so much edge and alertness that when a real attack did come, they couldn't defend effectively against it. They would slip, drop their guard, grow weary—and only *then* would the attack come. There was no way to prevent such slips, either; people grew tired.

The enemy wasn't using mages to predict when troops had gone stale; he didn't have to. The very children playing along the roads could do that.

Perfectly logical, a brilliant use of limited resources. The only problem was, it fit the pattern of a country that was *well*-organized, one with people fiercely determined to defend themselves against interlopers, not a land ravaged by its own leaders and torn by internal conflict.

He turned away from the tactics table and faced the window, staring into the teeth of the storm. *We never move in until and unless conditions inside the country we wish to annex are intolerable. The arrival of our troops must represent a welcome relief—so that we can be seen by the common people as liberators, not oppressors. King Ancar certainly created those conditions here!*

In fact, if half of what he had read in the reports was actually true and not rumor, Ancar would have had a revolt of his own on his hands within the next five or ten years. When Imperial troops had first crossed the border, in fact, they *had* been greeted as saviors. So what had happened between then and now to change that?

It can't be the tribute, we haven't levied it yet. Imperial taxes amounted to sixty percent of a conquered land's products every year—and the conscription of all young men between the ages of sixteen and twenty-one. But none of that had been imposed yet; it never was until after all of the benefits of living within the Empire were established. By the time the citizens had used the freshwater aqueducts, the irrigation and flood-retention systems, the roads, and most of all, the Imperial Police, they were generally tolerant of the demands the Empire made on them in return.

The taxes were adjusted every year to conform to the prosperity (or lack of it) in that year—the farmer and the businessman was left with forty percent of what he had earned, instead of having all of it taken from him—and he didn't have to worry about the safety of his wife, daughter, or sister. Women could take the eggs to market and the sheep to pasture without vanishing.

Which is definitely more than can be said for the situation during Ancar's reign.

If there was any grumbling, it was generally the conduct of the Imperial Police that changed the grumbling to grudging acceptance of the situation. Imperial citizens and soldiers lived under the same hard code as conquered people. Even in the first-line shock troops, the Code was obeyed to the letter. The Imperial Code was impartial and absolutely unforgiving.

The Law is the Law. And it was the same for everyone; no excuses, no exceptions, no "mitigating circumstances."

Assault meant punishment detail for a soldier, and imprisonment with hard labor for a civilian. A thief, once caught, was levied fines equal to twice the value of what he had stolen, with half going to the ones whose property he had taken, and half to the Empire; if he had no money, he would work in a labor camp with his wages going to those fines until they were paid. If the thief was also a soldier, his wages in the army were confiscated, and his term lengthened by however long it took to pay the fine. Murder was grounds for immediate execution, and no one in his right mind would *ever* commit rape. The victim would be granted immediate status as a divorced *spouse*. Half of the perpetrator's possessions went to the victim, half of the perpetrator's wages went to the victim for a term of five years if there was no child, or sixteen years if a child resulted. If the child was a daughter, *she* received a full daughter's dowry out of whatever the perpetrator had managed to accumulate, and if the child was a son, the perpetrator paid for his full outfitting when he was conscripted. That was a heavy price to pay for a moment of lust-anger, and rape was much less of a problem within the Empire than outside of it. The second Emperor had determined that attacking a person's purse was far more effective as a deterrent to crime than mere physical punishment.

And once again, if the perpetrator was some shiftless ne'er-do-well, who did not have a position, he would find himself in a labor camp, building the roads and the aqueducts, with his pay supplying the needs of the child for which he was responsible. And that responsibility was brought home to him with every stone he set or ditch he dug.

And if a perpetrator were foolish enough to rape again— *then* he underwent a series of punishments both physical and magical that would leave him outwardly intact but completely unable to repeat his act.

Tremane brooded as lightning flashed outside the window. *Compared to life under Ancar, all this should have been paradisiacal. So why the revolt and resistance now?*

Perhaps Ancar had not been allowed to operate freely long enough. *There may still be enough people alive who recall the halcyon days of his father's rule. They may be the ones behind the resistance.*

He grimaced. *Too bad they didn't have the good taste to die with Ancar's father and spare the Empire all this work!*

He would have to revise his plans to include that possibility, though. Somehow, he was going to have to find a way to counter their influence.

Perhaps if I fortify and protect select cities, and bring in the Police and the builders . . . no matter how golden the old times are said to be, the reality of Imperial rule will be right in front of these barbarians as an example. With Imperial cities prospering, and rebellious holdings barely holding on, the equation should be obvious even to a simpleton.

But what about Valdemar? The more he looked at it, the more certain he became that *they* were as much behind the resistance as these putative hangovers from an earlier time. But what could he do about them, when he knew next to nothing about them?

Then he gave himself a purely mental shake. *Stupid. I may know nothing now, and it may be very difficult to get current information out, but I have other sources of information.* He was a great believer in history; he had always felt that knowing what someone had done in the past, whether that "someone" was a nation or an individual, made it possible to predict what that someone might do in the future.

And I have an entire monastery full of scholars and researchers with me—not to mention my personal library. I can set them the task of finding out where these Valdemarens came from in the first place, and what they have done in their own past.

There was one rather odd and disquieting thing, however, that might concern the land of Valdemar. In all of the histories of the Empire, from the time of the first Emperor and before, the West was painted as a place of ill-omen. "There is a danger in the West," ran the warning, without any particular danger specified.

That was one reason why the Empire had concentrated its efforts on its eastern borders, taking the boundary of the Empire all the way to the Salten Sea. Then they had expanded northward until they reached lands so cold they were not worth bothering with, then south until they were stopped by another stable Empire that predated even the Iron Throne. Only *then*, in Charliss' reign, had the Emperor turned his eyes westward and begun his campaign to weaken Hardorn from within.

Tremane turned away from the window and walked back into his study in silence. The light from his mage-lamp on the desk was steady and clear, quite enough to give the feeling that no storm would ever penetrate these stone walls to disturb him. *Odd how comforted we humans are by so simple a thing as a light.*

There was an initial report on Valdemar from his tame scholars, hardly more than a page or two, lying in the middle of the dark wooden expanse of his desk. He picked it up without sitting down and scanned it over. He didn't really need to—he'd read the report several times already—but it gave him the feeling that he was actually doing something to pick it up and read the words.

The gist of it was that some centuries ago, a minor Baron of a conquered land within the Empire named "Valdemar" reacted to the abuses of power by *his* Imperial overlord in a rather drastic fashion. Rather than bringing his complaints to the Emperor, he had assembled all of his followers in the dead of winter when communications were well-nigh impossible, and instructed them to pack up everything they wanted to hold onto. Valdemar was a mage, and so was his wife; between them, they managed to find and silence all the spies in their own Court. Then Valdemar, his underlings, their servants and retainers right down to the last peasant child, all fled with everything they could carry. At last report, they had gone into the west, the dangerous west. Valdemar had probably known that the Empire would be reluctant to pursue them in that direction. *Presumably his quest for some land remote enough that he need no longer worry about the Empire finding him bore fruit.* The coincidence of names seemed far too much to be anything else, and according to the scholars, this present "Kingdom of Valdemar" bore the stamp of that original Baron Valdemar's overly-idealistic worldview.

That was all simple enough, and it could account for the animosity of the current leaders of Valdemar toward the Empire of which they *should* know very little. If they, in their turn, had a tradition of "fear the Empire," they would react with hostility to the first appearance of Imperial troops anywhere near their borders.

That much was predictable. What was *not* predictable was the shape that Baron Valdemar's idealism had taken. *Where in the names of the forty little gods did this cult of white-clad riders come from?* There was nothing like them inside the Empire or outside of it! And what *were* their horses? His mages all swore to a man that they were something more than mere horseflesh, but they could not tell him what they were, only what they *weren't.* How powerful were the beasts? No one could tell him. What was their function? No one could tell him that, either. There was nothing really written down, only some legend that they were a gift of some unspecified gods. Were they "familiars," as some hedge-wizards used? Were they conjured up out of the Etherial Plane? No one could tell him. Nor had the agent unearthed anything;

the riders themselves, when asked directly, would only smile and say that this was something only another rider would understand.

That was hardly helpful.

I never liked the idea of employing an artist as an agent, he thought with distaste. *When they aren't unreliable, they're ineffectual.*

Not that he'd had any choice; the agent was an inheritance from his predecessor, and there hadn't been time or opportunity to get another in place.

White riders and horses were bad enough, but worse had somehow occurred before Ancar took himself out in some kind of insane battle with an unknown mage or mages.

Valdemar had somehow managed to patch up a conflict going back generations with their traditional enemy, Karse. And *how* they had managed to make an ally of that stiff-necked, parochial bitch Solaris was completely beyond him! He wouldn't have thought the so-called Son of the Sun would ally herself with anyone, much less with an ages-old enemy!

And *where* had all the rest of Valdemar's bizarre allies come from? He would hardly have credited descriptions, if he had not seen the sketches! Shin'a'in he had heard of, as a vague legend, but what were Hawkbrothers? And *who* could believe in talking gryphons? Gryphons were creatures straight out of legend, and that is where they *should*, in a rational world, have remained!

His agent's report credited most of this to Elspeth, the *former* Heir. Former? When had a ruler-to-be ever lost his position without also losing his life or freedom? Yet Elspeth had abdicated, continuing to work in a subsidiary capacity within the ranks of the white Riders, the Heralds. Elspeth was too *young* to have made alliances with so many disparate peoples! She'd have no experience in diplomacy and very little in governance. In the end he'd simply dismissed the agent's report as a fanciful tale, doubtless spread about to make the former Heir seem more important and more intelligent than she really was.

He wished he could dismiss the gryphons as more fanciful creations, but there were others who had seen them as well as the agent. The gryphons worried him. They represented a complete unknown; in an equation already overcomplicated, they were a dangerous variable. Were there more of them? A whole army, perhaps? The idea of flying scouts and spies working for the Valdemarans was not one that made him any happier.

He groaned softly and flung himself down in a chair. Useless to ask "why me?" since he knew why all this was happening to him. *I want the Iron Throne. An Emperor must be able to deal with situations like this. If I want the Throne, I must prove to Charliss that I am competent.*

Of course, now that he had begun, it was impossible to bow out of this gracefully.

His nearest rival was also his nearest enemy, and if he failed here, or even gave it up and admitted defeat and resigned his position, his lifespan could and would be measured in months or years rather than decades. He *would* be dead, as soon as Charliss gave up the Throne. No new Emperor permitted former rivals to continue existing; the first few years on the Iron Throne were generally nervous ones, and it didn't make any sense to leave potential troublemakers in a position to make the situation worse.

No, now he must carry this through, or else flee—into the south, into the west, into those barbarian lands beyond even Valdemar, and hope to cover his tracks well enough that no agent of the Empire could find him.

I walk a tightrope above the vent of a volcano, he thought grimly. *And there is someone shaking the tightrope, trying to make me fall.*

Shaking? That was odd.... For a moment it felt as if something had just picked up the building and dropped it; the unsettled feeling in the pit of the stomach an earthquake caused. But there was no earthquake, and this was no physical feeling; this was centered in the mage-senses—

—as if something strange, terrifying, and *huge* was looming over him—

Before he could move from his chair, it struck.

All his senses failed; sight, sound, hearing, all gone. He floated in an ocean of nothingness, bereft of any touch with the real world. Mage-energy coursed through him, without truly touching him. Once, as a child, he had gone to the

Salten Sea on a holiday. A great wave had come in and picked him up, nearly drowning him, carrying him up onto the shore and leaving him gasping on the sand. This was another kind of wave, but he was just as helpless in its powerful grasp, and now, as then, he did not know if it would leave him alive or drag him under to drown. It tumbled him in dizzying nothingness, disorienting him further. He was lost. . . .

He thought he cried out in terror, but he couldn't even hear his own voice.

Then it was over. He *felt* the chair he was in again, heard his own harsh gasps for breath as the breath burned in his throat. His body shuddered with the pounding of his heart, and his hands ached as they spasmed on the arms of his chair. For a moment, he thought he was blind, but lightning struck just outside and illuminated the room for a moment, and he realized that the mage-light had simply gone out.

Simply? It was not *that* simple; the kind of mage-light he had created was supposed to endure anything save having the spell canceled!

He blinked. There was light in the next room, dim red light from the fire. He unclenched his hands with a rush of relief; at least he wasn't left in the dark! Odd. All his life he'd had mage-lights about him; even in a room darkened for sleep there was leakage from lights in the garden, lights in the hallway or the next room. He'd never realized how *dark* a truly dark room could be.

With shaking hands, he felt in a drawer of the table next to him, found a candle, and took it into the next room to light it at the fire there. Some enemy had sent a magical attack at him, surely! Magical assassins had been blocked by the protections he kept constantly in place—or was this meant simply to disrupt his concentration? This attack, if attack it was, certainly hadn't been very effective! And yet—to cancel a mage-light spell *within* his protections meant that someone had incredible power. He controlled the trembling of his hands and forced himself to think of who might command that kind of power.

That was all he had time for; aides burst in on him, sent by every commander in the camp, all of them carrying messages of varying levels of hysteria.

That was when he realized that the effect of the—whatever it was—had not been targeted solely against him.

Somehow he managed to assemble all of his mages within a reasonable time the next day, gathering them all into his councilroom to assess the damage. "So it swept the entire country?" Tremane asked his chief mage, Artificer Gordun. The homely, square-faced man nodded, as he laced his thick, clever fingers together.

"As nearly as we can tell," Gordun replied. "It was like one of those enormous waves that carries right across the Salten Sea; it came from the east and north, and is traveling into the west and south. We think it also washed over the Empire, but just at the moment, it is impossible to tell. We can't get messages to the Empire, and I would suspect that the reverse is true."

Tremane grimaced. Like those great waves, this thing that had come and gone had left devastation behind it, and the more something was connected to magic, the worse the effect was. *Every* spell suffered damage to a greater or lesser extent. Lines of communication were all gone until the mages found each other again; the Portals were all down, and only the forty little gods knew when they would be reopened. Defenses were gone, or shaken. Little things, like mage-lights, magical cook-fires, weather-cloaks, timekeepers, all the tiny things that made life run smoothly for the troops, were gone, the spells that created them shattered. There would be dark, cold tents and cold meals all up and down the lines tonight, unless the various commanders quickly found non-magical substitutes.

"It was a mage-storm, that much we are certain," Gordun continued. "Although it is not like any such storm we have ever encountered before. The storm itself did not last for more than a heartbeat or two. Mages encountered a physical effect, as you no doubted noted yourself. Non-mages experienced nothing."

"That was enough," Tremane muttered. "It's going to take days to set up all the spells it knocked down, and more time to inspect anything that survived for damage and repair it."

"That isn't all, my lord Duke." The thin, reedy voice came

from the oldest mage with Tremane's entourage, his own mentor, Sejanes. The old man might look as if he was a senile old stick, but his mind was just as sharp as it had been decades ago. "This mage-storm has affected the material world as well as the world of magic. Listen—"

He picked up the pile of papers on the table before him, with hands that were as steady as a surgeon's. "These are the reports I have from messengers I sent out on horses to the other mages in the army. The tidings they returned with were not reassuring. From Halloway: 'There are places where rocks melted into puddles and resolidified in a heartbeat, sometimes trapping things in the newly-solid rock.' From Gerrolt: 'Strange and entirely new insects and even higher forms of life have appeared around the camp. I cannot say whether they were created on the instant, or come from elsewhere in the world.' From Margan: 'Roughly circular pieces of land two and three cubits in diameter appear to have been instantly transplanted from far and distant places. There are circles of desert, of forest, of swamp—even a bit of lake bottom, complete with mud, water-weeds, and gasping and dying fish.'" He waved the papers. "There are more such reports, from all up and down the lines, and from behind them as well. You are well beyond my needing to prompt you, Tremane, but this *cannot* have been an act of nature!"

"And it isn't likely that it is residue from King Ancar's reckless meddling, either," Tremane agreed.

"I cannot see how," Sejanes replied, dropping the papers again. "Ancar was not capable of magic on this scale. There *is* no mage capable of magic on this scale. I can only assume that it must have been caused by many mages, working together. Perhaps that would account for the variety and disparity of its effects."

Tremane racked his memory for any accounts of *anything* like this "mage-storm," and came up with nothing. Oh, there were mage-storms of course, but they all had purely physical effects, and were caused by too much unshielded use of magical energies. *Those* storms were real storms, weather systems, very powerful ones. This was not like any mage-storm *he* had ever seen, and yet the term was an apt one. It had struck like a storm, or a squall line; it had passed overhead, done its damage, and passed on.

And there was only one place this storm could have come from.

"There is only one place this storm could have originated from," Sejanes said, echoing his own thoughts. "Despite the fact that it began east of us—well, any fool knows that the world is a ball! What better way to surprise us than by sending out an attack to circle the world and strike from behind?"

"You're saying that Valdemar sent this against us," Tremane replied slowly.

Sejanes shrugged. "Who else? Who else has access to strange allies from lands we never even heard of? Who else uses magics we don't understand? Who else has reason to attack us from behind?"

"Who else indeed," Tremane echoed. "They lose nothing by making life miserable for the Empire and the Imperial allies, and they could have warned their friends to erect special shields. Except that—according to all of you, Valdemar has the absolute minimum in the way of magic!"

He cast an accusatory glance around the table. Most of the mages cringed and averted their eyes, but Sejanes met him look for look.

"We still don't know what those horses are," Sejanes pointed out acidly. "And we don't recognize their magics. So how could we tell what they had and didn't have? We made our best guess based on the fact that they simply do not use magic in their everyday lives. There are no mage-lights or mage-fires; they have only candles, lanterns and torches, and physical fires. There are no Constructors; they build contrivances with no magic at all to haul water, grind grain. There are no Replicators; all documents are copied by hand, or printed with much labor. Messages are sent by those crude mirror-towers, or by human messenger. So what are we to think? That they have no magic, of course."

"But if they have no magic in daily use," Tremane pointed out, thinking out loud, "then they will not suffer from this attack as we have."

Sejanes nodded, his head bobbing on his thin neck like a toy on a spring. "Precisely. *As if they used this kind of attack all the time.* As if they planned for this kind of attack to be used against them."

It made sense. It more than made sense. If you expected someone to hurl fire at you, you built your fort of stone. If you expected catapults, you built the walls thickly. If you expected to be deluged with mage-caused thunderstorms, you built truly good drainage.

And if you expected to be attacked by something that twisted and ruined your spells, you didn't *use* any. Unless, of course, it was the spell intended to twist and ruin all other spells.

"But where did this come from?" he asked, thinking aloud again.

Sejanes shrugged, and the rest of the mages only shook their heads. "It passed roughly east to west, and at a guess I would say that if it came from Valdemar as we think, it truly *did* circle the whole world to get here. That is logical, and in line with the notion that it originated in Valdemar. Frankly, if I had such an attack, I would use it that way, because it would be at its weakest when it finally got back to me. It was certainly strong enough to wreak havoc for us when it reached us!"

That made sense, too. "You're saying you can't find a point of origin, though," he persisted. "If you could, we would know where their best mages were." *And that useless artist could find out who they are. Then we could neutralize them.*

"Not a chance," Sejanes said flatly. "At the moment, we're lucky to find the mages in the other camps, much less a point-of-origin for this thing. We are fundamentally disarmed at this point, and we'd better hope that neither the rebels nor the Valdemarans have anything planned for us, because we're so disorganized that we'll be lucky to hold the ground we've got."

The others chimed in with more tales of woe; he had already heard from his military commanders by now, and he was simply glad that so many of them were used to working under primitive and uncertain conditions. They had found substitutes for the magics that weren't working, but there was no substitute for the lack of communication. That was the worst.

Tremane was just grateful that he had called a halt to the attempt to advance *before* all this happened. If he had been in the midst of a military maneuver, it could have been a disaster.

Sejanes was the only one who really had anything useful to say, and what he had was all too meager. The rest simply floundered, out of their depth.

"I can only see one thing useful at this point," Tremane said at last. "Repair the damages, and armor the repairs against a repeat of this attack. Communications, first. Then the Gates; if this goes on too much longer, we'll be short of supplies in a week. Shield and reshield everything you do. Then check back with me; I'll determine what is most important."

Tremane finally dismissed his mages back to their work of repairing the damages after a little more exhortation, and slumped back into his chair, his temples throbbing. He hoped that he was the only one suffering from a headache, that it was caused more by stress than by the mage-storm; if all his mages were working under the burden of an aching head, they'd only be about half as effective as they were normally.

He rang for a page and called for strong wine. He seldom drank, but at this point he needed at least one cup of fortification.

He stared at the polished surface of the table and turned the cup around and around in his hands. One question was uppermost in his mind: *How did they do this?*

It was not just that the attack was like nothing he had ever seen before. It was not only the sheer size and scope of the attack. It was the randomness of it all.

Insane. Absolutely insane. Not even Ancar had been crazed enough to have developed a spell like this one.

And the effects—what *possible* use was there in an attack that ripped up circles of land and planted them elsewhere? Were the Valdemarans simply hoping that there *might* be strategic targets inside those circles? Or were they just striking for the effect on mind and morale?

Was there a meaning behind it at all? Or was the chaos really the meaning? Was *this* representative of how Valdemarans thought? If so, they were more alien than the gryphons they courted!

If they can do this, he thought to himself, sipping the bitter, dark wine, *what else can they do? Have I taken on even more than Charliss himself could handle? Or is this another of Charliss' little tests?*

That, too, was possible. Charliss and the Empire were in the east, and the storm had come from the east. The Emperor could be testing him under fire, to see how he handled such an attack.

It *still* could have been one of his enemies who had sent this; or more likely, several of his enemies working together.

As he reached the bottom of the glass, another thought occurred to him, one even more bitter than the wine, and more frightening than the mage-storm.

What if Charliss *wanted* to be rid of him? How better than to embroil him in a conflict he could not win?

Had he been set up to fail from the beginning?

Tremane ground his teeth as he pursued that thought. He had been under the impression that he was the Emperor's own choice for successor. Charliss could have been lying, or he could have changed his mind between now and when he had left. He could not ignore the possibility that Charliss now favored one of his enemies.

Could Charliss realistically get rid of him if he succeeded, against all odds and the Emperor's own opposition?

Probably not. A victory here would make him too popular to get rid of. Charliss would be forced to name him as his successor. *And once I am back in Court, at his side, I think I can repair any damage that was done while I was gone.*

That left him with new problems, though. *I am going to have to assume that there will be interference with my orders and requisitions once the orders reach the Empire. Supplies will come in slowly, not at all, or not enough. Reinforcements may not come in time. So I will have to assume the worst and issue my orders well in advance, for more than I think I will need, once our communications are back.*

And if communications could not be restored? That was another possibility.

I will have to plan to at least hold my ground with no help.

A grim prospect. *I have to find a way to throw as much inter-ference in the ranks of the Valdemarans as I can. . . .*

Well, what had made them able to turn the tide against An-car? What was enabling them to hold their own now?

If this *was* their doing, where had the magic come from?

Allies.

He ran his finger around and around the rim of the empty goblet. The new allies—that was how Valdemar was holding her own. So find a way to make those alliances fall apart, and Valdemar would probably have enough trouble at home to prevent any more interference in the situation in Hardorn.

He grimaced again, but this time with distaste. He used spies, he gathered unsavory information, but there was one aspect of this game of empire that he hated. Nevertheless, to buy himself time, he would use it, because he must win the game or die. It was not only his own life that lay in the bal-ance of whether he won or lost, but the lives of all of those who had linked their fortunes with his. If he fell, his family and all their retainers fell as well.

He rang the bell that summoned one of his servants. There was one certain way to ensure that the tentative alliance of Valdemar, Karse, and Rethwellan melted away like snow in the summer, and that was to put one of his own agents into play. It was time for his Spymaster to go to work.

It was time for his Spymaster to make use of those little copies of that souvenir of Valdemar that had come into the Emperor's possession.

"Send me Lord Velcher," he said to the man when the ser-vant arrived. "Tell him that I finally have need of his *particu-lar* services."

13

Karal sat quietly on his bed, his legs crossed beneath him, waiting. His eyes were closed and his breathing was steady.

Ulrich would have said he was "meditating," of course; in fact, that was precisely what most of his teachers would say he was doing. Karal felt uncomfortable with that word. It implied that he was trying to touch the Sunlord in some way. It also implied a certain quality of "holiness" he felt equally uncomfortable with.

He certainly didn't think he was very religious, even if he was an acolyte of the Sunlord. He hadn't really wanted to be in Vkandis' Service. It had just turned out that way, due to fate, Vkandis' Will, or luck.

Still, he *was* being visited by a Firecat, and he *had* agreed to give An'desha some kind of moral support. So while he really didn't want to call any further attention to himself, it seemed to him that if he was just quiet enough, and patient, Vkandis might, well, *dribble* some kind of guidance into him.

So he waited, keeping his mind as free of thoughts as he could, hoping for a dribble, and trying not to *ask* for one.

Nothing came, though, no matter what he thought of—concentric rings in a pool of water, raindrops sprinkling on a still pond—and he gave up when his feet began to go numb. He opened his eyes and stretched, and discovered that at least the mental exercise had relaxed his physical muscles, even if it had made his extremities pin-tingly.

He was just about to swing his feet down to the floor, when he was abruptly no longer alone.

Altra flashed into the middle of the room, every hair on end, eyes as round and wide as a pair of blue plates.

:It's happening!: the Firecat exclaimed. *:Brace yourself!:*

And then, as abruptly as he had appeared, Altra vanished, without telling Karal just what "it" was that was happening.

He sat there, staring stupidly at the spot where Altra had been, for two or three breaths. Then he didn't have to wonder what "it" was.

From his point of view, the entire room heaved and rolled for just a moment, as if he was a speck on a carpet someone had decided to pick up and shake. Even though there were no outward signs that any actual movement was happening, his stomach dropped, and he clung to the bed as a wave of dizziness overcame him for no more than three heartbeats.

Then it was over.

That was all? What had Altra been so excited about? It was strange, yes, and felt a little like an earthquake was supposed to feel, but nothing in the room was disturbed, so obviously the "quake" wasn't really physical. Unless—was this some symptom of a disease? Could he be falling ill? Could it be some kind of plague, and was Altra warning him that an attack was coming?

Could Ulrich have it? If Ulrich was sick—

He's not strong; something serious could kill him! Karal was trained in basic field surgery, as were all acolytes. If his mentor *was* hurt, he could at least diagnose major problems. He was off his bed and out of his room without another thought; he wrenched open the door to Ulrich's room, nearly separating his wrist from his forearm, to find his mentor sitting up so stiffly in his chair that he might have had a metal rod for a spine. Ulrich's face was pale, and beads of cold sweat trickled down his temples; his white-knuckled hands clutched the arms of his chair, and the pupils of his eyes were mere pinpoints.

Ulrich blinked and suddenly relaxed, slumping back into his chair. Color came back into his face, and he raised a trembling hand to wipe the sweat from his forehead.

"Master? Master Ulrich?" Karal said, uncertainly. "Shall I get you some help? A Healer? Are you ill?"

"No—no, don't bother, my son," Ulrich replied, his voice

tremulous with fatigue and other things Karal couldn't identify. "This is nothing a Healer can deal with. Did you feel
anything, just now?"

"I was dizzy for a moment, and I felt like I was falling,"
Karal replied promptly. "Nothing more, though. Should I
have felt something more?"

Ulrich managed a faint and tremulous smile, and shook his
head. "Not necessarily. Altra warned me in time to brace myself. *This* is what he has been waiting for, what he has been
warning all of us about, obliquely. And this may well be what
your friend An'desha has been sensing would descend upon
us. It was a mage-storm, Karal, but one unlike any we have
ever seen."

"That?" Karal shook his head; Ulrich wasn't making any
sense. "How could that be dangerous? It was no more than a
little moment of dizziness!"

"For you, perhaps," the Priest replied sharply. "But for
those of us who are mages—we just spent an eternity in that
'little moment' and for us, it was like being dropped into a
cauldron and stirred! I suspect that the more mage-power one
has, the worse one would be affected."

Karal gasped. "Then An'desha—"

"And Firesong as well," Ulrich replied, looking alarmed.
"They will have suffered worse than I. They may well have
injured themselves, falling—at the least they will be disori-
ented. Go to them! I can manage for myself."

Karal didn't need Ulrich to tell him twice; he shot off like
an arrow from a bow, and ran all the way from the Palace to
the secluded *ekele*.

It never occurred to him that he might find the two of them
in an—embarrassing position—until he actually reached the
door of the dwelling. He paused for only a moment, his hand
on the latch, before going in anyway. After all, he would be
embarrassed, and that hardly mattered, not when the other
two might be hurt. He let himself into the garden.

There was no one there.

He headed for the staircase. "An'desha?" he called over the
sound of falling water. "Firesong?"

"Here—" came a weak reply from above. It wasn't An'desha's
voice; it had to be Firesong. He dashed up the stairs and found

the silver-haired Hawkbrother lying in a heap with one leg twisted under him, his face as pale as his hair, and obviously dazed. His firebird was clenched to a chair arm nearby, scorching the wood in its agitation.

"My leg—" The Adept gestured at the offending limb. "I fell down."

"Don't move; I know some field surgery." This at least was something he could do. He knew enough to check for broken and dislocated bones, and if Firesong *was* hurt, he could go for a real Healer.

Firesong looked at him, and though his eyes were glazed, they held some recognition in them. And questions.

"What—who—" Firesong began. Karal answered the questions as best he could.

"My name is Karal, sir," he said, "I'm a friend of An'desha's. I'll tell you about that later. You've probably seen me during Council sessions, with my master Ulrich, the Karsite envoy. I think you've sprained your ankle, and it probably hurts like anything; can you flex your toes, then your foot, carefully?"

Grimacing with pain, Firesong did so. "I—ah!—if I can do this, nothing is broken. Find An'desha," the Adept ordered. "Tell me the rest when we know he's all right."

"Yes, sir." Karal left the Hawkbrother sitting on the floor of the *ekele* massaging his ankle, and sprinted up to the kitchen, calling An'desha's name as he ran. The third time he called, he got an answer.

"Here," An'desha said. "Here—" Karal found him in a small room, draped to look like the inside of a tent. His friend was curled up in a ball on the floor, but it didn't look as if he was hurt. Karal dropped to his knees beside the young mage.

"An'desha?" he said, touching the mage's arm tentatively.

"I am all right, Karal," An'desha whispered, slowly opening his eyes. "I believe it is over for now."

"You didn't hurt yourself, did you?" Karal asked anxiously.

"No; I felt it building, and something warned me to fall to the ground." An'desha blinked, as if he was forcing his eyes to focus again. "It is well I did so. I think—I think this, or something *like* this, is what I have been fearing." He blinked again, and astonishment and relief spread over his features.

"Karal? That dread I was feeling, waiting for something terrible to come—it is gone!"

"Can you stand?" Karal asked anxiously. "Can you walk? Your friend Firesong is hurt, and—"

He was not able to get anything more out of his mouth; An'desha scrambled to his feet, unassisted, and was already out of the door and running before Karal was standing. By the time Karal reached the two of them, An'desha had supported Firesong over to a couch, and was making distressed sounds over his rapidly-swelling ankle.

Karal blushed, his face and ears hot. "I'll—ah—get a Healer," he stammered, leaving An'desha to explain where and how he and Karal had met.

By the time Karal returned with a Healer, he was also full of other news. In general, there was no real physical damage to anything in or around the Palace, and the worst physical hurt seemed to be a couple of bruises, bloody noses, and Firesong's ankle. From all he had been able to make out, some of the weaker magical defenses about the capital had been taken down by the storm and would have to be put up again, but there wasn't much more to worry about. If this was what An'desha's attacks of fear and dread had been about, it was certainly anticlimactic.

Besides the Healer, Karal brought orders for Firesong and An'desha to come to an emergency meeting of the allies and the Council, though, which tended to make him think that there had been effects outside of Haven that were a lot more serious than disorientation and the disruption of weak shields.

He was right.

"Once you are outside the shields that Elspeth, Darkwind, and Firesong erected to protect Haven, there are places all across the country where very *weird* things have happened," said Skif. "I went out for a fast reconnoiter with Cymry, and I saw some of them for myself. There are places where rock turned to liquid for an instant, places where circles of land have been cut out as if someone was making cookies, and circles of land from somewhere else were fitted into the holes! People brought me insects, plants, fish—even animals, all strange, all things I've never seen before in my life! People are scared."

"Surely this was the work of the Empire," the Seneschal began, but oddly enough, it was the Lord Marshal who shook his head, and Kerowyn who echoed that headshake.

The Lord Marshal deferred to the Herald Captain with a raised eyebrow and a nod, as if to say, "After you."

"It can't have been the Empire's doing, unless it was some new magic they were trying that backfired on them," Kerowyn told them all, drumming her fingers nervously on the table in front of her. "I already have short reports from two Mindspeakers behind their lines, and word is that their forces have suffered *much* more damage than ours have. They depend more than we do on magic, and right now they are working with most of their support systems reduced. By that, I mean they have no means of communicating between groups except by messenger, and no Gates back to the Empire for supplies and reinforcing troops. In a word, gentlemen and ladies," she said, with a certain satisfaction, "at the moment, they are well and truly flattened. The only thing that could have hit them worse would have been an army-wide outbreak of dysentery."

Silence followed that pronouncement, and Queen Selenay sat back a little in her seat. "I trust you'll forgive me if I take some pleasure in that news," she said dryly. "Base though such a sentiment is—"

"Forgive me, Majesty," Darkwind said, interrupting her. "As a mage and an Adept, I cannot help but be more concerned, rather than less. These physical effects—it seems to me that they indicate something very serious. They worry me more than the effects upon magic. How do we know this thing will not come again?"

He turned to Firesong as if for confirmation, and the handsome Hawkbrother nodded in complete agreement. "If we cannot tell what it is and from whence it came," Firesong said gravely, "we cannot hope to judge whether it will fall upon us again, nor when."

He glanced aside at Karal, who was busy jotting down notes. Karal had caught a couple of strange looks from him, but otherwise, he had said nothing about Karal's acquaintance with An'desha.

"And you don't think this will be an isolated incident." Selenay's inflection made that a statement rather than a question.

"Absolutely," Firesong replied. "And before we can make any guesses as to what it may be, we need to know more about these physical effects—what they are, at what intervals—"

As the other mages chimed in, Elspeth and Treyvan, Hydona and Master Ulrich, and even An'desha venturing a word or two, it became obvious to Karal that for this, the rest of the Council and allies were superfluous. It must have been obvious to the Queen as well, for after regaining order and promising all of the resources needed for whatever the mages required, she ended the Council session and left the chamber to the mages and Prince Daren as her representative.

Karal remained as well, in his usual capacity, but he soon found himself drafted to serve another purpose altogether.

"We need a view frrrom above," the male gryphon said, flatly. "If therrre isss a patterrrn, we may only sssee it frrrom above."

"That's true enough, old friend," Darkwind agreed. "But you should have a human with you. You two aren't familiar enough to the average Valdemaran that some poor farmer is going to be able to take the sight of you lightly. I'd hate to have to pick arrows out of your rump. And it should be someone with hands, and at least a mediocre talent at drawing sketches of what you see."

"Rrr." The gryphon ground his beak, then glanced around the table. His eye lighted on Karal.

"*Him,*" the gryphon said. "He isss light and sssmall enough, and intelligent. He can take notesss. With yourrr perrrrmisssion?" he added, nodding graciously at Ulrich.

The Priest looked the gryphon straight in the eye, as Karal shivered with mingled shock and apprehension. The gryphons wanted to *fly* with him? *Fly!* Like a bird?

"It is up to my secretary to speak for himself," Ulrich said, with a nod to Karal. "I have no objections, but rumors to the contrary, we of Karse do not make slaves of our subordinates. If he chooses not to volunteer, I shall not force him."

"Well?" the gryphon asked bluntly, turning his huge eyes on Karal.

Karal swallowed hard. "Ah—yes, sir," he replied, managing not to stammer. "If you think I will be of help. I've never done anything like this. I might only get in your way."

I might die of fright before we go a hundred paces.

"Good. It isss done." The gryphon turned his attention back to the other mages, leaving Karal feeling rather dazed.

And feeling as if he had somehow been bowled out of his path by a very heavy object. *Now what have I gotten myself into?*

He had occasion to ask himself that question again, a few marks later, when he saw the object that Treyvan casually referred to as "the carry-net." He had envisioned something a little more substantial; this was hardly more than a wicker laundry basket in a cradle of thin lines of rope, with laminated wood spars here and there above it. It didn't look as if it would take the weight of a child.

It sat in the middle of a patch of lawn in the gardens; there were no trees of any size here. He gathered that it would take the gryphons time to haul him above tree level. That did not comfort him much, either.

"It's stronger than it looks," said Darkwind, who had come to the Karsite suite to fetch him.

Karal held back a grimace. "I'm sure it is, sir," he replied instead, politely. He was past having second thoughts about this expedition—now he was into fourth and fifth thoughts!

"Heh. I distinctly heard a tone of 'It would have to be stronger than it looks,' Karal. There's magic in the making of it," Darkwind continued blithely, as if they *weren't* out to investigate the effects of the failure of magic! "Don't worry, you'll get used to it. Treyvan told me that k'Leshya use carry-nets like this all the time, that they're as safe as the floating barges."

As if I knew what a "k'Leshya" is. Or a floating barge, for that matter. He looked the "net" over dubiously; each end of the rope sling was meant to fasten to a harness worn by each gryphon, and the basket in the middle was evidently supposed to supply more stability to the rider than he would get from the kind of hammock this resembled.

The rope was a lot stronger than its light weight suggested, and Karal discovered when he tried to tilt the basket while it was still sitting on the ground that it resisted all of his attempts to turn it over, even though he could lift it straight up quite easily. So, there was a great deal more to this contraption than met the eye!

Maybe this wouldn't be so bad, after all. But still, *flying?*

"The gryphons will be along in a moment," Darkwind said, glancing up at the angle of the sun. "I need to start my own search pattern with Vree, Firesong, and Aya, so I'll leave you here to wait for them."

"Wait a moment." Karal hesitated, then asked the question he'd had on his mind anyway. "If what they need is someone to record what they see, why do they need me? They have perfectly good memories."

"But no hands," Darkwind reminded him. "They read, but they can't write or draw—not easily, at any rate. That lets Rris out as well—I promise you, he was terribly disappointed. He wanted a ride through the air very badly; he said he would be the first of his clan to do such a thing, which would mean he would *finally* do something famous-cousin-Warrl hadn't!" The Tayledras mage smiled, and clapped Karal on the back. "Don't worry. After a few moments, you'll be glad they asked you to come. You'll do very well indeed."

Karal could not imagine what it was about him that prompted such assurance on Darkwind's part, but he nodded bravely.

A few moments after Darkwind's departure, Hydona appeared from inside the Palace, wearing her harness. It was a sturdy affair of leather and brass, and it looked a lot more substantial than the basket. The gryphon clacked her beak in greeting to him once she was within earshot, and sauntered over to stand beside him.

"If you would fasssten that clip herrre—" she said to him, indicating what he should do with a touch of her talon. "And that one herrre—" She nodded with approval as he engaged the two fasteners. "That isss good. When Trrreyvan comesss, do the sssame on hisss harrrnesss." She cocked her head to one side and studied him for a moment, then added, "If it isss any help, I have carrried my little onesss in thisss verrry net. They may be fledged, but they arrre not trrruly flighted, yet. They tend to plummet."

If she trusted her precious gryphlets in this— Hydona's maternal qualities were one of the first things anyone mentioned about her. She wouldn't risk her little ones. Relief made him relax, and he managed a tentative smile.

How had she read his expression so accurately? And how had she guessed the very thing that *would* make him feel that the net was flightworthy? "Thank you, my lady," he replied humbly. "It does help. I have never flown before."

With that, she chuckled. "I would be verrry sssurrrprrrisssed if you had," she rumbled smoothly. "But I think you will enjoy it."

Treyvan appeared from above, backwinging gracefully to a landing beside the two of them. "I have been aloft, and therrre isss a patterrrn, I think," he said cheerfully. "Ssso—let usss sssee if I am brrrilliant, or deluded!" Caught up in his excitement, which radiated from him like warm sunshine, Karal snapped the hooks of the other side of the net onto the male gryphon's harness, and got into the basket, suddenly eager to be off. He arranged his stylus and waxboard, and didn't even think about being afraid until they were several stories above the ground, skimming the treetops.

And at that point, he was too caught up in the incredible feeling of power and freedom to be frightened.

Like most people he knew, he'd had dreams of flying before, but it had never been like this. He was buffeted by wind from all directions—from the backwash of both gryphons' wings, and the maelstrom of their passage. They were moving *much* faster than the fastest horse he had ever ridden. He clung to the edge of the basket—which did *not* tip over, even when he dared to lean out to look straight down—and stared at the city below.

Was this how the gryphons always saw things? From this vantage, the city took on an entirely new look. Patterns emerged that he would not have seen from below. Now he could judge what houses were built about the same time from the way the roofs were constructed, for instance. Now he could tell that someone who had an otherwise impressive house might be either very careless or falling on hard times by the dilapidated state of what did not show from the street level. People in the poorer sections *used* every bit of space, too, which was not the case with those who were better off; roofs in the poorest parts of town held plants, vegetables grown in carefully-tended tubs of soil, and were strung with lines for hanging out wash. People gathered up there, women and children mostly, who gaped and pointed at him and the gryphons when they passed overhead. Children stopped in their games, and one woman even shrieked and flung her wet laundry over her head to hide.

A moment later, they were over a district of warehouses— and a moment after that, they were outside the city walls.

The gryphons strained for altitude, and climbed higher into the cloud-strewn sky. Karal watched those clouds worriedly; this would be a very bad time for a lightning storm to blow up! But, even if he were struck from the skies, he would die knowing what it felt like to be so close to Vkandis. . . .

"Look," Hydona called, over the thunder of her own wings. "Down therrre. That isss the firrrssst of the sssignsss."

Karal looked down obediently and saw exactly what she was talking about. Right in the middle of a green field was a circular space that held black sand. Sheep eyed it dubiously.

"We need morrre height to sssee the patterrn," Treyvan called back. She nodded and strained upward.

The sheep dwindled into white toys, then into clots of wool, then into small dots on the green field. The air got colder and thinner—not even while going through high mountain passes had Karal been this high up! His ears and nose were numb, and his eardrums popped again and again as they surged higher. Treyvan pointed, and Karal followed the direction of his talon.

A thrill of excitement touched him. There *was* a pattern! Beyond the circle of black sand, there was another discoloration in the middle of a field of grain, a place that appeared to be circular as well. And beyond that, a mere blot of color in line with the first two, there seemed to be a third at about the same distance as the interval between the first and second.

"Go down!" he shouted to Treyvan. "Land next to the sand-circle! I'll make some notes and take a sample; we'll go on to the next one and do the same. We'll measure that distance, and see if there really is a third and what the distance is to it—"

"And if therrre isss a fourrrth, and a fifth," Hydona added. "Good idea, Karrral!"

They dropped a lot faster than they had climbed. Karal clamped both hands firmly around the front of the basket, but felt like he would be better served by clutching at his stomach. Still, the basket landed with a controlled bump that rattled Karal's teeth but did no other damage. He hopped out and measured the circle of sand by pacing it, folded a bit of paper into a cone and scooped up a sample, then sketched and described the circle. There didn't seem to be anything alive in it; he stirred the center of it with a stick and came up with nothing but fine, black sand, completely uniform in makeup and texture. The sheep watched him with vague alarm on their silly faces but couldn't make up their minds whether to flee or stand. They were more afraid of him than they were of the gryphons and shied sideways, bleating each time he made a move toward them.

The gryphons watched, panting, sunlight glinting off their feathers. He made sure to take long enough at his tasks to allow the gryphons enough time to catch their breath.

"All right," he said, when he couldn't think of anything else useful to measure. "Are you ready?"

Treyvan nodded, and he climbed back into the basket. The takeoff was a little slower this time; with only sheep to impress, Treyvan didn't seem to be in as much of a hurry.

The next spot was, indeed, a circle—but this time, it wasn't of sand. This spot contained a short, wiry grass of an odd yellow-green; the soil beneath it was hard and full of reddish clay, so that the earth itself looked red. There were dead insects in this patch, but they didn't look any different from the ones Karal was familiar with. Nevertheless, he took a sample of the earth, the grass, and a little black beetle. Maybe someone else could make something of this.

The third circle held something quite unexpected; a section of ground that could have come from a Karsite meadow. The ground was exactly right; gray and full of stones. The plants were that tough gorse and mountain grass that only goats could eat, and in one side of the circle was a patch of kitten-paw flowers that Karal *knew* would not grow in Valdemar. He knew that because they were the common Karsite remedy for headache, and when he had asked for some, the Healers hadn't a clue what he was talking about.

Duitifully, he sampled this as well. He also took every kitten-paw bunch that was handy because he felt there would be a lot of headaches in his immediate future. He added notes and observations on the waxboard, and each page of paper. The distance between the first and second circles and the second and third was precisely equal.

They continued to follow a line of disturbances on away from Haven into the north; not all of the things they found were as obvious as those circles of alien earth. Several times they actually had to land to find that there *was* a transplant, for it was so similar to what surrounded it that only the neat circular cut-line around it betrayed that it was there. And once, they found, not a circle of transplanted soil, but a circle of fused sand.

Only once had Karal ever seen anything like *this*, and that had been as a child, in a place where lightning had struck sandy loam. That had left a mark about the size of his hand; *this* was a circle of blackened, cracked black glass, mottled and full of bubbles and irregularities, that was easily the size of a freight wagon. The three of them stared at the lumpy glass, and Karal wondered if the gryphons felt the same cold dread that he did. Something had certainly struck here with terrible force. What if it had struck within the city limits?

What if, somewhere out there, in Valdemar, Karse, or Rethwellan, it *had* struck within a populated area? What if it struck his father's inn, or Sunhame?

"Therrre werrre weaponsss that did damage like that in the old daysss," Hydona said softly. "Terrrible weaponsss, in the daysss of Ssskandrrranon. The Grrreat Adeptsss usssed them. We had hoped neverrr to sssee sssuch again in the lifetimesss of ourrr childrrren."

Weapons? It had not occurred to him that such a thing

could be a *weapon*. What could possibly guard against such a thing?

But remember the Sunlord; Vkandis can strike like this. Surely Karse, at least, is safe. Surely He can protect His people. But somehow, with this before him, it was hard to have faith that Vkandis would protect His people. This seemed too random, like a cosmic event, and even Vkandis Sunlord was said to be a part of a greater universe.

"We have enough, I think," Treyvan said in a louder voice, shaking himself as if to shake the terrible thought from his mind. "It isss time to rrreturrrn."

Obediently, if more than a little disturbed, Karal climbed back into the basket. But he was much too preoccupied with the thoughts called up by that circle of crackled glass to take any pleasure in the return flight.

As night fell, the mages gathered again to compare their notes in the Council Chamber, and once again, An'desha prevailed on Firesong to let him come along. To his relief, Firesong had accepted his explanation of how he and Karal had met with outward calm. Pointing out that it was *Talia* who had introduced them seemed to make the difference; An'desha had noted more than once that Firesong, who rarely gave deference to anyone, gave an immense measure of respect to Lady Talia.

That was just as well; An'desha had a lot more on his mind than explaining a simple friendship to his lover. The magestorm's first bluster had stirred something up from out of Falconsbane's deepest and oldest memories, and he was still trying to sort it out.

First and foremost, he was certain, as he had never before been certain of anything, that *this* was what both the Avatars and his seizures of fear had been warning him about. Secondly, he knew that a part of him recognized just what the mage-storm really was—or rather, what it was a symptom of.

There was a version of Falconsbane who called himself "Ma'ar" who was somehow involved with that memory, though without actually probing after it, he could not be sure just what that involvement was.

When Firesong went out with Darkwind to do a bondbird

aerial sweep to the south, An'desha stayed behind in the reassuring confines of the tiny Vale. Although he would have preferred to have Karal to talk him through this, he had
approached Karal's master, the Karsite Priest Ulrich, as a substitute to help him through another search through those
dreadful memories. When Ulrich agreed, the Priest suggested
his own quarters as the best place for such a search, and
An'desha had taken the suggestion with relief. Then he had
taken his courage in both hands, just as he had done when he
had tricked Falconsbane into walking out into the trap that
meant his death, and plunged into a trance to trace back the
memory.

It had taken a long time, and when he emerged from it, he
was too shaken by the experience to say anything. Ulrich did
not seem in a hurry to make him speak, though; the Priest
just sat there with him, pressing a cup of sweet tea on him,
letting him take his own time in recovering.

But by the time An'desha felt ready to talk, Firesong came
to tell Ulrich that the rest of the mages had already gathered.

"I should be there, too," An'desha said, as steadily as he
could, and felt a little glow of warmth at Firesong's glance of
approval.

*He's been trying for so long to get me to accept my powers
and responsibilities ... I suppose this makes him feel very
good.* In spite of the soul-churning effect of wandering through
the miasma of Falconsbane's evil memories, An'desha realized that it made *him* feel rather good, too. Shouldering the
burden—at least at the moment—was actually less onerous
than anticipating and dreading the need to shoulder it. It
made him feel the way he did when the Avatars had come to
him—that tremulous exultation, the sense of being a tiny but
bright light in a great expanse of darkness. He accepted what
he must do.

He followed the others into the Council Chamber again,
and waited with them while pages went around the room
lighting the lanterns set into the plaster-ornamented walls.
The Court Artist, who had apparently been sitting there and
sketching some of the mages under pretense of recording a
historical event, was sent packing out of the room by a scowl
from Daren. Karal was there, sitting with the gryphons this

time, bearing signs of windburn and chapped lips. His friend gave him a shaky smile. He seemed very disturbed by something, and somehow An'desha doubted that it had been the flying that had set that expression on his face.

Karal is brave, braver than I am. He wouldn't be afraid of flying. Something else has frightened him.

"Let Karrral ssspeak forrr the thrrree of usss," said Treyvan, when all the shuffling of papers and settling into seats was done. The great gryphon raised his head into the light, and his eyes glinted with reflections. "We have dissscusssed thisss, and he hasss the feelingsss of all three of usss."

Karal cleared his throat self-consciously as all eyes turned toward him. "Well, what we basically discovered, is that there is a regular pattern to the disturbances, the ones that we saw, anyway. They are all the same size, the same distance apart, and in a straight line. We went as far as we could before turning back, and we didn't see an end to them. Most of them are—transplants, I suppose you would say. They are circles of foreign soil; they look as if a gardener cut circles of land and replaced them with circles of land from somewhere else. Most of them were so similar to Valdemaran soil that if we hadn't been looking for signs of disturbance we wouldn't have spotted anything wrong. Some were from places I couldn't recognize—the one nearest the city going directly north from the Palace is of black sand, for instance. There was one piece that I would swear was right out of a mountain meadow in Karse; it even contained an herb I know grows only there. I took samples from all of them. But one—there was one at the end that was different. That strange one—it was fused sand, like badly-made glass." He swallowed, hard. "I—it would be very terrible if whatever did *that* has done it somewhere where there are people."

"Did you see any of the strange animals some people have described?" Elspeth asked.

Karal shook his head. "No, nothing that didn't seem quite normal, just out of place where we found it."

"I found some of the strange animals, and even a bird," Darkwind spoke up. "Or rather, Vree found them and caught them. I had the impression that the disturbances were not regular and not in a pattern, but it hadn't occurred to me that many of them would simply look just like the land around them."

An'desha listened with a sinking heart. Oh, this sounded far too much like that ancient memory for his satisfaction! *I had hoped they would prove me wrong, but they are only proving me more and more right!*

An'desha simply sat and absorbed it all, unable to garner the will to speak. Not just yet, anyway.

Darkwind described the creatures that he had caught and brought back; the other mages who had gone in other directions added their observations. Karal offered more comments of his own, calmly, though with obvious deference to the others. He wouldn't venture any conclusions, but based on his own figures and those of the rest, he began to plot the rest of the observations on a larger map of the land around Haven. Karal's relative self-assurance—and his and Ulrich's occasional glances of encouragement—finally gave An'desha the courage to speak up in a moment of silence.

"You all know—what, who I was," he said softly, his eyes fixed on a spot in the middle of the table.

Every eye in the place turned toward him. Karal stopped writing.

"I still have Mornelith Falconsbane's memories," he went on, haltingly. "And those of the lives he led before he was Falconsbane. I *knew* this mage-storm when it struck. I *recognized* it somehow, out of those memories, though I did not know what it was, exactly, nor how I recognized it." He swallowed; his throat and mouth felt terribly dry, and his hands were cold. "Please—please, do not think me crazy. What I say is true, as true as I can say it. With the help of Master Ulrich, I—I sought answers to that recognition. I believe I know what this storm was, what caused it, and even why."

The silence was so thick he heard the hiss of the lantern flames behind him. "Please be patient with me; this was the oldest memory I have ever touched, possibly the oldest that Falconsbane himself had. It came from a time when Falconsbane was a mage and a king called Ma'ar."

The gryphons hissed as one, hackles and crest-feathers smoothed flat to their heads, and sat straight up on their haunches. No one else moved.

"The memory of a storm like this one—it came after a Gate was destroyed. Not a temporary Gate like we know, but a *permanent* Gate—one that was held ready to be opened at any moment. It was a small storm, and the effects were limited, but they were very like what you have been describing here." He swallowed again; what followed had been very, very hard to cope with, even at the remove of several hundreds, if not thousands, of years. "But when Ma'ar—died—it was with the knowledge that *his* realm, and that of his enemy, were both about to fall to a suicidal cataclysm. Both realms, rich in magic, *built* with magic, were about to have every spell within them broken within moments of his death. *Many* permanent Gates, shields, devices, all—and all at once. He died before he himself experienced that cataclysm, but the effects would have been very like those we are seeing now, but much, much worse, lasting for days, and traveling across continents."

"Continents?" someone asked. An'desha nodded.

"Hence, that it is called 'the Cataclysm' in the old texts," Ulrich murmured as if to himself.

"But that wasss verrry long ago," Hydona said, puzzled. "What hasss that to do with usss?"

He took another deep breath. This was even harder to speak of, but for a different reason. "I do not often tell of this, but when I was entrapped within my body by Falconsbane, I was aided by two—presences." *Please, oh please, do not let them doubt my sanity!*

"Avatars of the Star-Eyed, he means," Firesong interjected, and reached under the table to squeeze his hand encouragingly. "The blade Need spoke to me of these, more than once. I believe they were what they claimed to be and so does she; after all, some of you saw them when they unmade both Nyara and An'desha, giving them back more human likenesses."

"An'desha has told me of these Avatars," Karal spoke up. "I believe them to be true Visitations also."

An'desha cleared his throat self-consciously, feeling his ears and neck growing hot with a flush he could not control. "They warned me then, several times, that there was something terrible in the future. Something that threatened not only Valdemar alone, but all our lands. *I* thought it was only Falconsbane, but I continued to have terrible dreams, and spells of great fear after he was gone. Now that this mage-storm has come upon us and I have searched out that old memory, I—I have—" he shook his head. "I am no great mage, for all the potential power that Firesong thinks I hold, but there are some things that are now making dreadful sense to me. The Avatars spoke to me once of 'power and chaos echoing back across time.' I thought that meant Falconsbane, but now I do not think so. I have the memory of *how much* power lay in all those spells that were released in that long-ago time of the Mage Wars. Ma'ar believed in his last moments that it was more than the fabric of the world could bear, to have it all released in a single moment—and as importantly, to have *two* such centers of power interacting with each other. I think that what happened *then* is about to echo back upon us *now*—but in reverse of the original. I think that the storm we just experienced is only the warning."

An'desha drew a halting breath, and summed it up as best he could. "What we experienced was the little chill breeze that presages a hurricane."

Firesong stared at him, stunned. Now it was Treyvan's turn to break the silence.

"It isss in the trrraditionsss of the Kaled'a'in k'Lesshya that therrre werrre weeksss of mage-ssstorrrmsss following the death of Urrrtho," the gryphon said with steady calm. "The old chrrroniclesss sssay that it wasss impossssible to desss-cribe how terrrible they werrre, in effect, and in ssstrrrength. The verrry land wasss torrrn asssssunderrr, and even time ssseemed to flow ssstrrrangely forrr the yearrr afterrr."

"There is an oral tradition of the same among the Tayle-dras," Firesong managed and shook his head. "I can't even be-gin to guess what effect the release of that much mage-energy would have. If it could turn the land around the King's Palace where Ma'ar was into a cratered lake, and the land around Urtho's Tower into a plain of glass, there is no reason to sup-pose it might not even travel through the fabric of time itself. So many spells and wards are linked to time as if it were a physical presence—and even small magical explosions wreck the latticework of magic for a dozen leagues around them."

The others turned their attention back to An'desha, who looked horribly pale. "I do not have the learning to guess at more," he said humbly. "And if you will please forgive me, I do not wish to delve more into those memories that might give me that learning—at least not tonight. They make me feel ill."

"I have knowledge of the old Kaled'a'in magicsss," Treyvan rumbled. "Asss passsed to Vikterrren and Ssskandrrranon by Urrrtho himsssself. The making of Gatesss warrrps time, asss waterrr warpsss wood; the making of perrrmanent Gatesss warrrps it morrre. Therrre werrre at leassst twenty sssuch Gatesss at Urrrtho's Towerrr, perrrhapsss morrre. Therrre werrre all the weaponsss that Urrrtho *would not* ussse, forrr they werrre too terrrible. Therrre werrre the prrrotectionsss on the Towerrr, and the magicssss of the placsesss we grrrryphonsss werrre borrrn."

Ulrich's brows knotted with thought. "I—this goes beyond what I have learned," he said at last, "but I can tell you this; I have myself had warnings from an Avatar of Vkandis that something of this sort portended."

Elspeth looked impatient. "You had *vague* warnings, An'desha had *vague* warnings, why didn't anyone get anything clear?"

An'desha winced. That was a perfectly reasonable question. And he didn't have an answer.

But Ulrich only smiled slightly. "Perhaps because even the Star-Eyed and Vkandis Himself did not know what the effect would be," he replied gently. "Hear me out. When the Gods granted mankind free will, They allowed uncertainty to enter the world. Some things can be predicted; others cannot. If I may make an analogy—I can tell you that a great storm is coming. With the knowledge I have that when the wind blows such-and-so, and the glass falls, and the sky looks thusly at this time of year, I can say that there will be a storm. But I cannot predict what places will flood, how high the floodwaters will rise, what homes will be battered to bits, and what keeps struck by lightning. As this power comes back to us, I think that even the Gods could not tell exactly what form it would take, *perhaps* because of what we and others have done with magic since then. They could only warn that there was danger."

"So—" Elspeth said slowly, after a long silence, "The good news is that this isn't anything we caused, and it isn't anything that the Empire is turning on us. The *bad* news is that this really isn't a 'mage-storm' as such. Not yet, anyway. It was—was one wave, created by the real storm that is out of sight of the land. It swamped boats and wrecked docks, but the real storm still hasn't come in yet."

An'desha watched as the faces of all the mages around the table sank as they all accepted that conclusion. If it was not the truth, it was certainly the closest thing they had to the truth at the moment. No, it wasn't a weapon, or anything *they* had caused. But it also wasn't anything they could stop, any more than they could stop a real storm from sweeping in.

"I should point out that there may be a bright side to this," Prince Daren said. "Kerowyn said it herself; the Empire relies *far* more heavily on magic than we do. The real mage-storm will hurt them *far* more than it does us."

"True." Elspeth chewed her thumbnail, a habit that made An'desha wince. "But it may destroy us all, Empire included. Well, there is one thing we *can* do, though whether it will do any good or not, I don't know. We *have* to get warnings out to every member of the Alliance about this, so that they will at least know what this last squall was, that it wasn't *us*, and that there's worse to come. There *is* worse to come, right?"

She looked at Firesong for the answer to that.

The Healing Adept shrugged. "My guess is that there will be. An'desha's prescient dreams were terrible things, and I do not think this little 'squall' as you called it could account for them. There were 'waves of mage-storms' before, and if the reverse of the past is happening, these squalls will build into a powerful climax."

"We have to collect every bit of information we can," An'desha insisted. "We have to know every spot of disturbance in Valdemar. If we have a pattern, maybe we can deduce the next places that will be struck."

"We—or, rather, the Tayledras—have another task before us first," Firesong interjected grimly. "Which is why I plan to send a mage-message to my parents as soon as we are done with this meeting. We *must* get the best shields ever created around each and every Heartstone, including the one here beneath the Palace. If that is not done, we, Valdemaran and Tayledras alike, could all find ourselves facing rogue Stones, and the storms will be immaterial for we will already be dead."

An'desha blinked in surprise as both Elspeth and Darkwind blanched. He had not thought there was anything that could rattle *those* two.

"Then Darkwind and I—all the Herald-Mages—had better get to work right now," Elspeth said, pushing away from the table and standing up. "Anything else can wait."

"I will help you, if you like," Ulrich offered. "I believe that I may know some shielding techniques you do not."

"We ssshall asss well," Treyvan said, with a dry chuckle. "Afterrr all, it isss *ourrr* tailsss in jeoparrrdy, too!"

"Shall—" An'desha began to add his offer to theirs, but Elspeth and Firesong both shook their heads.

"I know that you dread another walk through those memories, *ke'chara*," Firesong said quietly, "but if there is any more information in them, I wish you would look for it."

"I will be sssending a messsage to k'Lessshya, forrr acccurrrate copiesss of the chrrroniclesss," Hydona told them. "Therrre may be morrre anssswerrrsss therrre."

"Huh. *Rris* might even have something to add. But he's so selfish with his stories!" Darkwind raised an eyebrow as a chuckle of nervous laughter met his comment. "Well, he *is* a *kyree* historian; there might be an oral tradition about this among the *kyree*."

"True enough," Prince Daren said as he stood up, smoothing his white uniform in a gesture of habit. "Well, I think we have wrung the last drop of water from this for now. I will go report to Selenay; I leave you to your various tasks."

He paused for a moment before leaving, as his troubled eyes met each of theirs in turn. An'desha could not sustain that contact for long; he felt somehow guilty about all of this, as if he were somehow the cause of it.

"As unpleasant as my task will be, giving Selenay ill news," Daren said at last, "I do not envy any of you *your* jobs. For once, I am glad I am no mage. You must all feel like oarsmen trying to outrun a wave you cannot stop."

With that, he took himself out, and the rest of them followed his example. An'desha wasn't certain how the others felt, but so far as he was concerned, Prince Daren had summed up the entire situation *far* too accurately.

Despite Prince Daren's gloomy words, Karal was not about to give up the fight before he had even started! Surely there was something they could do about this! Even if they couldn't stop the storm itself, well, people built houses against storms all the time; why couldn't they build shelters against this one?

They survived back then, or we wouldn't be here now. What we need is more information. The more we know, the better we'll be able to prepare.

Maybe he was no mage, but he did know exactly where to go to find people who were absolutely, precisely ideal for the task of gathering and categorizing information.

As Ulrich followed Elspeth, Darkwind, and the gryphons to some mysterious room in the cellars of the Palace, he went off in a different direction entirely.

The clouds of this afternoon had thickened, and the air smelled damp, so he stopped just long enough to fetch a cloak from his room before heading out the side door to the little postern gate in the Palace walls that Natoli had shown him. The Guard there tonight wasn't one he knew, but it didn't much matter; most of the Guards probably knew how to get to any tavern in Haven.

His supposition wasn't wrong; the Guard was only too happy to give him exact directions to the Compass Rose, directions that matched very well with his own hazy memory of the way Natoli had led him the first time.

By the time the Guard was satisfied that he had the directions straight, thunder rumbled off in the far distance, and he thought he glimpsed a flash of lightning against the dark night sky. He set off down the street just as the first few fat drops of rain fell onto the cobblestones in front of him with audible *splats*.

The few drops had become a downpour by the time he reached the tavern door, and just before he opened that door, he had a horrible thought. *What if the rain kept everyone away? What if I can't find them all? What am I going to do then?*

But the blast of sound and warmth that hit his face as he opened the door against the rising wind told him that his fears were groundless. The Compass Rose was packed to the rafters; rather than avoiding the tavern because of the storm, the storm seemed to have had the effect of driving every Blue in Haven into the taproom.

Mouthwatering aromas hit his nose and made his stomach growl, but he ignored his hunger for the moment. Karal waited just long enough to get his senses used to the noise and light before pushing his way through the crowded tables in the general direction of the one Natoli and her friends generally used. He heaved a sigh of relief as he spotted the back of her head; one of her friends saw *him* and waved to him. Natoli turned around, saw who it was, and beckoned to him to join them.

He didn't need any further prompting; he increased his pace, leaving apologies to those he had unceremoniously shoved aside in his wake, and wedged his way in beside their table.

"Karal! We've just been talking about all the *weird* things that happened today," Natoli said, as several of the others edged over on a bench to give him a place to perch. "Some of us got dizzy, and a couple even thought there was an earthquake—and now there are all kinds of strange things outside the walls! It has to be magic, but none of us can figure out what in the Havens' name happened, or who caused it all." She eyed him with speculation. "*You're* in the thick of things at the Palace; I don't suppose you have a clue, do you?"

Karal silently thanked Vkandis for providing him with the most perfect opening that anyone could ever ask. "I am, I do, and I came here precisely because I need to talk to all of you about this."

That got their attention, all right. He became the center of a little island of silence in the middle of all the noise.

He wanted to blurt it all out at once, for the words were just bubbling up inside of him—but these youngsters were logical people, and he knew that the better organized his words were, the more likely they were to believe him. He knew that *he* would not have believed any of what he was about to tell them, if he had not been present from the beginning of it all. He would have to place *them* at the beginning, to prove to them that he was not deluded, or worse, making it all up out of whole cloth.

So that was how he told them, laying out everything that had happened and been said from the very beginning—starting, in fact, with An'desha's prescient fits of fear. He left Altra out of it, and the Avatars; these students were familiar with ForeSight and ForeSeers, but not Visitations from the Gods. He did not want to stretch their credulity with tales of Avatars and their ilk.

To his gratification, they listened to him, carefully and soberly, and did not seem inclined to doubt him, even when he spoke of the effects of magic reaching forward through thousands of years to reach them now. "I know this all sounds mad," he said finally, "But that's the conclusion even Firesong and Elspeth have reached. Prince Daren believes them—"

Natoli covered his hand with hers to still his plea. "We believe you, Karal," she said, then looked around the table. "Right?"

Nods all around met her question. "You've got no reason to lie to us," one of the others said. "And besides, it matches up too damned well with all the weirdnesses today. So, I've only got one question. We aren't mages, and everything we do deals with the strictly physical. Why did you come to us with all this?"

He heaved a sigh of relief and felt a huge weight lift from his mind. "Because I think you can help," he told them all. "And this is why. Right now, we're looking for patterns, patterns that will let us predict what is going to happen next, and maybe even when it's going to happen. Patterns are mathematical, logical."

"So who better to deal with math and logic than us?" Natoli finished for him, her eyes bright with enthusiasm. "Right! I think you came to the right people. We—" She paused for a moment, frowning. "Hang on, though, this is too important for just one tableful of students. This is something everyone should hear, *especially* the Masters."

With that, she leapt to her feet and shoved her way over to the fireplace. There was a large bell hanging there; Karal had never seen anyone ring it, so he'd assumed it was only there for decoration. Now, as Natoli seized the cord hanging from the clapper and rang it with vigor, he realized it had a real purpose after all.

The entire room fell instantly silent, so much so that the only sounds were those of the wind and rain outside, and the shoving back of chairs in the next room where the Master craftsmen were. Soon they, too, crowded into the taproom, pushing through the door in the rear wall; some looking annoyed, but most wearing expressions of startlement and curiosity.

"We have a friend among us, secretary to the envoy from Karse," Natoli called out into the silence. "He was introduced to me by my father, Herald Rubrik, and I was told I could trust and believe him. Tonight he learned of things he felt we should all hear, and having heard them, I believed they were important enough to sound the bell so that all craftsmen and students could hear them as well." She waved at Karal, who got to his feet, flushing with embarassment. "Karal, could you repeat what you just told my table?"

Still blushing, but obedient to her wishes, he did so, concentrating on keeping his words in exact chronological order, clear, and precise. When he finished, there was more silence, but there wasn't a single doubtful or hostile face in the room.

Finally, a wizened little man stepped forward from behind some of the other Master Craftsmen. From the way they all deferred to him and made way for him, Karal guessed that he might well be senior to all of them. He couldn't have been any taller than Natoli; his gray hair ringed a bald spot that took up most of his scalp, and his clothing was no richer than anyone else's here, but he had an air of competence and authority that no wardrobe could impart.

"Young lady—Natoli, is it?—you were right to ring the Silence Bell," he said, his old voice cracking. "This *was* a tale we all needed to hear—and a task too important for one table of students to deal with! And young secretary, you were right to come here with your tale." His eyes disappeared in a mass of wrinkles as he squinted in Karal's direction. "Magic is not the answer to all problems, as I have said in the past."

"Repeatedly," one of the boys still seated at Karal's left muttered under his breath.

"Whether or not magic will be the answer to this problem remains to be seen," the old man continued. "But if it is careful gathering of facts and measures, and equally careful advice that you want, then *this* is the place to look to find your experts!"

"Here, here," murmured several of the other Master Craftsmen; from the tone of their voices, Karal had the shrewd notion that they resented this intrusion of *magic* and *mages* into their world and would be very pleased to show that they could solve a crisis that mages could not cope with.

The old man paused and looked out over the taproom. "I know that there are tasks you have all undertaken and may not in honor leave unfinished—whether those tasks be study and learning, or the building of a road, a mill, or a dwelling. Nevertheless, as I can see at this moment, we all have hours of leisure that are at *our* disposal, or we would not be here, drinking our hosts' excellent beer and telling lies to one another. Can I request that until this crisis is dealt with, that you devote those hours to your Queen and your land?"

Karal honestly expected that no more than a third of those in this tavern would volunteer—which, philosophically, would be more trained hands, minds and eyes than he'd had when he walked in here, and far more than he ever anticipated! But without warning, Natoli jumped to the top of the table nearest her. She waved once, seizing the attention of everyone in the room, and stood there in a defiant pose, with her feet apart and her hands on her hips.

"How many of you spent your student days in the Collegium?" she asked, before anyone could make an answer, yea or nay, to the old man's question. "And how many of you saw the highborn brats looking down their noses at us, because we were going to *work* for our livelihood? And how many of you just twisted with envy every time one of those Herald-trainees rode by on their Companions? The highborn, the trainees, *they* were going to be important! All *we* were go-

ing to do was make *their* lives a little easier! Just one short
step up from peddlers, that's us!"

The students hissed and booed her words, and the sour
looks on the faces of the Master Craftsmen said all that
needed to be said.

"But now *we* can do something they can't!" Natoli cried
out in triumph. "Even those fancy mages, *they* don't have the
training or the organization—*they can't look at this problem
logically.* I don't think they can solve it! But *we* can! Can't
we?"

An angry chorus of "Aye!" and "Damn bet!" answered her.
She grinned with satisfaction.

"And we're *going* to solve it, if it takes every spare moment
we have, aren't we?"

Again, there was a chorus of assent.

"And how *better* to get the funding for our projects than to
show the Palace that *we* are the ones with the answers?"

This time the chorus was even stronger. Natoli's grin
widened, and she jumped down from the top of the table,
bowing slightly to the old man as she alighted.

"I believe you have your answer, Master Magister Henlin,"
she said, and made her way back to her table.

The old man shook his head, but grinned anyway, and his
eyes disappeared in his wrinkles again. He waited patiently
for the noise to die away, then gestured to the rest of the Master Craftsmen.

"Gentlemen, select your helpers; I assume you'll all be se-
lecting your own students, but don't overlook someone who
wants to work for you, or who hasn't been chosen. Master
Tam, Master Levy, please go with this young man to the
Palace and present our services to the Queen. I will organize
the groups for work tomorrow morning." He sighed and
shook his head. "I am too old to be traipsing out into a tem-
pest, I fear, or I would go myself."

"Master" Tam was actually a strong and squarely-built female of late middle age; she laughed and crossed her arms
over her chest. "Henlin, you haven't once left the Compass
Rose as long as there was a single drop left in the kegs in all
the years I've known you. I hardly expect you to start now."

Master Henlin shrugged but looked unrepentant. The other

Masters moved out into the taproom, but she and Master Levy headed straight for the table shared by Natoli's cronies.

"We'll take you scruffy lot, since you're already our students," Master Levy said, as soon as they got within an arm's reach of the table. "We're both used to you delinquents, and I wouldn't wish you on some poor, unsuspecting Master who has no idea what depravities you can get up to."

Natoli only nodded, unabashed. "Suits me. What *will* we be up to?"

"Dawn is what you'll be up to," Master Tam replied, and smiled evilly as the students groaned. "The logical, obvious thing is that first we'll divide up the area around Haven and each group will take one piece to study. We'll look at the obvious anomalies and look for ones the Heralds and mages missed, because I'll bet there will be some—once we've measured each anomaly to within a hair, we'll come here to collate the information. After that?" She shrugged. "My guess is that either we'll be sending individual students out with fast horses to get information from farther out, or we'll just make up a set of precise instructions based on what we find, and rely on locals to do the work. Then we'll start looking for answers that fit the information. We'll probably use the Rose as our headquarters, since it's set up to hold all of us."

"Just like a class problem," groaned one of the boys.

"Exactly." Master Levy fixed the offending party with a gimlet eye. "Don't you think you ought to cut the evening short, since you're going to be up so early?"

Obediently, the students started gathering up their cloaks; students at the other tables were doing the same, so evidently the other Masters had imparted the same set of orders to their groups. "I think Lady Herald Elspeth would be the one to take your offer, sir," Karal said to Master Levy, who was nearest him. "I know she'll still be awake. Would you like to go to the Palace now?"

"Between us, I'm pretty certain that Karal and I can get you both past the gate guard," Natoli added. "They've been letting me run tame at the Collegium since I could toddle, and every Guard and Herald there is my 'uncle.' "

Master Levy looked to Master Tam for advice. The woman nodded brusquely. "Sounds as good a plan to me as any." She slung her cloak around her shoulders and took a last swig of beer from a student's mug. "Let's go."

They slogged through rain that filled the gutters and soaked their cloaks; bent their heads against wind that drove the rain into their faces and threatened to pull their cloaks right out of their hands. The relatively short walk to the Palace was as exhausting as one of those dawn-to-dark rides he and Ulrich had endured on their way up here.

At long last they reached the postern gate, and the Guard there recognized all four of them. He waved them inside without any formality—which was a mistake, in Karal's opinion, for they could have been *anybody*, in very clever disguises. He resolved to tell someone about the lapse tomorrow. Alberich, maybe, or even Kerowyn.

Once inside the Palace, however, the Guards were a great deal more alert, to his relief. They were left to drip in front of a fire while someone went off to verify that they were who they *said* they were, and to fetch Herald Elspeth. Hot spiced tea arrived after a while, and towels, both brought by pages, who hung their cloaks over frames in front of the fire to dry them thoroughly. The air filled with the smell of wet wool.

Elspeth was not at all pleased to be fetched; she looked tired and rather frazzled. Her hair had escaped from its utilitarian braids, and her face was slack with exhaustion. But the moment that Master Tam and Master Levy introduced themselves to her and explained what brought them there, she brightened with relief, and actually apologized for her curt welcome.

"I'm dreadfully sorry I was so surly, but we just finished some very difficult work, and we're about to repeat it to double the effect," she said, pulling a damp curl off her forehead with an impatient gesture. "I can't even begin to tell you how much I appreciate this! Yes, we certainly *do* accept your offer, and I can't think of anyone better suited to try to apply logic to all of this." She favored Master Levy with a wry grimace. "Some of the others won't like it, but I can and will overrule them—and Mother will most *certainly* be relieved that someone is trying mathematics instead of intuition for a change!"

She continued for a little while longer, as both Masters glowed with satisfaction under the weight of her sincere thanks and praise. There was no doubt that she meant every word she said—and no doubt that both of them had been half-expecting to find opposition from someone who was a mage as well as a Herald. Not surprising; *they* didn't know her, after all.

I wonder if she's stretching all this thanks out a little—he thought, when she began repeating herself. Then he saw her take a surreptitious glance at the cloaks, and knew he was right. She was waiting for the cloaks to dry before sending them away!

Thoughtful, making up for being discourteous earlier? It could be. Elspeth, he had learned by watching, was like that.

"Well," Master Levy said, when Elspeth finished her speech, "if we're going to lead a team of unruly students out into the muck at dawn, *we* need to take our leave. As soon as we have anything of any substance, we will let you know, Herald Elspeth."

"Send me your measurements and charts, would you please?" Elspeth asked as the two Masters took up their now-dry cloaks. "They might help those of us who aren't applying strict logic to the problem."

"Certainly, my lady," Master Tam assured her, tossing the cloak over muscular shoulders. "Now, by your leave?"

"I've sent for a carriage; at least you won't have to walk back in this mess," Elspeth told her, and grinned at the gratified expressions they wore. "Masters, I promise you, no matter what you've heard, I didn't turn into a *complete* barbarian while I was gone!"

They laughed, and Elspeth called for a page to take them to the carriage she'd ordered up. Once they had gone, she turned her attention back to Karal, who was waiting quietly for her to dismiss him.

"Was this your idea, sir secretary?" Elspeth asked, with a stern expression that was entirely spoiled by her glow of amusement and the twitching of her lips.

"Yes, Lady," he replied. "I don't know a great deal about magic—but Altra, a friend, told me to trust my own good sense. You *all* said you needed measurements and facts, and my own good sense said that if you were going to need facts and figures, you ought to have people who specialize in them gather them for you."

"Well, your friend was right," Elspeth declared. "And I can't begin to thank you for going out and *acting* on your conviction. You do your order proud." And with that, to his immense confusion and embarrassment, she kissed him, much to Natoli's open amusement.

"Now, you've done more than anyone else but the mages tonight, and you deserve some rest, so you ought to go get it," she told him. Then she turned to Natoli. "You are just as much to be thanked for seeing that the task was too large for a small group of students and acting on *your* conviction," she added. "It isn't every youngling who'd sacrifice personal glory for seeing that the job is done right."

Natoli shrugged. "A Herald's daughter learns not to let self-aggrandizement get in the way of the job," she said.

"A Herald's daughter?" Elspeth looked at Natoli with speculation but did *not* ask *so why aren't you a Herald, too?*

"So that would be how you met Ulrich's young secretary?" she asked instead.

Natoli nodded. "Father was the one assigned to escort them. He thought I might be able to help Karal get settled."

Elspeth smiled. "I'd guess you succeeded, since he managed to find the Compass Rose and its taproom! Anyone could get settled with a couple of Rose pints in them!" Natoli lost control enough to giggle.

But Elspeth wasn't finished yet. "There's one thing I'd really like to tell you, Natoli. No matter what it may sometimes seem like, there are important, vital jobs that can't be done by Heralds, which is one reason why this land isn't hipdeep in Companions. You and your friends and Masters are and will be doing things as important as anyone who ever put on Whites, and don't ever let anyone tell you differently. We Heralds are there to be obvious symbols to the people, but the Guard and Bards deserve most of the glory we get."

As Natoli flushed with confusion, Elspeth gave her a little salute and then left.

"Well!" Natoli said at last. "What brought that on?"

Karal raised his hands and shook his head, although he had a good idea what had brought it on. Natoli's carefully veiled expression of envy on seeing Elspeth's uniform, and the flat tone of her voice when she mentioned that she was the daughter of a Herald. "Heralds. Who knows? It was something she thought you ought to hear from her directly, though, or she'd never have said it."

And given that little speech back there in the Compass Rose, I think you needed to hear it, he thought silently.

Natoli shrugged uncomfortably. "Well—I need to get back to my bed. Coming here isn't going to excuse me from going out with the others at dawn."

"Thank you," Karal said, very softly, catching her arm as she turned to go. "We couldn't do this without you. Elspeth was right. You did some very good things. I think you're going to do more of them. I really admire you."

Natoli blushed again and averted her eyes. "I've—got to go!" she blurted, and turned and hurried away. Karal watched her go and remained staring at the door for minutes after she was gone.

Karal made his own way back to the Karsite suite, his head so full he couldn't even begin to sort out his thoughts. He was only certain of one thing.

He'd better get some sleep, himself, no matter how much turmoil his thoughts were in. Whatever lay ahead of them— this was likely to be the last moment of peace any of them would have for a long while to come.

Altra

14

But the next morning, it might all have been a dream.

Except that Ulrich was up very early and left immediately after canceling all of his appointments, and when Karal took his usual lesson with Kerowyn, she was preoccupied and actually let him score on her without making him work himself into exhaustion to earn it. He waited for an opportune moment and told her of the Guard's laxness of the night before, which earned him a nod of approval.

But after that lesson was done, he found himself at loose ends. Ulrich had forsaken meetings and discussions in the face of this greater threat, which left Karal with nothing whatsoever to do as Ulrich plied his other avocation of Priest-Mage.

Ulrich reappeared for lunch, just long enough to snatch a hasty meal and ask Karal if he had taken care of the appointments that had been canceled.

"Yes, sir," Karal replied. "Is there anything else you want me to do?"

"Not really," the Priest told him. "Really, just take a rest; do whatever you want to do this afternoon. I'll be in conference with the rest of the mages. We're still mostly at the talking stage, now that we've reinforced all the shields and—well, never mind. Just take a little holiday."

With that he was gone, leaving Karal to trail forlornly around the suite, finally ending up in his own room.

For the first time in a very long time, he had leisure to be lonely—and, suddenly, homesick. Up until now, he'd been so busy that he hadn't had much time to think about himself.

When he wasn't actually working, he was encouraging An'desha, learning as much as he could about the land and the Heralds that guided it from the library and from Florian, or discussing what he'd learned with Ulrich.

He hadn't even had a chance to talk about this latest crisis with his mentor, and that bothered him more than he had thought it would. He sat on the bed, staring at the wall, feeling very much left out. No point in looking for An'desha, he'd be with the others. Natoli was out doing whatever her Master assigned her. Florian was like Altra—you didn't go to the Companion, *he* showed up when he wanted to. Karal wasn't a mage—and he wasn't one of the Blues, either. That left him with no purpose at all, and nothing useful to contribute.

:Oh, do stop feeling sorry for yourself!: Altra snapped, appearing out of nowhere and jumping up onto his bed. *:You've taken the initiative before. What's to stop you from doing it again? You're an adult, Karal, an acolyte, not a novice! Of course you have a purpose! You're supposed to be Ulrich's assistant, aren't you?:*

"Ah—yes, but—" Karal began, starting a little at the Firecat's sudden appearance.

The Firecat snorted. *:Well, go assist him, then! Do your job! Who's going to remind him to eat and rest if you don't? Didn't Solaris tell you to take care of him? All of the rest of them are younger than he is; if they don't feel tired, they'll keep going, and he'll feel he has to keep up with them. Who's going to take notes? Even if you don't understand all that mage-babble, you can take notes, can't you?:* Altra's tail switched from side to side, annoyance in every twitch.

Karal nodded, tentatively at first, then with more enthusiasm. There was a very good chance they wouldn't exclude him if he presented himself at the door of the meeting. He *was* Ulrich's assistant, after all. And there probably *wasn't* anyone else playing secretary in all the mage-conferences.

:Besides, what you learn there, you can take to Natoli and the others,: Altra added, narrowing his eyes, which gave him a very sly, self-satisfied look. *:The Seekers need that information as much as they need measurements. They really don't know how magic works, and the more you can tell them, the better they can do their job. Right?:*

"Right." Karal got to his feet, and gathered up his pouch of note-taking materials. "Thank you, Altra."

:*My pleasure.*: The Firecat twitched his tail again, jumped down off the bed—and vanished before he touched the floor.

Karal shivered. He really wished that Altra would at least get out of sight before he pulled one of those disappearing tricks. Having the Firecat *there* one moment and *not-there* the next was decidedly unnerving.

Oh, well. He knew where the meeting was going to be, since Ulrich had let that drop—not in the Council Chamber this time, since they couldn't keep usurping it from governmental business, but in the gryphons' suite, since it was the only other set of rooms large enough to hold the gryphons comfortably.

He had never been there, but it was easy enough to find a page to show him the way; they *all* seemed to know where the gryphons were. The tiny child who led him down the maze of corridors confessed as they walked that he often played with the young gryphons. Karal had to shake his head at that; how in Vkandis' name had his parents been persuaded to allow him to play with meat-eating raptors that could easily bite his hand off? That said a lot for the ability of Treyvan and Hydona to convince Valdemarans that they were as friendly as they claimed.

The chamber was at the end of a long corridor that looked vaguely familiar to Karal. It looked as if it had been originally intended for some other use than as guest quarters, with its huge double doors of carved wood. Had it been a lesser Audience Chamber, perhaps? Tentatively, he tapped on the door and was a little surprised when Ulrich himself answered it.

"Karal?" the Priest said, when he recognized who was there. He held the door as if he was thinking about shutting it again, a frown just beginning to crease his brow. "Didn't I tell you—"

"You don't have anyone here to take notes for you all, do you?" Karal interrupted, before Ulrich could chide him. "You don't have anyone here to fetch things for you; you'll have to call for a page and wait until one comes. You don't have anyone to run out and have meals and drink sent up. I can do all of that, and you already *know* that I won't get in the way."

He swallowed a bit, and let a little pleading creep into his voice. "Please sir, I want to help. I want to help *you*. It's not a duty, it's a pleasure."

Ulrich's frown faded when he heard Karal's intentions. "I didn't—think you'd care to be here," he replied, with a hesitancy he had never shown before. "You've been working hard, and I thought I'd been exploiting your good nature. I was afraid we'd overwork you—"

Karal coughed as his cheeks heated. "Master, one of my duties is to make certain that *you* don't overwork." He lowered his voice to a near-whisper. "You aren't exploiting my good nature, sir. I am proud to serve and honor you as I would serve and honor my own father."

Ulrich bowed his head, and he blinked rapidly for a moment. "Karal, you are a remarkable young man. I am proud to be here to help you when I can. Thank you. We can certainly use your services."

Karal slipped inside the door as Ulrich held it open just enough for him to get inside. There was no furniture, just the bare wooden floor and huge pillows and featherbeds; logical, actually, since this place was meant for the comfort of gryphons, not humans. Firesong was holding forth and did not even notice as Karal took a place on the edge of the gathering, got out his pens and paper, and began taking notes in the middle of Firesong's current sentence.

"—if all of you are really set on it, I can't see how it's going to hurt anything," the Healing Adept was saying, his voice full of contemptuous amusement. "But I repeat, I *don't* think that these—craftsmen of yours, these *engineers*, as you call them—are going to accomplish anything at all useful. Magic simply does not work the way they are used to thinking. Magic is a thing of intuition, of art; you can't dissect it, set down logic, make it march in step."

"But haven't *you* been teaching me the laws of magic?" An'desha objected stubbornly. Karal's eyebrows arched in surprise, though he kept quiet, true to his promise. Was An'desha actually *disagreeing* with Firesong? If so, it must be for the very first time!

"Yes, but—" Firesong floundered for a moment, then regained his poise. "But the 'laws' of magic are simply guidelines! Haven't Elspeth and Darkwind accomplished things the mages of k'Sheyna thought could not be done, simply because Elspeth was not aware that common thought was that they were impossible? That is because magic simply is not *logical*. It doesn't always answer the way you think it will. You can't call it to the glove like an imprinted falcon!"

"But you won't object if I assist the engineers?" An'desha persisted. "So long as I don't use time and energy we need to put into shields?"

He's opposing Firesong? *Has the moon started rising in the west?*

Firesong flung up his hands in defeat. "How can I object to what you do with your free time?" he asked sourly. "If you want to waste it, go right ahead. I simply don't see where you are going to accomplish anything concrete."

"Well, now that we have that out of the way, shall we get down to the business at hand?" Darkwind asked dryly.

Firesong shrugged and sat down again, settling into a more comfortable position against one of the huge pillows, a bolster of a green so dark it approached black. Karal noted with amusement that he had chosen the only pillow in the room that harmonized with his brilliant emerald costume.

"I asked Rris if there was any oral *kyree* tradition about the mage-storms that followed the Cataclysm," Darkwind told them all. "So here he is, and he's going to recite it to you."

Rris rose from his place at Darkwind's side where he had been lying like an obedient dog, stepped forward into the center of the room, bowed his furry gray head once to all of them, and sat down on his haunches with immense dignity. :*I trust you will not object if I tell it in the traditional manner?*:

"Go right ahead," Firesong said. "You might forget something if you break from tradition, else."

Rris nodded. :*Hear you all, from the times of the Change, from the times of the Falling of the Sky and the Stars,*: he began, his mental voice ringing in Karal's mind. It occurred to Karal at that moment, as he scribbled furiously to get all of the story down, that he himself had changed out of all recognition ever since he had come to Valdemar. Not that long ago, simply *seeing* the *kyree* would have put him into shock.

Now he was taking down what the creature dictated into his mind, without a second thought.

Was this a good thing, or a bad one?

Neither, he decided, as his fingers flew across the page, filling line after line with meticulous script. *It's just change. You change, or you turn into a dry old stick.*

And another thing occurred to him.

Dry old sticks break under pressure. So maybe it was a good thing after all. The last thing they all needed right now was one of their number who would snap like a twig.

It had been a long day; it was going to get longer before Karal saw his bed. Nevertheless, when An'desha intercepted him on his way out of the gryphons' room and asked him to make a map of the way to the Compass Rose, he volunteered to act as An'desha's escort instead, after they both had some supper. Ulrich was to work with the Tayledras and Elspeth, strengthening shields again; that left Karal free to make a hasty copy of the day's notes and show An'desha the way.

That was why they both found themselves trudging through a night made darker by the clouds still overhead, splashing through puddles left by the rain, with the sounds of carousing coming from the lantern-lit taverns all around them.

"Thank you for coming with me to where these engineers meet," An'desha said shyly. "I would be very uncomfortable, going there alone."

Since this would be the first time, to Karal's knowledge, that An'desha had *ever* left the grounds of the Palace, he suspected that "uncomfortable" was an understatement. *Terrified* might be more apt.

But An'desha was set on going. He felt that someone was going to have to try to explain magic to those without it, and that he was the best person for the task. That was the argument Karal had walked in on this afternoon. An'desha had volunteered his services, and Firesong had objected.

Firesong might be jealous; he might be afraid that An'desha will find someone else he's attracted to. I wonder if that occurred to An'desha as an explanation for all his objections?

"I have all these notes from our meeting to deliver, and I need to get copies of what they've done for our mages," he replied. "And besides—An'desha, I know you're shy, and I just couldn't let you walk in there alone, face all those people you don't even know. That's what friends are about, right?"

"I had hoped so." An'desha smiled tentatively. "But you are stretching yourself very thin, running errands for all of us, transcribing the notes of our meetings for us. I hadn't wanted to ask you."

"Before this is over, we're all going to be exhausted, so don't worry about it," he told the young mage. At that moment, they reached the door of the tavern, and he paused for a heartbeat on the threshold. "Well, brace yourself. This is not going to be like anything you've ever seen before."

An'desha did visibly brace himself, but he still winced as the door opened and a steady stream of babbling voices poured out over them.

But the voices all stopped when people noticed just who it was that was standing in the doorway. Natoli hurried over to them, and Master Tam was right behind her.

"We've got notes and charts for you," Natoli began.

"And I've got notes from the mages' meeting for you," he replied. "And more than that, I've got a mage with me who wants to show you some of how magic works." An'desha clearly wanted to shrink back away from all the people, but only his trembling hands betrayed his nervousness. "An'desha, this is Natoli, and this is Master Tam. Ladies, this is An'desha; he's both Shin'a'in and Tayledras, and he's one of the mages that works with Lady Herald Elspeth."

"Very pleased to see you, Master An'desha," Master Tam said, folding her hands together and bowing a little to him, rather than seizing his hand to shake it. That was a rather tactful gesture on her part, Karal thought. "We badly need someone to help us understand how these magic powers of yours work. Right now, we're in the position of trying to read the wind."

"I can understand," An'desha replied, so softly that Master Tam had to lean forward to hear him. "I am happy to be of help."

"Well, come over with us, then. Karal, I think Master Henlin wants your notes so he can have copies made; join us when he lets you go." Master Tam took charge of An'desha as if she were used to shepherding shy youngsters all the time. Perhaps she was; it occurred to Karal that many of her students might be just as shy and introspective as An'desha. Intelligent children generally got into trouble with their less intelligent peers; it had happened that way to him when he'd been taken by the Priests, after all.

I only hope none of her students have had half so exciting a life as An'desha. I wouldn't wish that on anyone.

He brought the notes to Master Henlin, who was in the Masters' Room at the rear of the tavern, presiding over a sea of paper, hundreds of sheets of it, covered with figures and diagrams. Then, relieved of his burden, he hurried back out to see if An'desha was still holding up well under the scrutiny of so many strangers.

He was; in fact, he was deep in a discussion of where magic energy came from.

"—so some mage-schools have built up reserves, like a cistern or reservoir, and that is what *their* Master mages can tap into when they need it," he was saying. "It all comes from the same source, though—the energy of life that is all around us. All of us living creatures shed it as we breathe and move."

"And what about the Adepts you mentioned?" Natoli asked. "Do they use something special? Or are there other reserves only they can use?"

"There are," the young Adept replied, nodding. "But they are not the reserves that have been built up by other mages. Rather, they are the reserves that exist where two or more natural lines of force meet. These are called 'nodes,' and they are *so* powerful that only an Adept can control the energy that pools in them. Anyone else trying would either be unable to touch the power, or would be engulfed by it and devoured. Charred."

One of the boys shivered. "Not a pleasant prospect."

"No," An'desha replied soberly. "It is not. But you see, now, that this all *does* respond to natural laws. The power comes from somewhere, and goes elsewhere, like water flowing to the sea. Where it goes eventually, is to a place we call the Nether Planes, where everything is made of chaos and energy. And I suspect that it comes back into our World Plane from there, through the medium of living things."

"Time to speculate about that when we have the leisure," Master Levy interjected, spreading a map out on the table in front of An'desha. "We've been over every thumblength of ground a half day's ride from Haven, and this is what we've found so far. Transplanted areas are in green, blasted areas are in red, transformed areas are in yellow."

An'desha bent over the map to study it; Karal whispered to Natoli.

"Transformed areas?" he asked. "What are those?"

"Places where whatever was there was changed," she whispered back. "Everything in them is the same as it was, but inside those circles, it's another season. We're in late summer right now; there, it's fall, winter, or even spring. Plants that should be in fruit are blooming, or dormant, insects are dead or in cocoons or eggs, and birds or animals are in winter or courting colors."

He blinked at her in surprise; she only grimaced. "Don't ask me, I have no notion what could have caused something like that," she told him.

He turned his attention back to the map, thankful that there were fewer red dots than green or yellow. There definitely was a pattern there; the dots were spaced out at equal intervals, and if you followed a line of them, they would sequence as three greens, a red, and three greens and a yellow. But there didn't seem to be a center to the pattern, or a point of origin.

"I wonder—" An'desha began, then stopped.

"Go ahead," Master Tam urged. "You know magic, and we don't. If you can suggest some kind of meaning or interpretation, I for one would be happy to hear it."

"Well—I wonder if what has happened is that with the transformed and blasted places, there was *too much* energy brought to bear, and that is why the damage?" Then he shrugged. "I am grasping at straws."

"That's no more than we've been doing," Master Levy confessed to him. "Let's follow that theory for a moment."

Karal couldn't understand more than half of what either of them said, but they seemed to understand each other, and that was the important part. Since An'desha didn't seem nearly as shy of these people as he had when he'd first walked into the room, and since Natoli was immersed in the discussion and ignoring everything else, Karal finally left them and assigned himself to one of the desks where others his age were making copies of the same chart that Master Tam had unrolled in front of An'desha.

I can make a copy of this to take back with me; that will save these others from having to make a spare. He helped himself to pens, ink, and paper, and when he had finished that task, he began making copies of his own notes for the other Masters, just as the rest were doing.

When his tired eyes threatened to unfocus completely, he finished one last page, and rolled up his map and the pages of descriptions of the "magic circles," and went to find An'desha.

Despite the latter's promises to Firesong, An'desha *had* been giving demonstrations of mage-craft to the engineers, and he was tired and ready to go back to the Palace. When Natoli declared her intention to defect as well, the whole group broke up, yawning.

"I'll walk back to the Palace with you," she said, as Karal handed An'desha back his cloak. "I've got a room in the wing where they put some Blues who don't have patrons or aren't highborn, and who also don't live in town. We share it with the Healer- and Bardic-trainees."

"I'd wondered," Karal admitted, slinging his cloak around his shoulders, as Natoli found hers in the pile of student Blues. "You kept popping up in the Palace and you acted as if you belong there."

"In a sense, it's the only home I have," Natoli admitted. "Father was Chosen after my mother died of complications of childbirth. No, it wasn't me," she added hastily. "It was a still-birth, and I was about four. He brought me with him to the Collegium since he hadn't any place else to take me, and I've spent all of my life here. When he went out on circuit, one or another of the Heralds would take care of me until he got back."

Well, it wasn't the worst sort of childhood, though it was nothing like the warm family situation Karal had enjoyed.

"It sounds lonely," An'desha said ingenuously as Karal opened the door and held it for the two of them.

Natoli only shrugged as she stepped out into the dark street. "Mostly, it was odd. When Father was *here*, he made sure I knew he wanted me there, and that he cared about me. For lack of anything else to do, once I got old enough, I took most courses in all the Collegia except the ones in Bardic that had to do with performing and composing, and the ones in Healer's that had to do with really *Healing* someone. Then one day I realized what I wanted to do; I went to Master Tam and asked to be taken on, and she asked *me* why I had taken so long to figure out what I was good at."

"She would," Karal said dryly. "I have the impression that Master Tam would never take an indirect route when there was a direct one available." Other students drifted along behind them, talking quietly to one another, voices murmuring across the otherwise silent street.

"She does tend to bludgeon things," Natoli replied, but smiled. "Father was just pleased that I'd found my avocation; he granted his leave, and I've been studying with Master Tam ever since."

"At least you had some choice in the matter," Karal replied, with some envy. "I was quite literally kidnapped by the Priests." He went on to describe his own childhood, while An'desha and Natoli both listened with interest.

"Odd that of the three of us, I am the one who had the most normal childhood," An'desha mused. "How very strange."

"Well, you made up for it." Karal slapped him lightly on the back. "Never mind; I've figured out that anyone who is more intelligent than the people around him has troubles as a child. The important thing is not to dwell on those troubles and make them into *all* you are. You should do what you can with what parts of your life you have personal control over!"

"That makes good sense," Natoli applauded, and changed the subject. "I wonder what late night food we can gain personal control over?"

Several days passed, with Karal serving double duty: to the mages and with the engineers. As the days went by, the engineers collected more and more information and added it all to

their charts, tables, and maps. Florian passed on a great deal
more of what Master Tam referred to as "data" from other
Companions out in the field with their Heralds—all of it was
pertinent, and most of it was much more accurate than the
information coming from humans. After the third day of this,
Karal paused in the midst of his copying, struck by the fear
that all this might *not* be the sort of thing Vkandis would approve of his acolyte doing. After all, he hadn't seen Altra in
days. Was the Sunlord annoyed with him?

At that very moment, Altra wandered through the room,
tail waving like a banner in a light breeze.

Karal froze, and not just because Altra had appeared the
moment Karal thought of him, but because it was here, in the
middle of a crowd of—well—unbelievers. What were *they* going to think? Altra wasn't exactly inconspicuous!

But the others did nothing unusual. The other students and
teachers *saw* him—they avoided trampling him when he was
in their path—but they didn't seem to see anything odd about
him. He jumped up onto one or two tables and surveyed the
figuring and charting going on with aloof interest, and none
of them stared at him. He might very well have been a perfectly ordinary tavern cat.

Considering that he was four or five times larger than any
domestic housecat that Karal had ever seen, that was certainly strange!

But Altra eventually made his way to the back of the room
where Karal sat staring at him, and gave Karal an approving
wink.

:*They see only what they are expecting to see,*: the Firecat
said cryptically. :*I have more information for you. The same
patterns are in Karse and southward. Tell the others. You'll get
the maps and so forth that Solaris has sent you in a few days.*:

And with that, Altra strolled underneath a table, and did
not come out on the other side. Karal sat there with his pen
still in his fingers for a long time.

Well—at least he approves, Karal thought, dazedly. That
was, after all, one less worry.

But given his current luck, with every worry that he lost,
four more rose to take its place.

* * *

A day later—and the half-expected second wave swamped them. It came exactly one day short of a fortnight, and at very nearly the same time of day as the first one.

This time the areas of disturbance were not as obvious until a few days had passed, and someone noticed that there were places where plants and insects had—changed. They weren't dead, but they certainly weren't the same anymore. The plants in particular had undergone a transformation that made them act like primitive animals. They reacted to the presence of other living creatures, some by shrinking away, but others by reaching toward whatever was near them. Some of the plants were observed trapping and presumably eating insects; others were growing strange new forms of defense; thorns and spikes, saps that had a terrible stench or were outright poisonous. And two days after the storm passed over, when a farmer found his child in a patch of the changed plants, crying hysterically, with hundreds of tiny thorns in her flesh that she swore the plants had flung at her, Selenay ordered that samples be sent to the Palace and the parent plants be destroyed wherever they were found.

The mages studied the changed plants without learning much—except that Firesong noted a definite resemblance to some of the dangerous "thinking plants" in the Uncleansed Lands of what Valdemarans called the Pelagir Hills.

One day short of a fortnight later, the third storm-wave arrived.

If this keeps up for much longer, I'd better think about growing gills. Karal trudged through yet another nighttime thunderstorm, his cloak already soaked, heading for the Compass Rose. But this time, he felt a little more cheerful than at any time before.

According to Firesong, this last wave was just a trifle weaker than the previous two. This time virtually no shields had gone down before the onslaught, and although even non-mages had experienced the disorienting effects of the wave, Firesong was positive that this mage-storm hadn't lasted as long as the previous two had. No one had reported in from the area outside Haven yet, but the mages were guardedly optimistic that the worst was over.

Such good news was more than compensation enough for a long slog through a driving rain, at least to Karal's mind. He couldn't wait until the others heard!

He opened the door of the tavern and stepped through into warmth and light, only to find virtually everyone clustered around a single table. They were ominously quiet, and when they all turned to see who had entered, there was not a single cheerful expression among them.

"I've got good news!" he said into the oppressive silence. "Firesong says this last storm was weaker!"

Their expressions did not change, and he felt his own spirits dropping. "It was weaker, wasn't it?" he faltered. "Firesong said so. We didn't lose any shields this time—"

Master Levy shook his head slowly. "I'm afraid your Firesong is mistaken," he replied. "Not only was it not weaker, it was actually a little stronger than before. The reason nothing magical was affected was because you've managed to build up good enough shields to protect everything magical that you still retain—and you've pared the number of magical things you need to protect that way to the absolute minimum. Come over here and look at this."

He gestured to something in a wooden box with a grate over the top of it. Karal couldn't see clearly what was in it, but it sat on the table next to Master Levy and had been the object they had all been clustered around. His mouth suddenly dry with trepidation, Karal edged over to the group and looked down into the box itself.

It was an animal, but no animal he had ever seen or heard of before. Mad red eyes stared up at him, and long, hairless ears flattened against a viperish skull covered with a thin coat of gray hair. It snarled at him, and he inadvertently backed up a pace.

"Don't touch it," someone warned. "It just about took Semon's hand off."

"What is it?" he asked, fascinated and repulsed at the same time. It looked vaguely familiar, somehow.

"Nearly as we can tell, it *was* a rabbit." Master Levy looked down at the creature and shook his head. "Or rather, most of it was a rabbit. We can't tell if this was just a case of several creatures being melded together into something new, or a rabbit that got turned into some sort of meat-eater. *That* is what your latest wave did; we've sent word to the Palace to warn people out in the countryside. We're just lucky that there generally aren't any large creatures inside those circles of change. I don't know what something as large as a dog would turn into. Just as a guess, I'd say our wave of disruption is now powerful enough to affect larger animals."

"Think what would happen if this hit a cow, or worse, a pig," someone added. Master Levy shuddered, and Karal didn't blame him.

"Or a human. Another evidence that this wave is stronger is the storm outside," Master Levy put in as an afterthought. "There's always a thunderstorm after the wave passes. This one is worse than the one before, which was worse than the one before that."

"There's always good news to go with bad news," Natoli said, as Karal finally shivered and turned away from the creature on the table. "With three waves, we have enough information to make some predictions. Now we know *when* the next wave will come, we know *where* the affected circles will be, and we know something else. We've been calling these storms 'waves' just as an analogy, but it turns out they really *are* waves."

"You can? They are?" The sick feeling in the pit of Karal's stomach cleared. "But that's wonderful! If we can predict these things, we can at least make certain nothing like *that* thing can happen!"

"For now," Master Levy said ominously. "The size of the affected circle is growing, too, as the duration of each wave increases with its power—"

"Wait!" Karal exclaimed. "Don't tell *me*. You'll have to tell the council of mages—and you ought to come with me and tell them *now*, while they're still congratulating themselves that Valdemar survived the worst of it and came through all right! They haven't told anyone else yet. We have to stop them before they tell Selenay."

"He's right," creaked Master Henlin, running a hand over his bald spot. "If we wait until tomorrow, they might not believe us, even with that *thing* in the box to back us up. Even if they did believe us, they might not want to appear like

fools, telling the Queen this directly after telling her everything would be fine. Right. Levy, Norten, Bret; you all go
with him. Take all the new charts and the wave-drawing, so
they can see for themselves how the waves are acting. Go!
We'll all stay here until you come back with word. Maybe
now that we know *how* these waves are acting, we can work
out a more effective defense against them."

Rolls of paper were carefully inserted into waterproof cases;
Cloaks were collected, and Karal found himself once again
leading a group of men who otherwise would never have
given him a second glance out into the teeth of a storm.

This physical storm was indeed *much* worse than the ones
that had followed the last two waves. "This alone ought to
show your mages that we're right!" Master Levy shouted over
the thunder. "That An'desha showed us how unshielded
magic-power can affect the weather, and if this isn't an example of just that, I'll eat my map case!"

Karal didn't think that the case was in any danger of becoming an entree, given the severity of the storm. He just
hoped that the others were still where he had left them. The
little parade struggled against wind and rain all the way to the
Palace, despite the sheltering effects of the buildings on either side of the street. Several times Karal was afraid they'd
be blown off their feet, but it never actually happened.

Kerowyn must have given the guards a fairly severe lecture;
some time was consumed in verifying that everyone was who
he said he was, but it was time that Karal didn't begrudge.
Master Levy did, though; he stormed up the path to the
Palace, grumbling under his breath, and Karal trailed in his
wake, followed by the other two Masters. Norten and Bret
were too busy trying to keep their cloaks around them to say
anything, which didn't make Karal feel any too comfortable.

But once they reached the doors of the Palace, Master Levy
allowed him to take the lead again, even though the Master's
expression was as stormy as the night outside. It was just for-
tunate that the gryphons' quarters were not very far; Karal
feared that another delay might well cause the temperamen-
tal Master to explode.

But maybe it isn't just temper; maybe it's worry. Worry
and fear made people sometimes act in ways that you wouldn't

expect. Ulrich just got more clever when he was worried. Maybe Master Levy had fits of bad temper when he was concerned about something.

Never mind, he told himself, as he reached up to knock on the door to the gryphons' rooms. *Temper-fits are hardly our worst problems at the moment.*

As the door opened, Karal recognized the voice just beyond as belonging to Elspeth, which meant that the single most important person they needed to convince was still here. He waved the others inside first, and wondered for a moment if he just might possibly be able to get away and let the Masters do all the explaining.

No, he told himself sternly. *That would be cowardice.* And, reluctantly, he followed them inside.

Karal listened to Master Levy speak about mathematics and theory with great envy for Natoli, who had such a good teacher. If *he'd* had teachers as good as this man, he might have had more understanding of and love for mathematics. Instead, math was as arcane a subject for him as magic, and he remembered his mathematics lessons as being ordeals.

". . . so you see," Master Levy said, with a certain grim satisfaction, "by using this mathematical model, I was able to predict the size and location of all of the areas of disturbance from this last wave. We will have parties out in the countryside verifying my predictions, of course, but the ones we were able to reach before darkness fell were all where I predicted they would be and the size I expected they would be."

"So these storms are really *waves*; they act like real waves?" Elspeth asked, weariness warring with the need to understand, both emotions mirrored in the set of her mouth and the tense lines around her eyes. Darkwind looked over her shoulder at the charts and maps, his brow creased with exhaustion and anxiety.

"In many ways," Master Levy told her and raised a sardonic eyebrow. "I take it that I have convinced you?"

"Just by virtue of the animal you found. I've seen the creatures in the Uncleansed Lands for myself," she replied. "This rabbit-thing you found sounds much too like them for me to disbelieve you."

"And I must agree, at least that the waves are growing stronger, not weaker," Firesong said with extreme reluctance. "They must be growing stronger to have had the effect of warping an animal in such a manner. But—still—mathematical models? Magic does not *work* that way!"

To Karal's surprise, the look that Master Levy bestowed on Firesong was one of understanding and sympathy. "Sir, I comprehend your feelings. Yours is an intuitive nature, and your understanding so deep that you *intuit* the formulas and laws. So must an artist feel when he picks up a shell, paints a sunflower or creates an image of a snowstorm—yet I can reproduce that sunflower in precise mathematical terms, and every snowflake is a mathematically exact shape. If I show you in such a way that you can understand me, will you believe that your magic *does* answer to predictable laws?"

Numbly, Firesong nodded. Master Levy had a force of personality—when he cared to exert it—that was easily the equal of Firesong's. This must have been a rare experience for the Hawkbrother Adept, to find someone who was his equal in personality and intellect.

"Look. This was your original Cataclysm," Master Levy said, pulling out a clean sheet of paper and a pen and drawing concentric circles on it. Karal marveled at that—there were not many people in his experience who *could* draw an even circle without the use of tools. Master Levy must be something of an artist in his own right.

"There were two centers of disruption," the mathematician continued. "One *here*, where the Dhorisha Plains are now, and one *here*, where Lake Evendim is. The force spread outward, in waves—each of these circles represents the apex of the wave—you see where they meet and touch as they spread outward? *That* is where your points of extreme disturbance are, where the apexes of two waves meet."

"So why were the areas of change so great in the original Cataclysm?" Firesong asked stubbornly. "They weren't little circles of devastation, they were huge swaths, reaching from Lake Evendim to beyond where the eastern border of Hardorn is now!"

Master Levy smiled patiently. "The very first waves had a period—a 'width,' if you will—that was enormous; roughly the equivalent of several countries. In areas of the apex of the wave, disturbance was powerful enough that there was no need for waves to interfere with each other to distort the real world, the wave itself was what did the initial damage, and created what we call the Pelagir Hills and what you call the Uncleansed Lands—and yet, entire nations who happened to be in the trough of the wave remained relatively unscathed. I suspect that you would find that where the apexes of the first two great waves met, you *would* find areas of such damage that nothing lived through it."

Firesong bit his lip, as if Master Levy had triggered a memory of something, but he remained silent.

"Now—this is another guess, but I believe that the first wave of shock, the one from the initial destruction of the two centers, was followed by waves of successively shorter period and lesser strength." He cocked his head at Firesong, as if to ask if Firesong understood.

"Perhaps—" Firesong murmured reluctantly.

Master Levy flashed Karal a conspiratorial glance. "Now look; I am drawing the circles closer together, for a reason. The next waves had a period that was shorter, and the next, shorter still. The areas of overlap were correspondingly more frequent, and smaller, until the last of the waves of disturbance passed. As the waves grew weaker, and the period smaller, the disruptions were confined to the places where the wave-apexes intersected. That is why we are finding little circles of disturbance at regular intervals; the intervals represent a combination of the period of the two sets of waves. And the periods presumably lessen due to effects analogous to how the troughs of waves in deep water reduce when they 'drag' the floor of the body of water. Expenditure of energy."

Firesong studied the rough diagram and nodded slowly, then began twisting a lock of his long silver hair in an uncharacteristically nervous gesture.

Firesong? Nervous? The sun will surely rise in the west tomorrow!

"Now, if what I believe turns out to be the truth, these waves of disturbance are returning through time, in a mirror image of how they occurred in the first place." Master Levy waited, like the teacher he was, for someone to volunteer the next piece of the puzzle.

"Do you mean that they are beginning small and weak, and will end enormous and enormously powerful?" Darkwind hazarded.

"I do," Master Levy replied, nodding at Darkwind as if the mage was a particularly good student. "And I also mean that they are traveling in the opposite direction; instead of radiating *out* from the Plains and Lake Evendim, they are *converging* on the Plains and Lake Evendim. Which means that all their force, in the end, will be concentrated in those two spots."

"Oh." Elspeth held her knuckles to her mouth in stunned silence.

"And as the waves increase in strength, the areas of disturbance will no longer be confined to the points of intersection, but will be as wide as—" Master Levy paused for a moment, "—at a guess, I would say roughly a third of the wave's period. Once again, that could be an area the size of a country, or larger."

Firesong sat down slowly. "You have convinced me, mathematician," he said, his face blank. "Your proofs are too good. And you have told me that my people are doomed, mine and the Shin'a'in. They lie directly in the area that will be affected the worst. No shields can ever withstand the force of the kind that is mounting against them."

"Feh!" snorted Master Norten into the heavy pause that followed. He was a short, squat fellow who had remained silent during all of this. His exclamation pierced the ponderous silence, making all of them start.

"What?" Elspeth faltered.

"I said, begging your pardon, *Feh*. No one is *doomed*, young man." Master Norten favored Firesong with a sharp glare, as if he had caught Firesong being impossibly dense. "We have enough information to *predict* the period of the next waves! We have enough information to *know* what the strength will be, and where the intersection points are! Right now, the danger is only at the intersection points; we can keep people and animals out of them; we can destroy the plants inside them. But haven't you been paying attention? We *have* a temporary solution, enough to buy us time to find a real solution!"

"You have?" Elspeth gasped.

"We *have?*" Master Levy gaped.

Master Norten took the cane with which he had been supporting his bulk and rapped Master Levy with it. "Of *course* we have, you dolt! All you ever see are your damned mathematical models! *Think*, man! You're the one who pointed out that these spurts of magic are acting in a way we recognize! Can't you understand that these—these magic-waves—are acting *exactly* like waves of water? And can't we protect harbors and anchorages from *real* waves with breakwaters? So why can't these mages come up with magical breakwaters to protect important places, places like cities and those nodes of theirs and all?" He glared at all of them, as if he could not believe they had not seen what to him was so obvious. "Hell and damnation! Why can't they just build a magical breakwater to protect every country in the Alliance?"

"This is why I am a mathematician and not an engineer," Master Levy replied, with chagrin. Master Norton snorted again, and looked very pleased with himself.

"I—I suppose it ought to be possible," murmured Darkwind, his brows knotted as he thought.

"Well, then, you ought to damn well *do* it, boy!" Master Norten retorted. "We can surely give you the dates and times and interference points. We can calculate the strength and period if you help us establish scales. With all that, I don't see why you can't do the rest, instead of sitting on your behinds, whining about being 'doomed'!"

"But magic doesn't work that way," Firesong whispered— except that it sounded more like a plea than a statement of fact.

"I'm sorry, Firesong," Karal replied, not at all sorry to see Firesong at last convinced that he was not the greatest expert in all things. "It does." He handed Firesong a set of all of the tables for the last two waves, his own copies that he had been keeping with him. In the face of all the neat rows of dispassionate, logical figures and formulas, finally even Firesong had to concede defeat.

"All right," the Healing Adept said at last. "It does. And I

promise that I will learn how to use all of this. How long do
we have before the *real* mage-storm breaks?"

"We haven't calculated it yet," Master Levy responded instantly. "We only now have enough information to predict
how much stronger the next waves will be from the ones pre-
ceding them. It would *help* if we had an idea how strong the
original waves were, and what their period was."

"Farrr enough that the Kaled'a'in werrre engulfed in the
rrresultsss of the Cataclysssm, dessspite the grrreat distancsse
they had gone frrrom Urrrtho'sss Towerrr," Treyvan rumbled. "Howeverrr—we alsssso trrrraveled to a point outssside
that, beforrre we finally found a placsse wherrre the land
wasss clean. Therrre we ssstopped. Perrrhaps we can give you
an essstimate."

"An estimate will do," Master Levy told the gryphon. He
had started when Treyvan first spoke, but he seemed to have
accepted the fact that the gryphons could speak with intelligence.

"I can send a mage-message," Firesong volunteered instantly. "And—wasn't there something in that history Rris
recited about how long the original—ah, I suppose we could
call them 'aftershocks'—lasted?"

"It was fairly vague," Karal replied after a moment, check-
ing his notes from that first meeting. "I've got it here. He just
said, 'many moons.' That's not much help."

Firesong blinked, as if he had forgotten that Karal had
taken notes for all their meetings.

"Except that we know we have at least a few months to figure something out before the monster comes upon us," Master Norten was quick to point out. Then he yawned hugely
and looked surprised. "Gods and demons, it *must* be late, or I
wouldn't be yawning! Look, none of us are fresh enough to do
any good right now. What if we three meet with you mages in
the morning, and we'll see what we can work out from here?"

"That—would be good." Firesong bowed his head. "I hope
you will forgive me. I am not used to being wrong. It sticks
like a barb in my crop."

"I can understand that." Master Norten favored him with a
sardonic smile. "I'm not used to being wrong, either, and I
hate it like poison when I am."

"So we understand each other." Firesong gingerly took the Master's hand as Elspeth and Darkwind watched, the former with approval, the latter with amusement. "Tomorrow, then?"

"Tomorrow." Master Norten favored Karal with his stiletto glance now. "I trust you'll be there, with nimble fingers and sharp pens? I want notes on *everything,* even if at the time we think we've gone down a dead end. It might be useful."

Karal sighed. It was going to be a *very* long day.

"Yes, sir," he promised. That made yet another group he was taking notes for. At this rate, his fingers would be worn to the bone! It was just a good thing he had glass pens now, instead of the old quills or metal; the glass hadn't worn out yet.

Well, I did volunteer. And with luck, maybe Natoli will be impressed with all this diligence. I get the feeling that nothing impresses her quite like competence.

Only after he was well on his way down the corridor, walking next to his master, did he wonder why he'd had that particular thought. . . .

Grand Duke Tremane listened to the tales of woe from his commanders with a blank expression and a churning gut. They had all ridden here—*ridden,* as if this was some barbarian army rather than the proud Army of the Empire. Most of them hadn't ridden any distance in years, but with all the Gates down—again—there was no other way for them to reach him.

It was very clear to everyone that the Imperial forces were in a state of barely-controlled panic. No sooner did the mages manage to fix all the things that had gone wrong, than another wave of disruption came along and knocked everything magical flat again. There wasn't even time to set up shielding around things! This was the third time, and it was worse than the last two; shields that had held through the first two waves had broken before this third onslaught.

Not one of his commanders cared a bean about gaining more ground in Hardorn anymore. All *they* wanted was for things to get back to normal! Even the weather-workers were having problems; they couldn't even begin to control the storms and were just trying to keep the worst effects off the camps themselves.

Add to that the panic and the disruption in services of all those terrible storms that dumped purely physical chaos down on the camps, and you had a recipe for disaster if he didn't *do* something to increase the troops' confidence. Rumors running through the camp right now were enough to cause even hardened campaigners to worry; new recruits were often panicking, and had to be restrained by their more experienced fellows. There were tales that Hardorn had bought the services of the Black Kings in the south, stories that some mage in the Empire itself had caused this by accident, rumors that Valdemar was unleashing the hidden powers of their Heralds and white horses. No one knew, but everyone had a theory. Most of those theories painted a grim picture of the first defeat that the Imperial Army was likely to face in centuries, if Tremane didn't pull some answer out of his sleeve.

The only trouble was, he hadn't the foggiest notion how to do that.

I pledge you a tonne of incense and a gross of candles each, he silently told the forty little gods, *if you will just grant me some inspiration on what to do in this situation!*

But inspiration and intervention, divine or otherwise, was clearly in short supply at the moment. None of the forty vouchsafed him a reply.

"We have to do something," General Harde said, at last. "No matter what your orders are, you have to order us to do *something,* or the troops will assume you've lost your nerve and we've lost the situation."

"Consolidate," he said finally. "Everyone pull your men in, and consolidate our forces around this keep. To the coldest hell with the battle plans; I want every soldier right here where we can stay in contact by runners if we have to. With all the men we'll have here, we can build purely physical fortifications. Abandon the front line; the Emperor is hardly in a position to find out what we're doing right now, anyway."

Oh, if only the Empire is suffering the same effects that we are! he prayed. *Chaos there will save the situation for me here. Chaos there will convince the Emperor that I am not exaggerating my troubles to cover my own incompetence. And if this is something that Charliss unleashed on me, on his own loyal soldiers—*

He did not finish that thought; it would be treason, no two ways about it. He was not ready for treason.

Not yet.

"But what about supplies?" one of the commanders asked. "How are we going to keep such a huge force fed?"

"I don't know yet; I'll have an answer for you when we finally bring them all in," he promised. "I have supplies here for the whole Army for about two weeks before we'd have to go on lean rations. Meanwhile, there are rebels out there, and they are still picking at us; we're better off with all the men in one place, rather than stretched out along a line that reaches across half this benighted country. I *don't* want to lose any units by having them cut off from me."

That put some spine back in them; with firm orders to carry out, his commanders were a lot more comfortable. And with a march ahead of them, followed by the physical labor of building fortifications, the men should remain tractable until the work ran out.

Better get the engineers to work on designing a wall using only the materials on hand, and mostly hand-labor. And after that, well, if I have to, I'll march the whole damned lot all the way back to Imperial soil, he thought grimly, dismissing his commanders. He turned his attention to the reply to last night's urgent request for information from his tame scholars. He'd literally ordered them out of their beds, and set them to work all night. *I may go down in disgrace, but I won't leave these men to be picked off two and three at a time by a pack of barbarians.*

At least he'd transported his whole library here before everything went to hell. Somewhere, some time, *something* like this must have happened in the past. He'd ordered his scholars to abandon their search for information on Valdemar and concentrate on looking for just that. He was, by the gods, going to find out *when* there were disruptions like this, where they occurred, and most important of all, what the people back then did about it!

My lord; the letter read—the Chief Historian had been im-

pressed enough by the salty language of his order to keep his
report concise and omit all the flowerly nonsense usually
pasted into such documents. Then again, the Chief Historian
was now working without mage-lights, mage-fires, running
water, or any of the other comforts he was used to. That
alone must have impressed him that the situation was urgent. *These disruptions that we are now experiencing were
unusual enough that we were able to eliminate most of the
texts in your library immediately. I and my three colleagues
are familiar with the history of the Empire, and we knew
that there would be nothing in the Official Chronicles—
which meant that we began our search in the copies of texts
we had that predated the foundation of the Empire itself.*

Well! Tremane sat back in his chair, taken aback. He knew
that the fact that he actually owned copies of pre-Imperial
texts was something of a fluke, and due only to his own interest in history. Most people didn't own anything nearly so old;
he'd paid a healthy sum in bribes above and beyond the cost
of the books to get some of those books, too, and now he was
very glad that he had.

*First, I must caution you that these texts are a jumble of
many archaic tongues, and it is going to take some time to
translate them precisely. We have all agreed on the general
gist of what we found, however.*

*Second, the texts themselves are the personal papers of a
mixed group of ancient warriors. Some were—we think—
mercenaries, and others were liegemen to a Great Lord of
some kind.*

Well, that certainly fit in with the official history of the
Empire. Tremane cupped his chin in his hand and read on.

*We have gathered from the papers that this group was part
of a much larger force; that they were cut off from the rest
when their enemy gained an unexpected and decisive victory. They were warned by their Lord that they must flee as
far and as fast as they could, by means of a Gate.*

Interesting. That was not part of official history, which
stated that the group had marched off on its own to carve out
conquest for themselves.

*Why they fled, we do not yet know; our guess, and it is
only a guess, was that the Great Lord intended his enemy's*

victory to be an empty one, and meant to ensure his enemy claimed only ashes by destroying everything before he actually took it. Be that as it may, it is clear that they did build a Gate to reach a location they knew was relatively safe, far eastward of the place where they had retreated after being cut off. Then something happened as they were passing through the Gate, and a catastrophe of—we believe—a magical nature, flung them farther away than they had ever intended to go. This landed them in completely unfamiliar territory—territory that became, as you have probably anticipated, the heart of our Empire. In the days that followed, a series of disruptions that one writer terms "magic-quakes" occurred; another writer describes them as "aftershocks." These disruptions seem on first blush to match the kinds of troubles we are experiencing now.

This was exactly what he had been hoping to find! Elation built in him—

—only to be crushed, abruptly, by the words that followed.

You were most urgent in your orders that once we found a match to our circumstances, we should discover what those ancients had done to remedy their situation. I have no good news for you, my Lord. Once again, my colleagues and I are unanimous in our understanding of these papers.

Our ancestors did nothing. They could do nothing. They simply waited for the magic-quakes—or aftershocks—to end, or destroy them. Eventually, of course, the disruptions ended, they consolidated their position, and the rest is official Imperial history.

Tremane buried his face in his hands.

They waited it out. This was *not* good news.

But I am going to have to deal with it. He was not one to try to pretend that bad news wasn't the truth. If anything, he tended to act as if bad news was only the shadow of worse to come. It would be a good idea to act that way now.

His mages were in a panic; the waves of disruption were growing stronger, not weaker, as each one passed. His instinct to get the Gates up *first*, and start hauling supplies through them as soon as they were up, had been the right choice. They had supplies enough to last them well into the winter at half rations, now, and if they could just get the

Gates back up a few more times, they might get enough to last all the way to spring on *full* rations.

No. That was the wrong choice—get the supplies, yes, that should be the priority, but why waste time on getting *several* Gates up, when he only needed one? Just the one to the westernmost Imperial supply depot, the one for foodstuffs. Forget weapons; he wasn't going to allow his men to waste a single arrow until he had decided what his long-term plans should be. Forget reinforcements; he had all the men he needed to hold firm, and too many for an orderly retreat, if it came to that. He would have all his mages concentrate on getting that one single Gate back up, and he would forge the orders he needed to loot the depot, and to the coldest hell with honesty and procedure, and anyone else who might need supplies from it.

It's easier to apologize than get permission. He could make amends to the Emperor later, if he needed to.

At least he knew one thing; it was less likely now that Charliss was actively sending this against him. However, it was still possible that Charliss had known this would happen, and had sent him off on a doomed mission to be rid of him.

And condemned hundreds of thousands of good soldiers with me. That made him angry; the loyalty of the Army to the Emperor was legendary. To have that loyalty betrayed so callously was a betrayal of everything the Empire held sacred.

Which isn't much. When he thought back on the state of the Court, of the corruption deep in the bureaucracy, perhaps he shouldn't be angry *or* surprised.

He shook his head. It didn't matter. What *did* matter was that while he was maneuvering to get his army into a defensive position, there was Valdemar, virtually unscathed, poised, and waiting.

If I were the Queen, I'd strike right now. I'd bring in Karse, hit the Imperial lines at a dozen places and break us up into manageable pieces, and then wipe the pieces out at my leisure. I wouldn't hesitate. Just arm the natives, and they'd probably take care of most of it for me. That would give me Hardorn with a minimum of effort—and I might even be able to penetrate into Imperial territory before it got too expensive.

He had to do something to keep Valdemar so busy with its own troubles that it wouldn't have the leisure or the coordination to strike now.

Unfortunately, that meant using a weapon that he'd held in reserve because he hated it so much.

But a man threatened will use anything to stay alive. I am fighting for not only my life, but the lives of my men. I cannot hesitate. I will not hesitate.

He would not entrust this to an aide or a messenger. Instead, he unlocked a drawer of his desk, and removed a square of something heavy wrapped in silk. He laid the square in the middle of his desk and unwrapped it, uncovering a piece of polished black obsidian-glass, perfectly square and perfectly flawless.

This was another reason why all candidates for the Iron Throne should be mages. Some messages were too important for anything but personal delivery.

He reached into the drawer again, and brought out a hand-sized portrait of a man; it was an excellent likeness, though the man himself was hardly memorable. This was a good thing; it was not wise to employ a man who was distinctive as a covert agent. With the portrait was a lock of the man's hair; the physical link needed to contact him.

It was also the physical link that any decent mage could use to *kill* him if he became uncooperative, as all agents knew very well. There was nothing like having a little insurance, when one dealt with covert operatives.

Using the portrait, he fixed the agent's image in his mind, and reached for the energies of his own personal reserve of magic. He did not care to trust the lines of power hereabouts; his mages had already warned him that they were depleted and erratic. What these disruptions had done to them, he did not care to speculate. While he relied on his own protected pool of power, he should be immune to the disturbances around him.

He stared into the black glass, emptying his mind of everything except the agent and the need to speak with him, flinging his power out as if it was a fishing line, and he was angling for one fish in particular.

His power slowly drained out as he sought and waited; sought and waited. This might take a while; he was prepared to wait for as long as it took. His agent was not in command of his own movements, and it could be some time before he was free to answer the call. That was fine; a mage must learn patience, first and foremost, before he could build any other skills. A mage must learn concentration, as well, and Tremane had ample practice in both virtues.

The marks crept by and the candle burned down, and at long last, past the hour of midnight, the answer came to his call.

The agent's face formed in the glass, expression anxious and apologetic. Tremane thought, with a curl of his lip, that the fool looked even more ineffectual than he did in his portrait. *Why* had anyone ever chosen an artist as a covert agent? *"My Lord Duke!"* the man cried, his lips moving in the glass, his voice as thin and weak as a fly's buzzing whine. *"I beg you to forgive me! I could not get away! I—"*

"You are wasting my time with apologies," Tremane said curtly. "Here are your orders. Release the little birds."

The agent's face went dead white. *"My—my Lord?"* he faltered. *"All of them? Are you certain?"*

"All of them," Tremane ordered, curtly. "See to it."

Before the fool could waste his time and resources further by arguing or pleading that this would place him in danger, Tremane broke the spell. The agent's image vanished from the glass, quickly as a candle flame is blown out. Tremane paused for a moment, massaging his temples, before he folded the silk around the obsidian and put glass, hair, and portrait back into the drawer.

Would the agent survive his appointed task?

He would if he was careful, Tremane decided. There was nothing about the job that left him vulnerable to discovery. The "little birds" should already be in place, and setting them free could be done at a distance. If he was stupid, he might be caught, though.

Then let him suffer the penalty of stupidity, Tremane decided with uncharacteristic impatience. *If he is caught, he has done all he need do, and he is expendable.*

He was rarely so ruthless with an underling, but this man was no agent of *his* choosing, and he had not been particularly useful until now.

He clenched his fist for a moment, as a pang of regret for what he had just ordered swept over him. This was—ugly, unclean, and underhanded. It was neither honest nor honorable. It would be the first real stain on his conscience or soul. He had ordered the deaths of men before, but they had always been death in battle or other circumstances where both sides knew what they were getting into. He knew that he would spend at least one sleepless night over this and probably more to come.

This was the death of innocents, noncombatants. Yet an Emperor had to be ruthless enough to order just such an action to save the lives of his own people.

But I had no choice, he told himself, staring up at the black glass of his window, so like the black mirror he had just used. *I must save my men. This is war, and I had no choice.*

So why did it feel as if he had betrayed, not only his honor, but some significant part of his own soul?

Florian

15

There were seven days left before the next wave, and Karal was not altogether certain he was going to live that long. There were simply not enough marks in the day to do everything he had to. Then again, he was not the only person working to exhaustion; the mages and the engineers were all walking around with dark rings under their eyes. The only reason *he* was getting any sleep at all was because he was seeing to it that Ulrich got a decent rest every night, and then dropping into slumber shortly thereafter.

The mages did their shielding work in the morning, when they were all fresh; then came a break for lunch, then their meeting with the Master Engineers, and then their own meetings. Karal was not always present at the latter; the mages needed his reports on what the engineers were doing, more than the reverse, since An'desha was making himself available to them for explanations and demonstrations. Karal had to wonder where *he* was getting the energy.

Generally he kept himself as unobtrusive and invisible as possible—except where Ulrich's health was concerned. It had taken a major effort of will to march right in on the mages and demand that Master Ulrich be allowed to get some rest, the first time he'd gotten back to the suite after returning from the Compass Rose only to find that Ulrich was not in his bed. He was nothing more than the merest secretary; *he* had no standing and no authority among such luminaries as Elspeth and Darkwind! But Ulrich's welfare was the most important job he had; *Solaris* had entrusted him with seeing that his mentor remained hale and well, and staying up until dawn, snatching an hour or two of sleep, and getting up to work complicated magics was going to wear him to nothing in a very short period of time. He didn't think the others, being much younger than Ulrich, were aware of how quickly he could be exhausted. So he had gathered up all of his courage, walked straight into the meeting, and respectfully "reminded" Ulrich that his master had left orders to be told when midnight arrived so that he could get enough rest to work the next day.

Ulrich had looked momentarily startled, then had given Karal a long, hard look. Karal had done his best to wear an expression of bland implacability.

I won't go away, sir, he'd thought hard at Ulrich. He'd never known whether or not his master could read thoughts as he had often suspected, but if Ulrich could, he was certainly getting an "earful" now. *Whatever it takes to persuade you to get some rest, I'm going to do it, even if I have to fabricate emergencies, even if I have to recruit Altra.* Though how he was going to persuade the Firecat to go along with the scheme, he hadn't had a clue at the time.

He still didn't know if Ulrich could read thoughts, but his mentor had risen with thanks for the "reminder," and had excused himself from the meetings whenever Karal appeared after that, and all without a contradictory word thereafter.

Still, if Karal felt as if he was constantly on the verge of exhaustion, how must Ulrich feel?

He knew what was driving them all; he felt it himself. Beneath it all, underscoring every waking moment, was the sense of urgency. *Hurry, hurry, hurry,* whispered a tiny voice. *Don't waste any time. You don't have time to waste. Find the answer; find it now, before it's too late.*

Some time, soon, too soon, scant months from now, it would *be* too late. The real storm would break over their heads, and Valdemar was closer to the center of one of the two places in peril than any other land and people—

Except for the Shin'a'in.

And except for the small group of Kaled'a'in that had made their new home on the very edge of the Plain. Those were the gryphons' people, and although Treyvan and Hydona said nothing about it, Karal knew that they were as grimly worried about their little group as the Shin'a'in ambassador was worried about her own people.

There was an option that no one liked, but which would at least save the lives of those in peril. Before the Storm actually hit, the people themselves could move. It wouldn't be easy, though; by then, disruption-waves would be arriving daily, making it impossible to set up Gates. They would all have to move the hard way; overland, by foot and horse, and even the Kaled'a'in "floating barges" would be useless unless the mages spent all their time and energy in holding shields against the disruption.

By then, though, the lands around the area would be the next thing to uninhabitable. There would be no possibility of anyone leading a normal life, not when your crop plants were suddenly warping into things that could kill you with flung thorns or poison, and the beasts of your fields had turned into rabid killers.

Karal had the latest maps spread out on the table in front of the fireplace and was studying them while he waited for Ulrich to return for lunch. These were the maps predicting the areas of effect from the next disruption-wave. It would come exactly one and one-half days short of a fortnight, and the circles of "change" would be twenty hands across—enough that now a large animal *could* conceivably be caught inside one.

A Shin'a'in horse, for instance. Or a Valdemaran bull.

Or a wild deer; it didn't matter. The "rabbit" had nearly taken off someone's hand; anything larger would be deadly to whatever was within its range of movement.

Karal shivered at the thought. With luck, and the help of all the Heralds out on circuit, they could warn people to keep their livestock at home that day, or confine them away from danger zones. That was in Valdemar, and it still left the possibility that some large game animal would be caught in a change. Altra had taken a copy of the map this morning as soon as he had made one, and had vanished with it; evidently now the Firecat had no problems acting as a messenger to Solaris. That took care of Karse—again, except for wild animals, and they would just have to chance that.

Presumably Firesong could send the information to the

Hawkbrothers by magic—and they in turn would pass it to the Kaled'a'in and the Shin'a'in.

Prince Daren had sent a Herald off last night to Rethwellan, but there were no Priests or Heralds in Rethwellan to distribute the warning. There were none in Hardorn either, nor in the icy wilderness up above the Forest of Sorrows, nor in Iftel. There was no way to tell anyone farther south than Rethwellan, except if the Shin'a'in got around to it, nor were there any ways to distribute warnings there. *Their* only hope was that the wave centering on Evendim would be so weak by the time it got that far, that the combined effect with the one centered on the Plain would be negligible.

It wouldn't remain that way for long, though. Sooner or later the waves would be strong enough that the warping effect would be felt even farther away than Ceejay, and at that point, the waves would be coming more often, too.

Somehow, someone had to spread the word. Somehow, *they* had to find the answer to stopping this thing.

Hurry, hurry, hurry, before it's too late. . . .

Nothing could be done about the Pelagirs or the northern mountains. What would happen when the beasts that were already strange and deadly, out in the Uncleansed Lands, encountered these warping forces a second time? One wag of a student had suggested that they *might* just go back to being rabbits, mice and tree-hares. That was an amusing thought, but unlikely.

And what about the Empire? There was still an army out there. What if whoever was in command decided that Valdemar, Karse, or both were the cause of all this? *They* had command of far more magic than either land did, and an unlimited supply of troops, or so it seemed. What if they decided this was an attack, and decided that it was worth carrying the battle to the enemy?

As if that thought had been a cue, the door opened, and Ulrich stepped in.

The sound of his limping footstep made Karal turn, with a frown of worry on his face. Ulrich should not be limping, not unless he was so exhausted that even walking was an effort.

His frown deepened when he saw the pale, translucent skin above Ulrich's beard, and the dark circles beneath his eyes.

"You've been overworking again," he accused.

"I've been undersleeping," Ulrich corrected. "I had troubling dreams last night, and this morning I urged that our work consist of sending out warnings, maps, and the formulae to calculate the schedules, not only to the Tayledras, Shin'a'in shaman, and Kaled'a'in, but to every mage-school any of us knew of. It occurred to me that in the schools there is *always* someone teaching or practicing a scrying spell, and we needed only to "interrupt" what was already in place. The Blue Mountain and White Winds mages were particularly helpful there." He smiled wanly. "We covered quite a bit of ground, so to speak."

"That's all very well and good, but—" Karal stopped himself in midscold, shaking his head at himself. "I'm sorry. I sound like your mother, or at least a nagging son, and I'm only your protégé and secretary. Forgive me, Master Ulrich."

But to his shock and delight, Ulrich not only did not take offense, but he smiled again, this time with real warmth. Wan sunlight relected from the white plaster-adorned mantel fell on him, accentuating his pallor. "You have every right, and if I had a nagging son, or any kind of son, I would hope he would be precisely like you. You are a never-ending delight to me, Karal. I had thought when I first took you as my protégé that I would always be a little disappointed in you because you were not a mage. I was wrong."

"Wrong?" Karal replied vaguely, more than a little stunned by the sudden turn this conversation had taken.

"Very wrong." Ulrich limped across the floor to him and hesitantly put one hand on his shoulder. "You are something more important than a mage, and much rarer, my son. You are a warrior of the spirit and a healer of the soul. You have more compassion than I can begin to understand, and you are already showing the beginnings of true wisdom. People trust you instinctively, and instinctively you sense that and try to help them, even as you do your best not to betray that trust. You will be a great Priest in the purest sense one day, the sense that has nothing to do with magic, power, or politics; that, I think, is why Altra was sent to you."

Karal trembled under Ulrich's hand; this was *not* anything

he had ever expected to hear, and he plainly didn't know what to think.

"Yours will not be an easy path, I fear," Ulrich continued. "But I can tell you one that you should make the time to speak to. Herald Talia is one who is very like you; her abilities differ in that she is a healer of the heart, rather than the soul, but otherwise she will understand you better than anyone else you are ever likely to meet."

"B–but—Solaris—" he faltered, blurting out the first thing that came to mind. *Why is he talking like this? He sounds as if he thinks he might not be here while I still need him—*

Ulrich shook his head. "Solaris is something else entirely; the Prophet and the Leader are concerned with the needs of the people as a whole, and not with the needs of individuals. Solaris will not be able to help you—although you may be called upon one day to help her."

Karal dropped his gaze to the floor, a lump in his throat, confusion in his heart. Ulrich put a finger under Karal's chin, and raised his face so that Karal was forced to look into his eyes. "In one thing, Talia will not be able to help you, and you will have to find your own way. The way of the true Priest is often solitary; he can sometimes tread a parallel road with another, but sooner or later, their ways must part, and they may not come together again. Your life belongs to others, and I think you already understand and accept that, although you have not put it into words for yourself. If you are very lucky, you may find a partner who can understand or accept that. If you are not, there will be heartache. If the heartache comes, *remember* what you are, and that if you may not be the lover of one, you *will* be beloved by many."

Karal blinked up into Ulrich's eyes, trying his best to understand what his master was saying, and not quite grasping it. Ulrich looked down at him for another heartbeat or two, then released him with a dry chuckle.

"Ah, my dreams have made me fey, a little mad, or both," he said lightly. "Either that, or I am so hungered that I am seeing shadows of a future that may never happen. Did you bespeak lunch?"

Karal released a sigh of relief and nodded. "And it's odd that you should have mentioned Herald Talia; she wanted to talk to both of us about An'desha. She says that he is all knotted up over something, and she thinks we can help him."

"Well, perhaps we can," Ulrich began, just as a light tap signaled someone at the door.

"Come!" Ulrich said immediately; the door opened and the Lady Talia herself stepped inside, followed by the page with their lunch. For a moment, there was a little confusion, as Karal quickly cleaned the papers off the table, the boy maneuvered the tray onto the waiting surface, and everyone sorted themselves out. The boy bowed quickly and left, Talia and Ulrich exchanged greetings, and Karal *started* into the other room to fetch a third chair.

He never even got as far as the door.

Something—some strange sound, or maybe not a sound at all, just a feeling—made him whirl around, every nerve afire with the certain knowledge of *danger*, deadly and imminent.

The fireplace was decorated with plaster ornaments much like the Council rooms and most of the other suites in the Palace. They were set into the wall on either side and above the mantel, a series of whorls and scrollwork, with four larger whorls, one just off each corner of the mantelpiece.

A shrill trilling sound split the air just as the plaster of those whorls split and shattered, releasing *something* that sprang out into the room and hung, hovering, in the air.

Karal didn't get a good look at them; they made his eyes hurt, and no matter how he concentrated, the very air blurred around them. He only had an impression of a diamond-shape of sharp blades, frightening and deadly.

He didn't think, he acted, instinctively flinging himself in front of Talia, keeping his own body between her and them. If anyone in this room was in danger, surely it was Talia!

In the next instant, Altra was in front of *him*. Every hair on the Firecat's body was on end, and the Cat howled a piercing battle cry that rivaled the whining trill of the devices.

The diamond-blades *moved*; the two nearest Karal flew at him as fast as a pair of glittering dragonflies. He flung himself backward, trying to knock Talia to the floor to shield her. He expected at any moment to feel one or more of those blades piercing his heart—

But there was a sharp *crack*, and two of the devices vanished altogether in a flash of fire, one that originated from Altra's extended claws. The third went careening sideways, into the path of the fourth, deflecting it—

But not enough.

The device slammed into Ulrich's chest with enough force to knock him to the floor, as the second device embedded itself in the wall.

The trilling stopped, leaving silence, and the sound of harsh, bubbling breathing.

"Ulrich!" Karal screamed, as he scrambled to his feet and flung himself down beside the Priest. Talia was right behind him, and stopped him before he could pull the damnable device out of Ulrich's chest. The Priest was still breathing, but he was unconscious, and a thin trickle of blood appeared at one corner of his mouth and ran down the side of his face.

"Don't touch him," Talia ordered. "I've called for help. I know some Healing, let me—"

Obediently, he moved aside and let *her* be the one to remove the device. Fearlessly, she pulled it out, and the wound whistled for a second until she slapped her hand over it, blocking it. "It's a lung-hit, that's bad," she muttered under her breath, distractedly. "Very bad—where *is* that damned Healer?"

Karal hovered beside her, in an agony of helplessness, wanting to do something, *anything*, and unable to aid her at all. "Ulrich, Master," he whispered, one hand on his mentor's forehead, the other on his shoulder on the uninjured side. "Please, help is coming, don't leave me, I need you, *don't leave me.*"

Time just did not feel like it was moving right. *Nothing* felt like it was moving right. This couldn't really be happening, Karal thought through a mental sludge. The sounds of their voices and movements seemed truncated, as if they were down a well, and Ulrich's halting, gasping breaths were too loud.

Then, finally, the door burst open, and a dozen or more people crowded into the room, at least two of them in the green robes that denoted a senior Healer in this land. They swarmed over Ulrich, shoving aside both Karal and Talia. A moment later, they carried the Priest away, leaving Karal and

Talia behind, with one other person. Karal started to follow, but a hand on his shoulder stopped him.

"Let me go," he spat, grabbing the hand to pull it off. But another hand grabbed his wrist and made him turn, and he found himself looking into Kerowyn's sober green eyes.

"You can't help Ulrich, and you'll only get in the Healers' way," she said, bluntly telling him the truth that he didn't want to hear.

"But—" He looked at her, and unexpectedly burst into tears.

Talia put her arms around him—and strangely enough, so did Kerowyn. Both of them held him while he sobbed hysterically.

"Why?" he wept. "*Why?* He never hurt anyone! He was an old man! He never *hurt* anyone! *Why?*"

Neither of the women said anything to him, which was just as well, since he wouldn't have been able to hear them or respond. They simply made soothing sounds at him and supported him as time wobbled and spun. After a moment, or a candlemark, Kerowyn detached herself and left him to bury his head in Talia's shoulder while the Herald stroked his hair and swayed back and forth with him in her arms.

Terrible grief shook him; he couldn't see, couldn't hear, couldn't even think. The only things in his mind were the dreadful sound of the blade-device thudding into Ulrich's chest, never-ending, and the sight of Ulrich's body hitting the floor. . . .

It was exhaustion that finally brought him back to himself. His tears stopped, mostly because his eyes were too sore and dry to produce another drop. Dully, he allowed Talia to lead him to a chair, and he sat down in it.

Kerowyn knelt in front of him, the two devices in her hands. "Ulrich wasn't the only one attacked," she said gently. "The Shin'a'in ambassador was killed outright, and it was just pure luck that the other mages were with the gryphons when more of these things came after *them;* they all managed to knock the things down, though Treyvan and Darkwind each took a wound. It looks, at the moment, as if someone hid these damned things in plaster ornaments in the rooms of every single one of the foreign mages."

He blinked at her, his eyes gritty and swollen. "Why?" he asked stupidly.

She shrugged. "Either *someone* wanted to eliminate all the ambassadors, or that same *someone* wanted to eliminate all the mages, and he settled for getting the foreigners because the rest of them live in the Herald's Wing and he didn't have access to that part of the Palace." She tilted her head to one side, and frowned. "Come to think of it, he wouldn't have access to Firesong's place, either. Maybe that's why there were four in here; the other two might have been meant for Firesong and An'desha."

He shook his head again. *"Why?"* he persisted. "Why try to kill anyone? And who would it be?"

Kerowyn's mouth tightened. "Figure it was the Empire that planned this, and you'll probably have your answer. Since I don't recognize these things, and I thought I knew every kind of assassins' weapon there was, the Empire would be my first choice for *who* did this."

Her words set his frozen mind in motion again, and almost against his will, a myriad of possibilities occurred to him. "If I wanted to break up the Alliance, I'd kill all the ambassadors," he said reluctantly. "If Valdemar couldn't protect the envoys in the Palace itself, the allies might assume it was too dangerous to ally with Valdemar against the Empire. It's possible that *some* of the allies, like Karse, might even blame Valdemar for the deaths. It might only be incidental that the targets were mages."

Talia's eyes went wide, and Kerowyn's narrowed in speculation. "That hadn't occurred to me," she admitted. "But it's an even better reason than killing them to lessen our magepower."

His mind was still working, out of long habit and training with Ulrich—

Oh, Ulrich—I've lost you. We've all lost you—

"The Empire would believe that this is an ordinary alliance, especially with Karse and Valdemar," he continued; now that his thoughts were set in motion, they wouldn't stop until he followed them to the end. "They can't know that Solaris is working under a divine decree; they'd assume that the death of her envoy would mean she would go back to the old assumption of Valdemar-as-the-Land-of-Demons. That would be why there was a device in here for me, even though I'm not a mage—so that there would be no witness to the contrary."

Kerowyn's lips thinned, and she nodded once. "That makes the best sense of all. Good work, Karal. I'm going to take these to Elspeth and Darkwind, and maybe they can take them apart. *You* are being moved to another room, as quickly as I can get *my* people in here to move your things."

He saw immediately why she had said that. "There's an Imperial agent in the Palace, isn't there," he stated flatly. "Someone who had access to all the rooms, and the *ability* to hide those things in the plaster."

"And I bloody well don't know who it is," she agreed. "So I want you and the rest of the foreigners out of here and into the Herald's Wing. Or better yet, I'll move *you* in with An'desha and Firesong, if they'll take you. Firesong got at least five of those things all by himself."

He looked up at her as she stood, and he felt his lower lip starting to quiver, his eyes starting to burn. "What about—" he began.

"Ulrich's in the best of hands, Karal," Talia said gently. "It's too soon to tell—but he *is* an old man, and we both know that he's been overworking, putting himself under a lot of strain."

He nodded and looked quickly down at his hands, before Kerowyn could see the tears starting to form in his eyes again.

Kerowyn left, but Talia stayed, so that when he began to sob again, this time quietly, she was there to hold him.

Talia stayed with him for the rest of the day; later in the afternoon Kerowyn returned with her hand-picked crew of tough-looking mercenaries from her own Company, packed up everything in the suite, and carried it out—off to Firesong and An'desha's *ekele*, she said. Karal stifled his tears when they came in; he just didn't want to cry in front of these hardened soldiers. They'd think he was being childish; surely they'd look on him with contempt.

But one of the toughest-looking turned in the middle of the

packing when Karal saw them carrying out some things of Ulrich's and choked back a sob. The man put down the robes he had draped over his arm and dropped down onto his heels in front of Karal's chair.

"Don' be 'shamed t'be a-grievin', boy," the man said, patting his hand awkwardly, his speech slow and so thickly accented that Karal barely understood him. "This kind'o thing don' get any nor easier e'en for the likes o' we. Gie yer tears t' a man who deserves 'em, an' take ye no shame i' the weepin', aye? Sure, an' we won' think th' less o'ye."

He stood up, as soon as Karal nodded numbly, and picked up his burden again. Karal just let the tears flow, then, and ignored all the comings and goings until the sun set, and the now-empty room filled with darkness.

"Do you want to go to the Healers' Collegium to wait, Karal?" Talia asked gently. "Or would you rather wait here?"

There was nothing for him here; the rooms held not even the scent of incense from Ulrich's robes—not that he could smell much after all the raw-nosed sniffling. "I'd like to go to Healers', I think," he said thickly. "If I won't be in the way."

"Of course you won't be," Talia replied warmly. She offered him her hand. "Come on, I'll take you there."

Somewhere he lost track of the walk, or else it was all swallowed up in misery. The next thing he knew, he was sitting down again, in another room, this one full of well-worn, ancient benches. The whole place had a sad air of *waiting* about it, interminable waiting. Talia was walking toward him as he looked up, suddenly aware of his surroundings again; she must have left him here without his noticing.

"There's no change, Karal," she said, and bit her lip. "I won't lie to you; you'd know it if I did. That's not a good sign. He hasn't even regained consciousness."

He nodded; she rested her hand on his shoulder.

"I'll stay with you if you want me to," she offered, and he knew that she meant it.

Just as he knew that she had much more important things to deal with than one boy's pain. Thanks to Florian, he knew what she was now, and how important she was. He knew that eventually he would be touched and grateful that she had given him so *much* of her time today, but right now, there was room for nothing but grief.

"You have to go," he told her. "I—I understand. I'll manage."

She searched his eyes for a moment. "You do understand, don't you?" she asked, wonder coloring her voice. "Thank you for that, Karal. If you can't bear it, send for me."

He nodded, and she walked off quickly, but with a slight limp. He watched her go, then turned his thoughts inward.

He prayed, even though he wasn't quite certain what to pray for. It would be no kindness to Ulrich to force him to live, if living meant he was trapped in a helpless body that held nothing but pain. Those blades were long—long enough to have pierced through the chest and damaged the spine. Perhaps that was why Ulrich had not awakened. . . .

He tried to remember what Ulrich had taught him—that Vkandis was neither some cosmic accountant, who weighed and measured a man before deciding if he lived or died, nor was He a grand torturer, inflicting punishment after punishment upon the living to find their breaking points. *We have free will, all of us, and Vkandis interferes very little in our life in this world,* Ulrich had said. *He does not play with us as a child plays with toy soldiers or dolls, nor does He test us to see what we are made of. He allows us to live our lives and make our own choices, and only after we cross to join Him does He judge us on the basis of what we have and have not done with the life and free will we were granted at birth—and how well we have kept our word in promises made to Him. What we choose to do intersects with what everyone else in our lives chooses to do; sometimes those choices mean joy, sometimes sorrow, often a little of both. That may be why good things sometimes happen to evil people. Most assuredly, with no cause by the Sunlord's hand, bad things sometimes do happen to good people.*

So it was by free will that *whoever* it was had laid those deadly traps, and Ulrich and he had been the ones to encounter them. It was by sheer circumstance that there had been four of the things, one too many for Altra to deal with. In fact, had Altra not *been* there—by the Sunlord's own will—*he* would be dead right now.

But I wish it had been me and not him! he cried to Vkandis. *Oh, Sunlord, I wish it had been me!*

The marks crawled by, tedious and slow as an ancient tortoise, plodding painfully toward midnight, and then toward dawn. People came by at intervals, presumably to see if he was all right, but they did not disturb him, and he did not speak to them.

Finally, though, someone *did* stop, and touch his shoulder.

He looked up, and the sympathy in the Healer's face told him everything he needed to know.

He could not show his sorrow before all the strange faces, sympathetic though they might be, and he could not burden Talia further by asking someone to disturb her rest and bring her to him. Instead, he refused all offers of consolation and stumbled blindly away from the building, shaking with sobs he could not give voice to, throat so choked with grief he could not even swallow.

It was not yet dawn; frost-covered grass crunched underfoot as he wandered out into the waning hours of the night. He had to go somewhere . . . life *would* go on, and now he was the sole representative of Karse here. Where had Kerowyn said she was moving his things?

The ekele. An'desha and Firesong—

That was bearable. Better them, than to try to make a place among strangers, Heralds whose names he didn't even know.

Now that he had a destination, he set off through the darkness. Once he was out of sight of the Healers and their unwanted, professional sympathy, he allowed the tears to come again. Blinded as much by his weeping as by the dark, he felt his way along the path to the gate in Companion's Field; got it open, and slipped inside—

And there he stopped; or rather, collapsed against the gate post, shuddering with great, racking sobs that did absolutely nothing to ease the agony of his loss.

:Karal—: the voice in his mind was hesitant, but the sympathy was real. *:Karal, I am not Talia, but I am here for you.:*

Blindly, he turned and buried his face in the white shoulder that lowered to meet his trembling body as the Companion lay down. His tears trickled through the silky white mane that presented itself to him. He clung to Florian's neck and wept and wept until his throat was sore, his eyes were nothing more than slits, and his nose was so swollen and stopped up that he *had* to stop sobbing because he couldn't breathe.

The breathing of the Companion at his side was steady and soothing, and after what could have been a candlemark, the pace of his own breathing matched Florian's.

:Karal, I am with you. This might not be the best time, but there is someone who sorrows as much as you do,: Florian said hesitantly. *:He needs you very badly, and right now he has no one to comfort him.:*

Unlike me . . . The unspoken implication had not escaped Karal. "Wh–who?" Karal asked dully, wiping his nose.

:Listen,: was Florian's only answer.

Obediently, Karal stifled his sniffling for a moment. As he strained his ears to listen over the sound of the river nearby, he heard what Florian was talking about—a high-pitched wail so much like a baby's cry that he was startled.

A baby? But what would a baby be doing out in the middle of the Field?

The wail came again, so full of heartbreak and pain that Karal had to respond to it; he walked in the general direction of the sound, Florian following behind. A few moments later, he knew what it was—not a baby, but a cat.

"Is that Altra?" he asked, incredulously.

:Yes,: Florian replied. *:He hasn't told you the whole truth, Karal. The Firecats are almost exactly like us—like Companions, except that they have magic to protect themselves, and they can move themselves the way someone who has the Fetching Gift can move an object. They are mortal, they eat—he's been stealing food from the kitchen—and they have no more idea about what is going to happen in the future than you or I do.:*

"That was why he didn't know that the disruption-waves were coming, he only knew *something* was going to happen." Karal replied absently, distracted for the moment from his grief by this revelation.

:Yes. And that was why he didn't know you were going to be attacked until it happened. Nor does he know who your

attacker was. He blames himself.: Florian's mental voice was saddened and subdued. :*I can understand that only too well. I had thought about urging you to take a break this morning and come out here for a ride on Trenor; you haven't seen him for days. I keep wondering what would have happened if I had done that instead of just thinking about it.:*

"What's the point in rasping away at yourself with might-have-beens?" Karal retorted. "All you do is make yourself hurt more—"

:*I know that. You know that. It is Altra who needs to hear that.:* They were practically on top of the wailing now, and Karal made out a white form curled into a ball of misery, wailing disconsolately into the night. Karal's heart and his resolve to stay controlled broke at the same time.

"Altra—" he cried, flinging himself down in the grass beside the Firecat. He took the Cat into his arms exactly as Talia had taken him into her comforting embrace, and his tears started again. "Altra, Altra, it wasn't your fault."

:*I had to choose,:* the Cat cried in his mind. :*I had to choose, and I was sent for you, so I had to choose you.:*

"And you almost saved both of us anyway," Karal told him, holding his furred body tightly, as the Firecat shivered with more than physical cold. "You aren't the Sunlord, Altra, you can't know everything or be everywhere at once. *You did your best.* I *know* that."

:*But I couldn't—save—him!:* The heartbreaking wail began again. Altra had no way to shed tears, so Karal did the crying for them both.

Florian stood vigil over them, a solid, comforting presence in the dark, until they were finally too tired to weep anymore.

In the end, Karal picked up the exhausted Firecat—who must have weighed nearly half what he himself did—and carried him to the *ekele*, with Florian walking beside them. Firesong was still awake, but he said nothing when he met them all at the entrance to his home, neither about the lateness of the hour nor Karal's odd burden. He only gestured for Karal to follow and led the way to that peculiar room draped to resemble the interior of a tent.

And this was where Karal talked to Altra until the sun rose, telling him all the things he had tried to tell himself, and in so doing, seeing the truth in those things. That was where they finally slept, spent and exhausted—but neither one alone.

When Karal awoke, he knew by the sun that it was well into the afternoon. He'd slept far later than he had thought he would, and Altra was still curled against him. The Firecat woke as soon as he moved, though, and raised his head to look at him with shadowed blue eyes.

"Altra?" he said, quietly.

:*I will be all right,*: the Firecat replied. :*The pain—it is bearable, now. We have things we must do; you especially, and he would not thank us for neglecting them.*:

Karal rubbed at his eyes; they were sore and gummy, the lashes all stuck together. His nose and cheeks were tender from scrubbing at them. Odd how such little discomforts distracted a person from grief, but not enough to be more than one more burden.

He had awakened with a heaviness of soul that cast a gray shadow over everything. He knew that he ought to be hungry, but he had no appetite whatsoever.

He scratched Altra's ears; the Firecat didn't seem to mind being caressed like an ordinary cat. All of his things were here, piled into baskets at the sides of the fabric-draped room. Was this supposed to look like the inside of a Shin'a'in tent? Probably. So this would be An'desha's room, though he doubted An'desha used it much.

Now he wondered what it was about An'desha that Talia had wanted to talk about. If she hadn't come to their suite, would things have fallen out any differently?

No matter. He should follow his own advice, and not torture himself with might-have-beens. The danger from the disruption-waves hadn't gone, just because Ulrich was—

His eyes stung.

There was still work to do. He should get changed and do it.

"Altra, you ought to stay here and rest." The fur under his hand felt harsh and brittle, and Altra looked in poor shape, as if the events of yesterday had completely depleted him. "I'll be back after I find out what everyone else is doing."

"Everyone else—the mages and the Prince, that is—is—

are?—coming here," Firesong said from the doorway. Karal's head snapped up and he started; he hadn't heard anything at all to indicate that Firesong was in the hallway. "With an unknown agent somewhere in the Palace, the others are reluctant to trust that he or she might not be somehow listening. The *ekele* is safe enough; I supervised every bit of the building myself, and before you arrived I checked for more such little gifts as were distributed yesterday."

The Hawkbrother entered the room and sank down on his haunches beside the pallet that Karal and Altra shared. He studied Karal for a very long time without saying a word; Karal didn't say anything either. He was too tired, and too grief-laden to play at verbal fencing with the Healing Adept. If Firesong wanted to know something, then he could damned well ask it.

"I think I understand, now," Firesong said, out of the blue.

"What?" Still less was Karal ready to trade non sequiturs.

"What An'desha sees in you." Firesong continued to sit on his heels, watching Karal measuringly.

Karal traded him back look for look. Firesong was baiting him, and he was not going to rise to it. Maybe the Hawkbrother meant well, trying to distract him from his sorrow, but he'd chosen a bad tactic to use.

"Talia wanted to talk with you and—" Firesong hesitated, then went gamely on. "She had already spoken with me. An'desha is in the midst of a crisis, she thinks; he is afraid of setting his feelings free, and he is afraid of losing control of himself if he keeps examining those 'Ma'ar' memories. Evidently they are the most powerful and the most seductive of all. Falconsbane was mad, purely and simply, but Ma'ar was as close to sane as anyone of his ilk is ever likely to be. He had reasons and rationalizations for everything he did, and I suppose that is what makes his memories so seductive." Firesong shrugged. "An'desha is afraid of much, and I have lost patience with his timidity. Frankly, I do not think he is going to be of much use to us unless he can face what he has inside him without being afraid of it, and I know he will not be of much use—ah—to us, if he keeps shutting off how he feels."

"That's what you told Talia?" Karal asked.

"And now you," Firesong confirmed. "Now, more than ever, we cannot afford to have anyone handicapped, and at the moment An'desha is like a hooded falcon."

"Or a racehorse with hobbles and blinders." Karal nodded. "Let me think about this."

"Fair enough." Firesong stood; today he had chosen to dress all in white, as if to represent the winter that drew nearer with every passing day. "I—I am not always this insensitive. If I had a choice, I would not have mentioned it until you were feeling better. It is a burden you could do without."

"But we don't have the time for sensitivity," Karal acknowledged. "I understand."

"You can bathe in the pools below," the mercurial mage said then, changing the subject completely. "There is food in the kitchen. The others will be here shortly."

And with that, he turned in a swirl of long sleeves and crystal-bead fringe, vanishing as silently as he had arrived.

Food. No, he still didn't want to even think about food. Nor about all the times that Ulrich had teased him about how much he ate—

No, wait. This is all wrong. I should think about things like that. He should remember as much as he could; there was good advice buried in nearly everything that Ulrich had told him, and now he was going to have to glean as much of it out of his memories as he could.

:*He used to offer me cat-mint, you know, as a kind of joke, as if it would affect me as it does a real cat.*:

Altra looked up at him from the pallet.

"And what did you do?" Karal asked obediently.

:*Asked him to make it into tea, and serve it in a civilized fashion.*: Altra sighed. :*It was funny at the time.*:

"It will be funny again," Karal promised warmly. "I'll bring you something to eat, if you like."

:*So Florian spilled my secret, did he!*: Altra actually snorted, and looked annoyed for a heartbeat. :*Ah, well, I couldn't stay mystical and inscrutable forever, I suppose. Please bring me something that isn't breadish or vegetablish.*:

"I'll be glad to, as soon as I have a quick bath." At least Altra still had an appetite. That was something, anyway, a sign that the Firecat was on the way to recovering.

He found that he felt better after a bath and a change of clothing. It did help that there was nothing at all here to remind him of Ulrich. He didn't think he would be able to maintain his own fragile stability if there had been.

He still had no appetite, though; rummaging around in the larder didn't do anything to remove the lump of cold grief from his stomach. He confined himself to taking care of Altra; he found some fish that was so fresh it must have been caught that very morning, and decided that someone in the two-person household had seen Altra for what he really was. And while the Firecat didn't precisely fall on the offering as if he was half-starved, he certainly polished every scrap off during the time it took Karal to change into clean clothing.

I'm the only Karsite representative, now, he thought, as he examined his clothing. *Until Solaris sends someone else—it's me or no one. I'd better look the part.*

He chose one of his formal robes, and carefully arranged his sun-disk pendant over the front placket. He wished there was a mirror.

:You look very impressive,: Altra observed from the bed. *:You've grown since you came here. You're a bit young for an envoy, but as old as some ruling nobles I've seen, even as old as some reigning monarchs. I've even heard of Sons of the Sun no older than you:*

Karal tugged his tunic straight. "I'll have to do," he replied. "There isn't anyone else for the moment."

"You'll do very well." Once again, Firesong had appeared out of nowhere. He eyed Karal carefully and nodded with satisfaction. "No longer the retiring little secretary. Very good. Let's go down, the others are waiting."

:You'll be fine,: Altra murmured.

Well, he would, if appearance was all that counted. He only hoped he could be so confident of his abilities.

The subject, inevitably, was the attempt to uncover a presumed agent of the Empire.

"I've checked and rechecked the servants under Truth Spell," Elspeth told them all as Firesong and Karal took their places in the circle. Beside her, Darkwind nursed a bandaged shoulder, and the male gryphon had a stitched-up cut in his right wing. "They're all exactly what they seem to be, so it can't be one of the regular servants."

"It could be one of us, you know," Karal put in reluctantly.

Prince Daren grimaced. "That had not escaped me. It could also be any of the other ambassadors and envoys, including those of long standing. Whoever this agent is, it is likeliest that he has been among us for a very long time, and he could be one of a number of foreigners we trust. It is a bit difficult to persuade *them* to be examined under Truth Spell."

"Difficult?" Firesong put on his best sardonic look. "Only if you are not willing to risk an incident."

"Selenay is not," Daren replied flatly. "We have enough of an incident on our hands already, although mage-messages have come from Solaris this morning saying that she is aware of what happened and that it changes nothing."

Only that Ulrich is gone . . . and I promised to take care of him. Karal tucked his head down so that his grief would not show until he got his face back under control again. *Altra must have gone to her with the news, before he fell apart. No wonder he looked so depleted.*

"That leaves—what? Something like a hundred possible suspects?" Kerowyn hazarded. "And a good chance that whoever this is will do something again."

Karal frowned. Perhaps associating with the engineers had put an edge on his reasoning ability, but he was certain he could narrow the field down more than that. "Wait a moment. It can't be that many. It has to be someone who is *high* enough in rank that no one would question seeing him anywhere in the Palace, but low enough in rank—or *apparently* ineffectual enough—that no one would ever notice him. It also has to be someone who would have a reason to be in and out of people's rooms at least once this year. If this is an agent of long standing, then surely the Empire is using him to gather information—so it has to be someone who has a reason to receive and send packages at intervals of more than once a year. He *couldn't* have sent his information by magic-messengers before this year, remember? You had a guard against magic until then." Once again, his own intellect had seduced him into concentrating on something besides grief. "That virtually eliminates all of the Palace servants."

Kerowyn gnawed on her lower lip. "That does eliminate most of my suspects," she admitted. "It could be one of the personal servants of one of our own nobles, though."

"Yes, and it could *be* one of your nobles." Darkwind was quick to point that out. "It would not be the first time that Selenay had had her own intrigue against her."

"The weapon, though—it had a residue of magic that made me think it was targeted to a specific individual," An'desha said shyly. "That would imply that your agent is a mage himself, or more likely, found a way to gain access to something personal from each of his targets to imprint the weapons with their intended victims."

"Then planted them into the walls." Kerowyn looked baffled. "Now you open it up to everyone in the Palace *except* the servants."

Karal pondered his next words long and hard before speaking them. *How expendable am I? Realistically, very. And I have Altra, who will try to protect me. I think that I must do this.*

"I can offer a possible trap," he said carefully. "With myself as the bait. Two of those weapons were meant to eliminate me; let me place myself where our agent can come at me. I honestly do not believe he will try to take me again, so soon. I think that he will try to ascertain what Solaris' position is, and whether or not the Alliance is in jeopardy, due—"

He couldn't say it; he choked up. The others gave him time to recover.

After a struggle, he got control of his voice again. "If disrupting the Alliance was this agent's primary goal, he will want to talk to me almost as soon as I appear in the halls of the Palace. Let me go walk there, and see who comes to offer condolences and fish for information."

"And what if this agent decides to ensure the Karsite defection by eliminating you?" Kerowyn asked quietly.

He twitched his mouth in what was supposed to be a smile. "Have you not been training me in enough self-defense to keep myself alive until help can come? Magicked weaponry is difficult to come by; if this person wishes to strike again so soon, I think he will have to do so through conventional means. That requires skill, opportunity, and time. I will assume he has the first, I will give him the second, and I will deny him the third." There. Hopefully, he sounded like the self-confident Karsite envoy. He certainly didn't *feel* like the self-confident Karsite envoy.

Kerowyn continued to gnaw her lower lip. "I like it, and I don't like it at all," she said finally. "I don't like it, because it puts you in so much danger, Karal. I like it, because it has a good chance of winkling out our agent. I wouldn't ask it of you, but if you are volunteering—"

:As am I,: Altra said, for Karal's benefit alone. :You were right in thinking that I can roam the corridors with you and protect you. I shall do better this time.:

"I am," Karal said firmly. "What is more, I am ready now."

"Well I'm not—or rather, my men aren't." Kerowyn reached over and patted his knee. "Give *me* a chance to get set up, say, after dinner. Don't come to formal dinner; that will make it look as if there might be trouble with the Alliance. Then come on over and roam to your heart's content. Among other things, you can reassure some of our own people that things haven't deteriorated to the point of war quite yet."

Karal sat back and let them discuss the weapon itself; they were mages, he was not, and what they had found did not mean a great deal to him. At least he could *do* something now, though. That helped, a little.

Only a little, but it was a beginning.

In the evenings, after formal dinner, Ulrich had often strolled in the gardens with the rest of the courtiers. During inclement weather, the same leisurely strolls took place in the hallways and the small informal audience chambers. The weather was barely warm enough for both to be in use, so Karal resigned himself to a long evening with a great deal of walking.

Most of the Valdemarans did not seem to know quite how to treat him; he *had* been the insignificant secretary, and now he was the only Karsite representative at Court, and he had dressed to reflect that rise in position, though the velvets were too warm for the indoor venue and not warm enough for the gardens. Most of the courtiers eventually opted for brief and uncomfortable expressions of regret and condolence, approaching him, making graceful but painful short speeches, and scuttling away again.

For the first few marks, no one even mentioned the fate of the Alliance, and as Karal alternately sweated and shivered, he began to wonder if this had been a fool's errand.

The first person who did was the Seneschal, a situation so absurd that Karal almost burst into hysterical laughter. The only ones that were privy to Karal's little ruse were the mages; Prince Daren had decided that it would be better not to let any of the Councillors in on the subterfuge, on the grounds that they were very bad actors, and would probably give the whole thing away. The Seneschal was pathetically transparent in his attempts to divine Solaris' position from Karal's attitude, and to keep up the illusion that Solaris was still undecided, Karal was forced to be distinctly cool to the poor man. It took all of Karal's ability to keep from revealing the whole trick with his reaction to the poor fellow's disappointment in learning nothing.

He eliminated the next few "fishers" on grounds that they were not likely to have a pretext that would let them move in and out of private rooms at will. Then came another long, dry spell; his sober face and black robes seemed to put people off, making their expressions of sympathy hurried and nervous.

He resigned himself to a fruitless, boring evening.

Ah, well, at least I tried—

"Master Secretary?" said a squeaky voice at his elbow.

He turned, and had to think long and hard before he could identify the fellow who had greeted him. He was utterly nondescript to begin with, and had the demeanor and apparently the personality of a mole—

"—ah, my condolences, Master Secretary," the mole said, squinting at him and twisting his hands nervously together. "You probably wouldn't recall me, I suppose, I'm not important or wealthy or—"

The spot of green paint caught in the cuticle of one finger gave him away.

"Of course I recall you, sir," Karal replied, in a properly subdued manner. "Master Celandine, is it not? The painter?"

"The artist, yes, and I was *terribly* grieved to hear about Master Ulrich, *terribly*," the mole replied, his fingers knotting together until his hands resembled a nest of worms. "I hope—I pray—that your gracious mistress will not take this incident badly—oh, dear, no—that would be dreadful, dreadful—"

"I suppose from the Valdemaran point of view it would," Karal replied, with careful neutrality. There was something about this man ... something nagging at the back of his mind.

"Oh, I'm not from Valdemar, but it would be *personally* dreadful for me all the same," Celandine replied. "My pigments—so difficult to obtain, you understand, and before the Alliance so terribly expensive—"

A tiny thread of warning slipped down Karal's back, and his hands went cold. *He's always sending people off after pigments and colors, I remember him saying that when Ulrich sat for a portrait. He must have at least one package coming in every fortnight or so! Could it be? Oh, surely not! This fellow was so ineffectual he couldn't possibly be their quarry! Everyone at court made fun of him and his pretensions of genius!*

Then again, came the nagging response, *wouldn't that make him ideal for the part? How better to observe people than when they think you're insignificant?*

"—I wondered if your mistress would still be interested in that official portrait, or if she would prefer to wait until the next envoy was assigned or even have *your* little sketch turned into a portrait instead?"

Bright Sunlord! Didn't An'desha say the mage must have had something personal in order to set the weapons, or some kind of image? This man paints portraits, he sketches people in Court circles all day long and no one ever thinks anything about it!

:*Karal,*: said Altra carefully, :*I think you may have something in this one. Can you get him to take you to his studio? I may be able to find real evidence, rooting around like a cat.*:

"Perhaps," he said, assuming more dignity. "I have been given to understand that if the Alliance continues, the latter would be the most likely option."

The mole's tiny black eyes lit up, but before he could say anything else, Karal continued.

"That portrait of my—my Master, though, the one you mentioned," he continued, and it did not take any acting at all for his eyes to mist over. "I would like to have it for myself. Is it anywhere near completed?"

"Oh, yes! Yes, it is!" The mole was positively babbling. "Would you care to come to my studio to view it?"

:Excellent,: Altra applauded. :I'll warn Florian and he can warn Kerowyn through Sayvil. Go with him now, before he changes his mind!:

"I would very much like to see it," Karal said in complete and sincere honesty as he wiped his eyes. "Please."

The mole eagerly led the way down the hall toward the quarters of those who were not *quite* highborn, but were not servants, either. Altra padded along behind, tail in the air, pretending to be a housecat. The mole either didn't notice him or didn't care.

The mole's studio lay at the farthest end of the corridor, and Karal had a moment of trepidation when he realized that there was no way that Kerowyn could have them followed down here without it being painfully obvious. And if the mole left the studio door open, he would see if Kerowyn sent anyone down after them. Celandine might look like he was short-sighted, but as Karal already knew, there was nothing wrong with his eyes.

:I'll shut the door behind me,: Altra told him. :Just enough that he won't be able to see down the corridor. With luck, he'll be so excited that he won't notice.:

That was exactly how the next few moments played out; Celandine ushered Karal into the cluttered, crowded studio with much bowing and scraping, and Altra slipped in behind them, nudging the door closed without Celandine noticing. The place was a mess, with easels and half-finished sculptures on pedestals everywhere, supplies piled on top of furniture and spilling down onto the floor, blank canvases stretched onto frames and leaning against the walls, and dust all over everything. Karal doubted that the servants ever even tried to clean in here.

In fact, the mole was only interested in getting Karal to the area where several canvases stood on easels, covered with drop cloths. He positioned Karal in front of one of them, and made a great deal of fuss about getting the lighting absolutely right, before whisking off the cloth.

Karal did not have to simulate his reaction. Whatever else the mole was, he was also a genuine and superb artist. He had captured Ulrich in one of his rare moments of relaxation; good will and humor glowed in his face, and a half-smile played on his lips.

Karal's eyes filled, and two tears ran down his cheeks unheeded. He took an involuntary step forward; the painting only improved on closer inspection.

Celandine smiled, baring tiny teeth in an expression of greed and satisfaction at Karal's reaction.

"My—good Master Celandine, you are—" Another tear escaped down Karal's cheek, and he shook his head as he wiped it away. "There are no words. There are just no words. I *must* have this painting."

Celandine fussed over the canvas, preening, as he dusted the easel unnecessarily. "Well, I must admit, I was rather pleased with the way the robes came out. You folk who affect black—oh, forgive me, but it is *so* difficult for an artist to render properly! This particular shade of *sebeline* along the crease for instance, that is my own little secret for simulating the sheen of good black velvet—"

He nattered on, but Karal had frozen in place at the foreign-sounding word for the streak of blue-white pigment that ran along the top of one of the sleeves in the portrait. That was *not* a Valdemaran term!

:No. It's not.: The murmur of quiet noise in the background ceased, as Altra froze as well. :Stall him, Karal! I need time to have Mindspeech with an expert!:

"How did you make the eyes look so—so—" Karal choked out.

That was enough to set Celandine off again, this time on a much longer dissertation, about reflection and transparent colors and glazes. Meanwhile, Karal waited, the back of his neck prickling, as he tried to recall if Celandine had ever been in their quarters.

Then, as Karal leaned forward to look at the painting more closely, and noted the distinctive whorls of the background, he remembered. *He was. Not only to make the preliminary sketches, either! I found him there poking at those decorations one afternoon, complaining that every time some plaster decoration cracked, the Seneschal ordered him to repair it on the grounds that he was an artist!*

Celandine was a sculptor, who could probably reproduce anything he chose at will. He had access to plaster. He had put himself in a position to plant whatever he cared to by allowing the Seneschal to order him to fix broken decorations!

And all he had to do to be called into a particular room was to crack the original himself—before, during, or after the portrait-sitting.

:Karal!: Altra called, panic in his mind-voice for the first time since Karal had met him. *:That word, it's Imperial tongue—what's more, the pigment is only mined somewhere east of Hardorn!:*

Celandine had worked his way in behind Karal as he spoke of colors and pointed this or that effect out. The prickling on the back of Karal's neck had become an agony. He tried to watch the mole out of the corner of his eye without being obtrusive.

:KARAL!:

Karal did not need Altra's mental scream to warn him; he had sensed Celandine's sudden movement half a breath before. Karal ducked under the blow and whirled at the same time, then dodged past the easel and the painting it held, winding up facing the artist.

No—the *agent.*

The artist was gone; in his place was someone far more dangerous, and nothing at all like a mole, more like a cornered rat. Celandine's beady black eyes glittered dangerously; he had a mallet in one hand, and a sharp palette knife in the other. The edge of the knife had a nasty, sickly green tinge, and Karal had the sinking feeling that it wasn't paint. "He'll kill me, you know," the artist said, his voice deceptively calm.

"Who?" Karal asked urgently. "What's wrong? Why would anyone kill you?" *Stall for more time. Help has to be on the way.*

"The Grand Duke. Tremane. I'm not *his* man. I'm expendable. I didn't finish the job. The little birds flew, and only pecked out the heart of one of the targets." The glitter in Celandine's eyes wasn't danger, it was madness. He feinted with the knife, and Karal winced backward. "He'll kill me; he has my likeness and my hair, he can do it. Unless I finish the job, right now."

He feinted again, and Karal flinched. He obviously knew what he was doing; he had all the moves of an experienced knife fighter. Karal's best bet was to keep him talking.

But Celandine rushed him; he ducked and sidestepped and barely managed to avoid the knife *and* the mallet blow aimed at his head.

"If I get you, I can leave you in the garden with one of Elspeth's knives in your heart," he continued. "We made copies, you know, just in case. You know the one I'm talking about."

"Actually, no I don't—"

Altra's mind-voice was frantic. *:Karal! I can't get him! You're in my line of attack!:*

Karal stepped to the side at once, but Celandine lashed out viciously with the mallet, and he stepped back again hastily.

"The one Elspeth left in the heart of *our* ambassador, of course!" Celandine said, as if he was some kind of dolt. Then he blinked. "You're playing for time!" he accused, and slashed at Karal with the knife.

:Karal! There's poison on that knife! Stay out of reach—use something as a shield.:

A shield—something Celandine wouldn't want damaged!

He grabbed one of the canvases at random as Celandine drove him back, and held it in front of him as he backed toward the windows. Celandine's mouth twisted in a snarl.

"Put that thing down, you idiot!" he screamed. "How *dare* you put your hands on—"

He never finished the sentence.

There was a crash of glass as all the windows shattered at once. Karal ducked instinctively, crouching and making himself as small a target as possible as shards of razored glass went everywhere. Celandine came up out of his fighting crouch in shock and glanced around wildly—

Then a dozen crossbow bolts hit him at once from the di-

rection of every window; his body jerked wildly in a gro-
tesque parody of a dance—

—then he dropped to the floor, eyes already glazing in
death.

Karal dropped to the floor as well, as his knees gave out.

"Karal!" Kerowyn leapt through one of the broken windows and crashed through the easels to get to him, knocking
paintings in all directions. "Karal, are you all right? Did he
scratch you? Sayvil said there was poison on his blade. Are
you—"

"I'm all right, I'm fine," he replied weakly. "Oh, dear Sunlord, I have *never* been as grateful for any lessons in my life as
I am for yours." He hugged the painting to his chest, and took
deep, steadying breaths. "He was going to kill me and leave
me with a copy of one of Elspeth's knives in me. He said they
got it when she left one in *their* ambassador."

He was babbling and he knew it, but he couldn't stop himself. Altra finally wormed his way through the tangle of art
supplies and tumbled easels, and began winding around and
around him frantically, purring loud enough to make both of
them vibrate.

"Elspeth's knife?" A large man climbed over the windowsill with a crossbow in each hand; after a moment, Karal's mind put a name to him. *Skif.* He wasn't a mage, but he
often sat on the Council with Kerowyn.

"Elspeth's knife?" the man repeated, scowling ferociously.
"Demons take it, I *knew* that thing was going to come back
to haunt us!"

Karal started to shiver, when he happened to look down to
see just what painting he had snatched up as an impromptu
shield.

Ulrich's warm, amused eyes gazed up at him; he froze for a
moment, then burst into tears.

Karal at the Iftel Border

16

:*Are you sure that you're ready for this?*: Altra asked anxiously. :*This is going to be very dangerous for you.*:

Karal shrugged, and shook his head.

"Actually, I'm quite sure that I'm not at all ready for a confrontation like this," he admitted to the Firecat. "But we just don't have a choice. An'desha needs help; besides being afraid of allowing his emotions free play, he's locking down his anger because he is certain that if he lets it go, he'll *use* his powers to hurt whoever he's angry at. The problem with doing that is that it just makes things harder for him the next time he's angry." Karal rubbed the side of his nose thoughtfully. "He has to discover that 'control' doesn't always mean 'containment.' He's got to see that the simplest solution isn't always the right one."

The Firecat washed a paw thoughtfully. :*I saw how he was when they told him how near you'd come to being killed—both times,*: he said. :*Terrible anger—then nothing. He just turned it all inside himself.*:

"Terrible anger is dangerous when you are—or were—an Adept who specialized in destruction," Karal said grimly. "Someone has to prove to him that he can lose his temper and his self-control, vent his emotions, and not hurt anyone in the process. *Then* he'll feel safe enough to go after those very emotional memories of Adept Ma'ar and learn all the destructive magic that Ma'ar knew. Firesong thinks the Ma'ar memories are important; I *know* that they have to be the key to this situation. I can't tell you why I'm so certain, I only know that I am."

Hurry, hurry, hurry. That sense of terrible urgency made *him* as tight as a strung crossbow. The sense that time was running out on them was stronger than ever.

:*But are you the best person to do that?*: Altra asked, with complete logic. :*Shouldn't it be someone who's also a mage, who can defend against his attack if he should lash out? He* can turn you into a cinder, and you haven't got any kind of protection.: The Firecat looked up at him with large, bottomless blue eyes, full of candor and concern. :*I'm not completely certain even I could protect you against his full power, in a killing rage.*:

Karal sighed. "That's why it has to be me. It has to be someone so completely vulnerable that An'desha *knows* that person is defenseless. It has to be someone who knows An'desha well enough to make him rage with anger in a very short time. Firesong won't do; Firesong could hold his own against any attack An'desha could launch, and what would that prove? And it has to be done, because if it isn't, I think he'll be incinerated. Talia and Firesong both agree with me. If he keeps turning his anger inward, one day his power will turn inward as well, and it will consume him."

:*And besides,*: Altra added, :*he's your friend.*:

"That's right," Karal agreed. "He's my friend. Friends help friends. We're both strangers in this Valdemar place. Sometimes friends are all we have."

He didn't have to mention all the nights this past week that An'desha had held him while he wept out his grief for Ulrich; Altra knew all about that, since he'd been there. He didn't say a word about the thousand little kindnesses that An'desha had shown him since—and the way he had gently deflected Firesong's resulting jealousy. None of that really mattered anyway. What did matter was that An'desha needed help, and it was help that Karal could give him.

In the larger picture, if he *didn't* help An'desha, they might never have their "breakwaters" to use against the disruption-waves. The latest one had caught at least one large animal that Karal knew of, turning it into a monstrous killer that had savaged an entire herd of cattle before twenty men shot it full of arrows. Word had trickled back that the Tayledras Vales were suffering damage to their special shielding. According to

Master Levy, the engineers and mathematicians had constructed a pattern of increasing power to these waves. Natoli had explained it to him, and he had felt the jaws of time closing on them. *Something* had to be done, and done quickly.

It had taken Karal the better part of the afternoon to work up the courage to face this particular trial. It had been relatively easy to steel his nerve to face a possible enemy, but to have to face a friend who just might kill him—that took a different kind of courage altogether.

Now, though, he was as prepared as he was ever likely to be. An'desha was hiding down in the tent in the garden, already shaken by a preparatory confrontation with Firesong, carefully planned and choreographed by Karal and the Healing Adept beforehand. The effects of the last disruption-wave were over, which meant there would be no interference from that quarter. Now, if ever, was the perfect moment.

As always, his eyes met the painted eyes of Ulrich in the portrait he'd hung on his wall. *I hope I'm doing the right thing, Master,* he told the painting silently. *I'm not as sure of this as Altra and Firesong think I am.*

He really didn't expect an answer from the portrait, and he wasn't surprised when he didn't get one. He tugged his tunic into place, and headed down the stairs into the garden.

An'desha had been getting alarmingly predictable in his reactions to emotional confrontation; now that Karal had the fabric-draped room—for Kerowyn did not want to risk another assassination attempt and ordered him to stay in the *ekele* for the duration, or at least until Solaris sent official word of what she intended to do—An'desha had no other refuge than the small tent in the garden. Whenever he was upset or had an argument with anyone, that was where he went.

He had been spending a lot of time in that tent, and the number of times in a given day he was retreating to it was increasing.

Karal nodded to Firesong, who was lurking just out of An'desha's hearing. Firesong's jaw tightened, and he nodded curtly back. Firesong didn't like this any better than Altra did; he liked *his* part in it even less. *He* was going to have to create a very tough mirror-shield around that tent to hold in whatever An'desha let loose.

If there're going to be any victims here, let's keep it to one. The expendable one. I am expendable. I am stupid. Here I go.

He pulled the tent flap aside and dropped down on his heels next to An'desha, who was sprawled on his back with his arm over his face, cushioned by a pallet identical to the one that Karal now used for a bed upstairs.

"Down here again?" Karal said incredulously. "What's wrong this time?"

An'desha didn't even remove his arm. "Firesong. He does *not* understand. He wishes me to sift through the memory fragments of Ma'ar again." An'desha's hands clenched into fists, and his mouth tightened, sulkily. "He will not understand. Those memories are very old, and to read them I must grow *very* close to them."

"So?" Karal let scorn creep into his voice. "I think that Firesong is right, An'desha. You aren't thinking of anyone or anything but your own self. You are, quite frankly, becoming a spoiled brat. We have been coddling you, making allowances for you, and now you have no more spine than a mushroom!"

An'desha sat up, suddenly, his mouth agape with shock, staring at Karal with a dumbfounded expression. "Wh–what?" he stammered.

"You are *spineless*, An'desha!" Karal accused. "You know yourself that what we need lies in *your* mind, and you are too frightened to even *try* to look for it!" He let his own expression grow pitiful and petulant, and pitched his voice into a whine. " '*Those memories are dangerous, they might hurt me, I am afraid of them—*' as if we all aren't afraid of much worse than a few paltry *memories!*"

"But I—" An'desha began, his eyes glazed with shock at the way Karal had abruptly turned on him.

"But *you*. Always *you*. What about the rest of us?" Karal asked. "What about all that we have been doing? What about the *losses*, the harm that we have suffered, while you have been curled here in your little cocoon of self-pity, feeling, oh, so put-upon? What about the Tayledras, who are trying to piece their Vales together again, the Shin'a'in who fear their

herds of precious horses will turn into herds of monsters—
what about the Shin'a'in ambassador who *died* a few days
ago? What about them? What about Karse? And Rethwellan?"

An'desha was on his feet now as he tried to push past Karal.
Karal shoved him back rudely, not letting him leave the tent,
and evidently it never occurred to him that he could just turn
and slash his way through the walls to get away. An'desha
backed up a pace, and Karal shoved him again, getting right
up close and shouting into his face.

"You are a spineless, lazy, selfish *coward*, An'desha," he
spat. "You've been playing the poor little wounded bird for
too long! I have had quite enough of this, and so has everyone
else! It is about time *you* started doing something to help, instead of whining about how *afraid* you are! We're *all* afraid,
or hadn't you noticed? *I* was afraid, when Celandine nearly
killed me, but you didn't see *me* whining about it, did you?
You don't hear Firesong whining about how exhausted he is,
even though he is working on shields until he is gray in the
face!"

An'desha's face had flushed to a full, rich crimson.

But he wasn't angry enough yet, and Karal kept right at him.

"You don't hear Darkwind whining about how put-upon he
is, even though his shoulder still isn't healed and he is working night and day with the other mages! It's time to stop
whining and start doing something, An'desha—or go find
someone else to whine at, because *we* are all tired of *you!*"

An'desha's face was contorted out of all recognition, but
Karal continued the verbal abuse, continuing to attack him
for being cowardly, selfish, and spoiled.

An'desha's hands were clenched at his sides, and he stood
as rigidly as a tent pole—

—and there were colors swirling around those clenched
fists; brilliant scarlets and explosive yellows, mage energies
that, if they were visible to *him*, were probably quite potent
enough to flatten an entire building.

He'd seen Ulrich strike down something by magic once,
and the powers gathering around An'desha's hands right now
were twice, perhaps three times as bright.

He wanted to run. Every nerve in his body screamed at him

to turn and flee. Every hair on his head felt as if it was standing straight on end from the power in this little space.

But instead of fleeing, he did the hardest thing he'd ever done in his life; harder than facing Celandine, harder than coming to this strange land in the first place.

He stepped back a pace, spread his hands, and *sneered*.

"Well?" he taunted. "I'm right, aren't I? I'm right, and you're too spineless even to admit it!"

And he waited for An'desha to strike, still holding that merciless sneer on his face.

The air *hummed* with power; he'd read of such things, but he'd never experienced it. Now every hair on his head *did* stand straight on end—

And An'desha's control finally exploded.

"Damn you!" An'desha screamed. *"Damn you!"*

There was a flash of orange and white, and the energy dissipated, draining away into the ground so quickly that in one breath it was completely gone.

An'desha collapsed down onto his pallet, folding up as if he was completely exhausted, his face pale and pained. "Damn you," he repeated dully, as Karal dropped down to his side in concern and a fear that he'd managed somehow to make An'desha burn himself out. "Damn you, Priest, you're right."

He looked up, as Karal tentatively touched his shoulder, eyes bleak. "You've been coddling me, and I've been unforgivably selfish."

Karal grinned, which obviously astonished him, for An'desha gaped at him. "I'm right twice," he pointed out. "I *told* you that you were underestimating yourself, believing that because you have the memories of a Falconsbane or a Ma'ar, you also have their ways. You thought that if you 'lost control' of an emotion, you'd lose control of everything. Well. You lost control of your temper, didn't you? You were afraid to learn everything that lay in your old memories, because you were afraid that if you got too angry with someone, you'd use it. You just *got* angry, and there you are, after doing nothing more than curse me—and here *I* am, unsinged, unflattened. Falconsbane would have sent me through a wall, or incinerated me. *You* are sitting there, back in control again, and your own man. Right?"

An'desha stared at him. "You mean—all that was just to prove to me that—" He reddened again. "Why, I should—I—"

Karal raised an eyebrow at him. "And?" he said impudently. "Why don't you, *Adept?*"

"Because *you* aren't worth the effort it would take to blow you through the wall, *Priest*," An'desha retorted, a ghost of a smile lurking around his eyes. "And because it's not worth taking on your vengeful god as an enemy just so I can get some satisfaction! Damn you! Why do you have to be so *right?*"

"It's not my fault!" Karal protested. "I can't help it!"

"Pah!" The young mage mock-hit his shoulder. "You revel in it, and you damn well know you do! One of these days you'll be wrong, and I'll be there to gloat!" The ghost of a smile had become a grin. "Just wait and see!"

"I'll be looking forward to it," Karal replied, and he meant every word. A moment later, Firesong looked in on them both, with a small but loving smile on his handsome face.

After all that, though, he felt an obligation to be there along with Firesong when An'desha worked up his own courage and took the plunge into those old, dangerous memories. It became something of a vigil for the two of them; An'desha lay in a self-imposed trance, looking much like a figure on a tomb, while the two of them watched, waited, and wondered if they *might* have been wrong in urging him to this. Firesong hadn't expected it to take more than a mark or two, but the afternoon crawled by, then most of the evening, and still the trance showed no signs of ending.

"Is this getting dangerous?" Karal asked in a whisper, as Firesong soberly lit mage-lights and returned to his seat beside An'desha's pallet.

"No—or not yet, anyway," the Adept replied, although he sounded uncertain to Karal. "I have been in trances longer; for two or three days, even."

But those were not trances in which you pursued the memories of power-hungry sadists, Karal added, but only to himself. Still, nothing had gone overtly wrong yet. There was no point in conjuring trouble.

He wished that Altra was here, though. The Firecat had

waited just long enough to be sure that he had survived An'desha's anger, then had vanished without an explanation. He could have used Altra's view on this; if Solaris' behavior was anything to go by, a former Son of the Sun should be much more familiar with trances and their effects than he was.

A hint of movement riveted his attention back on An'desha. Had his eyelids moved? If the lights had been candles, he would have put it down to the flickering shadows, but mage-lights were as steady as sunlight. Yes! There it was again, the barest flutter of eyelids as the sleeper slowly, gently awakened.

A moment later, and An'desha opened his eyes and blinked in temporary confusion; Firesong poured the tea that had been steeping all this while, and helped him to sit up, then offered him the cup. An'desha took it, his hands shaking only slightly, and drank it down in a single swallow.

"How late is it?" he asked, as he gave the cup back to Karal, who poured more tea for him.

"Evening. Not quite midnight," Firesong told him.

An'desha nodded. Karal watched him covertly, and was relieved to see nothing in his expression or manner that was not entirely in keeping with the An'desha that he knew. "I discovered that we have been laboring under a misconception," he said, finally. "Before Ma'ar died, there *was* a time when he had to deal with the kind of situation we have now, although the initial destruction was of a single Gate and the spells of the area around it, and nowhere near so cataclysmic as what came later."

Firesong nodded with excitement in his eyes, and Karal leaned forward. "So what did he do?"

An'desha sipped his tea before replying. "It isn't so much what *he* did, as what his enemy did," he said. "He wasn't concerned with the effect of the waves outside his domain, so *he* simply built the sort of shield that I *think* we've been assuming we'd need all along." An'desha shook his head. "That would be a dreadful mistake," he continued. "A shield wall alone would simply reflect the waves again, and the reflected waves have the potential for causing more harm than the original waves!"

Karal sat back for a moment, and pictured the physical model that the engineers had constructed, a large basin filled with water, the bottom covered with a contour map of Valdemar and most of the surrounding area. He thought about the experiments that Master Levy had been making, dropping large stones into the basin over "Evendim" and "Dhorisha Plains" and watching the wave-patterns, seeing how those patterns interacted.

And when the waves reached the edge of the basin, the experiment was over, because they reflected from the edge and made new and different patterns that had nothing to do with the ones he was studying.

"I see it," he replied, "but—"

"But it was what Ma'ar's enemy did that was interesting—and more importantly, appropriate," An'desha interrupted. "Instead of making a flat shieldwall he literally created a breakwater, exactly what Master Norten has been talking about; something that not only stops the waves, but absorbs their force. Ma'ar studied it and knew how to recreate it, but he considered it a waste of his time and resources." He paused. "Because *he* knew how to recreate this, so do I. What's more, I also know how to recreate his 'shieldwall.' If we combined both—we can absorb the waves coming at us, *and* we can reflect the rest back at the Empire!"

Firesong sucked in his breath, and Karal sat back on his heels.

"I don't know if we ought to do that," Karal said at last, troubled by the implications. "Does the Empire deserve that?"

Firesong shot him an incredulous look. "You say that after what they've done to you?" he exclaimed.

But Karal shook his head. "*They* didn't do anything. There are two, perhaps three people who are responsible; Celandine, who got what he deserved, this Grand Duke Tremane, whoever he is, and possibly the Emperor. *They,* the whole of the Empire, is very large, and composed mostly of people who aren't even aware of the existence of Karse." He sighed. "Firesong, don't make the mistake that we of Karse did for so long with Valdemar. Don't make the Empire into a vast conspiracy of faceless enemies who are all personally responsible for what the leaders do and do not do. There are thousands of perfectly innocent people in the Empire, who do not deserve to have their chickens turns into child-eating monsters just because a few ruthless people caused us harm."

Firesong shrugged, but Karal could tell by the troubled look in his eyes that he *had* listened to what Karal had said.

"And don't make another mistake," he continued. "Don't assume that because a leader ordered something be done, that he had any idea what the consequences were going to be. Unless you have someone like a Herald or Solaris, who has a—" he grinned wanly, for he sensed Altra padding in the door just at that moment, "—a rather insistent and altogether meddling four-legged conscience always at his side, leaders are just people, and they frequently forget to think before they act."

:Indeed,: Altra said sardonically. *:A very nice speech. Meddling, am I?:*

He only reached out and scratched Altra's ears, a caress that the Firecat "submitted to" quite readily.

"That's all very well, but we still need to do something about the next wave coming in, don't we?" An'desha replied pragmatically. "Once I can think properly again, we need to get all the mages together. I can explain this once, and get the questions over with."

"Should I bring over Master Levy and Master Norten as well?" Karal asked, assuming that it would be his task to find everyone and notify them that their presence was needed.

An'desha considered that for a moment. "I believe so," he said finally. "They can find the key points where we can place our defenses to do the most good; I think their formulas will be useful there."

Karal was struck, suddenly, by the fact that An'desha sounded different somehow; it was nothing very obvious, and he wasn't saying things that he wouldn't have said before, but it was the way he said them that had changed.

He's—by the Sunlord, he sounds older, *that's what it is! He doesn't sound like a half-child anymore! He sounds—yes, and he acts—his true age!* Karal didn't say anything, but the change delighted him; so far as he was concerned, this was *all* to the good.

:One wonders what Firesong is going to make of an independent An'desha,: Altra remarked, as if to himself. The

same thought had occurred to Karal, just as Altra made the comment.

Well, there was nothing to be done about it. Firesong was just going to have to cope. Whether the Adept liked it or not, Karal was certain that this change in An'desha was not going to be temporary. Firesong should be allowed a little time to recognize it and deal with it in private.

:Or not,: said Altra. Karal aimed a sharp thought-jab at the Firecat; once in a while it *would* be nice to have a private thought or two!

"I'll go tell the others that we'll have a meeting in the morning," he said, getting to his feet. "And I'll be back only when I find them all. Don't bother to wait for me."

He trotted off down the hall and down the stairs without giving either of them a chance to reply.

But was it his imagination, or did he actually hear An'desha say "We won't," and chuckle?

By the time the morning was half over, the Master Craftsmen had narrowed down the "necessary" key points for the new shields from several dozen to the absolute minimum. There would be three major, essential points of blockage, and several minor points. The minor points could all be handled by sets of Master Mages, and all of them were within a few days' ride of Valdemar.

"We have enough mages here, between Herald-Mages and the envoys, that we can post people to each of those minor points," Elspeth said, pursing her lips over her list of available personnel. "This shouldn't be a problem."

"But here, here, and here—" An'desha pointed on the map to the three major points—north, in the heart of the Forest of Sorrows—south, at the border of Karse—and east, at the place where the borders of Iftel, Hardorn, and Valdemar all met. "These are problems. The breakwaters are unstable in their first stage; they actually require the energy from a wave to stabilize them and make them self-supporting. You will *have* to have either two Adepts or one Adept and two Masters to create them, join them to the two others, and hold them until the wave comes." He studied the map, and put his finger on the third point. "This one will be the easiest, but the most vulnerable; it's like the keystone of an arch. It will need less power, and more craft. And the mages will *have* to be at the site in order to create the breakwater and join it into a whole."

Elspeth grimaced. "We only have four Adepts," she pointed out gently. "And we only have a few days to get them in place, before the next wave comes."

An'desha took a long, deep breath. "You have two Adepts, one Healing Adept—and me."

Firesong turned to stare at him, and it was as clear to Karal as the color of his eyes that he had *no* idea what An'desha meant.

"You have a Sorcerer-Adept," An'desha elaborated. "A creator. The kind of mage who actually *made* living beings. All of Ma'ar's knowledge is mine, now. I know how to build these breakwaters because in a sense, I've done it before. I can work with two Masters; you don't have to pair me with Firesong."

Firesong paled but said nothing.

Elspeth's mouth formed a silent "oh," but she wisely bent her head over her list. "Right, then—let's think about *how* we get the Adepts in place." She bit at the end of her quill, and looked at the map. "For obvious reasons, at least to some of you," she said, finally, "I think that Firesong and I should go north. We can Gate there—"

"We'll probably have help," Firesong muttered. Elspeth's mouth quirked, although Karal had no idea what he meant; evidently this was a private joke.

"Hydona and I arrre Masssterrrsss," Treyvan said. "Darrrk-wind can Gate parrrt of the way, then we can carrry Darrrk-wind in the basssket. We have done ssso beforrre." He cocked his head at Hydona. "Ssso, sssouth orrr eassst forrr usss?"

:You will go south.:

Everyone's head came up at the imperious mind-voice. Al-tra jumped into the center of the group, landing right on top of the location of the eastward key-point. The Firecat posed like a statue, holding a folded and sealed parchment packet in his mouth; with the exception of An'desha and Firesong, the rest of the group gasped, and Karal guessed that they were finally seeing the Firecat as he *really* was, and not in the guise of a household pet.

:You and the gryphons will go south, Darkwind,: Altra repeated. *:For reasons I am not permitted to reveal at this time, Karal and I will accompany An'desha to the east.:*

"Karal and you?" Elspeth said incredulously. "But he's not even a mage! He's not even an envoy!"

:He is an envoy now.: Altra dropped the parchment packet on the table. *:Solaris has decided. Karal will replace Ulrich. He is a full Sun-priest now, and a channel for magic as Ulrich recognized when he was a child. I am a mage. Karal, one Companion, and I will accompany An'desha.:* Altra stared her down, and she finally dropped her gaze.

"So *that's* how all those miraculous documents of Ulrich's were getting here!" Prince Daren exclaimed.

Altra favored him with a faintly approving look but said nothing.

"Wait a moment. You said one Companion," Elspeth objected. "Who is the Herald?"

:There is no Herald. Florian is unpartnered. He, too, is a mage and will use Karal as his channel as well,: Altra shot back. *:Although we may not work magic as a human can, we are mages and can support as Masters with Karal as our channel.:*

Elspeth looked back up at him, her face showing nothing but disbelief. "This is impossible!" she cried. "You're breaking all the rules!"

:And who made those rules?: he countered, just as swiftly.

Karal cleared his throat. "This is Altra," he interjected mildly. "He is what we call a Firecat; and he is—something like an Avatar. I don't think any of you are aware that there were *four* of those Imperial weapons targeted for Ulrich and myself. Altra dealt with two and deflected the third."

Everyone in this room had seen the swiftness and deadly power of the weapons at firsthand; they stared at Altra with surprise and growing respect.

"We of Karse generally consider it wise not to argue with a Firecat," Karal concluded as the silence grew. "They are often acting on orders."

:As I am now,: Altra stated. *:There are reasons for what I*

*have said. Those reasons do not yet concern you, and may
never concern you. The future is fluid and subject to change.:*

And you are being your most inscrutable and infuriating,
Karal thought hard at the Firecat. Altra turned his head
slightly in Karal's direction, and dropped one eyelid in a
quick, but unmistakable, wink.

Elspeth was clearly fuming. "Look, you—Avatar or not, I
won't be manipulated on some grand playing board of—"

She stopped in midsentence as Altra turned to face her
directly.

:I understand,: the Firecat told her with surprising gentleness. *:Please believe me, Lady Elspeth. What I have been ordered to tell you is not meant to manipulate you all like so
many game pieces—it is to ensure that you have the opportunity to exercise your free will.:* He sighed, and somehow conveyed the impression of a burden of terrible grief. *:The future
holds the secrets, not I, Solaris, or even Vkandis. Ulrich
should have been here. He was an Adept, although he seldom made that known. It would have been he who accompanied the gryphons in the east, Elspeth and Darkwind
together in the south, and An'desha would have gone north
with Firesong. This is not optimal; now Florian and I must
serve as the suppliers of power—you have not enough Master
Mages to cover all the minor points and send two with
An'desha. Besides, there is another consideration. Karal is
the most acceptable substitute for a—a guardian—that must
be placated by a presence it will understand. The guardian is
not intelligent, but it will recognize Karal. I am not yet permitted to tell you why. Be assured that when I can, I will—
although—:* His ears twitched. *:—I have the feeling that by
that time, you will have deduced the reason for yourself.:*

"Guardian," Elspeth muttered to herself, and her eyes
dropped to the Firecat's hindquarters—or rather, where those
hindquarters were set. "Bright Havens!" she exclaimed. *"Iftel!"*

The Firecat bowed his head to her. *:Precisely. Check Master Levy's calculations. You will find that the middle key-
point stands at the exact joining of the three countries.
Because of the mages who are available at this moment, this
key-point requires a certain diplomacy where that guardian
is concerned. You will be working Great Magics that will be-*

come one with the border of Iftel, after all; the guardian must be reassured that this will cause no harm. Originally, this would have required two Adepts, or Ulrich and the gryphons. Now it requires a balance of four workers. Two will stand in and for Valdemar—:

"That will be Florian, obviously," Elspeth stated. "The other would be An'desha?"

:Yes—and two will stand in and for Iftel. That must be Karal and myself. The Vkandis Priest-mages still in your land would not be recognized by the guardian as legitimate; although they are good men and women, they are mages first and Priests only as an afterthought. Talia—: the cat paused. :If Karal were not here, Talia might possibly be an acceptable substitute, but I am not willing to risk the chance of failure. It must be Karal; he is the only one besides myself available that the guardian will allow to pass the border. And since he is not a mage, but is a channel, he can support An'desha with help from myself and Florian.:

"This is beginning to sound like a religious ritual," Prince Daren said, finally, with a chuckle. The chuckle died when Altra turned those fiery blue eyes on him.

:You are not entirely wrong,: Altra replied. :The circumstances are extraordinary. If Karal had died along with Ulrich—: he paused again :—it is possible that Solaris herself would have been with you at this moment, at whatever cost. The situation is that grave.:

"Oh, no." Elspeth said hastily. "No, no, no! Talia has told me quite enough about Solaris, and I don't even want to think about that possibility!"

Altra actually shrugged, although a cat's body was not particularly suited to that gesture. :Think on this, then. It is also true that if you had been able to learn the magics for the breakwater-shieldwall before this last wave, the key-point would have involved only the borders of Valdemar and Hardorn. If you wait until this wave is passed, however, the next will involve only the borders of Valdemar and Iftel. You will still need Karal, which means you would still need me and Florian.: He shrugged again. :This is simply the way that things fell out. There is no Great Destiny involved, if that comforts you any.:

"Great Destinies generally involve great funerals," Elspeth muttered, as if she was quoting someone. Both gryphons laughed. "All right; I can accept all this, then. Thank you for taking the time to explain."

:*Well*,: Altra replied, standing up again and walking carefully to the edge of the table. :*Your dislike of manipulation is well-established. Infamous, even. Had I not explained, you might well have found some way to subvert my orders entirely. In this case, that would have been a disaster for all concerned.*:

"I guess he does know you," Prince Daren whispered roguishly to his stepchild. Elspeth blushed.

"Cats," Elspeth muttered. "They always know. Why don't we get back to the business at hand, then?" she added hastily.

"I don't care what that cat is, or what it *says* it is!" Firesong said waspishly. "I do *not* like the idea of you holding the middle key-point all by yourself!"

An'desha suppressed the response that had been second nature to him; to give in to Firesong and defer to his judgment. *We can't afford that now*, he thought, chillingly aware of how little time they *did* have. As blithely as Altra had spoken of "waiting until the next wave," he and Master Levy both knew that would be a very bad idea. The wave that was approaching *would* have intersection-points ·in several populated areas.

He knew, as no one else did, what that would do to the humans in those areas—and not all of those populations were in places that could be warned in time.

"I don't like it either, *ke'chara*," he said instead, very quietly. "To tell you the truth, I'm terrified. I'd much rather it was you beside me; Karal has never served as a channel before, and no matter how well Altra prepares him for it, this will still be an entirely new experience for him. What's more, *I* don't like the idea of *you* being at the most volatile of the key-points! Elspeth may be an Adept, but she is very young in her power, and I had much rather that you had someone experienced beside you."

"You aren't experienced—" Firesong began, then coughed

sardonically. "Of course. You have all that secondhand experience to draw on, correct?"

He had not been distracted by An'desha's own, very real, concern for *him*. *Ah, well,. I tried*, An'desha thought.

"You were the one who rightly insisted that I learn to use those memories," he began.

Firesong interrupted him. "Oh, well, throw my own words in my face!" he replied angrily. "And what next? I suppose now that you have all this experience at your behest, I am no longer interesting to you! Shall I expect to find myself left by the wayside, with the rest of the unwanted discards?"

There was more in the same vein, and it was a very good thing that Karal and Talia had seen the signs of this turnabout in Firesong and had warned An'desha. This would have been very hurtful, had An'desha not understood what was behind it all.

Firesong, possibly for the first time in his life, was jealous and afraid—afraid that An'desha *would* simply walk off and leave him behind. He could, now. He was no longer frightened and dependent. Firesong had never been in the position of the courter, rather than the courted, and he had no idea how to deal with it.

Firesong was also afraid *for* An'desha; the substitution of two mages and a channel for a real Adept was dangerous enough to make An'desha's hair stand on end when he stopped to think about it. Only his faith in Karal allowed him to even consider it.

Karal will allow himself to be burned out before he breaks, he thought, as he let Firesong continue to rant. *He has changed, too.*

He knew what Firesong's conscious intention was—to make him so emotionally wrought up that he would give in, and let Firesong find some other solution to the situation.

There was only one problem with that idea. An'desha had spent too much time with Karal. *I suppose a sense of responsibility must be contagious*, he thought, a bit wryly.

"Aren't you even listening to me?" Firesong cried desperately. "Don't you care what I'm saying, what I'm going through?"

"Yes," he replied, reaching out to catch Firesong's hands in his own. "But more importantly, I have listened to everything you didn't say, but meant. You are afraid for me, and you think I am in great danger. You are afraid I will leave you, that I no longer care for you. You are right in the first instance, and completely, absolutely, utterly wrong in the second."

Firesong's hands tightened on his; Firesong's silvery eyes begged for something he could hold in his heart.

"I am in danger; *all* of us are in danger. If we do nothing, your people, mine, and all these friends in this adopted land of ours will suffer, and maybe die." His eyes, he hoped, told Firesong that this was wholly the truth, nothing held back. "If we try to change this plan—" He sighed. "I must tell you that I do not know what difference the changes will make. Altra swears that this is the optimal use of our powers, and that anything less will not guarantee success. With all of my so-called 'experience,' I cannot tell you if he is right or wrong, but I am willing to trust him."

Firesong nodded, reluctantly.

"*I will not leave you.*" He said that with such force that Firesong winced. "I am not tired of you, nor bored with you, nor do I find you less than my equal." He allowed a hint of a smile to flick across his lips. "I *do* find you my superior in more than you know." Now he tightened his hands on Firesong's. "I have never said this in so many words, *ashke*, and I believe it is time that you heard it."

And take this with you, to hold in your heart.

"I love you." He said it softly, simply, and with all the conviction in his body, mind, and soul, and not entirely sure that even this would satisfy him.

But the truth is often enough in itself. So it was, now.

They made an odd little group; Altra beside Florian, An'desha in his Tayledras finery beside Karal in his sober black, holding the reins of Trenor. An'desha would have to ride Florian as soon as they got through the Gate; he wouldn't be fit to sit on an ordinary horse afterward. They would need to ride for about two days to get from the place An'desha knew—where he and all the others had crossed into Valdemar from Hardorn, fleeing the destruction of the capital—to the place where all three borders met. All three groups would have to travel about two days to get to their ultimate destinations, once they Gated as far as they could. And for the first day, whichever mage had created the Gate would be altogether useless for much of anything.

Firesong and Elspeth had gone first, then Darkwind and the gryphons. Now it was An'desha's turn.

He turned to Karal, as if to say something, then turned back to the stone archway in the weapons-training salle they would all use as their Gate-terminus.

Karal had heard of Gates, but he had never seen one. And after a few moments of watching An'desha build his, he never wanted to see one again.

It wasn't that the Gate itself was so terrible to look at; it was actually rather pretty, except for the yawning Void in the archway where the view of Kerowyn's office should have been. No, it was because Karal sensed that the Gate had been spun out of An'desha's own spirit; An'desha was a pale shadow of himself, as this Gate fed upon him, a lovely parasite draining his very essence. It was quite horrible, and Karal wondered how *anyone* could bear to create something like this.

Suddenly, the gaping darkness beneath the arch became the view of a forest—a place where the forest had taken over the ruins of a farm.

"Go!" An'desha said, in a strangled voice. Altra bolted through. Karal set Trenor toward the Gate; Trenor fought the bit. The gelding did *not* want to go in there!

Karal started to dismount, then looked back at An'desha and saw the terrible strain holding this Gate was costing him. With a silent apology, he wrenched Trenor's head around and dug his heels into the gelding's sides.

Although he wasn't wearing spurs, the startled horse acted as if he was; Trenor neighed frantically and bolted through the Gate.

It felt as if the ground dropped out from underneath them. For no longer than it took to blink, Karal's body swore to him that he was falling; for that long, his senses swore to him that the entire universe had vanished and he was blind, deaf, and frozen.

Then they were through, and Karal spun Trenor around on

his heels as soon as they had cleared the immediate area. He saw that this side of the Gate was the remains of a ruined stone barn, with only the frame of the door and part of a wall still standing and a view of the salle where only weeds and tumbled stones should have been. A moment later, Florian and An'desha came barreling through, and the scene of the salle vanished behind them.

An'desha swayed in the saddle; someone had thoughtfully strapped him in so that he wouldn't fall. He clutched the pommel with both hands, leaving the reins slack on Florian's neck; his face was alabaster-white, and his eyes were closed. He opened them slowly as Karal rode Trenor up beside him.

"I never want to Gate anywhere ever again," Karal said, putting such intensity into every word that An'desha sat up straight in surprise. "I *never* want to put you through something like that again!"

"It won't be so bad, next time," An'desha replied weakly. "I promise you. Next time, we will make the journey in several smaller portions, over several days."

"There won't *be* a next time, if we don't," Karal replied acidly. He looked down. "Florian, is he fit to ride?"

:Even if he weren't, I am fit to carry him. That is why he is bound to the saddle,: came the reply. *:We have no choice. Time is speeding.:*

"So we had better speed ourselves." He reined Trenor back and gestured. Florian knew the way without a map; he was the best guide they could have had. "If you would lead?"

He steadied Trenor, and Altra leapt up to the padded platform where a pillion-saddle would have been. Rris had sworn that his "famous cousin Warrl" often used such a contraption to ride behind the Shin'a'in warrior Tarma shena Tale'sedrin, and in the interest of making the best speed possible, Altra had agreed to try it. Trenor didn't seem to mind too much, although he'd tried to buck a little the first time Altra had jumped up there.

Florian swung off into the deeper woods, and if he was following a trail, it wasn't a trail that Karal could read.

Then again, I'm not a woodsman, am I?

There must have been a trail there, though, since Florian pushed through the brush and rank weeds with no real problem. He was making good time, too; not quite a canter, but certainly a fast walk.

Poor Trenor. Two days of this is going to wear him out.

But there was no choice; every mark that passed was a mark that brought the next wave nearer—and Natoli had confided to him that there were several small villages lying where interference-points would fall. The ones in Valdemar had been evacuated, of course—but there could be no such guarantees of the villages elsewhere.

They *had* to stop this wave. They *had* to be in place in time.

When we have done all we can, then it is time to add prayer to the rest. That was one of Master Ulrich's favorite proverbs. Well, they had done all they could; Karal shut his eyes, trusted to Trenor to follow Florian, and sent up fervent prayers.

Whenever Karal sensed that Trenor was tiring, they stopped for a brief rest, water, and food; other than those stops, they rode right on through the night and on into the next day. This country was all former farmland, now gone to weeds and desolation; Karal didn't really want to ask why it had been left like this. He had an idea that the answer would involve the war with Hardorn, and the little he had learned about Ancar from An'desha did not make him eager to hear more.

Hurry, hurry, hurry. There isn't much time.

The countryside was desolate in other ways, too; there didn't seem to be a lot of wildlife. Birds were few, and mostly oddly silent. Although it was late fall and frost soon crusted every dried, dead leaf and twig, there *should* have been night sounds; owls, the bark of a fox, or the bay of a wolf. The only sounds were the noises they themselves made, and that very silence was more than enough to put up the hair on Karal's neck. An'desha slept in the saddle, as he had since they left the area of the Gate; Altra was not disposed to conversation, and Florian had his mind on finding their way. That left him with nothing to do but half-doze, worry, and try another prayer or two.

When dawn came, it brought a thin gray light to the gray landscape, and matters did not improve much. Trenor was tiring sooner, now, and it hurt Karal to force him on, but he knew there was no choice. They only had until two marks after dawn tomorrow to get into place.

But not long after the sun rose, An'desha actually shook himself awake, and looked around.

"I remember this," he said quietly. "This was land that Ancar held briefly, and he drained it while he held it. It has made a remarkable recovery."

"This?" Karal replied incredulously. "Recovered?"

"You did not see it before," the Adept told him grimly, turning in the saddle to face him. "Nothing would grow; *nothing.* By next year this may be back to the kind of land it once was." His eyes were shadowed by other memories than of this place, and finally he voiced one of them. "Ma'ar made places as desolate as this. The truly terrible thing is that he *thought* he was doing right in creating them."

"Because in creating them he served some kind of purpose?" Karal hazarded.

An'desha nodded. "He served his own people very well; he made them into a great and powerful nation. The only problem is that in doing so, he turned other nations into stretches of desolation that are still scarred by his wars today. For him, nothing mattered except himself and his own people—who were extensions of himself. He did horrible things in the name of patriotism, and thought that he was in the right. I do not *like* Ma'ar, but I understand him. Perhaps I understand him too well."

Karal heard the self-doubt creep into An'desha's voice again, and answered it. "Understanding is the essence of not making the same mistakes, An'desha," he replied. "I rather doubt that Ma'ar ever understood himself, for instance."

An'desha actually laughed. "Well, now that is true enough," he said cheerfully. "So, once again you unseat my problems before they can dig spurs into me. How far to the key-point?"

:Most of the day, if we are not delayed,: Florian replied—

—just as they topped a hill to find themselves staring down at a gorge many hundreds of hands below. The gorge held a river—a river so full of whitewater rapids that it would be insane to try and cross it.

:This should not be here!: Florian exclaimed.

They all stared down at the river below, all but Trenor, who took the occasion to snatch a few mouthfuls of dried weeds.

:*And here, right on schedule, is our delay*,: Altra said finally.

"Not necessarily," Karal pointed out quickly. "There may be a bridge. Do we go upstream or down to try and find it?"

"Upstream, I think," An'desha said, after a moment of consideration. "It takes us nearer the Iftel side that way."

In the end, they *did* find a bridge—a narrow, shaky affair of old logs and rough planks. Karal had to blindfold Trenor to get him across, after Altra tried the footing by carefully padding over first. But that put them several marks behind schedule, and it was nearly dawn before they finally reached their goal.

Karal had wondered just how they would know what side of the border was the Iftel side, and what was the Valdemar side. As the sun rose, he had the answer to that question.

"What *is* that?" he asked in awe, staring at the wall of rippling light that lay along the top of the ridge, just above them. He couldn't see the top of it, whatever it was; it wasn't air, unless there was a way to solidify air and make it into a curtain of refraction. It wasn't water, although it moved and rippled like water with a breeze playing over it, and Karal was just able to make out large masses of green and gray-brown on the other side of it that *could* be trees and bushes.

:*That is the border*,: Florian replied warily. :*It wasn't always like that. Before the war with Ancar, it looked just like the border between Valdemar and Rethwellan, but once Ancar tried to bring an army across it, that was what sprang up. Anyone who tried to cross it was forced back. Anyone who tried to drive their way in with magic—died. I've heard that there are some very select traders who are allowed to come and go between here and there, but they are a close-mouthed lot, and they won't talk about anything that they've seen over there.*:

"I thought they had an envoy at the Valdemar Court," An'desha observed.

:*They used to, a very long time ago. Not anymore.*: Florian let out his breath in a sigh. :*It's tradition to keep their suite ready for them, but no one has come to claim it in anyone's lifetime.:*

Karal swallowed as he contemplated that shimmering wall of—of—

Of power, that's what it is. Pure force. And I'm supposed to walk across it! And anyone who tried to cross it is dead!

What was more, he was supposed to walk across it *right now*. There couldn't be more than a mark to go until the next wave was upon them!

"Come *on*," he urged, as his hands shook. "We have to get moving *now*. We haven't got any time at all to spare!"

To set an example, he urged poor, tired Trenor into a clumsy trot, sending him down the valley, through the knee-high grass, and up the ridge. The wall just loomed larger and larger; it didn't change at all except for the continuous rippling of the surface as he drew nearer to it. He sensed An'desha and Florian at his back, but the sheer power of the wall drove them mostly out of his thoughts.

There wasn't time for finesse, for study, for anything other than what he was already doing—running headlong into the thing, and hoping that it didn't decide to kill him, too.

Fear held him rigid and made a metallic taste in his mouth. He closed his eyes and shouted at Trenor to drive him the last few spans remaining—

—opened his eyes again, just as they actually reached it, and passed into it—

Something seized and held him.

****what****

He could not move, not even to breathe. He was surrounded by light, yet could not see. He could only wait, while whatever it was that held him examined him, inside and out.

*****Priest!*****

Was he a Priest? An'desha had named him "priest," but it had been in jest. Or had it? Solaris had named him "priest," but he thought it had merely been expedience. What had he done to earn the name?

****ah****

Suddenly, it let him go. He found himself still in Trenor's saddle, looking at An'desha and Florian through a curtain of rippling light that seemed thinner here than elsewhere.

:It is thinner. That is so we can reach them,: Altra said, urgently. *:It is coming, Karal, take your position. Don't just stand there thinking,* move!:

He tumbled off Trenor's back and took the stance he'd been coached in, bracing himself and holding both his arms out and up.

:Now. Into the trance I taught you.:

Obediently, he spoke his keywords and fell into a light trance; not so deep that he was unaware of everything around him, but too deep for him to move on his own now. He wasn't sure what was going to happen after that; Altra and An'desha hadn't gone into it—

A fraction of a heartbeat later, he realized *why* they hadn't gone into it. If they had, he'd have been too terrified to go through with it all.

From Altra's side, a torrent of power poured into him; from Florian's, another. There was *something* in him that managed to join those two streams of energy and actually hold them— even though from his point of view, it was like the one time he'd foolishly mounted an unbroken stallion. He was not controlling the power; it was permitting him—briefly—to hold it!

Then An'desha somehow reached out to him from across the border, and the two streams of power that had been made one found their outlet.

Now An'desha did something with that energy that Karal could not see, and could only sense, very dimly, as a blind man might sense a mighty fortress being built beside him. He arched his back and closed his eyes to concentrate on holding the power steady; the longer the power "permitted" him to hold it, the more control he actually had over it.

It was not easy, and he sensed something else. If he slipped, it was going to do terrible things to him, and if he survived the experience, the likelihood that he would regret surviving was very high.

He no sooner had that unsettling revelation than the disruption-wave hit.

It was worse than all the others combined.

The ground heaved and buckled under him, as if this was the earthquake that would end the world. He went entirely blind, but not in the sense of being immersed in total darkness. Instead, there was nothing to see *but* color and light, swirls and whirlwinds and cascades of color and light. The light was something he could hear; it roared and rushed in his ears. The color had flavors; iron, scorched stone, and copper. Somewhere out there he knew that Florian and Altra were still pouring energy into him; he felt it, hot and primal, deep inside him—and An'desha needed that power. So he held to it, even when the light turned into a million serpents that threatened to crush him, even when the colors tried to wash him away, right up until everything collapsed and he was all alone in an unending darkness, and he knew he would never, ever find his way out again—

—that was when he faltered.

Fear overcame him; he felt the power slipping through his tenuous grasp.

I can't take this! he thought, gasping in panic. *I can't do this! This was for someone like Ulrich, not me! I can't—*

His control slipped a little more, and he flailed in confusion.

I don't even know what I am anymore.

His heart raced in panic, and he *wanted* Ulrich. He wanted to be *like* Ulrich.

Then from deep within him came a feeling of conviction, of responsibility, too strong for even fear to shake.

I have to. There's no one else.

He held the power, though it writhed and threatened to escape. He ignored his confusion, fought his panic, and held.

Then, as suddenly as it began, it was over. Abruptly, he found himself back on the Valdemar side of the barrier, knee-deep in dead grasses, staring into An'desha's eyes from a distance of no more than an arm's length. How he had gotten there, he had no clue.

:*The other breakwaters are up,*: Florian said, his voice so faint with exhaustion that it might have been nothing more than a whisper of Karal's own thoughts. :*All three are joined. The Iftel border is part of it all. We did it, Karal.*:

Karal sat down in the grass; Altra was already lying down beside him, completely drained, one very flat Cat. "We did, didn't we?" he said, wonderingly.

:Ah.: That was Altra. *:I believe that I will lie here for a while. A month would be good. Maybe two. How do you manage with the limits of these bodies?:*

"I manage very well, thank you," An'desha replied sharply. "I had a taste of doing without one, remember? Don't complain."

Karal decided that Altra's idea of lying flat was a good one. He felt—he felt as if someone had filled him full of light, then drained him; as if someone had turned him inside out, left him under the desert sun for a while, then turned him right-side out again.

:There is help coming.: Florian said. *:A Herald on circuit. Just rest now, until he comes.:*

"We did it," he said again, wonderingly.

:We did. The barriers will hold for now. We have bought some breathing space.:

Breathing space. Time. He blinked, and looked up at the blue sky. Maybe a little rest. All three sounded impossibly good.

Never mind that *he* was truly going to be the Karsite envoy now, a position he didn't want, and wasn't sure how to fill. And never mind that there was a young engineer back in Haven who made him think very uncomfortable and yet delightful thoughts.

There was still the Imperial army out there—and no telling what they would do. Karal himself was now a potential major target for them. And the cataclysmic mage-storm was yet to come.

But at the moment, it doesn't matter. For now, they *had* time; and a little time—and each other—could be all they needed.